SOPHIA

by the same author

EMAIL FROM A VAMPIRE

SOPHIA

NIGEL COOPER

GENERIC POOL PUBLISHING

Copyright © Nigel Cooper, 2014
All rights reserved

Published in Great Britain in 2014 by Generic Pool Publishing
www.genericpool.co.uk

This book is a work of fiction. Names, characters, places and incidents are either a product of the author's imagination or are used fictitiously. Any resemblance to actual people, living or dead, events or locales, is entirely coincidental.

No part of this publication may be reproduced, stored in any information storage and retrieval system, or transmitted in any form or by any means, electronically or mechanical, including photocopy and recording, without permission in writing of the author.

A CIP catalogue record of this book
is available from the British Library.

ISBN 978-0-9573307-3-3

Cover design by Nigel Cooper.
Cover photo by Lawrence Randall.
Colour retouching by Dean Feast.

Set in Garamond 12.5/14.75 pt.
Typeset by the author.

Printed and bound in the UK by
TJ International, Trecerus Industrial Estate, Padstow, Cornwall. PL28 8RW

This novel is also available as an eBook, details of which
are available on the author's website at:

www.nigelcooperauthor.co.uk

Dedicated to my beloved sister, Lynda Ann Cooper (29th December 1963 - 26th June 1968) - rest in peace my darling. Although you died when I was just two years old and I don't recall your physical being, I know I had a beautiful sister. I felt you then, and I feel you now. You are in my heart.

Chapter 1

With the taste of a recently eaten banana still lingering on her tongue, Sophia lifted her cello bow and struck the opening G of Bach's delightful Prelude from the Cello Suite number 1 in G Major. Even though the cellists, musicians and critics among the evening's audience at the Wigmore Hall in London were well aware that the opening prelude is by far the easiest, technically speaking, than the remaining five suites for unaccompanied cello, they, along with the rest of the audience, sat in silent awe of Sophia's sheer musical brilliance. For those in the audience who had never seen Sophia Beckinsale perform at a live recital, it didn't take long before they bore witness to her musical genius and alluring stage presence. By the end of bar eleven of that first simple prelude, the sell-out audience were spellbound by both the music and the intense emotional connection she made with them.

Sophia patiently progressed through each movement, unhurried, allowing the audience to soak up and appreciate every single note as the horsehair on her bow glided smoothly with grace, elegance and unparalleled perfection, across the strings of her cello, reverberating through the auditorium the smoothest, sweetest, beautifully soulful sounds imaginable.

The sounds that emitted from her cello came not only from the stage, but they also seemed to wrap around the audience, coming from the sides and back of the auditorium, almost three-dimensionally, encapsulating the audience from all sides like a surround sound system. Only here, at the Wigmore Hall, there was no such electronic audio system, just Sophia Beckinsale and her cello and the natural acoustics of the hall. Yet, if you closed your eyes, she had an uncanny ability to project her sound to the back of the auditorium, giving the illusion of the music creeping up on you from behind.

When Sophia played, the audience listened – intently. She was like the Pied Piper, only Sophia did not lead children away from a town, instead she took the audience on a musical journey – her musical journey, the composer's musical journey, a journey never to be forgotten by those who heard her play.

The audience were so spellbound that they did not applaud between suites, which was most unusual. During this uncommon silence, Sophia paused momentarily to turn the octagonal adjuster at the end of her bow, making miniscule adjustments to the tension of the horsehair, allowing her bow to sit more seductively into the strings for certain suites, looking introspective and lost in her own personal world of music as she did so.

What was she thinking? Where did she go in her mind when she was playing? One could be forgiven for thinking that she had her own personal built-in telepathic transmitter with the ability to communicate directly with the composer to whose music she played – even when that composer had long since passed.

Then, paused motionless, bow in hand, she slowly and intently viewed the audience, first from right to left and then from front to back, while gracefully lifting her bow and positioning it a few millimetres above the strings – just hovering there, as if waiting for the audience's approval to continue onto the next suite. During this ritual, the audience remained perfectly still and quite silent. Nobody fidgeted in their seat and nobody coughed – the silence and stillness was eerie, yet beautifully serene at the same time. As the cliché goes, you could hear a pin drop – quite literally.

With each passing suite Sophia left the audience even more mesmerised. Her cello had a dark side to its tone, but it was very clear and had a vast dynamic range. Her musicianship was pure and honest and she appeared to have absolutely no technical boundaries whatsoever and her intonation was pitch-perfect from one note to the next.

The sounds she produced were nothing less than exquisite. Her body acting as a musical transmitter, passing the music from the composer directly to the audience – untainted, interpreting it exactly as the composer intended, all wrapped up in her own unique musical signature. This was honest playing, it was sincere and it was rare. It's what music should be, and it's what the classical music world had been waiting for. Nobody had heard sounds quite like this since Jacqueline du Pré.

Sophia's slower movements were purposeful, but

always played with the delicate respect that is often required of Bach's music. In other movements her bow attacked the strings with precision and speed; yet the sound was always articulate, measured, sweet and never harsh.

Sophia doesn't move her body much while playing, just the required amount of arm, shoulder and torso movement – no less, and certainly no more. Every movement she makes is either unconscious or is in the service of her relationship with the music, the composer and her cello.

Unlike some other female – and sometimes male – soloists, Sophia has no use for over sensualized or glamorous body movements while playing. Gazing romantically toward the ceiling revealing her beautifully long pale neck and closing her eyes is a facade Sophia does not need in order to impress her audience – she is a musical genius and her audience knows it. She relies only on the sounds she produces, the music, the notes, and playing them back the way the composer intended – all neatly wrapped up in Sophia's unique and inimitable musical ability.

Although Sophia is attractive, a tall slim dress size eight figure, long legs and beautiful long auburn hair with a hint of deep vibrant red, pearl white teeth, and the most exotic cheek bones you've ever seen, she does not need, or use, her physical looks to win the affections of her audience. The most visual movement an audience at a Sophia Beckinsale recital is ever likely to witness is when she occasionally shifts her weight from one buttock to the other, and even this is done with a graceful inertia.

SOPHIA

To watch her play is like witnessing an angel sent from heaven to personally deliver to our eyes and ears a large helping of musical utopia.

One journalist even said that she's like somebody who possesses some kind of ethereal dimension. She also claimed that if you stare at her long enough and hard enough without blinking, you could actually see the faintest opaque pearl white halo around her body while she played. Other music critics have compared Sophia Beckinsale more than favourably to Jacqueline de Pré and Mstislav Rostropovich.

Another critic, after seeing twenty seven of Sophia's hundred and thirty four recitals during the previous twelve months, went as far as saying – with the greatest respect to Jackie – if Jacqueline du Pré was a cello-playing force of nature with few musical inhibitions, then Sophia Beckinsale is the musical equivalent to the second coming, with absolutely no musical inhibitions whatsoever.

Sophia has an energy and willingness to invest herself beyond where any other musician dare – she pushes the envelope to its absolute limits, taking risks and pulling them off consistently and without effort. She puts maximum energy – to the point of exhaustion – into every recital she performs. To Sophia, the music deserves and requires this sort of input and anything less is cheating! She doesn't know what it's like to have technical difficulties, or what it means to play safe. She gets inside the music and totally devours it. Sophia has a principal belief that not a single moment, not even a millisecond of the music, or the silences, can be overlooked or undervalued.

After Sophia finished the Gigue, the 36th and final movement of Bach's Six Cello Suites, the audience didn't even wait for her to complete her bow stroke of that final note D before jumping to their feet and breaking out into rapturous applause. The capacity audience gave Sophia a standing ovation as she stood to curtsey. Flowers were thrown onto the stage around her feet to the deafening cheers and whistles and shouts of 'bravo!'

Sophia made a huge deal out of her curtsey, taking her time. She took her pearl white satin dress with her right hand. Her left hand held her bow and cello upright by its neck as she slid her left foot across the stage floor to position it behind her right. Then, in her own pool of the spotlight, she stylishly knelt and went all the way down to the floor, leaning into one knee and balancing with the grace and elegance of a white swan. Finally, she slowly lowered and bowed her head. She held this position for what seemed like an inordinately long time – the audience enjoyed her beautifully graceful routine as much as the music they had just heard.

Sophia stood up and looked to her right where she noticed the backstage usher had opened the door on the curved rear stage wall and was holding it open for her. Standing just behind the usher she saw her beloved boyfriend, Spencer, standing there watching her, with a loving and knowing smile on his face. She smiled at him in a way a woman smiles at the man she is desperately in love with – the man she knows she is going to spend the rest of her life with. She faced the audience and took another brief curtsey before eagerly pacing off the stage and into the arms of her cherished Spencer. They embraced and she kissed him on the lips, delicately, but purposeful, relinquishing all her love and passion upon him – butterflies fluttered in her stomach, along with other wonderful sensations, as she did so.

They could hear loud roars and whistles and more shouts of 'bravo!' coming from the auditorium. Spencer delicately, and grudgingly, pulled his lips away from Sophia's while he cupped her cheeks in both his hands. He smiled at her with his big ocean blue eyes, in which she could happily swim forever.

'It would appear that you're desperately wanted by about five hundred other people as well,' he said. Sophia smiled at him.

'Don't go anywhere, I'll be right back,' she said. The usher opened the stage door for her and she walked back out onto the stage and stood facing the rapturous audience holding her cello upright to her left. She then performed her slow ritual curtsey once again, and as before, held her low bowed position with grace and elegance for about ten seconds before slowly returning to an upright position – the audience loved every second. She smiled at them, and then turned and walked off stage and through the door, and again into the arms of Spencer while the usher closed the stage door behind her. They embraced tightly, as tightly as Sophia was able to one-handed, while the other hand held her cello by its neck.

Even though Sophia and Spencer had known each other for ten years, since they were both twelve years old, and have been in a serious relationship together since they were sixteen, they kissed each other with the kind of brand new passion and deep love that is more akin to something out of a great love story. Sophia and Spencer were two lovers like no other – they were childhood sweethearts, they were always meant to be – the meant-to-be soulmates. As they stood there entwined and engaged in a long dreamlike kiss, it was as if the world around them had faded away into the background and no longer existed. The only thing that mattered during that moment, or any of their other moments together, was the two of them and the depthless, undying love they had for each other.

The roars of the audience grew deafeningly loud as they continued to shout and whistle and cheer. Multiple roars of 'encore' echoed around the auditorium.

'Don't move, I'll be back in a tad over two minutes,' she said as she kissed him again, harder this time – passionately and with vigour, and then she walked back out onto the stage with a definite spring in her step. The cheers and roars escalated to decibel levels previously unknown at this venue.

She took her seat and positioned her cello spike precisely onto the rubber-dimpled strip that was attached under her left/front chair leg. The audience fell silent and waited with anticipation. The silence was electrifying as Sophia lifted her bow once again, holding it just a few millimetres above the strings. Then, without pause, she lunged straight into Popper's Elfentanz, playing it considerably faster than its customary tempo and without the usual piano accompaniment either. Sophia's interpretation, coupled with her lightning speed bowing and fingering techniques, totally blew the audience away as she effortlessly ate up the relentless prestissimo semiquaver passages at an impossible speed. Her bowing hand was quite literally a blur. Considering how technically demanding this piece was, even at its typical metronome mark, made it all the more astonishing. The words: technical brilliance, impeccable intonation, musical mastery, unparalleled virtuosity and utter showmanship all sprang to mind.

Sophia completed the Elfentanz in exactly two minutes and two seconds, which was blisteringly fast – even more so than Rostropovich ever played it. There was absolutely no doubt that Sophia Beckinsale was a virtuosic genius. She produced not so much a sound in her playing, but a voice, a voice that has a character that is immediately recognizable. It was a voice that you remember, in the same way that you would remember the voice of Janet Baker, Kathleen Ferrier or Maria Callas. The fact that the cello has a similar range to the human voice makes Sophia's astonishing musicality touch all those who heard her all the more so.

As more flowers landed on the stage to a noisy soundtrack of whistles and roars and more shouts of 'bravo!' Sophia stood up and took her final curtsey, then strutted off the stage and back into the arms of her dearest Spencer, squeezing him tight and kissing him repeatedly – many short purposeful kisses, followed by a longer more meaningful one.

'I've missed you so much!' she said, eventually pulling her lips from his. 'Can you spend the night?'

'How about two nights?' he said, smiling. Sophia could hardly contain herself and let out a shriek of happiness and hugged and squeezed him for all she was worth.

Chapter 2

It was a beautifully crisp, yet serene, Saturday morning in Hampstead, North London. The sunlight streamed in through the main bedroom window of Sophia's two bedroom apartment, projecting a diffused impressionistic pattern from her net curtains across the duvet, adding an extra dimension to the two entwined slender bodies that lay beneath it. The blindingly harsh morning sunlight, although diffused by the opaque net curtains, penetrated Spencer's eyelids, which caused him to gently stir. He turned his head and watched Sophia sleeping. Her pale porcelain-like blemish-free skin looked as angelic as ever in the pure directional sunlight. Her lips were slightly parted and she was breathing through her mouth. Spencer watched her chest gently move up and down with each delicate breath she took. He leant over so his face was positioned just a few inches away from hers, and then moved in even closer, as if he was going to kiss her. But he didn't. Instead, his lips stopped just a few millimetres from hers. He parted his lips slightly and breathed in as his beautiful Sophia breathed out. Their synchronised breathing filled his lungs with each of her outward breaths, feeding and absorbing her very essence into his own lungs and bloodstream and body.

Spencer could never be too close to Sophia, and vice-versa. They were constantly looking for ways to be even closer – spiritually, mentally and physically, while their love continued to deepen, even after all this time.

Sophia first met Spencer via her father's good friend, Philip. Sophia's father, Andrew, is a Harley Street skin specialist and Philip, who is an orthopaedic surgeon specializing in disorders of the hand and wrist, has worked in the same Harley Street building as Sophia's father for ten years.

At the beginning, Sophia and Spencer only saw each other every few months or so when Sophia's parents got together on the occasional Sunday for dinner with Philip and his wife. But when Sophia and Spencer were fifteen years old, the two families went on holiday together to a large villa with a swimming pool in the South of France. It was during this up-close-and-personal holiday time while relaxing by the pool that their friendship transitioned and they fell in love. At first their parents thought it was just one of those teenage love things, but it soon became apparent that their love was something else entirely – it was special. Sophia and Spencer bonded stronger than Araldite during that double family holiday vacation and they never looked back.

The next few years were very special for Sophia and Spencer, even though they were both busy with their studies, their love deepened, even when they weren't together. Spencer followed in his father's footsteps by gearing his studies and exams towards a career in medicine. While Sophia, after demonstrating incredible musical talent on the cello from a very early age, studied at the Purcell School for gifted young musicians in Hertfordshire, where she had been since she was 9-years old.

During these vital years of study in their mid to late teens, Sophia and Spencer managed to carve occasional opportunities to spend time together; learning more and more about each other with each encounter. Their love for each other continued to deepen and they developed an uncanny two-way telepathy. Then, eventually, on Sophia's eighteenth birthday, they spent their first weekend together in a beautiful riverside hotel in Stratford-upon-Avon. Exactly what happened between them that weekend, nobody really knows – nobody except Sophia and Spencer. But when they returned home, they were like two physical bodies sharing one soul. A single energy bound by love. Everybody could see it, it was magical and their love for each other was hugely contagious. It forced those around them to re-examine their own relationships and re-introduce and inject a large helping of romance back into their average passionless marriages. That weekend away together was the defining moment. From then on, Sophia and Spencer knew that they were going to spend the rest of their lives together – and beyond.

Over the next four years, Sophia and Spencer continued with their studies. Spencer went to medical school, while Sophia left the Purcell School at eighteen and went on to the Royal Academy of Music in London, where she studied until she was twenty-one.

Spencer inhaled one last breath from Sophia, and then kissed her tenderly on the lips, causing her to let out a quiet moan of pleasure, while stirring slightly. He quietly got out of bed and went to the kitchen to make some coffee while Sophia rolled over onto the warm spot where he had been laying and buried her face into his pillow – taking in his blissful aroma.

By the time Spencer returned, Sophia was fully awake. 'I thought I could smell coffee,' she said, smiling as he walked over to the bed and placed a tray on her bedside table. On the tray sat two cups of coffee and a single red rose. At first, Spencer felt a little embarrassed buying red roses for Sophia, in case the florist thought it was cliché. But Sophia loved the smell of roses and the way the velvety petals felt between her fingers when she delicately touched them. So after a while Spencer stopped thinking about what the ladies in the florist shops may or may not have been thinking and simply thought about how happy it made his treasured Sophia.

Her hands held the rose and with delight she smelled the exquisite aroma emitting from its petals, breathing in deeply through her nose. She then delicately stroked the petals with the tips of her fingers while smiling at Spencer.

'Here you go,' said Spencer, handing Sophia a coffee in her favourite cup.

'What did I do to deserve you,' she said.

'I could say the same about you,' he said, as he leaned forward and kissed her before picking up his own cup of coffee.

'What time is it?' she said.

'Half ten.'

'Wow, I can't believe I slept in so long.'

'Well we didn't get in until after one.'

'Yes, I could have done with coming home straight after the recital, I was pretty exhausted anyway and could have done without standing around chatting to people for another two hours.'

'Well you didn't seem that exhausted when we got into bed at half past one in the morning – where did that sudden burst of energy come from Miss Dominatrix,' he said, with a wicked smile on his face.

'Well, I hadn't seen you for two weeks. I'd missed you.'

'I should say, one minute I'm kissing you and saying "goodnight" and the next your throwing me onto my back, jumping on top of me, pinning me down and locking your knees either side of my waist like a professional wrestler.'

'I hope you're not suggesting I look like a professional wrestler?' she teased as she leaned over and placed her coffee cup back on the tray.

'Well, perhaps one of those stunningly attractive female ones with a great body,' he said, leaning forward to kiss her again.

'Hmmm, I like the sound of that. So how would you like to go another round, Mr Spencer Seymour-Duncan,' she said, as she wrapped her arms around his neck and pulled his face closer to kiss him. She forced a gap in his slightly parted lips with her tongue and venturing sensually into his mouth. They spent the next hour making love – slow and meaningful.

Even though it had been several years since they first had sex together, every time was just like the first – those lovely tingly feelings of anticipation you get in your stomach, your heart pounding faster in your chest when you know it is leading somewhere, the exciting adrenaline rush, the sharp intake of breath at the first sensual touch, the sheer pleasure of discovering each others bodies, the stroking, the hands venturing, the kissing, the sexual tension building to the point that you simply can't take it anymore. Then finally, that moment, that first slow and deep sexual moment that causes you to let out a groan of immense sexual pleasure as you connect and become one and truly feel each other for the first time – this is as close as two people can physically get. Then there is no stopping the sexual pleasure from building as the immersion and feelings deepen, there are no limits to the heights of this incredible sexual awakening as the arousal and satisfaction builds with more and more movement and energy until that universally recognisable moment happens that leaves two motionless bodies locked together in a state of total sexual satisfaction – paused in a moment in time just before every muscle in your body slowly falls into a state of complete relaxation as your body comes down from the greatest physical high there is known to man and woman.

Then comes the afterglow, gently touching and caressing each other's bodies, kissing, gazing into each others eyes while stroking each other's face and hair – words are no longer necessary. During this *coming-back-down-to-earth* time, there is an unspoken language that is as close to telepathy as two humans can get, and Sophia and Spencer have their own special brand of telepathy. They are more than capable of having an entire conversation without ever opening their mouths.

Multiply these emotions and feelings by a thousand and this is how Sophia and Spencer felt every time they engaged in any one of the multifaceted variations of sexual intercourse: making love, having sex, fucking. But more than this, Sophia and Spencer are in love – deeply in love. They are the quintessential love story, he is her Marc Anthony and she is his Cleopatra. They are the modern day fairy tale, a Romeo and Juliet.

After fully coming back down from their sexual utopia, Sophia got out of bed and went to make some fresh coffee. When she returned, she put the tray next to the bed, slid her dressing gown off her shoulders and allowed it to drop to the floor. She walked naked across the bedroom, took her cello out of its case, pulled her dressing table stool out into the middle of the floor and started to play one of Spencer's favourite pieces of music – the Melody from Gluck's opera, Orpheus and Eurydice. As she sat there playing the slow romantic melody naked, Spencer propped himself up on one elbow and watched her, admiring the perfect form of her body, the feminine lines, her neck, her shoulders, her collarbones, her breasts, waistline, legs, feet. The way she moved, so gracefully, as her bow moved slowly across the strings of her cello. His entire vision was filled with Sophia; his peripheral vision had shut down – just for her.

'You're so beautiful,' he whispered to himself.

Sophia read his lips and smiled at him as she continued to play, making her physical movements more sensual with a suggestive glint in her eyes. Spencer got out of bed and walked, naked, across the room and knelt down behind her, stroking her shoulder blades and running his fingers down her spine as she played. He moved her long lustrously tumbling auburn hair to the side to reveal her slender neck then started to plant delicate kisses on it. She responded by tilting her head to the side, giving him full access to every inch of her beautiful neck. He continued to kiss her neck, more slowly now, while moving his right hand up the side of her body so it came to rest just under her right armpit while his left hand navigated its way around her waist to her belly button. Sophia let out little gasps with each of his kisses and gentle touches.

As she continued to play, *those* feelings started to stir up deep inside her again. Spencer's fingertips delicately stroked Sophia's taught tummy, causing her to shudder with pleasure. Had her legs not already been wide open due to her cello being placed between them, she would have parted them right about now. Instead, she gracefully shifted her position on the stool, pulling in her tummy and pulling her buttocks upward, inviting his hand to venture lower. Spencer obliged and slid his hand down into her warm moistness. Sophia gasped out loud; the Melody she was playing suddenly went from piano to forte in the space of half a bar while Spencer's fingers did the most incredible job of pleasuring her.

The tempo of her playing started to increase, as did

the tempo in her body. If her heart was a metronome, Gluck's slow Melody was now most inappropriate. As Spencer's hand increased in speed and pressure, Sophia's bow lifted off the strings and her right arm stretched out slowly like a swan stretching its wing out to dry in the sun. Her left hand slid down the neck of her cello until it came to rest on the hollow wooden body. Her lower body writhed and squirmed like an eel out of water, while her buttocks thrust back and forth on the stool faster and faster. Her orgasm was on its way, speeding full steam ahead. Nothing could stop it now. Her writhing and thrusting became stronger and more intense. Then, finally, she let out a long loud moan of pleasure as she pushed her cello from between her legs and clamped her knees together hard, locking Spencer's hand and fingers right were they were.

'Oh my god!' She gasped as she leaned forward and rested her forehead on the body of her cello, panting deeply, totally satisfied.

Chapter 3

Sophia and Spencer enjoyed the familiar scenery as they drove from Sophia's apartment in Hampstead along Spaniards Road and past the Toll House and into Hampstead Lane before turning off into the road where Sophia's parents lived.

Sophia took a small remote control device out of her handbag and depressed it as they approached the tall wrought iron gates, which opened electronically allowing Spencer to drive through and up to the entrance of the large white six-bedroom house. He parked alongside Andrew's Mercedes S-Class. Before either of them got out of Spencer's car, Andrew had opened the front door to come out and greet them.

'Hello my darling,' said Andrew.

'Hi Daddy,' she said, wrapping her arms around him enthusiastically and kissing his cheek.

'Spencer,' he addressed, extending his hand for Spencer to shake. 'How's the young doctor doing?'

'Absolutely perfect, Sir, couldn't be better.'

'Good, I'm glad to hear it,' said Andrew, shaking his hand firmly while giving him an authoritative pat on the shoulder with the other. 'But do stop calling me Sir,' he smiled, 'you've known me long enough – Andrew will do just fine.'

'Ok, I'll try and remember.'

'Well, perhaps after your official engagement party to my daughter next weekend you'll feel more comfortable with it,' he said, smiling at them. 'Anyway, come on in. Go through to the back garden, Spencer – Diana's in the gazebo. Sophia and I will bring out some drinks.'

'Hello Spencer,' said Diana, 'how nice to see you. Come and sit down,' she said, patting the seat next to her.

'Thank you Mrs Beckinsale.'

'Oh please, my darling, after all these years I find it hard to comprehend that you still can't call me Diana – endearing and well-mannered as it is, you really must try and get into the habit. After next weekend I'm going to insist you know.' Sophia and her father emerged from the house and strolled across the garden to the gazebo.

'Ah, there you are. I was beginning to wonder if Spencer here had left you at home,' said Diana.

'Hello Mummy,' said Sophia, leaning down and kissing her mother's cheek.

'Where's Grandma, I thought she was going to be here today?' said Sophia.

'She was,' said Diana, 'but she's feeling a little weak. She said she wants to save all her energy for next weekend.'

'Oh,' said Sophia, looking a little concerned.

'Don't worry,' said Andrew, putting his hand on Sophia's shoulder. 'She has off days like this. She's in good hands and she's surrounded by people who love her.'

'I know, but I still can't believe it, when I think about it I ...'

'Look darling, Grandma's perfectly content and she's comfortable in every way. And above all, she's *really* looking forward to hosting your engagement party next weekend.'

Just then Sophia's younger sister, Charlotte, came trotting across the lawn enthusiastically.

Charlotte is twenty years old, two years younger than Sophia. She still lives at home with her parents where she spends most of her spare time, when she is not at Uni, in her room studying to be a dentist. She is in year two of her dental degree and spends a lot of time studying anatomy, physiology, biochemistry and pathology, along with learning anatomy on cadavers – *not* her favourite part. She is not treating patients yet, but she spends a lot of time practising on, what the university call, phantom heads, with synthetic jaws set in them that dental students, well, cut their teeth on. Charlotte is tall and slim, like Sophia. But unlike Sophia, her hair is only shoulder length and is light brown in colour. She's a happy-go-lucky girl who always has a smile on her face. Sophia and Charlotte have never fought or argued, not even a little disagreement. Sophia really loves Charlotte and they have a deep caring sisterly love for each other. No matter what else is going on in their lives, they always have time for each other.

'Hey, I thought I heard people arriving. How are you Sis?' said Charlotte, giving her sister a big hug. 'How do you manage to look so radiant and fresh with all those recitals you do. You must have done a hundred during the past year?'

Sophia

'A hundred and thirty four, and that's not including the master classes she's given,' said Andrew, proudly. 'But you can't sustain that amount of recitals forever you know, sooner or later, you're going to have to slow down,' said Andrew

'I know, Daddy. But Meredith's inundated with calls for bookings.'

'Meredith's a great agent and she protected you well when you were young, but these days I wish she'd leave you a little more breathing space between recitals, especially the international ones.'

'Don't worry, Daddy, I'm fine. Whenever one recital finishes, I can't wait to get back on the stage to perform the next. I love my music.'

'Hey, you got a great review in The Guardian,' said Charlotte, picking the paper up off the wooden table. 'I love this part, "Sophia Beckinsale can play quieter than any other musician in the world and she can make an entire concert hall practically stop breathing to listen to her perform delicate pianissimo passages." And further on it says "I haven't heard such an honest and sincere musician since Jacqueline du Pre".'

'That reminds me, you'd better make sure you don't have a recital booked on your birthday next month. It's only three weeks away you know,' said Andrew. 'Know what you're going to do yet?'

'Spencer and I are thinking something small and quiet. I don't think I could handle two large parties back-to-back.'

The family pleasantries continued as they discussed

Diana's mother's terminal illness and Sophia and Spencer's up-coming engagement party the following weekend.

Diana's mother, Lizzie, was diagnosed with cancer a month ago. Lizzie wanted to tell everybody personally and Sophia was one of the first people she told. It was quite advanced and she was told she had three or four months to get her affairs in order. Sophia is Lizzie's favourite granddaughter and she is desperate to see Sophia engaged to be married before she passes away. Sophia has a deep love for Lizzie and has always had an amazing relationship with her. She and Spencer are happy to oblige and get engaged, which will not only make Lizzie the happiest grandmother alive, but it will also help lift some of the sad darkness that is currently weighing heavily on the family.

Lizzie has pulled out all the stops for Sophia and Spencer. She is hosting their engagement party at her large house in rural Kent. She has spared no expense for her dearest granddaughter and Spencer. She found a superb party planning company and insisted on paying for everything herself – her final parting gift. She has loved every minute of it and has told the family that her life will be well and truly complete after Sophia's engagement party.

'Have you spoken to Eleanor this week?' asked Diana.

'Briefly. She's coming over to my place for an hour on Thursday evening,' said Sophia.

'An hour, I'm glad she could create a little window for you, that's only two days before your engagement party,' said Diana.

SOPHIA

'Oh Mummy, Eleanor's got a lot on at work at the moment,' said Sophia, defending her older sister.

'Well, so are you dear, between all your recitals and a diligent practice schedule, you still manage to find time for your family.'

'Come on, Diana, you know Eleanor's got a lot on with work at the moment,' said Andrew, grounding his wife.

'I know, I'm sorry. I'm just anxious about next weekend. I want it to be perfect. For everyone, especially Mummy, she's so looking forward to it. Ignore me, darling,' she said to Sophia.

'It's ok, Mummy. Everything's organised. It's going to be fine. Hey, I almost forgot, DJ knows a professional harpist and she's agreed to play at our engagement party. Just a little gentle background music while the guests arrive and before the main band.'

'That's wonderful darling, Lizzie will love that,' said Diana.

'How is young Django?' said Andrew.

'Busy. He's got lots of international recitals booked in the coming months. Then he has a break so we can do the recording of Beethoven's Five Cello Sonatas. The record company are chomping at the bit for us get into the studio and start working on it as soon as possible.'

'I thought they wanted you to record the Elgar Concerto?' said Diana.

'Well …' she didn't quite know what to say.

'They did,' said Spencer. 'Sophia's still mentally preparing for the inevitable comparisons.'

'Oh come on, darling. You know you've got nothing to worry about in that department,' said Andrew.

'Daddy's right Sis, you should record it and blow the classical music world away.'

'I agree, it's not like you haven't played it before,' said Spencer.

'I know, but the only other person in the room was DJ accompanying me on the piano.'

'Yes, and he told everyone that he'd never heard anybody play it like that before. "Pure Elgarian" he said. He's heard Jackie's recordings. Both with Barbirolli and Barenboim, and he still said you do it better,' said Spencer.

'Well, I don't have time right now, even if I wanted to. I've got too many recitals lined up and the Beethoven recordings to do.'

'What do you think, Spencer. You're the one closest to her these days. Why do you think she won't perform or record the Elgar?' said Diana.

'Well … I don't really know.'

'Oh come on, you must have an inkling?' said Andrew.

'Well, perhaps she's showing Jackie respect. By not performing the Elgar in public and keeping a dignified silence – I guess it's a kind of tribute.'

'Well I think if Ms du Pré was alive today, she'd be telling you to go for it,' said Charlotte. 'Lots of other cellists have recorded the Elgar.'

'Yes, and they've all failed. None of them can touch Jackie's version,' said Sophia.

'So why don't you change all that, honey?' said Spencer.

Chapter 4

Sophia heard her doorbell ring and went to answer it.
'Hi Sis,' said Eleanor.

'Hey, right on schedule,' said Sophia, looking at her watch. 'That's a first.'

'Well, I thought as it's your engagement party the day after tomorrow I'd at least free up my schedule a little and get out of work on time.'

They hugged briefly and then went through to the living room. Hugs between Sophia and her older sister were always brief and slightly awkward. It's not that they don't love each other. Sophia just never quite bonded with Eleanor in the same way she did with her younger sister, Charlotte.

Eleanor is 24 years old. After doing a degree in business studies she soon found herself working for an insurance company before moving into their fraud investigation department. She works long hours as an insurance fraud investigator, which often takes her all over the country, and sometimes into Europe. She's really good at her job, is career-minded and is moving up the ladder fast. At five feet four inches, Eleanor is the shortest of the three sisters. Although Eleanor's exterior demeanour is corporate and business-like, she does have a sensitive side, which she goes out of her way not to show, preferring instead to come across as a hard power suit woman. She lives in a 3-bed semi-detached house in Primrose Hill, North London, which she was fortunate to have had left to her in a will by her godfather who died two years ago. She lives there with her boyfriend, Michael, who recently moved in with her. When Eleanor and Michael are together in public or family get-togethers, they don't share public displays of affection. They almost look and act like business partners. Sophia and Charlotte always wondered what it would be like to be a fly-on-the-wall in their bedroom – usually during a giggly moment.

'Here you go, one cup of tea, just as you like it.'

'Thank you,' said Eleanor, taking the cup. 'So, where's Spencer, I thought you two were going out to dinner with friends later?'

'Yes, he'll be here at eight.'

Sophia and Eleanor spent the early part of the evening catching up and talking about Grandma Lizzie and the upcoming engagement party.

They heard a key in the apartment door as Spencer let himself in. 'Hi baby,' said Spencer. Sophia jumped up off the sofa and skipped across the living room to meet him halfway. They hugged, tightly. Spencer lifted her a few inches off the floor and they kissed as Sophia kicked her feet up and down with excitement.

'Oh please, have they not made a movie about you two yet?' said Eleanor.

Spencer gave Sophia one last kiss then put her down.

'They wouldn't be able to find an actor handsome enough to play my Spence,' said Sophia.

'Eleanor, how are you,' he said, going over to kiss her on the cheek.

'I'm good. I don't know how you two do it, you're always so naturally happy and in love. Don't you two *ever* argue?' Sophia and Spencer thought about this for a second. Then they both said in unison, 'no.'

'You mean you've never argued, not even a mild disagreement or misunderstanding?'

'Never,' said Sophia.

'Wow!' said Eleanor.

'So how are things going with Michael, since he moved in?' said Sophia.

'Oh, great. Sometimes he can be a little *middle-of-the-road*, in that *accountant* sort of way. But he doesn't drink or smoke, he's clean and tidy and he's devoted to me.'

'You love him though, right?' said Spencer.

'Yes, of course. A little more *excitement* every now and then wouldn't go amiss – if you know what I mean – but I guess I should thank my lucky stars. Most women would give anything to have a decent caring man like Michael. Speaking of which, I'd better get home; he's cooking dinner tonight. I'll see you two on Saturday.'

Sophia and Spencer's evening out with Spencer's friends was perfect. The restaurant their friends had chosen had a great atmosphere and the food was superb. Later, when Sophia and Spencer drove back across London toward Hampstead, the streets were considerably quiet and free of traffic. High noctilucent clouds floated by the almost full moon. And for once, in London, they could see the bright stars through the sunroof of Spencer's BMW. Although it was almost midnight it was relatively warm so Sophia opened the sunroof for a clearer view. She reclined her seat slightly and leaned her head back on the headrest and gazed at the bright stars while listening to the dream-like voice of Diana Krall as she elegantly sang her way through the tracks on *The Look Of Love* CD that played on the car stereo.

The light wind in her hair, the bright stars, the light music, holding Spencer's hand while he drove smoothly across London – it was perfect, like it always was. She looked across at him and soaked up his side profile, his short neatly cut, light mousy brown hair and handsome features. She felt a love so strong as she gazed at him.

'Woah!' shouted Spencer as he yanked hard right on the steering wheel. Sophia was instantly yanked back into reality and looked through the windscreen to see a fox running across the road in the path of the BMW. Spencer swerved at a severe angle to avoid hitting it. He wrestled with the steering wheel and tried to straighten up the car, but he lost control and the car spun sideways and bounced up onto the kerb on the opposite side of the road. Spencer braked hard while still struggling with the steering wheel. The car bounced back down the kerb and came to a halt, sideways on, on the opposite side of the road right in the middle of a bridge over a canal. The panting Spencer looked at Sophia.

'Are you ok?' he gasped, adrenaline rushing.

'Yes I'm ... oh my God, SPENCER!' Sophia looked beyond Spencer out of his driver's side window and saw a lorry hurtling around the blind bend towards them. The driver was clearly speeding and there was no way he was going to be able to stop in time. Spencer turned just in time to see the lorry's large headlights blinding him. The driver hit the breaks and the lorry skidded momentarily before slamming hard into the offside of their car. The impact obliterated the driver's side of the BMW, while sending the car crashing up onto the kerb, flipping it onto its side and up onto the barrier. The BMW toppled and finally settled upside-down on its roof, teetering on the barrier hanging over the edge of the bridge with the canal thirty feet below. Sophia was stunned and in shock. Upside down, her head was wedged against the opening of the sunroof. She was disoriented, but conscious. She struggled to turn her head to the right, and then she saw Spencer. When she saw his motionless body, she started to hyperventilate and shake violently. He hung suspended by his seatbelt with copious amounts of blood dripping from his crushed torso down onto his face. His neck was clearly broken – he was dead. The chest of his torso was twisted and faced square on to the driver's window while his face and lifeless eyes faced the opposite direction staring straight at Sophia. Sophia's body went into involuntary spasms as she screamed emotional screams. The car rocked tentatively like a seesaw, threatening to go over the edge of the bridge at any second.

'Keep still,' shouted the driver of the lorry, who had got out and was unscathed. 'You have to keep perfectly still. I'm going to call for help.' The lorry driver dialled 999 and demanded all three emergency services, giving the operator the exact location.

'Help will be here soon, try not to move.' But Sophia could not hear him. She was in her own dark world of horror; unable to comprehend anything outside the half crushed metal box she was cocooned in.

The police were the first on the scene. After quickly assessing the situation, the larger of the two officers tried to put his bodyweight onto the boot end of the upside-down BMW to prevent it from tipping over the edge. Minutes later an ambulance and the fire brigade arrived. Just as the firemen jumped out of their truck there was a sound of metal twisting and scraping. The barrier collapsed under the roof of the BMW and the police officer could not hold the weight of the car to prevent it from tipping up. All he could do was watch, in horror, as the BMW tipped up and plummeted straight down into the cold dark canal below.

All of the emergency servicemen hurtled over the barrier at the side of the bridge and down the sloping bank to the water's edge. The car was upright in the middle of the canal, slowly sinking. Without hesitation, and against the rules, one of the firemen jumped into the canal and waded, up to his chest in water, out to the sinking car. He could see Sophia, screaming in a frenzied

SOPHIA

emotional state, trapped inside the car. The fireman struggled to open the door against the pressure of the water, eventually winning the battle and pulling the door open. He cut Sophia's seatbelt with his emergency tool and pulled the hysterical Sophia from the car.

'Spencer, I want my Spencer!!' she screamed. The fireman waded back to the bank with Sophia kicking and screaming in his arms. 'Spencer, Spencer!!' she screamed with tears flooding down her face. She looked back towards the sinking car, now almost totally submerged with just the rooftop barely visible. Water poured into the open sunroof. 'SPENCER!!!'

Chapter 5

'Hello,' said Diana, answering the telephone on the bedside table.

'Who is it?' said Andrew, stirring next to her. 'It's one o'clock in the morning.'

Diana listened intently to the voice on the other end of the phone, and then took a sharp intake of breath, 'NO!' Andrew shot bolt upright in bed.

'What … what's happened?'

'NO, NO, NO!' Tears started to flood down Diana's face as she continued to listen while sobbing hysterically. She put the phone to her chest and looked at her husband, unable to talk and in a clear state of shock. Andrew took the phone off her.

'Hello,' he said. He listened to the doctor at the hospital. 'Oh Lord, no, please no.'

Diana went to Charlotte's room and woke her up. 'Darling, it's your sister,' she said.

A doctor entered the relative's room at the hospital. 'Mr and Mrs Beckinsale?' he enquired.

'Yes,' said Diana.

'I'm Dr Harris—'

'How is she?' said Andrew, bounding to his feet.

'Your daughter was very lucky – just a few superficial cuts and bruises. She's still in shock, but she's going to be fine.'

'How is she going to be fine, she's just lost the love of her life. She'll never recover from this,' said Diana, crying hysterically. Andrew put his arm around her and tried to console her – to no avail.

'Can we see her?' said Charlotte.

'Soon. She's upstairs being treated by the Gynae team.'

'Gynae team? I don't understand, why would she need to see a Gynaecologist?' said Andrew.

'I'm sorry, I thought you knew. Your daughter was ten weeks pregnant.'

'Oh no,' said Diana.

'Was?' said Andrew.

'Sophia was holding her stomach in pain when she was brought in. Then a nurse noticed she was ... bleeding.'

Diana put her hand to her mouth. 'Oh Lord, no!'

'She miscarried. The impact and trauma of the accident could have been responsible, or it could have been totally unrelated.'

'I don't understand. She's on contraception,' said Diana.

'Well, they're not one hundred per cent. Some women still fall pregnant,' said Dr Harris.

'Mummy, I want to see my sister,' said Charlotte, crying and shaking her mother's arm.

'When can we see her?' said Andrew.

'I'll go and find out for you. I'll be back shortly.'

Dr Harris went upstairs to the Gynae Ward, leaving Andrew, Diana and Charlotte alone in the relative's room. The next twenty minutes seemed like a day. The three of them paced up and down while they tried to absorb the horror of the accident and Spencer's death. Their minds were overwhelmed as their world was abruptly thrown into a living nightmare. Diana reached into her handbag and took out a packet of cigarettes. With her shaking hands she struggled to manipulate one out of the packet. Eventually she did and placed it between her lips, then noticed the NO SMOKING sign on the wall. She tried to put the cigarette back in the packet, but with her shaking hands she broke it in half. This small insignificant act was enough to send Diana into further floods of tears. Andrew relieved Diana of the cigarette packet and dealt with her frustrating situation by removing the broken cigarette from the pack and discarding it by accurately tossing it into the wastepaper basket in the corner of the room. He held his sobbing wife and daughter as they all stood there thinking about the things that Dr Harris had just told them about Sophia, the accident, the miscarriage, Spencer's death, the horror of it all. What's going to happen now? Sophia is on the Gynae Ward upstairs having a gynaecologist make sure that everything has come away while her beloved Spencer is lying dead on a slab in the hospital mortuary. Who are they going to call first? What about Grandma Lizzie? What about Spencer's parents? Were they here? Did they even know?

There was a light knock at the door and Dr Harris entered.

'Please, follow me, I'll take you up to see her.'

In the elevator, Dr Harris continued to explain what still had to be done.

'The gynaecologist is satisfied and has given your daughter the all clear. However, due the mechanism of her injuries I'd like to carry out an abdominal CT scan. I'm happy there's no serious injury to her head and neck, apart from the cut on her temple where she scraped her head. But she does have some bruising across her abdomen.' The elevator arrived and the doors opened. Dr Harris led them down a short corridor to the ward.

'Remember, your daughter's not very communicative, understandably. She's still in shock.'

Dr Harris drew back the privacy curtains. Sophia was sitting upright on the narrow bed wearing a hospital issue gown, her wet clothes in a bag on the floor next to the bed. There was a small butterfly stitch on her temple taking care of the deep cut from where she hit her head on the car door during the struggle with the fireman. Apart from that and a few small grazes and a light bruising, she was fine; at least physically. Mentally, however, was a very different story. Her expression was inert to say the least as she stared blankly into an imaginary space a few feet in front of her face.

Diana put her hand up to her mouth and cried. 'Oh, Sophia, my darling,' she said. She put her arms around Sophia and held her, but there was no response. Sophia's arms remained by her sides and her puffy red bloodshot eyes remained fixed straight ahead.

'Oh, dear God,' said Andrew. Sophia remained unresponsive and motionless as her parents and younger sister hugged and held her. Charlotte could not control her sobbing.

'Can you hear me, honey?' said Andrew. Nothing. 'Please say something my darling,' said Diana. Nothing. Diana looked at Andrew, mortified.

A nurse arrived with a wheelchair and advised Andrew and Diana that they were ready to do the CT scan and given Sophia's state of shock the wheelchair would make things easier.

The abdominal CT scan was clear and Dr Harris was happy, knowing Sophia's father was a doctor, to discharge Sophia into the care of her parents. Andrew used the wheelchair and managed to get Sophia to his car then drove her home to their house in Hampstead. Once there, they sat Sophia on one of the sofas in the lounge. Charlotte sat with her while Diana got her old room ready and made up her bed. The doorbell went and Andrew went to let Eleanor in.

'How is she?' said Eleanor. Andrew just shook his head with tears in his eyes.

'She's in the lounge with Charlotte. Your mother's upstairs making up her bed.'

Eleanor went though to the lounge and couldn't believe what she saw. In a physical sense, the person sitting on the sofa next to her younger sister vaguely resembled Sophia, but Sophia was simply not there.

Andrew phoned Spencer's father, Philip, and spoke very briefly on the phone. There was a lot of crying through the early hours of the morning. There was an endless flood of emotions, thoughts and feelings. There was simply too much to think about, too much to comprehend. How could this horrific devastation have happened to them? How could it ever be fixed, how could their lives ever be normal again? After this, they doubted their lives would ever return to normal. Andrew carried Sophia up to her old room and gently laid her on the bed. Diana stayed with her. Sophia eventually fell asleep at around six in the morning. Diana fell asleep on the chaise-longue in Sophia's room shortly after.

Over the next four days Sophia was unreachable. She hadn't left her room, she didn't speak, and she didn't eat anything. The family GP told Andrew and Diana that if she wasn't eating, they at least needed to get a protein milkshake down her, but Sophia barely took a few sips when they tried. She just sat upright in bed, clutching a pillow to her chest imagining it to be Spencer. There she remained, locked in thought, staring at the wall. She longed for Spencer's touch. She thought about the unborn child she didn't know was developing inside her and if she hadn't miscarried, she could at least have had Spencer's child. But now, she couldn't even have that small consolation. Often tears would escape her eyes and run down her cheeks and onto the pillow that she desperately grasped and hung onto.

Sophia's love for Spencer was so deep and intrinsic she didn't know how she was ever going to survive without him. He was everything to her. He was her reason for living. Before, when she woke up beside him in her apartment, she would feel his presence lying next to her. She would snuggle up close to him and feel the warmth of his skin against hers. She would inhale the smell of him, his cologne still faintly present from the day before. She'd run her fingers gently through his neatly cut mousy hair while listening to his gentle breathing. She imagined the two of them married with, first a baby girl, then perhaps later a boy. Even with children she would make time for her beloved Spencer and one day the children would grow up and she would have him all to herself again. They would be the perfect family, the perfect couple, the definitive soulmates. But now Spencer was dead, gone, and none of this would ever happen.

Sophia missed him with physical pain, he should be there, he had become part of her, she was not fully functional without him. Without him, there was a roaring silence, a gaping chasm, without him, there was nothing.

Her younger sister, Charlotte, spent most of her time in Sophia's room doing everything she could to comfort her older sister. She took her portable music system with its iPod dock and tried playing light classical music in the background. Those soft and soothing middle adagio movements from Baroque pieces. Charlotte wasn't sure if they helped, or simply made things even more melancholy.

She also tried reading to Sophia. Charlotte had soft vocal tones and read beautifully. Every day she read Jane Austin to her, but it didn't help. Perhaps romantic fiction was the last thing Sophia wanted to hear. So, in the end, she just held her older sister in silence with a box of tissues at the ready to gently wipe away any tears that Sophia shed.

'It's been four days and she hasn't come out of her room or said a single word. When she's not sleeping she just stares at the wall. She won't eat and she barely drinks. Any food we take to her she barely touches. I'm really worried. What are we going to do, Andrew?' said Diana.

'I'm not sure ... well ... there's a psychologist I can call.'

'A psychologist? Don't you think that's a bit much?'

'I don't know. The initial shock should have worn off by now; I think she's suffering form post-traumatic stress disorder. And if she is, it's better that she sees somebody sooner rather than later, to prevent any long term effects.'

'How well do you know this psychologist?'

'He's a friend of Philip's.'

'Philip, as in Spencer's father?' she quizzed.

'Yes. His name's Jacques de Beaumont. Philip says he's a brilliant psychologist. I met him once, briefly, about a year ago. He might be able to help Sophia.' Diana paced up and down contemplating the idea.

'Look, darling, I'm a skin specialist, not a psychologist. I just feel that we need to call somebody in, somebody who knows more about this than we do, somebody we can talk to. I'm not saying we should send him straight up to see her, but we should at least get his advice.'

'Ok, you're right,' she said.

'Look, I've cancelled all my appointments for next week, but the week after I have to be back at work,' he said.

'I can stay with her,' said Diana. 'Lisa said to take all

the time I need. She can manage the gallery without me for a few weeks, maybe more. If an emergency comes up she'll call me.'

Diana opened the kitchen door to the patio and took out a cigarette.

'Ok, call him,' she said, exhaling a large puff of smoke in the direction of the garden.

Chapter 6

'Dr de Beaumont, come on in,' said Andrew, opening the electronic gates. Andrew and Diana stood at their open front door as Dr de Beaumont drove up and parked his car outside the house alongside Diana's Audi A6 Avant.

'Dr de Beaumont, it's so good of you to give up your time and come out in the evening,' said Andrew, shaking his hand. 'This is my wife, Diana.'

'Good evening,' he said, shaking her hand. 'Please, call me Jacques.'

'Come on in, can I get you a drink?' said Diana.

'A glass of water, please.'

Andrew and Jacques sat in the lounge and waited for Diana to return with the glass of water. Jacques admired the tasteful modern décor, especially the painting on the wall, which he instantly recognized as a Robert Antoine Pinchon. But he wasn't about to make small talk about post-impressionist landscape paintings or interior design.

'Thank you,' said Jacques as Diana placed the glass of water onto a small circular placemat on the coffee table in front of him.

'I saw Philip and his wife yesterday. As you know we're good friends,' said Jacques.

'Yes ... I can't begin to imagine what they're going through right now,' said Andrew.

'It's difficult. They've started making the funeral arrangements. I'm sure they'll be in touch to give you the details. Look, why don't you tell me about Sophia.'

Andrew and Diana gave Jacques the whole story in great detail, not only about how Sophia had been since the accident, but also the back-story, how long Sophia and Spencer had known each other and what they meant to each other. During the conversation, Jacques scribbled down notes onto a leather-bound A4 writing pad.

'I'd like to go up and see her,' said Jacques. Diana looked at Andrew unsure of what to say.

'She's ...' Diana searched for words, but didn't find them.

'Look, this is an area I specialise in. I need to see her to evaluate exactly where she is.'

'She won't talk,' said Diana.

'It doesn't matter, I don't need her to talk, not just yet.'

Diana looked at Andrew again and read his eyes. 'Ok, I'll take you up to her,' said Diana. Andrew followed them up to Sophia's room.

Sophia was wearing her nightclothes, but was sitting on the bed with her arms hugging her knees to her chest. She was rocking faintly back and forth as her insensible eyes stared at the end of her bed. Charlotte sat next to her with her arm around her shoulder.

'Charlotte, honey, this is Jacques. He's going to try and help Sophia.'

'Would you mind leaving me alone with her,' said Jacques. Charlotte got up.

Sophia

'We'll wait downstairs in the lounge,' said Diana. They hesitantly made their way downstairs as Jacques closed Sophia's bedroom door and sat on the chaise-longue by the foot of her bed.

Ten minutes later Jacques came down and entered the lounge.

'How did it go? Did she say anything?' said Diana.

'No ... at least not audibly.'

Andrew, Diana and Charlotte waited with bated breath for Jacques to speak.

'Sophia's transitioned from being in a state of shock into a state of post-traumatic stress disorder. During this process she's possibly developed mild selective mutism; it's not common, but it's not totally unheard of. It's important that I help her straight away. The sooner PTSD is confronted, the easier it is to overcome. I need to get Sophia speaking as soon as possible, so she can confront what's happened to her and accept it as part of her past,' he explained.

'What do you suggest?' said Andrew.

'Trauma-focused cognitive-behavioural therapy.'

'Are you happy to do this?' said Diana.

'Of course,' said Jacques. 'I have deep knowledge in this area. I think it's the best option for Sophia right now.'

'Ok,' said Andrew. 'If you think that's the best direction to go.'

'Of course, I have some initial groundwork to do first as she's not talking. Then I'd like to see her every day initially. I'll come here to start with, then when I'm happy with her progress she can come to see me at my office maybe twice a week to continue.'

'When would you like to start?' said Andrew.

'Right away,' he said, taking out his diary. 'I'd like to see her tomorrow afternoon, at one o'clock. Will you be here?'

'Of course, Andrew's off work for the next few days and I'm going to be around for the next few weeks. Charlotte's sometimes around as well, she's re-worked things at Uni so she can do more study at home over the next few weeks.'

'Good. I'll move some appointments around so I can see her every day for the next week.'

'How long do you think ... I mean ... she will be ok won't she?' said Diana.

'Yes,' he said, in a soft reassuring tone. Diana managed a weak smile. 'I'm going to pencil her in every day for the next week, then depending on how she progresses I'll continue to see her for a further four to six week period. I'm optimistic I can get her to come to terms with what happened so she can function again and rebuild her life.'

'Thank you, thank you so much,' said Diana.

'Mummy, I'm going back upstairs,' said Charlotte, keen to be with her sister.

'Ok, honey,' said Diana.

'Well, I must get home. I'll see you tomorrow,' said Jacques.

'Thank you so much for taking the time at such short notice,' said Andrew, shaking his hand.

The following day, Jacques arrived at 1 p.m. sharp and

spent an hour with Sophia in her room. Naturally, Andrew and Diana were keen to hear how his initial session went, but Jacques explained that it was going to take him a little time to gently draw Sophia out. He wasn't going to force anything.

The days went by. Andrew couldn't cancel any more appointments and had gone back to work. Eleanor had only managed to come to the house to see Sophia and to help out a few times due to her busy work commitments that she couldn't get out of. But Eleanor could hardly connect with Sophia at the best of times, so her efforts proved awkward and somewhat unnatural for her. Lisa had shown signs of anxiety at Diana's art gallery in Kensington. They had a big exhibition fast approaching for a well-known contemporary Italian artist and there was much work still to do. Lisa needed Diana's leadership with such an important event, so Diana had reluctantly started going over to Kensington to run things again on a part time basis. Andrew and Diana had been to Spencer's funeral and they did everything in their power to get Sophia to go, but Sophia clammed up, shook violently and screamed every time her parents mentioned it. On top of all this, Sophia's agent, Meredith found out about the accident when Sophia missed an important recital. The venue had phoned Meredith when they didn't hear from Sophia. The promoter was not happy; issuing ticket refunds is not something any promoter likes doing. After speaking with Diana on the phone, Meredith decided to cancel Sophia's recital bookings for the next four weeks and let the relevant venues and promoters know. She prayed for Sophia, but hoped she would pull through soon and be able to get back to her busy recital schedule.

Jacques was starting to get concerned. His CBT therapy wasn't working out the way he had hoped. In fact, he had barely scratched the surface with Sophia and was making little to no headway. She was still barely communicative and never came out of her room. However, during the past week Jacques had witnessed the occasional facial expression from her. She was also picking more at the food her parents took to her. Jacques could sense that something was stirring within Sophia. The way she was at the beginning was somewhat different from how she was now. Her body movements and facial expressions were shifting slightly. It was like she was morphing. Something wasn't right, but he was unable to fathom what it was – he needed more time.

Although Andrew and Diana had returned to work, Sophia was not alone during the day. Andrew had hired a professional carer/nurse to be there Monday to Friday during the day and Charlotte was freeing up as much time as she could to be with her sister. The cleaner was also around during the day twice a week and she was very sweet and understanding.

Andrew's schedule had freed up, so he had taken the afternoon off work. He thought if Sophia heard him around the house it might help her. Just when he was thinking of going up to her room to check on her, the intercom rang. Andrew looked at the small LCD monitor on the wall by the front door and noticed a man leaning out of the window of a pristine white car waiting for a voice to come over the intercom system.

'Hello,' said Andrew.

'Mr Beckinsale?' said the man.

'Yes.'

'I'm from Finchley Road Audi, we've come to deliver your car.'

Oh Lord. With everything that had been going on he had totally forgotten. Andrew and Diana had bought Sophia a brand new sparkling white Audi A3 hatchback for her birthday – which was just a few days away. Although when they ordered it ten weeks previously it had proved quite problematic. Andrew and Diana knew that Sophia wrestled to fit her cello into her existing car, which was getting quite old now, so they thought a logical gift for her twenty second would be a nice new car. However, Andrew had to loan a Stevenson cello case to take with him to the dealership to make sure it was going to be easy to load in and out of the car. All that thought and effort had somehow paled into insignificance now. But ten weeks on their daughter's birthday present was sitting at the entrance gates to their house with its engine idling.

'Ok, I'll open the gates for you. Come on up to the house.' The white A3 led the way, followed by his colleague in a silver A5. The A3 driver went into the house briefly to give Andrew the keys and finalise the paperwork, while the A5 driver waited in his car outside the house, ready to give his colleague a lift back to the dealership.

Diana arrived home at 5:40 p.m. Having noticed the

new Audi parked on the driveway outside the house she went to Andrew's office.

'They delivered the car? I forgot it was today,' she said.

'Me too. What are we going to do, Diana? Our daughter's sitting up there in her room all day going through Lord knows what and Jacques doesn't seem to be getting anywhere.'

'Has she eaten anything today?' said Diana.

'The carer took some breakfast up to her this morning and a sandwich at lunchtime. She ate half of it.'

'Well that's something. I'm going to make myself a cup of tea and go up and sit with her for a while,' she said.

Diana knocked lightly on Sophia's door before entering.

'Hello, darling,' she said, sitting on the corner of the bed. 'Can I get you anything?' But Sophia just stared at the wall and was unresponsive. 'Do you want something to eat or drink?' asked Diana. But Sophia didn't even acknowledge her mother's presence. Sophia was there in physical presence only, but her mind was not.

'Look, Sophia, it will be ok, it'll get easier, in time–'

'Shut up, just shut up,' she snapped, 'it won't be ok, it'll never be ok, it won't get easier and I'll never forget him. Spencer's gone, he's dead, and nothing can ever come to any good anymore.'

'Sophia, I know what you must be going–'

'Don't you dare, you haven't the faintest idea what I'm going through or feeling. Somebody's ripped open my chest and torn out all my insides. Now all that's left inside me is a huge empty void where Spencer used to be – he was the very fabric that was woven into my life.

I'll never get over this, I'll never be able to live without him – I can't live without him! Nothing means anything anymore; everything's empty and soulless. He was woven into every part of my life and I can't detach myself. There's nothing you can say or do that's going to make me feel any better, Mummy – so don't say anything, please, just leave me alone!'

'Ok, darling,' she said.

Later that evening Andrew and Diana were talking in the lounge when Diana became aware of a draught on her legs.

'Do you feel a draught, darling,' she said.

'No.'

'I can definitely feel a draught coming from somewhere.'

'Maybe you left the kitchen door open earlier when you went out onto the patio for a cigarette?' he said.

Diana got up to go and check, while Andrew took a sip of his drink.

'ANDREW!' she shouted.

Andrew jumped to his feet and raced through the house to the kitchen. The door to the patio and back garden was wide open. He ran through it and saw his wife kneeling down next to Sophia, who was sitting in the muddy flowerbed wearing nothing but a skimpy nightie. There had been an unexpected thunderstorm and a downpour of rain the night before so the ground was sodden and muddy. Sophia sat in the middle of a muddy flowerbed hugging her knees. Her bare feet had sunk into the muddy ground. She'd smeared wet cold muddy earth from the flowerbed all over her legs, arms, chest, neck and face. She had even caked it into her long hair. Andrew and Diana couldn't see an inch of her beautiful white skin; all they could see was a muddy mound that physically resembled a female human form.

'Oh my darling, what have you done,' said Diana, as she tried to wipe away the mud from around Sophia's eyes. Sophia grabbed Diana's wrist to prevent her clearing away any mud from her face. She looked intently into her mother's eyes.

'I wanted to look on the outside how I feel on the inside,' said Sophia.

'Oh my poor darling,' said Diana, holding her mouth. Seeing her daughter like this was too much, Diana broke down and cried. She was overwhelmed with mixed emotions, sad, shocked, but also strangely happy that her daughter had come out of her room for the first time since the accident.

'Come on my darling, let's get you into the house,' said Andrew as he bent down to pick her up. She was calm as Andrew carried her through the house and upstairs to the bathroom. Charlotte came out of her room to see what was going on.

'Oh no, what happened?' said Charlotte.

'Honey, can you get me some fresh towels and a robe,' said Diana.

Charlotte went to get them while Andrew stood Sophia in the shower and left Diana alone with her to help shower her down.

Sophia stood in the shower, oblivious, as her mother started at her head and washed the dark earthy mud down her daughter's body. Eventually, the thick dark muddy water around her feet started to dilute, like the final remnants of gravy being washed down a sink. The water finally turned from murky brown to just murky and then finally clear. Diana got her daughter dried and settled in her room. Sophia's expression had changed somehow and Diana thought she was about to start talking. She looked at Sophia expectantly, her face willing her to speak. After all, just twenty minutes earlier in the muddy flowerbed she had spoken an entire sentence, which, for all intents and purposes, sounded quite normal. But, the words never came. However, Diana noticed that Sophia had lost the vacant look in her eyes, she detected life in them again, but not the life that was there before the accident, this was a different look altogether – a look that worried Diana.

The following afternoon the carer took some food and drink up to Sophia's room. As usual, she knocked quietly on her door before entering. She leant forward to place the tray onto the table next to the bed.

'I have some food for you, sweetheart,' she said in her calm nurse-like voice.

Sophia lunged forward and smashed the tray out of her hands, sending the food and drink in every direction. The glass of water shattered against one wall and the bowl of soup smashed against another, its contents ended up dripping off the ceiling and walls.

'I DON'T WANT ANY FUCKING FOOD,' shouted Sophia.

The carer stood there clutching her chest, her heart beating so hard it felt like a stallion was trying to horse-kick its way out of her chest. Sophia's eyes bored into hers. The carer ran out of the room and down the stairs and out of the house.

Andrew got home first and saw the carer sitting on the steps outside the front door of the house. The carer told him that she would not go back into the house. She explained what had happened and that the incident had scared her so much she couldn't continue working for them. She told him that Sophia had the look of a possessed manic devil in her eyes. As she was talking to Andrew, Diana's car drove through the gates and up the drive.

'What's going on?' said Diana.

'There's been an incident,' said Andrew.

'What sort of incident, Sophia?'

'Yes,' he said.

Diana rushed upstairs to check on Sophia. Andrew joined her after paying the carer for the work she had done, plus a token bonus.

From what Diana and Andrew could see, Sophia seemed perfectly calm as she sat on her soup-splattered bed winding a lock of her hair around her index finger. Diana collected up the broken glass and cleared up the worst of the soup. The cleaner would have to carry out a more thorough job tomorrow.

Diana made sure Sophia was ok and settled, and then went to leave the room. As she turned and walked towards the bedroom door, she sensed Sophia's head turn and she felt her eyes on her back. When she got to the door, she turned, but Sophia was looking in the other direction. She closed the door and went back downstairs.

Later that evening, Charlotte returned home and joined her parents in the lounge.

'How was your class?' asked Diana.

'It was great. How's Sophia?'

'I'm not really sure,' said Diana. She went on to explain the incident with the carer to Charlotte.

'Is she ok, can I go up to see her?' said Charlotte.

'Sure, honey,' said Diana.

Just as Charlotte got up off the sofa, they heard a car start up outside the house on the driveway.

'What's that?' said Diana, looking towards the window.

Andrew got up to go and look out through the curtains, Diana and Charlotte followed. Andrew pulled back the curtain just in time to see the sparking new white Audi A3 speed down the driveway and through the electric gates; its wing mirrors marginally missing them before they had fully opened.

'SOPHIA,' shouted Diana. She ran out of the front door. But it was too late; the sound of the Audi's engine had vanished. Diana ran back into the house and up to Sophia's room, hoping that a car thief had stolen the car. She burst into Sophia's bedroom only to find it empty – Sophia was gone.

As Sophia accelerated along Hampstead Lane she found that the trauma of her recent car crash had not put her off getting into a car. In fact, at this precise moment, she felt quite invigorated by the driving experience – even reckless. She sped through the narrow gap in the road at The Spaniards Inn and Toll Gate House at 60mph, not bothering to be courteous to the annoyed oncoming driver. She had no intention of slowing down to give the oncoming driver priority. As Sophia sped through the narrow gap, the woman driver shook her fist and gave Sophia an angry look. She yelled something through the windscreen, which Sophia did not hear, nor care about.

Chapter 7

'Wow, it looks so amazing,' said the young female hairdresser standing behind Sophia, looking at her all-new shockingly vibrant hair colour in the mirror. Gone was Sophia's beautiful long natural auburn hair. After three hours in the hairdresser's, a bleach dye process, a thorough rinse, two shampoos and another rinse, Sophia now had bright bleach blond hair that was more akin to a cheap brainless bimbo than an upper middle class concert cellist.

'You look so different, what a transformation,' said the scatty hairdresser.

'Transformation, yes, this is the new me,' said Sophia.

She left the hairdressers and crossed the road and made her way back down the high street to where her car was parked. As well as a new hair colour, Sophia had also been shopping for new clothes and shoes. Everybody, and I mean everybody, turned to look at Sophia as she walked down the high street with her long blonde hair and new clothes. Her new skin-tight black leather trousers did an excellent job of showing off her long legs, great hips, and attractive behind.

On her feet she wore black stylish shoes with

vertiginously high metallic silver stiletto heels that looked frighteningly like the stiletto daggers they were named after. With heels like those she had to adjust her deportment and walk differently; so she walked with a graceful feline sway.

Her top half was scantily covered with a partially see-through sexy white lace blouse. Although this attire was more common during the 1980s, Sophia somehow made it look bang up to date and her new lightly tinted Maui Jim sunglasses also made her look super cool. She looked striking to say the least, tall, thin, long blonde hair, and a beautiful porcelain white blemish-free completion with big brown doll-like eyes. Other women looked at her with envy as she passed, while the men drooled. One young man found himself taking some serious wrath from his girlfriend, who had caught him checking out the behind on the stunning blonde as she walked past; to the amusement of the other passers by.

After stopping off at HMV to bring her music collection up to date, she eventually arrived back at her apartment in Hampstead. Her telephone answering machine was inundated with messages from her parents, her two sisters, her good friend and piano accompanist, Django, her agent, Meredith, as well as other concerned friends.

For the past few days, since Sophia sped off the driveway from her parents house, she had pretty much been off the map and unreachable, in more ways than one. Her mobile phone was still at her parents house, somehow, she hadn't really needed it, or missed it.

Sophia

But now she was back at her apartment looking at the flashing number 17 on the answering machine. *That's a lot of messages*, she thought. She kicked off her stilettos and went into the kitchen to make herself a cup of tea. Just as she settled on her sofa, the phone rang; no surprise considering nobody had heard from her or seen her for the past few days.

'Hello,' she answered.

'Oh, thank goodness. Sophia, where've you been? We've been worried sick,' said Diana.

'I'm fine, Mummy. I just needed a few days on my own that's all.'

'I must have called you a dozen times over the past two days. Why didn't you answer?'

'I haven't been here. I guess I just needed to be somewhere else. I didn't feel like talking.'

'I know that, I've been over to your apartment five times. We even called the police. Where have you been darling? We've all been worried sick. Your mobile's here so we couldn't even contact you that way. Where were you?'

'I stayed with a friend.'

'Which friend?'

'Mummy, I'll pop over this evening and tell you then. I'll pick up my phone at the same time.'

'Sophia, don't get me wrong, I'm thrilled that you're back at your apartment now, but you sound ... well, calm and normal.'

'That's good isn't it?' she said, matter of fact.

'Well, I suppose it is,' said Diana, puzzled and concerned.

'Great, well I'll see you about eight?' said Sophia.

'Ok,' said Diana. Sophia hung up the phone. Diana stood in her kitchen, not really knowing what to think or feel.

Sophia opened the electric entrance gates to her parents' house with her remote control and drove up to the house. Her mother came rushing out in anticipation. As Sophia parked outside the house, Diana stopped in her tracks and stared at the unrecognisable blonde girl sitting behind the steering wheel of the brand new white Audi A3. Sophia got out of the car, looking like a superstar in her new clothes. She casually closed the car door, seemingly without a care in the world. She swaggered over to her waiting mother, who was stunned and speechless as it dawned on her that this blonde girl wearing somewhat questionable attire was in fact her daughter.

'Oh dear Lord, what happened, what have you done?' said Diana.

'Are you talking about my hair, Mummy?'

'Everything, I'm talking about … everything,' she said, looking her up and down. 'Look at your hair, and those clothes, what's happened to my sweet daughter?' she said, clearly repulsed by her artificially dyed hair and choice of clothes and shoes.

'I fancied a change, it's the new me. Don't you like it?'

Just then, Sophia's father, Andrew, and her younger sister, Charlotte came out.

'Thank God you're ok,' said Andrew, coming over to hug his daughter.

'She's hardly ok, just look at her,' said Diana.

'Wow, you look great, sis,' said Charlotte, all excited that her sister was back, and with this incredible new, if somewhat different, look. 'Wow, those shoes are so cool,' said Charlotte.'

'Well, this is an exciting new look,' said Andrew, just pleased to see his daughter was ok.

'Andrew, please, don't encourage her, just look at her hair, and those shoes,' said Diana.

Come on inside, darling.' said Andrew, 'have you eaten?'

'Actually, I am a bit peckish,' she said, smiling while sauntering into the house with her father and Charlotte.

'How about one of those toasted ham and cheese sandwiches that you love so much?' said Andrew, opening the fridge door.

'Oh yummy,' said Sophia.

'Can I have one too, Daddy?' said Charlotte, giving her father her best cute puppy dog look.

'Sure you can sweetheart,' said Andrew.

Diana stood at the kitchen door giving Andrew one of her, *what are you playing at?* looks. She then went into the lounge, but not before giving Andrew a final, *I want to talk to you right now* look. Andrew placed two sandwiches onto the electric sandwich maker and dropped the lid.

'Back in a minute girls. Keep an eye on those will you?' he said, pulling a silly mock-scary face as he headed into the lounge to face whatever music his wife had cued up for him.

'What do you think you're doing?' said Diana.

'Making my daughters ham and cheese sandwiches,'

he said.

'You know exactly what I mean, just look at the state of her, she looks like … well, something you'd expect to see streetwalking around a red light district.'

'Oh come on, darling, she doesn't look that bad, you're overreacting.'

'Overreacting, how can you say that. Look what she's done to her beautiful hair, and those cheap clothes she's wearing.'

'Look, she's suffered a great loss, not only Spencer, but an unborn baby too. Perhaps this is her way of dealing with it. She's expressing herself.'

'Well, I don't like it one bit.'

'You never did,' said Andrew.

'What exactly is *that* supposed to mean?'

'Well, let's face it, you never let any of them express themselves when they were growing up. You wouldn't let them try make-up and you always decided what they could and couldn't wear.'

'Not all the time,' she said. Andrew looked at her and raised an eyebrow.

'Well this is different, this isn't just a little bit of make up. She has enough make-up for five supermodels plastered all over her face.'

'Look, if this is her way of dealing with Spencer's death and it helps her function then I'm all for it. Besides, I'm sure it'll be temporary; it's just a process she has to go through. Why don't you try and forget about what she looks like, she's still your daughter. Come into the kitchen and have a drink with us.'

SOPHIA

Diana couldn't hide the fact that she deeply disapproved of Sophia's new look. But, she eventually saw the positive side, in that she was up and about, eating, and seemed quite normal – at least outwardly. Sophia explained that she just felt a sudden urge to get out of the house and be on her own for a day or two. She spent two nights at her friend's house. Isabella was a music teacher from the Royal Academy who Sophia had stayed in touch with. Isabella was older than Sophia, but she had lost her own husband tragically two years earlier, so she understood exactly what Sophia was going through.

'Honey, you could have at least let us know where you were, and that you were ok,' said Diana.

'I'm sorry, Mummy. My mind feels like it just hasn't been my own recently,' said Sophia.

'It's ok, darling. We totally understand,' said Andrew. 'So, how are you enjoying your birthday present,' he said. Sophia looked slightly embarrassed.

'Thank you, Daddy, I love it,' she said, kissing him on the cheek and hugging him.

'Thank you Mummy,' she said, hugging her.

'Well, we knew that you struggled to get your cello case in and out of your car,' said Diana.

'Yes, and it was getting a little unreliable too,' said Sophia.

'Well, we hope you enjoy it,' said Andrew.

'Oh, before I forget, here's your mobile,' said Diana, picking Sophia's iPhone up off the kitchen table and putting it firmly into her hand. 'Please, keep it with you, darling' she pleaded.

'I will, Mummy.'

Sophia didn't stay too long. It was about thirty minutes after she first arrived when Andrew and Diana watched Sophia get into her new car and head off down the drive and through the gates in the direction of Hampstead Lane.

'I'm a little surprised that she would even want to get into a car after what happened to her,' said Andrew.

'Yes, it does seem a little unusual. Does this mean she's no longer suffering from post-traumatic stress?' said Diana.

'I'm not sure. It certainly looks that way. I'll call Jacques in the morning and speak to him.'

Chapter 8

The next morning Sophia woke up in her own apartment for the first time since Spencer's death. As she stood in the shower with the hot water beating a wide area of skin between her shoulder blades, everything felt quite different. Physically, she seemed to feel more energetic than usual. She held her hands up in front of her, spanning her fingers as the water came over her shoulders and jetted onto her palms rinsing away the soapsuds. She closed her fingers and clenched her fists tight observing the lines of the taught muscles in her wrists and forearms. She felt strong and invigorated – at least physically. However, her head was pounding as something hammered away at the front of her brain – a headache sent straight from hell. She turned and stood close to the showerhead allowing the water to blast hard against her face and forehead, but there was no relief from the headache. The soapsuds drained down her body and washed away down the plughole. The thoughts of Spencer and his voice in her head, however, did not.

Sophia had slept lightly the night before and had been woken twice to the sound of Spencer's voice calling her name. The first time, during that delicate moment just as she was falling asleep, she heard it as clear as day. It was like he was standing right there in her bedroom. 'Sophia' said Spencer's voice. It was so vivid it yanked her right out of the sleep that she was just seconds from falling into. She gasped and reached for the lamp switch next to her bed. She scanned the room and said 'Spencer?' but he was not there. Convinced she'd actually heard him calling her name, she got out of bed and looked in the living room and then the kitchen and then the bathroom. She even looked in the cupboard in the hallway and just outside her front door, but Spencer was not there. It took her two hours to get to sleep after that as she lay in bed listening out for his voice.

Eventually, she did hear his voice again; waking her at six a.m. As before, she got up and searched her apartment for her beloved Spencer, calling his name. But as before, he was not there.

She tried to get back to sleep, but couldn't. So she took a shower, put on her robe, bunched her all-new blonde hair up and fixed a small towel around it and went to the kitchen to make a drink.

She took her cup of tea into the living room and took a large pile of CDs out of the carrier bag that she'd bought from HMV in Oxford Street the day before. Heavy rock wasn't Sophia's typical taste in music. In fact, with her classical music upbringing her collection was largely made up of music from the baroque, classical and romantic periods, with a smattering of contemporary; the majority of which was on vinyl.

SOPHIA

Sophia had finely tuned musical ears and she could hear the extra detail and *je ne sais quoi* that you only got from a piece of vinyl spinning around at thirty three and a third. Although she had a CD player for the twenty percent of CDs that made up her collection, it was a rather high end one. The only other music she had in her collection that deviated from classical was some jazz and blues and a sizable collection of female singers such as Nora Jones and Diana Krall. But now, for some strange and inexplicable reason, Sophia was developing a taste for heavy rock and metal music.

Not knowing an awful lot about rock music she had asked one of the salesmen at HMV if he could be kind enough to pick out a selection of about two dozen really great rock and metal CDs. She said she wanted a selection of classic rock/metal albums from over the years, as well as some up-to-date stuff. She struck lucky. The salesman she asked just so happened to be something of a metal head, who loved metal and rock and generally good music with an element of muscle and edge to it – definitely nothing lame. He was in his early-twenties, skinny, quite short and wearing skinny fit chinos and a black t-shirt. He wasn't what she'd call a good-looking guy, but he had an endearing charm about him, which she liked. He was enthusiastic about rock music and was keen to help Sophia. He even loved the classic stuff from the 70s, 80's and 90s, as well as all the more modern bands. He was thrilled to walk around the store with this beautiful tall blonde girl, helping and advising her on various rock, metal and goth bands.

He'd grabbed a basket and was leading Sophia through the many rows of CDs. Each time he picked up a CD he would proudly show off his knowledge to Sophia before putting it into the basket.

'Ok, AC-DC, you gotta have these two, Highway to Hell and Back in Black. Bon Scott's last studio album for the band before he died, and Brian Johnson's debut album with them; both are superb.' Sophia just looked at him and smiled, oblivious to what he was talking about.

'Led Zeppelin. The first four albums, you've gotta have them. It needs no explanation. It's a no brainer. Just listen to them and you'll see what I mean,' he said, dropping them into the basket before moving on and cherry-picking more albums.

Two of his male work colleagues saw him being overly helpful with Sophia. When he glanced across the shop floor, he noticed them standing there, arms folded, shaking their heads and laughing with a look of, *you really don't stand a chance, dude,* on their faces. He ignored their mickey taking and got back to helping Sophia, who had also noticed them teasing her little helper. To give his two teasing co-workers something to talk about, Sophia put her arm around her little helper's shoulder in a flirty manner and whispered in his ear 'what about this?' picking up a CD with interesting cover artwork of something that resembled a pig with fangs.

'Classic Motorhead. That's their debut album. It's a bit raw sounding with questionable production values, but it still hits the spot,' he said, slightly nervous and thrilled at the same time as this beautiful blonde girl stood in such close proximity to him.

'Sounds great,' she said, dropping it into the basket he was holding. 'Where now?' she said, as she dropped her arm down and around his waist. She led him along the shop floor, catching the gob-smacked look on his two co-workers in her peripheral vision. Her trendy young helper's nostrils were now filled with Sophia's incredible scent and perfume. He continued to pick out CDs and drop them into the basket for her. He could feel her warm arm and hand around his midriff. All his senses were going into overdrive. His legs started to weaken as he struggled to concentrate on the job in hand. *N, O, P, Q* he thought as he mentally went through the alphabet, desperately trying to concentrate on coming up with bands he thought Sophia might like. It was no good. By now he was totally mesmerized by Sophia's beautiful perfume. Right at the end of the row he spotted an album.

'Ah, ZZ Top, Eliminator. How could I forget this,' he said as Sophia took the CD off him and analysed the cover.

'Hmm, not familiar with them,' she said.

'Well, they were more famous in the 80s. This album was from back then, but look,' he said, turning the CD over in Sophia's hands so he could read the track listings, 'there are some classic tracks on this album. You must have heard *Gimme All Your Lovin'*,' he said.

'No, perhaps I'd recognise it if I heard it,' she said.

'Well, there are loads of great hits on this album, *Sharp Dressed Man, TV Dinners, Got Me Under Pressure, L*

... *Legs*,' he said, stuttering on the last one and turning a slight shade of crimson. Sophia dropped the CD into the basket.

'I think that's twenty four,' she said. 'You've been really helpful.' She gave him a friendly kiss on the cheek. 'Where do I pay for these?'

'Oh, just over here, I'll show you.' Sophia and her helper walked right past his two co-workers, who were no longer teasing him.

'Pick your tongues up off the floor guys, you're staining the carpet,' she joked. They didn't know where to look.

Sophia's little helper had picked out some great CDs from the likes of: Led Zeppelin, The Who, AC-CD, Metallica, Guns N' Roses, Nirvana, Faith No More, Rage Against The Machine, Radiohead, Foo Fighters, Muse, My Chemical Romance, The Killers, along with more recent bands like Avenged Sevenfold, Asking Alexandria, Max Raptor and Heaven's Basement.

Moving the CDs one at a time from the large pile on the right side of her coffee table, she built a new pile to the left as she studied the covers of each one in turn. A few of the bands she'd briefly heard of, Led Zeppelin, who hadn't? Even people who move in classical music circles have heard of them, and most people would be familiar with the famous picked guitar chord progression on *Stairway To Heaven*, but *who the hell are The Cooper Temple Clause?*

She flicked through a few more. *What the hell*, she thought as she peeled away the shrink-wrapping from a CD entitled *Wretched and Devine* by a band called Black Veil Brides. She pulled the door open on her CD player, placed the CD onto it and dropped the magnetic CD clamping puck into place. She didn't really know what to expect as she pressed the play button. But her little helper at HMV had said they were quite new and pretty cool. He also told her that they'd stolen their dress sense and make-up ideas from an 80s band called Kiss. She turned the volume up and waited.

After a brief build up of what sounded like electrical hum and bass rumble with a male voice saying something about the kingdom of God, the first song, *I Am Bulletproof,* kicked in and assaulted her loudspeakers. It sounded like a wall of sound with a male vocalist anti-singing. Sophia increased the volume further still in an attempt to drown out the horrifying memories and images of the car crash that led to Spencer's death. She also wanted to shut out her feelings and the sound of Spencer's voice that echoed around inside her head.

Chapter 9

After finishing up drying her hair she turned off her hair dryer. She thought she heard the doorbell so she jumped up and went into the living and turned the music down a little, and then she stood still and listened. The doorbell rang again. She opened the door and saw Django standing there. Django was a smidgen taller than Sophia and of slim build. His neatly cut hair was mousey blonde and he had an impeccable completion that a lot of women would die for. With his seductive grey/green eyes, chiselled cheekbones and blemish free complexion, women thought he looked attractive in a boyish kind of way. Django was always being hit on by young women and occasionally, young men too. He didn't only have unique attractive looks, he also had a natural endearing charm about him and he was a true gentleman, which made him all the more appealing.

'Hi … Oh wow,' said Django.

'What is it?' said Sophia, holding her front door open.

'Your hair.'

'Oh, do you like it,' she said, running her fingers through it proudly.

'It's … different,' he said. 'I've been ringing the bell

SOPHIA

for ages.'

'Oh, sorry. I was drying my hair and playing music. It's great to see you,' she said, giving him a big hug. 'Come on in, how was America?'

'Erm ... good.' Django could hardly believe what he was seeing. The hair, the clothes, the metal music playing in the living room. Sophia strutted across the living room to turn the music down a little more. She was acting as if nothing had ever happened, like there had been no accident, like Spencer had never existed.

'What is it?' she said, as she turned and saw Django standing motionless with a concerned expression on his face.

'I've come to see Sophia, is she home?' he said.

'Look, DJ, don't worry, everything's ok. I'm fine,' she said.

'Really?' he said.

'Yes. I had a tough time of it to begin with, but now I'm getting my shit together.'

'Wow,' he said, shocked and surprised. DJ had never heard Sophia swear before. 'Are you sure ... I mean, I've just never heard you swear before.'

'Well, this is the new me – fuckin' eh,' she said, joking around. 'Oh, come on, DJ, lighten up a little.'

'Sophia, you know I'm here for you, if you need me?'

'I know, DJ. You've always been good to me; you're a real gentleman,' she smiled.

Sophia first met Django – who she calls DJ for short – at the Royal Academy of Music when they were both eighteen. They started at the Academy at the same time. Django studied classical piano, to his parents' disappointment. They wanted him to be a jazz guitarist.

They'd even named their son after the legendary Belgian guitarist, Django Reinhardt, but Django had fingernails like paper, which kept splitting on his right hand when he plucked the strings. Also, he just didn't really like or understand jazz, especially modern jazz, which he positively hated. However, when he first played a piano at his friend's house it appeared that he had a natural talent for it. It was obvious from a young age that Django had a special gift for the piano and classical music, so his parents eventually came to terms with it and encouraged him.

From a young age Django won many piano competitions and, like Sophia, he also went to a specialist music school when he was nine years old. Then in his late teens he went to the Royal Academy of Music in London. During his three years at the Academy Django excelled and was soon snapped up by a major record company. His debut recording of Tchaikovsky's Piano Concerto Number 1 has been hailed as the most exciting performance since the Horowitz/Toscanini recording. One music critic said that Django performed with adrenalin-fuelled vigour and jaw-dropping virtuosity.

During the first year at the Royal Academy Sophia and Django became good friends and he accompanied her whenever she needed a pianist. Musically, they were the perfect combination. Django knew Sophia's playing style intimately. He had an uncanny knack of knowing exactly how loud she was going to develop any given crescendo, or how fast she was going to race into an accelerando, or how long she was going to hold a note

SOPHIA

under a pause symbol. Sophia also had the same intimate knowledge of Django's piano playing. Sophia's singing cello sitting on top of Django's smooth piano tones was a musical marriage made in heaven. Fellow students and professors at the Academy said they were the modern day Barenboim and du Pré. They also assumed that Django and Sophia were romantically involved because they looked and sounded so perfect together. They had a natural rapport both musically and as friends.

When they first met, Django did quite fancy Sophia, but he soon learned that they would not be suited romantically and they would be better off maintaining a professional working relationship as a musical partnership and just being good friends. Django couldn't quite explain it but he saw Sophia more like a sister. A romantic involvement just wouldn't have felt right for him, even if Sophia was not already in a relationship with Spencer. Sophia also felt the same way about Django, like he was the brother she never had.

They were strictly friends, be it very good friends. If there was any love shared, it was their shared love of music.

'So come on, how did it go in America?' she said.

'It was ok.'

'Just ok?'

'Well, the first recitals went perfectly, but I couldn't really concentrate during the final ones – I played them on autopilot. I still got great reviews though.'

'It's not like you to lose concentration during recitals. What happened?'

Django paused in thought for a moment. 'I got a

phone call from your father. He called to tell me what had happened.'

'Oh, I'm sorry, DJ. I wish he hadn't done that. It's not like you could have done anything – especially from over there.'

'Sophia, I'm so sorry. I'm so sorry about what happened and I'm so sorry that I couldn't get back sooner … to be there for you.'

'DJ, really, don't beat yourself up about it. I understand that you had several major recitals booked – you couldn't just drop everything and fly back to England.'

'I'm sorry,' he insisted.

'It's ok, really. Besides, you're here now,' she said, walking over and giving him a big hug.

'Sophia, if there's anything I can do, anything. If there's anything you need–'

'I know,' she said, putting her index finger over his lips.

'That's not a platitude Sophia, I mean it, anything at all.'

'DJ, I know you're sincere but I'm really ok.' She wasn't, she was pretty far from ok and Django could see it. On the outside she was doing a brilliant job of acting normal. Everything about her, the blonde hair, the clothes, the rock music, it was all some sort of facade. On the inside it was a different story – only Sophia knew what was going on there, or did she? Even Sophia had moments where she couldn't quite understand what was happening to her state of mind. She could feel something dark, lurking dormant, deep inside a faraway corner of her mind. *What is that?* She thought. It felt like her mind was going through some sort of transition, but

Sophia

into what? It was like something was trying to possess her and take over her mind. It felt like something deep inside was going to rear its ugly head at any given moment. Although this idea scared her, it also excited her. *This must be how it feels when you do something bad and you know it's wrong, but it's exciting at the same time?* she thought.

'Sophia … Sophia,' said DJ, causing Sophia to snap out of it.

'Sorry, I was miles away.'

'Do you feel like discussing the Beethoven Cello Sonatas?' he said.

'Oh yes, of course. We've got to start rehearsing.'

'The record company are keen for us to record them as soon as possible. But everyone will understand if you're not up to rehearsing just yet,' he said.

'No, I'm ready. Let me get us some drinks then we'll go over the details.'

Django knew Sophia well and he could see that although, to the rest of the world, she was giving an award-winning performance of being back to normal, she was definitely not normal. Something was wrong, and it had nothing to do with Spencer's death. There was something else happening here and Django knew it.

They discussed rehearsals for the up-coming studio CD recording of the Beethoven Cello Sonatas. All the while, Django was acutely aware of Sophia's shifted personality. This wasn't the Sophia he knew before he went to America five weeks previously.

Chapter 10

Sophia was playing through some Popper studies as part of her morning warm up exercise routine when she heard the phone ring.

'Hello,' she said.

'Hello, Sophia, it's Meredith.'

'Hi Meredith.'

'Look, I'd like to come over and see you.'

'Sure, when?'

'Well, when would be convenient?'

'Anytime, I'm at home during the day.'

'Are you home this afternoon?'

'So soon, is anything wrong?'

'No, not at all. If you're busy I'll totally–'

'This afternoon will be just fine, Meredith.'

'Wonderful, about one o'clock?'

'Ok.'

'Great, I'll see you later, darling,' said Meredith.

Meredith Cameron-Jones had been Sophia's agent since Sophia won the BBC Young Musician of the Year competition when she was fourteen years old. Meredith was a sympathetic agent and she had not pushed Sophia. Instead, she had gently nursed her and protected her future career. She had shielded this talented young cellist from the wolves and kept her recitals to a minimum during the early years allowing her to develop naturally – not forced.

Meredith paused outside Sophia's apartment door momentarily before ringing the doorbell. She could hear her playing Beethoven's Adagio con molto sentimento d'affetto from the fifth Cello Sonata. Meredith was overwhelmed, yet she felt strange at the same time as she stood there listening through the door. She realised that in all these years, she'd never actually heard Sophia practising before. Sure, she'd attended many recitals and competitions, but she had not once heard her practise. She sounded different. With no piano accompanying, the Adagio sounded quite dark and haunting, even scary. *Was it supposed to sound like this?* thought Meredith. She'd heard Sophia play this piece at recitals before but never interpreted quite like this. A shudder shot through her spine as if somebody had walked over her grave. Meredith's finger hovered a few millimetres away from Sophia's doorbell. Part of her wanted to interrupt Sophia's dark haunting interpretation. But it was just too infectious and she felt compelled to listen to the end. It was like Sophia's playing had cast a spell on Meredith as she stood frozen to the spot, listening intently. It was hypnotic to say the least. Finally, Sophia's cello fell silent as she finished the movement. Meredith paused for a moment longer, just in case Sophia was going to play the final Allegro movement; she did not. Safe in the knowledge that Sophia was not going to continue playing, Meredith rang the doorbell.

Sophia opened the door. 'Hi, Meredith.'

Meredith tried to hide her look of shock/horror at the sight of Sophia's bleached blonde hair, heavy black eye make-up and deep purple lipstick, all of which were so uncharacteristic of Sophia – at least until now. Instead, knowing that Sophia had suffered a great loss, she stepped into the doorway and gave her a heart-felt and sympathetic hug. 'How are you, my darling?' said Meredith, as her nostrils filled with Sophia's gorgeous, but somewhat overwhelming, perfume.

'I'm good,' said Sophia. 'It's good to see you, Meredith, come on in.' Sophia led the way down the corridor and into the living room. Meredith took the opportunity to study her clothing, which consisted of tight fitting black jeans and a gothic-style black lace blouse. All she needed was a black leather bomber jacket and she would look like a biker girl.

Meredith, with her usual grace and elegance, sat down on the sofa. She was 48-years old, and although she looked younger, she acted much older. Meredith was as upper middle class as you could get. She had old-fashioned values and spoke with refinement and had an air of sophistication. She had the kind of sharp attractive looks that attracted men: tall, slender, long chestnut hair, plump lips and sharply defined cheekbones. Men would sometimes approach Meredith but, as soon as she spoke, they would be on the back foot threatened by her intellect and headmistress-like tones. One minute she was an attractive challenge, like Angelina Jolie, and then when she spoke, she turned into Margaret Thatcher and the physical attractiveness vanished along with the man trying to chat her up.

Meredith tried to delicately bring up the subject of Spencer so she could be compassionate and supportive but Sophia didn't want to talk about it, insisting that she was getting over it and dealing with it in her own way. Sophia insisted that she just wanted people to stop fussing and let her try to move on. They spent the next few hours discussing Sophia's up-coming recitals – especially the Carnegie Hall concert in the USA. Meredith wanted to be sure that Sophia was ok to get back to her booked recitals and that she was ok to do the long-haul flight to America. Meredith knew that it was vital that Sophia got back to her recitals, and recording programmes. But she also knew that she had to nurse her back gently after her loss. Sophia had convinced Meredith that she was fine and ready for her imminent recital bookings, at least verbally. But Meredith had concerns over Sophia's hair and newfound dress sense.

'So, when did you get your hair done?' said Meredith, seemingly making polite conversation now that the business end of the conversation was over.

'You're concerned aren't you?' said Sophia.

'No, not at all, dear, I'm just–'

'Worried about what the audiences will think at my recitals?' said Sophia.

'Well, as long as you're going to dress appropriately,' she said, gesturing towards Sophia's black gothic lace blouse and jeans.

'Meredith, people come to listen to me play the cello not to look at my clothes. I'm sure they won't judge me for what I wear or what colour my hair is.'

'I'm sure they won't, dear,' she said, happy that she had at least made her aware and planted the seed.

'Don't concern yourself, I'll wear what feels right. You worry too much.'

'Ok. Have you spoken to Django recently?'

'Yes, he was here yesterday.'

'That's good. Django's a nice young man.'

'Yes he is. He's being very supportive. We're making plans to record the Beethoven Cello Sonatas.'

'That's excellent news,' said Meredith, with genuine enthusiasm.

Sophia showed Meredith out and spent the next few hours practising various movements from the Beethoven Cello Sonatas.

Chapter 11

Later in the evening, with her practice out of the way, Sophia felt restless and decided to meet one of her friends in Highgate. They met in the Prince of Wales pub to catch up over a few drinks. The only trouble was, for Sophia, a few drinks turned into a few more and before long she was getting uncharacteristically boisterous to the embarrassment of her friend. This was not like Sophia. She had never, until now, been much of a drinker; perhaps a small glass of something at Christmas and maybe a glass of Champagne on special occasions. But out-and-out drinking like this, and in a pub, was way out of character. Sophia didn't even like pubs. Well, maybe a nice quiet country pub for lunch but certainly not a High Street pub full of football supporters drinking pint after pint while watching a match on a large plasma screen.

A barman walked past as he was collecting empty glasses.

'Excuse me,' said Sophia. 'Could you be a sweetie and pop another shot of Vodka in this for me please?' she said, handing him her half empty glass of Vodka and Coke.

'Sophia, don't you think you've had enough?' interrupted her friend.

'Jane, when did you become such a square?' said

Sophia, handing the glass to the barman. 'In fact, make it a double,' she shouted after him.

Her friend, Jane, could see that Sophia was getting a lot of looks from some of the football fans in the pub. Her long blonde hair, skimpy black blouse and tight black jeans revealed her perfect slim figure. Well, it was all too much for the Arsenal supporters, who could hardly take their eyes off her. Jane was aware of the attention and looks that Sophia was getting and was starting to feel a little uncomfortable with it. The barman returned and put Sophia's drink on the table in front of her.

Looking at her watch, Jane said, 'Look, I'm really sorry, but I've got to be up at six. We should really get going.'

'Oh, come on. We've still got time for a couple more. Just another half hour,' said Sophia.

'I'm sorry, I've really got to go, Sophia,' said Jane, hunching on her coat and throwing her handbag over her shoulder.

'You know what, Jane, you've become a real fucking bore. Whatever happened to you?' snapped Sophia.

'I could say the same thing about you, Sophia. That's it, I'm leaving.' Offended, Jane marched out of the pub not looking back for a second.

Within seconds, a good-looking tanned man in his early thirties approached Sophia's table. He was impeccably dressed in a smart suit and his dark hair was neatly cut. His shave was close, so close it looked like he had shaved just minutes earlier.

'Having trouble with your friend?' he said.

'Not anymore, obviously,' she said.

SOPHIA

'You know, I couldn't help overhearing the end of that conversation. How about I buy you another drink. I promise you I won't be a bore,' he said.

Sophia looked him up and down. 'Why not,' she said.

Surprisingly, Sophia's new drinking friend was a true gentleman. He kept the conversation polite and interesting. Even through his Spanish accent, Sophia could tell that he was an educated man.

They talked for the next hour over more drinks. Sophia listened to him talk about his business trip to London but whenever he asked about her, she was a closed book. She just didn't feel like talking about herself or getting into anything deep. Though, when she told him she was a concert cellist he wanted to hear more. In the end, Sophia told him to Google her on the Internet. Everything about her as a cellist could be found there and it would save her having to tell him the whole story.

'It's getting stuffy in here, I want to go outside,' she said. The Spaniard accompanied Sophia out of the pub and into the night-time air.

'Oh wow, that feels so good,' said Sophia, spanning her arms out wide and looking up at the pitch-black sky.

The Spaniard couldn't help but admire her shapely neck, as Sophia continued to look up at the sky while the gentle breeze soothed her face and neck after being in the stuffy pub for over two hours.

'Let's walk,' she said, snapping her head down and looking straight into the Spaniard's eyes.

'Walk, where?' he said.

'Anywhere. It's a beautiful night and I feel like walking.'

'Ok,' he said. 'Let's walk.'

Sophia grabbed his hand and paced ahead, swinging his hand up and down as she did so. Although she'd had several Vodka and Cokes, she certainly didn't have any trouble walking. If anything, she had too much energy as she strode rapidly along.

'Wow, what's the rush, you got somewhere to be?' he joked.

They walked down Swain's Lane. Sophia sang out loud, in her own world and almost oblivious that she was dragging this man along for the walk. They eventually came to the gates of Highgate Cemetery.

'Wow, I've never been down here after dark. Kind of spooky, don't you think?' she said, looking through the black wrought iron fences at the various marble headstones, crosses and tombstones. She noticed part of the wall and fence had been pulled down and was in the middle of being replaced. There was some orange tape forming a temporary barrier with a sign reading 'DANGER Keep Out Building Work In Progress.'

'Let's go inside,' said Sophia, pulling the Spaniard towards the deconstructed part of wall.

'What?' he said. 'I don't think we're allowed in there.'

'Oh come on, it'll be fun. Besides, it's good to break a rule every now and then,' she said, winking at him wickedly.

The Spaniard looked around, feeling uncomfortable about breaking into a cemetery. *What the hell*, he thought. Led by Sophia, they lifted the orange tape and went under it. They carefully clambered over the rubble of the broken section of wall. Once inside, they walked between the various headstones and made their way to the public pathway. Sophia skipped along happily, almost dragging the Spaniard along by his hand. While the Spaniard pretended to be excited by the venture, he was actually quite uncomfortable about being there and Sophia could see his nervousness.

'Lighten up a little, it's perfectly safe, there's nobody in here. Well, nobody living anyway,' she said.

'Ha,' he said, letting out a nervous sigh.

Sophia started to sing the song 'I Think We're Alone Now'. She sang with a laugh as she skipped along the narrow pathway through the cemetery with her somewhat unwilling companion.

'Hey look, its Karl Marx's tombstone,' she said, dropping the Spaniards hand and running over to it. She kicked off her shoes and ran around the tombstone, lapping it three times before stopping at the front and leaning her back against it. She spread her arms out wide with the palms of her hands up high and flat against the marble either side of the gold lettering spelling out KARL MARX.

'Workers of all lands unite,' she said, posing in a extremely seductive manner as she dropped one of her hands and placed it on her stomach. She slid her hand down a little and tucked her middle finger under her tight black jeans below her navel and winked at him, suggestively.

'What are you doing?' he said, walking up to her.

She grabbed him by his waist and pulled him close and whispered into his ear, 'I'm trying to seduce you.'

'You couldn't have picked a more romantic spot,' he joked.

Sophia grabbed his hair with both hands and pulled his face to meet hers. She plastered her open mouth against his and proceeded to almost eat his face off.

'Wow, take it easy,' he said, pulling his face away.

Sophia kissed him again, this time a little more gently. She could see that this man wasn't the type to dive straight in; he needed to be eased into it until he was aroused and in the mood. Sophia's mind was all over the place. In her drunken state her emotions were off the charts. Spencer's voice was in her head and she didn't want it there. As she sent her tongue deeper into the Spaniards mouth she looked over his shoulder and saw Spencer leaning against a tombstone in the distance. He looked very pale and very dead. His lifeless eyes gazed at her with no emotion.

Sophia grabbed the Spaniard and spun him around so his back was up against the Karl Marx tombstone. The dead Spencer was now behind her and out of her line of vision. She lowered her hands and frantically fumbled with his belt and trouser button.

'I don't have any condoms,' he said.

'Don't worry, I'm safe,' she said.

'Are you ok with unprotected sex?' he said.

'You have honest eyes, I'm sure you don't have anything,' she said, as she continued to grab and pull hard at his belt.

'Ok, ok. Take it easy,' he said, lowering his own hands and undoing his belt for her.

'I want you to fuck me right now,' she said, frantically

pushing his trousers down while she continued to kiss him with her tongue out porn style. Spencer was in her mind's eye but there was something else there too, something dark, fighting for her attention. Whatever it was, it was rearing its dark ugly head and was taking over her mind. Spencer was struggling in her head against such fierce and powerful competition.

Sophia reached inside the Spaniards Calvin Klein's and grabbed his stiff cock, squeezing and tugging at it frantically.

'Fuck me, fuck me now,' she said. She manoeuvred herself between him and the twelve-foot high marble tombstone so that her chest and face were pressed up against it. She undid the button and zip on her jeans and pulled them down to her knees. She parted her legs slightly and stuck her backside upwards, encouraging him. With her left palm pressed up against the marble, she reached around behind her with her right hand and grabbed the Spaniards cock, which was now as hard as the cold marble tombstone that her right cheek was pressed up against. She pulled him towards her, encouraging him to penetrate her.

'Come on, fuck me,' she said, getting impatient.

'Are you sure about this?' he said.

'Yes, I'm totally fucking sure – I need this,' she said.

She held the tip of his cock hard up against her wet vagina and moved up and down a few times to make sure it found its way in. The Spaniard gently pushed himself deep into her, causing her to let out a groan of satisfaction.

'Fuck me hard,' she said, spurred on by the new dark demon in her mind. The Spaniard obliged, thrusting into her.

'Harder, fuck me harder,' shouted the demon in her. She was getting angry with him for not giving it his all. The Spaniard sensed this and slammed into her with everything he had.

'Oh fuck yeah, keep going, keep going,' she cried. She thrust her backside back and forth – hard – to meet him in perfect rhythm, both her hands flat up against the cold marble of the tombstone either side of the Karl Marx gold lettering.

'Faster, faster,' she cried. 'Oh yes, I'm coming ... don't stop.' The Spaniard's legs were tiring now, but he daren't stop. He summoned all his reserve energy to fuck Sophia harder and faster, right up to the point where she let out that globally famous loud moan of orgasmic pleasure. Then he slowed, but not before finally coming himself.

'Fuck me, that was good,' she said.

'It was different,' he said, slowly withdrawing.

'Oh no,' he said, as he noticed semen running down the inside of Sophia's thighs. 'I don't have anything to clean up with,' he said.

'Who bloody cares,' said Sophia, pulling up her knickers and jeans.

They left the cemetery and walked back up the hill to Highgate before going their separate ways. He went back to his B&B while Sophia called a cab from her mobile. The Spaniard could see that Sophia was not interested in seeing him again, so he didn't push it.

SOPHIA

Sophia got home to her apartment, took a shower, then filled the bath with hot water and lay there soaking away the evidence of her night's outrageous antics.

Chapter 12

Sophia delayed leaving her apartment until the busy school run and rush hour traffic had cleared. She left her apartment at 9:20am to go and meet Django to start rehearsals for the upcoming Beethoven Cello Sonatas CD recording. With Django being a Steinway artist, securing the Recital Room at Steinway Hall in London was painless. The fact that both Django and Sophia had record company contracts opened many doors for them.

Django lived in a detached two-bedroom annex in Elstree, Hertfordshire, on the grounds of his music professor, who was sympathetic to Django's needs for an environment where he could practise for many hours during the day without upsetting the neighbours. He practised on his professor's spare Yamaha six-foot grand piano, which was in Django's spare bedroom. Luckily for him, both bedrooms in the annex were quite large. Large enough for Sophia to rehearse there with him if required. In this instance, Django wanted to rehearse on a Steinway piano with Sophia. They both felt the tonal qualities of the Steinway better matched her cello. Although the Yamaha that Django practised on was six years old and well played in, it was still a bright sounding

Sophia

piano and this rehearsal was far too important.

Sophia didn't dislike Yamaha pianos, but she felt Django's professor's C3 was too brash. Django agreed totally. In fact he had been trying to source another practice piano, but with his busy schedule he hadn't managed to find a replacement he was totally happy with.

Django had spent a lot of time at Steinway hall practising in the past so he was familiar with their pianos. It's because Django spent a lot of time at Steinway Hall practising, coupled with the fact that he didn't actually own the Yamaha he practised on at home, that they allowed him to remain a Steinway Artist. They turned a blind eye to the fact that his practice piano was not a Steinway. Sophia had also spent time at Steinway Hall practising with Django, so it was an environment they were both comfortable in.

Six miles and thirty minutes later, Sophia arrived at Marylebone Lane with ten minutes to spare, which was enough for her to park her car and carry her cello case into the building. When she entered the recital room, Django was already there organising sheet music on the piano.

'Hey you,' said Sophia.

DJ walked over to great her. 'Hi. How are you?' he said.

'I'm good. So, you ready to get started?' she said.

'Oh yes. It'll be a walk in the park.'

Sophia and Django had played Beethoven's Five Cello Sonatas together at the Academy. They'd also played them just five months before at a recital that lasted nearly two hours. Because they knew the sonatas intimately they had only booked the Recital Room for four weeks, with the intention of rehearsing there three to four hours per day, four days per week. Even this was probably more than they needed. Sophia had played them with another pianist in Germany when she was twenty, at a time that Django could not be there due to his own busy schedule as a concert pianist.

Sophia had three pianists who she worked with regularly. Django was the one she worked with the most and there was no doubt that he was the one she gelled with on every musical level. They had so much respect for each other and they were both sympathetic to the other's musical needs and requirements when they played together. They treated each other as musical equals. There was never any one-upmanship and they never tried to outdo each other – it was unnecessary, especially with duo pieces, and neither of them ever felt the need to try and steal the limelight.

Django wasn't simply *the accompanist* when he played duo pieces in public with Sophia. A lot of music-goers often, mistakenly, see the pianist in this way at duo recitals. The same could be said of Sophia. When playing with Django, she wasn't the *soloist*. Both the piano and cello parts were equal – they both had an important role to play when it came to sonatas and other duo pieces. Of course, concertos for cello were a different story, as the pianist would play a transcribed version of the orchestral parts, which would have been written as an accompaniment. When Sophia and Django played duo recitals together they had a magnetic musical connection.

They blended and connected completely. It was like witnessing a unique musical amalgamation. Even their physical presence had a graceful unifying harmony in the same way a soft swaying coral reef has harmony with the blue ocean current.

'Where do you want to start from?' said Django.

'Why not go from the top. Number one, adagio sustenuto?' said Sophia. Django smiled a knowing smile.

Sophia got comfortable on her chair. Although her cello spike would not slip on the carpet, she still used a spike block, as she didn't want to mark the tasteful short pile red carpet with its gold Steinway logos.

After treating her bow with rosin and tuning her cello to the piano she quickly whizzed up and down a few scales and arpeggios to warm up. Then, after a brief conversation, they made a start on the first sonata.

This was the first time Sophia had played with Django since Spencer's death. It somehow felt different; but then everything had felt different since Spencer died. Although their combined musicianship was as sublime as ever and their usual musical rapport was spot on, there was a slight shift in the atmosphere. Outside of their usual musical energy, there was another kind of energy and it wasn't coming from Django, it was coming from Sophia. It was neither a good or bad energy, just different. She was seeing Django in a way she had never seen him before and it excited her.

After three hours of rehearsing, with short breaks and discussions, Sophia's emotions were in turmoil. She shouldn't be having these sexual feelings towards

Django; she never had before. She should be mourning Spencer still, shouldn't she? How many months does it take to get over a beloved boyfriend dying unexpectedly? She shouldn't be over Spencer so soon. He was more than just a boyfriend, much more. He was her world, he completed her life, and without him she could not function. But here she was, fucking a stranger in a cemetery and having uncontrollable sexual feelings towards her good friend, Django, who she'd always seen as the brother she never had. How could this be? Django was her best friend and musical partner. She had never thought of him in any other way. She watched his fingers caressing the piano keys and his slender, but firm, forearms moving up and down the piano, his strong shoulders. All she could think about was walking over to him and putting her hands on them and gently massaging them as he played. But something told her that would not go down well at all. She struggled to fight it, to suppress her urges. She knew that Django respected her and did not see her that way. Besides, Django was a true gentleman and even if he wanted to, he would never be so disrespectful to Spencer.

Halfway through the Rondo movement of Beethoven's second sonata, Sophia suddenly stopped playing. Her emotions were in a spin and she was worried she might say, or do, something stupid. What was happening to her? The mixed emotions, the detached feelings, erotic stirrings and thoughts, all this Jekyll and Hyde nonsense and randomly flying off the handle.

'Is everything ok?' said Django.

'I'm sorry, do you mind if we stop for the day?' she said.

'Sure, are you alright?' he said.

'Yes, I just need to get some air ... I think I might have done something last night that I shouldn't have,' she said.

'Oh, you wanna talk about it?' he said.

'I don't think so. Trust me, you wouldn't want to know. Even I'm disgusted with myself.'

'I'm confused, what did you do?'

'It doesn't matter,' she said, realising she'd let something slip that she wished, in hindsight, that she hadn't. 'I'm confused too, DJ. I feel like something's changing inside me ... like something's taking me over.'

'Can you elaborate?'

'Not really, no. Just these past few weeks I've been aware of it.'

'It?'

'This ... change. One minute everything's fine, then the next I feel ... sort of reckless. I find that I'm doing things that I wouldn't normally do and I have thoughts ... that I would normally never have.'

'What kind of thoughts?'

'I don't know, just thoughts ... sexual, dark, bad. But when I'm in that state of mind, they seem perfectly normal. Then I'll get a moment of clarity and I'll think, "What the hell was that all about"'.

'And last night was one of those ... dark moments?' said DJ.

'Yes, but at the time it felt like perfectly normal behaviour – in fact it all felt great. But this morning when I woke up I was disgusted with myself behaving in such a way.'

'Look, I won't press you for details of what you did, but I just want you to know you can talk to me, Sophia – about anything. I'll try to understand.'

'Thanks, I appreciate that, DJ.'

'Sophia,' said Django, suddenly looking quite sad.

'What is it?' she said.

'I know I've said it before, but I'm so sorry I couldn't get back to England to be there for you.'

'DJ, it's ok. You had important recitals and I'd never expect you to cancel them and fly back to England. You're a busy concert pianist, I understand that. We've had this conversation already, DJ so stop worrying about it.'

'I know, but I just want you to know that I'm here for you now. I feel I need to make it up to you somehow, I should have been there for you … if there's anything I can do, you know–'

'DJ, stop,' she said, walking over to hug him. 'I'm aware that you're here for me, DJ, and I really do appreciate that. Now pack your music up and we'll continue our rehearsals when *I* get back from America.'

Django gathered up his sheet music off the piano while Sophia packed her cello away. They arranged to meet for their next rehearsal ten days later, when Sophia got back from her Carnegie Hall concert in New York.

Chapter 13

Sophia had packed her clothes into her suitcase. Her cello was secured in its case all ready to go. She had a cake of her favourite Andrea Solo cello rosin and her rubber spike mat, her indispensable microwavable wheat bags to keep her hands warm while in the green room immediately before the concert, passport, handbag, money, etc. She looked around her apartment and searched her mind for anything else she might be forgetting. *Nothing else.* She was all set for her flight to New York early the next morning for her Carnegie Hall concert, where she was going to be performing the Haydn Cello Concerto in D major for the main work.

She looked at her wristwatch – 6 p.m. She went out to her car and made the short journey up Heath Street, along Spaniards Road to her parents' house off Hampstead Lane. As usual, Sophia let herself in through the electric iron gates with her remote controller and up to the front of the house. Her father opened the front door.

'Hello, darling. How are you?' he said, giving her a hug and a kiss.

'I'm fine, Daddy.'

'Come on in, your grandmother's in the lounge.'

'Look who's here,' said Andrew, leading the way into the lounge.

'Oh, darling. Come and give me a big hug,' said Grandma Lizzie getting to her feet.

Grandma Lizzie was looking a lot frailer since Sophia last saw her. Her plump, cuddly Grandma Lizzie was rapidly being replaced by a frail gaunt figure cruelly eaten away by cancer.

'It's so good to see you, and you're looking so well.'

'Thanks Grandma.'

'Wow, and look at that hair,' said Grandma Lizzie, with a beaming smile on her face.

'You like it?' said Sophia.

'I think it's wonderful my darling,' said Lizzie. 'What do you think, Diana?' she said.

'It's ... daring,' said Diana, forcing a smile. Grandma Lizzie adored everything about Sophia. She could do no wrong in her eyes. For Lizzie, Sophia was the perfect granddaughter. Diana knew this so she wasn't about to dampen the mood by expressing how she really felt about her daughter's shocking hair colour. Besides, Lizzie was dying of cancer, so it was all about *her* and what made her happy and comfortable.

'It certainly is,' said Lizzie. 'It's a pleasant evening, how about you and I go and sit in the garden for a lovely chat?'

'I'd like that,' said Sophia.

Andrew and Diana left Grandma Lizzie and Sophia alone out in the garden gazebo to have a talk. Lizzie had a way with Sophia that was calm and soothing. She knew just what to say, especially with delicate issues like Spencer's recent untimely death. Lizzie was incredibly selfless. Not once did she bring up her own terminal illness and imminent death, nor did she mention her own husband's death two years ago. She only had Sophia in her thoughts; she was all she cared about right now.

Lizzie knew Sophia so well she could see right through the brave face and façade she was putting on. What other people saw as genuine smiles and a young woman functioning again and doing so well overcoming her boyfriend's death, didn't fool Lizzie for a second. No, Lizzie could see that something was seriously wrong and Sophia was far from ok.

'Darling, you know you can't fool me for a second,' said Lizzie.

'I know Grandma.'

'So, would you like to talk about what's really going on?'

'I can't.'

'You can't because you don't want to?'

'No, Grandma, it's not like that. I mean … I don't really know what it is that's going on myself.'

'Your father told me about a psychologist you're seeing. A Dr de Beaumont?'

'Yes.'

'Is it helping?'

'I'm not sure. Sometimes it feels like it helps, but then sometimes …' Sophia went into deep thought momentarily.

'Darling?' said Lizzie.

'I don't know. Sometimes I just don't feel like myself. Strange thoughts and feelings keep creeping into my head.'

'What kind of thoughts?'

'Dark thoughts.'

'Do they disturb you?'

'That's the thing. Although they're quite shocking sometimes, I feel compelled to embrace them. Its like there's nothing I can do about it.'

'Its barely been six weeks, darling. Your mind's bound to be a little mixed up.'

'I guess so.'

'Listen, dear. It'll get better. Trust me, I know. You'll never forget Spencer and he'll always be in your heart. But in time the pain will dilute and then eventually that pain will stop hurting so much and all you'll be left with are the good memories and all of Spencer's love in your heart.' Sophia smiled at Lizzie and took a sip of her drink.

Sophia told Lizzie she would see her the minute she got back to England. Lizzie insisted that she call her from New York to let her know she had arrived safely.

Chapter 14

After parking her new Audi in the long-stay car park at Heathrow terminal five, Sophia headed for the terminal check-in area. Everything went smoothly and without a hitch. The drive from Hampstead, around the North Circular Road and along the M4 had been speedy and painless. Finding an easy-to-remember space in the long-term car park was easy. Wheeling her small suitcase and cello into the terminal was a manageably short distance. Even the checking-in part went without the usual cello case explanation. Luckily for Sophia the lady who checked her luggage was familiar with cellists and their unorthodox routine of taking their cello on the airplane with them as a fellow passenger.

After Sophia's cello case had gone through the x-ray machine, one of the checkers asked her to open the case so they could check inside. He looked at her cello briefly, and then plucked a couple of strings, causing Sophia to shoot him a *look*. He told her she could close the case. It was as if hearing a few crudely plucked open strings was enough to confirm it wasn't a bomb, or that the cello body wasn't packed with cocaine – though the latter would probably have altered the pitch somewhat.

Although a typical cello in its case would be way too big for hand luggage, Sophia got around this problem by purchasing a seat ticket for her cello so it could be right next to her throughout the journey and not down in the hold or getting thrown around by careless baggage handlers. Sophia had done this many times in the past when she gave international recitals. She simply booked two tickets with the airline. She would fill out the first ticket in her own name with her date of birth and passport number. For her cello she would put *Musical* for the first name and *Instrument* for the surname. As cellos don't have a date of birth – well, not in quite the same way that people do – she would put her own date of birth. For the cello's ticket she would also put her own passport number.

Most of the time, like in this instance, there wouldn't be too many issues checking in. If the check-in staff had never come across a cello having its own paid seat, Sophia simply explained that she always bought a ticket for her cello as it was a very expensive instrument and she could not risk it turning up either broken, or ending up on another flight to another country.

Once on the airplane, the cabin staff would insist that the cello case had to be seated in the window seat and they would also have to bring the extension seat belt to fit around the case's wider-than-human girth. Sophia always thought it was unfair that the cello case got the best seat - it's not like it could appreciate the view. But it was probably for safety reasons so that Sophia didn't have to squeeze her way around it in an emergency.

However, this time things didn't quite go according to plan. The airhead of an airhostess was young and new to the job and had never heard of a cello being allowed on with a passenger. She insisted that Sophia let her take the cello case and have it put in the cargo hold down below. Sophia's new dark side was starting to get very irritated and bored with this little airhead repeating herself like a stuck bloody record.

'Madam, its just too big. It could be a danger to other passengers. It will have to go in the hold,' said the airhead, for the fifth time.

'Yes, so you keep saying. But for the fifth time, this is a valuable instrument and it's staying right here with me,' stated Sophia.

'Madam, I can assure your cello will be quite safe in the hold,' said the airhead.

'Look, I'm not letting you put my cello in the fucking hold; end of story.'

By now, the immediate passengers were entertained by the exchanges between Sophia and the stewardess. One man even found it mildly amusing, while another woman made a tutting sound, then she spoke.

'Look, why don't you just let the lady do her job so we can take off already,' she said, in an annoying New York accent.

Sophia gave the American woman a, *don't say another fucking word or I'll stab you in the heart with this pencil*, look. Reading Sophia's demonic eyes, the woman kept her mouth shut and focused on a spot on the headrest directly in front of her. Meanwhile, the stewardess returned with one of her fellow cabin crew workers; the more experienced male steward assessed the situation. He looked at Sophia, then at the cello case seated next to her in the window seat.

'This is fine, Bailey. It's within the airline's regulations. Go and get one of the extension belts so we can strap it in securely, would you,' he ordered. She trotted off to fetch it.

'Bailey, like the drink?' asked Sophia.

'Spelled the same way too,' smiled the steward.

'Why am I not surprised,' said Sophia, just as Bailey returned and handed the extension belt to her colleague.

'Thank you, Bailey,' he said.

'Yes, thank you, *Bailey*,' said Sophia, with a detectable hint of sarcasm in her tone.

The steward strapped in Sophia's cello case and smoothed the situation over so everybody could have a pleasant flight. Sophia got back to the crossword puzzle in the airline magazine.

Just under eight hours later the airplane touched down at JFK airport. After sitting on the tarmac for an age, Sophia and her fellow passengers were eventually allowed off the airplane and into the terminal. Sophia was one of the last ones off as she had to let the other passengers past before making her way into the aisle with her cello case. This meant that she was also near the back of the very long queue of passengers waiting to go through immigration. And immigration at JFK dealing with international incoming flights were not only methodical, they were slow. *This could take all bloody night*, she thought, as she watched the immigration officials wave the next person forward. The time it took for them to check the passport, do the fingerprint scan and ask stupid questions was preposterous. Sophia was slowly losing the will to live.

Eventually, she ended up at the front of the queue and then a rather well built African American customs lady motioned Sophia forward.

'Do you have your passport?' she said, in a tired, almost monotone voice, as if she had said it a million times before. Sophia handed over her passport, unable to manage any kind of smile after the long flight.

'This doesn't look much like you, ma'am,' she said, studying Sophia's passport picture.

'I dyed my hair,' she said. The woman studied the photo then studied Sophia, then the photo again, then Sophia again two more times.

'You are aware of the concept of dyeing your hair, I'm sure people do that in America too?' said Sophia. The woman placed Sophia's passport down.

'Place your four fingers flat on the screen,' she ordered, gesturing towards the electronic fingerprint scanner. Sophia could not believe how devoid of any human emotion this woman was. She was like some sort of robotic military experiment. Sophia went through the motions, anxious to get out of the airport immigration hall and out into the open air of New York.

'I'm sorry, ma'am. Could you *please* place your fingers so they're flat against the screen?'

'They are flat,' said Sophia, not breaking eye contact with the woman's cold stare as she adjusted her hand position on the scanner. Again, military woman was not happy because she was not getting a clean scan of Sophia's fingerprints.

'Ma'am, I'm going to have to insist that you place your fingers perfectly flat against the screen so they can be scanned,' she said, louder this time and with military tone to demonstrate her supreme power.

'Look, my fucking fingers *are* flat against the screen,' she shouted. With this, military woman hit a button in her cubicle to alert security. Then she sat back, folded her arms across her chest and gave Sophia a smug, *you're fucked,* look.

'You know, we don't treat your citizens like this when they visit England. And for your information, we're not *all* fucking terrorists you know,' she said. Just then a firm hand was placed on Sophia's shoulder from behind.

'Ma'am, you're going to have to come with us,' said another military-toned male voice. Sophia turned to see a tall stocky black man in full security uniform and another rather official looking white man in a suit. 'Right now,' ordered the black security guard.

'Look, I just want to get out of here, get a cab and go to my hotel, ok. I'm tired,' she said.

'Don't make this any harder on yourself, ma'am. Come with us right now,' said the black security man, more sternly.

Sophia

'Let me take that for you,' said the white man, reaching for Sophia's cello case.

'Don't touch that,' she said, grabbing the handle. She reluctantly went with the two men, who led her through a security door, through a couple of short corridors and into a large room. There was a long counter with a woman and two men standing behind it. The women and one of the men were talking to a passenger who had recently arrived from the UK. She could just about make out what they were saying to him. Something about him ticking the box NO on the ESTA application under section B. Sophia could hear brief snippets of their conversation. Something about criminal convictions and crimes involving moral turpitude and the fact that the man should have ticked YES because their system showed that he had a criminal record. The passenger was in his forties and was getting quite upset. He tried to convince the immigration officials that it was only one joint he smoked at a party when he was very young. But the immigration officials were doing everything by the book and were following their strict protocol to the letter. He was told that the USA had a zero tolerance of people with drug related convictions and he was going to be deported back to the UK and would not be allowed to enter the USA. The man broke down and started to cry.

Holy shit, thought Sophia. Imagine flying all this way only to be marched straight back onto the next airplane back to the UK. *That's going to be a very long flight home.*

'This way, ma'am,' ordered the white man. He escorted

Sophia to a free space at the counter. The black security guard explained to the official behind the counter what had happened while the white man handed him Sophia's passport.

'Ma'am, you do realise that you can be deported back to the UK for showing aggressive behaviour towards immigration staff?' he said.

'I *wasn't* being aggressive. I didn't do anything wrong. It's your damn fingerprint scanner that has the problem,' she said.

'Ma'am, I'm not going to ask you again. Calm down,' he stated, giving Sophia a serious look.

'I'm perfectly calm,' she said, in her quietest most calm voice.

'Good,' he said, looking down and scrutinizing her passport.

'Jesus fucking Christ,' Sophia mumbled to herself. The immigration official heard, he looked up from her passport. He gave Sophia a long hard look, as if he was about to make a judgment call.

'If I'd have been shown just a little civility by that soulless cow out there then I wouldn't be in here. But no, she had to take her tiny little bit of power and lord it over me like a total bitch,' she said.

'I'm sorry, ma'am, but I'm going to have to refuse you entry.'

'What! You've got to be fucking kidding me,' she shouted.

Just then another suited white male poked his head around a door over to the right after hearing Sophia's vocal objections. He seemed to be looking closely at Sophia. Then he came out of the door altogether and walked past, checking her out as he did so. The man stood next to one of the other immigration staff further down the counter, studying Sophia and checking out her cello case. Sophia noticed him looking at her and whispering to the man next to him. Just as the black security man and the white official were about to lead Sophia away, he came over and asked them to wait a minute. He was obviously a higher-ranking official than the two who were about to deport Sophia back to the UK, *for apparently having human emotions.*

This smart suited official looked at Sophia's passport and then studied her. Sophia couldn't help noticing his vibrant red and black tie against his white starched shirt.

'You're Sophia Beckinsale,' he said, smiling. 'I didn't recognise you at first, with your new hair colour I mean.' The other two officials looked at him, somewhat confused.

'The famous British cellist,' he said. The other officials spun their heads to look at Sophia, as if they'd missed something the first time around.

'I'll take it from here,' he said to the immigration officer standing at the counter, who in turn walked away and left his superior to deal with Sophia.

'What exactly seems to be the trouble?' he asked the white official, who went on to explain about Sophia's aggressive behaviour towards immigration control.

'Explain to me how this came about,' he said, turning his attention to Sophia. Sophia could see that this man was more human than the others and had a sympathetic look in his eyes. So she trod very carefully, and in her most polite tone she went on to explain why she got agitated and she was sorry about the whole mess.

She wasn't sorry at all, but Jekyll had stepped in to relieve Hyde momentarily; and just in the nick of time until this mess was sorted out.

'I've got your recording of the Bach Cello Suites,' said the new friendly vibrant tie-wearing official.

'Oh, I hope you like it,' she said, keeping up the polite pretence.

'It's absolutely brilliant,' he said, 'Paul Tortelier's 1966 recording was always my favourite,' he said, 'But since I bought your version on CD last year, I've changed my lifetime's tune.' The two men standing either side of Sophia were lost for words. The conversation was going way over their heads. 'You know, I never thought I'd ever hear anyone play those Suites better than Tortelier,' he said. 'Your interpretation is impeccable. It's like I'm listening to old Johann playing it himself.'

'That's a very nice compliment,' she said.

'Well, its quite true. You're making quite a noise over here young lady.'

He got Sophia to place her hand on the scanner on the counter and, lo and behold, it scanned perfectly. A few minutes later everything was in order. He smoothed things over with the two men standing next to Sophia and stamped her passport.

'Welcome to America,' he said.

'Thank you. You've been most kind,' she said.

SOPHIA

'Well, I have to let you in,' he said. Sophia looked at him slightly puzzled.

'My wife and I have tickets to come and see you play at Carnegie Hall next week,' he said, smiling. Sophia took her passport and was directed out of the airport by security.

'She's famous?' asked the immigrations official in the white suit.

'Oh yes,' said vibrant tie official.

'She's a cellist?' said white suit official.

'Cellist is too small a word for Sophia Beckinsale. She's an ambassador of the cello,' he said.

Once outside, Sophia jumped into one of those world famous yellow taxis.

'West 55th Street please.'

'Certainly, ma'am,' said the taxi driver.

'Is it far from here?' she said.

'It's about fifteen miles; we should be there in about an hour, ma'am.'

Chapter 15

When Sophia woke up in her hotel room the next morning the long flight had left her with a pounding headache, which she could well do without, as this was the first day of rehearsals with the orchestra. After a quick shower and some *questionable* breakfast she grabbed her cello case, left the hotel and headed off to Carnegie Hall, which was conveniently located just two blocks away. The short walk and fresh air – if you could call it that with all the traffic – did a good job of clearing her pounding headache, to her relief.

At the hall she met the conductor, who introduced her to the lead violinist and the principal cellist. Everybody seemed friendly and rehearsals were going well enough as Sophia, the conductor and the orchestra worked at gelling together musically. By late afternoon the gelling process had hit a brick wall. Sophia and the conductor had some differences of opinion as to how the Haydn Cello Concerto should be interpreted. The conductor, on the face of it, appeared to be co-operative and sympathetic to Sophia's playing. But, when all was said and done, he was not moving very much to accommodate her. And there was no way on earth that Sophia was going to back down and give in to this musical idiot.

The conductor suspected that Sophia was a little irritable from jetlag so he decided to wrap up the rehearsals for the day. Sophia didn't bother sticking around to chat. She was not in any mood for discussion and the conductor could see this so he didn't try and force anything. Instead, he simply wished her a pleasant evening and that he would see her for rehearsals the next morning.

Sophia took her cello back to her hotel room and after getting assurance from the hotel manager that it would be safe locked in her room, she went out to do a spot of sight-seeing.

She walked down 8th Avenue, along West 57th Street, then down 7th Avenue towards Central Park. As she was walking she saw Spencer across the road, standing perfectly still in an otherwise busy street, looking straight at her. Sophia's eyes locked with his momentarily until a FedEx truck sped past and broke her line of sight. The instant the FedEx truck passed, Spencer had vanished. Sophia, forgetting she was in New York, walked straight into the road to cross to the spot where she had seen her dead boyfriend.

BEEEEEEEP! A bright red Chevrolet Captiva screeched to a halt stopping just a few feet short of Sophia. The sound of the screeching tyres and the loud horn froze Sophia to the spot in the middle of the road.

'Hey, get out of the road, lady!' shouted the driver while shaking his fist out of the window. Sophia was non-responsive. She just stood there motionless.

She was not there, at least mentally. She was back in Spencer's BMW, upside down and teetering on the edge of the bridge over the canal. She saw Spencer's body, twisted and mangled in the driver's seat. He looked at her through his dead bloody eyes then, all of a sudden, his eyes blinked and he smiled at her, blood oozed out of his mouth and his eyes rolled up into his head as he said, 'It's great to see you again, baby.' Sophia screamed and frantically tried to undo the seatbelt that bound her like a prisoner inside the BMW. She couldn't break free. Spencer smiled at her, wickedly. Sophia looked out of the window and saw the fox they narrowly missed standing in the road looking straight at her. It was as if it was trying to tell her something, willing her to get out of the car quickly. She finally managed to press the seatbelt button. The belt sprung open and her body slumped free. She opened the door and scrambled to get out. She was almost out of the car when Spencer's hand grabbed her shoulder to pull her back in. She screamed and flung her fist around to hit the demonic Spencer. But the hand that grabbed her shoulder didn't belong to Spencer; it belonged to the angry driver of the Chevrolet, who had got out of his car to get Sophia out of the road. She had spun around to hit him, but he had fast reflexes and managed to grab Sophia's wrist to prevent it impacting with the side of his head.

'Easy, lady,' he said. Sophia was shaking and disoriented.

'Are you ok, lady?' he said. 'Come on, you've gotta get out of the road.'

SOPHIA

Once back on the sidewalk, Sophia pulled her arm free of the man and rushed off down 7th Avenue with the haunting memories of the car crash and Spencer's death etched firmly in her mind. It was all there, she could see it and hear it all over again. She could smell the radiator fluid leaking out of the BMW. She could smell the warm blood pouring out of Spencer's dead body. She trotted along faster, breaking into a run. She put her hands up to her ears to try and block out the sounds of the lorry slamming into the side of Spencer's BMW as she continued to run away from it.

Eventually, she stopped running and found herself near the Apple Store on 5th Avenue. She removed her hands from her ears and went inside, where she bought an iPod and some Bose headphones. Outside the shop she sat on a bench and connected to the iTunes store wirelessly. She clicked on Music/Store/Genres/Rock, and proceeded to download some rock and metal albums. Wearing the headphones, she cued up an album called 'Sempiternal' by a band called Bring Me the Horizon. She pressed play and turned up the volume and allowed the first track, 'Can You Feel My Heart' to blast through her new headphones and directly into her brain with no interruption from the outside world.

As she walked back to her hotel, she found Bring Me the Horizon's loud blend of rock/metal music and screaming vocals strongly soothing. It did a great job of dispersing the horrifying memories and images of the car crash and Spencer's death. It was just her and the loud rock music – nothing else could get in.

Still on UK time, Sophia was totally exhausted and had fallen asleep at 9 p.m. with her headphones on and with rock music still playing. The next morning her headphones had snapped off her head and fallen onto the floor next to the bed. She looked at the time and realised her alarm was not due to go off for another hour. She took the opportunity to take a long relaxing shower. The shower was revitalising and felt good as the water jetted onto her back and shoulders. As she studied the tasteful eggshell white rectangular tiles and chrome shower control fixings on the wall she felt relaxed and at ease – encapsulated in her own world between two tiled walls and two opaque Perspex doors. She felt safe in the generously sized four by three foot shower cubicle. It was her world and nobody could get in or out. The sound of the water was soothing and hypnotic. The shower cubicle's acoustics were just right. Although she'd brought her own toiletries, the hotel's complimentary body wash and shampoo was high quality and had a nice rose scent. The lather felt nice against her skin as she gently moved the soapsuds around her chest and navel. *I could stay in here forever*, she thought.

The morning's rehearsals started off badly and got worse as the day went on. Sophia was getting agitated with the conductor who, in turn, was getting more and more stubborn about the interpretation of the Haydn. They had locked horns over the second Adagio movement. The conductor thought Sophia's tempo was too slow. Sophia was banging her head against a brick wall when she tried to explain to him that the tempo was *adagio*, as per the movement's title, and not Haydn's more usual *andante*. Sophia thought the conductor lacked musical depth and he obviously didn't understand Haydn's classical elegance. And to add insult to injury, the principal cellist had made a few snide remarks. It all came to a head when, during a break, the principal cellist told Sophia that her vibrato was too organic and needed to be more focused. Sophia lost it. She had had enough. A conductor who was a musical idiot and a prima donna of a principal cellist who had a big chip on her shoulder because she didn't quite make the grade as a soloist.

Sophia grabbed her cello case, opened it and started packing her cello away.

'What are you doing? We still have the entire afternoon to rehearse,' said the conductor.

'No, you're the ones who need to rehearse. I'm going home,' she said.

'Well, ok. Go and do some sightseeing, get some rest. Do whatever it is you need to so you can be in the right frame of mind in the morning.'

'Maybe I'm not being clear. I'm going home to England.'

'What,' he laughed. 'You can't do that, the concert's in five days, it's sold out, Sophia.'

'Well, unless you can find me another orchestra who understand the definition of *concerto* and a conductor who isn't a musical idiot, I'm not prepared to stay here a minute longer.'

'This is preposterous, you can't do this – *this is America*,' he stated, as if those final three words somehow obligated her to stay and do the concert.

'You know what?' said Sophia, as she picked up her cello case and walked across the stage to the exit, 'you can stick America up your arse.'

So, nobody in the USA got to see Sophia perform, apart from a few patrons and some friend and supporter members who had rehearsal passes to attend the open working rehearsals.

Chapter 16

Sophia arrived back in England. As soon as she set foot into her apartment she was greeted by the flashing digit on her answerphone. One of the messages was from Meredith; she was *not* a happy agent. Sophia, being a musician, could hear the subtle change in her tone, which suggested she was displeased about something. Sophia sensed that underneath the seemingly pleasant tones of her answer machine message, Meredith was furious. The Carnegie Hall concert had sold out and now Meredith had the event management to deal with and tickets that had to be refunded. The fall out of this was not going to bode well at all.

Meredith was on the phone for three hours tidying up the mess and desperately trying to set things right. She had a good rapport with one of the event managers so she managed to smooth it over – just. Although Meredith managed to calm the waves across the pond, she couldn't do anything about the headlines of a story a major London daily newspaper had printed the very next day.

ENGLAND'S FAVOURITE CELLIST SNUBS AMERICA!

How the paper had found out, she didn't know. Fortunately the story wasn't unkind to Sophia Beckinsale. In fact, the newspaper was on Sophia's side – thankfully. The British media saw Sophia as an English Rose classical music icon and they were determined to protect her and show her in the best light. Meredith explained to Sophia that if it had gone the other way it could have been very bad for her career. In this instance, Sophia had not been put across in a bad light and had come up smelling of roses. It was a lucky escape – this time. Sophia decided that was a conversation she didn't want to get into with Meredith, not yet, so she ignored the message.

'Do you want to talk about what happened in America?' said her psychologist, Jacques.

'No,' said Sophia.

Dr de Beaumont had come to Sophia's apartment at 11 a.m. for a scheduled appointment, which had totally slipped Sophia's mind. Lucky for him, she was home. But not lucky for her being caught at home like this. She was not in the mood for a fucking psychologist's session today.

'Sophia, how about you come to see me at my office from now on?'

Great, he wants me to continue with these stupid bloody sessions. How can I break free from this?

'You know, I really don't think that'll be necessary,'

she said.

'Well, I'd like you to consider it. Perhaps after a couple more sessions here?'

'I'm sorry, what I meant was, these sessions aren't necessary. I'm doing fine on my own and you dragging up the accident every five minutes isn't helping.'

'Sophia, it's important that you come to terms with what happened. So, you can accept it and move on with your life.'

'I don't want to move on. The best I can hope for is to move forward. Spencer's *dead* and he's never coming back, and neither is my unborn child. Why the hell do you have to keep banging on about it, it's not helping me.' Sophia was getting progressively annoyed.

'Sophia, Spencer's death–'

'AAARRRRRRR,' she screamed, putting her hands over her ears, which only blocked out the voice of the psychologist but not the sound of screeching truck tyres as it hurtled towards Spencer's BMW. The sounds of the loud crash as it slammed into their car. The metallic creaking as the car teetered precariously on the edge of the bridge. Sophia was right back at the crash site, living it all over again, all thanks to the fucking psychologist for poking and prodding away at her mind.

As the BMW gently swayed back and forth on the bridge, the bones in Spencer's broken neck crunched and cracked as he turned his head to look at her. Sophia could hear the high-pitched barking of the fox. It sounded horrific, like it was screaming. But neither the car or the truck hit the fox. It was simply a spectator looking on at the aftermath of the crash. Spencer had a sinister look on his face and smiled, which fitted the soundtrack of the screaming fox. Then, his mouth opened slightly and he delicately sucked in a small lungful of air. The barrier on the bridge gave way. The car was free-falling towards the canal below. But the impact of the water didn't come – not yet. The car continued to fall, but it wasn't going to hit the water until Spencer said what he had lured her here to say.

'You can't move on – you'll never move on,' he whispered. Then his face became even more sinister and his dead eyes turned blacker than a moonless prairie night. They widened and he leaned across so his face was just inches from hers. She was trapped by the seatbelt, again, and her head was pressed against the roof lining of the car with her shoulder pressed against her door. She could not escape the plummeting car. Spencer grabbed Sophia's shoulder and squeezed it tight. Everything was happening in ultra slow motion. Her mind was incapable of speeding up this horrific scene. She wanted out, but it was not going to happen. She felt like she was in a horrible nightmare and she was struggling and willing herself to wake up from it.

'YOU'RE MINE' shouted Spencer, as the car hit the water, engulfing it in a dark cold watery hell. The car started to go down, taking Sophia with it, deeper and deeper into the bottomless canal. Sophia screamed out loud and jumped when Dr de Beaumont shook her shoulder.

'Sophia, Sophia,' he shouted. She jumped to her feet

and hit Jacques hard in the chest with the palms of her hands, sending him scuttling backwards. He stumbled and fell over the coffee table.

Spencer's dead voice was screaming away in Sophia's head and it was all Dr fucking de Beaumont's fault.

Beaumont eventually left and over the next few hours Spencer's voice had subdued into a distant echo. *I've got to get out of here*, she thought. Just as she was grabbing her coat and handbag, her mobile rang.

'Hello.'

'Hey sis, how are you?' said her older sister, Eleanor.

'Not good, not good at all.'

'Daddy told me about what happened in America. I'm so sorry.'

'It's ok, Meredith smoothed everything over. Jacques has just left.'

'The psychologist?'

'Yes.'

'How's that working out?'

'It isn't. The last session was horrible.'

'You want to talk about it?'

'No, I don't think so. It was because of Jacques making me talk about it that I had a horrible nightmarish flash-back about Spencer.'

'I'm sorry, sis, I really am.'

'I know. I really don't know what's happening to me. I'm really confused.'

'Confused?'

'Yes. I keep seeing Spencer everywhere I go, and … well, I keep having these nightmares about him. Even during the day I keep having horrible flashbacks.'

'What kind of nightmares?' asked Eleanor.

'Its hard to explain. But in my dreams it's like he's somebody else. He's like the devil or something. He definitely isn't the caring loving Spencer that I knew and spent all those years with.'

'You poor thing. Look, what are you doing right now?'

'Nothing really, I was about to go out. Nowhere in particular, just need to get out of the apartment.'

'Good, so why don't you come and meet me at work and we'll go and have something to eat?'

'Sure,' said Sophia.

'Ok, I'll see you at five?'

'See you then.'

After getting stuck in a traffic jam on her way across London she was almost certainly not going to get to her sister's work place by five. She could murder a coffee so she pulled out of the traffic jam and into the retail park and a drive-through McDonalds. *Well, this is new*, she thought, having never visited a McDonalds drive-through before. But, she only wanted a black coffee. Surely nobody could screw that up. She told the metallic sounding voice coming out of the metal box what she wanted. She paid at the next window, collected her coffee, then drove out and re-joined the queue of traffic. She eventually crawled closer to the temporary roadwork traffic lights. She sat there listening to the pneumatic road drills power-driving into the lane on her side, sending white smoke up into the air. Sophia was concerned that small fragments of concrete would spray

Sophia

across and chip her new Audi, which was only a few feet away. She took a sip of her scalding hot black coffee. The lights changed to green, not a moment too soon. She put the cardboard coffee cup into the cup holder on the dash and sped through the work lights and attempted to make up for lost time. But a hundred metres down the road a set of traffic lights changed to red, forcing her to break hard as she approached them. 'Oh, come on,' she said. She watched cars cross the junction for bloody ages before the flow eventually came to a halt and her light changed to green. Again, she sped off the lights and raced down the road.

'Oh for crying out loud,' she said, as the next set of lights changed to red, as if to inconvenience her on purpose. She sat at the red lights, indicating right. She still had about two miles to go and it was already quarter past five. *Shit*, she thought, looking at the clock on the dash.

Finally, the lights changed to green. Sophia accelerated so hard it caused her car to wheel-spin as she raced around the corner and floored it down the road. Within seconds she heard sirens behind her. She looked in her rear view mirror and saw blue lights flashing on the roof of the car with the word, POLICE, sprawled across the bonnet in large blue letters.

'Shit.' Sophia pulled over to the left. The yellow and blue Battenberg patterned police car pulled up behind her and left the blue lights flashing. There were two officers in the car, a man and a woman. The woman stayed in the car while the man approached Sophia's window and rapped it with his knuckles. Sophia opened the window and looked at the very official looking policeman.

'Can you turn your engine off and put the car into neutral,' he ordered.

Sophia obliged, reluctantly. She let out a sigh, hoping this wasn't going to take long.

'Do you know why you've been stopped?' he asked.

'No, officer, I don't,' she said, letting out a sigh and looking at her watch.

'In a hurry to get somewhere, madam?' he said.

'Yes, I am actually, so can I be on my way?' she said.

'I'm sorry, madam. Can you step out of the car for a moment,' he said.

In the meantime, the WPC got out of the police car and came to join the fun and games.

'The WPC took the male officer to one side and whispered something in his ear.

'Is this your car, madam?' he said.

'Yes it is.'

'What's your full name?' he asked.

'Sophia Beckinsale.'

'Do you have your driver's licence with you?' he asked.

'It's in my handbag in the car.'

'May I see it?' he asked.

Sophia got into the driver's seat and took her licence out of her handbag that was on the passenger seat and handed it to the officer. She remained seated and took her black coffee out of the cup holder and took a gentle sip.

'Madam, can you get out of the car please,' said the WPC, looking slightly annoyed at Sophia's casual laid-

SOPHIA

back attitude as she sat there sipping her coffee. She got out of the car again, coffee in hand.

'Madam, you've been pulled over for reckless driving,' said the WPC.

'Excuse me?' said Sophia.

'You pulled away from the lights back there so fast your wheels skidded as you went around the corner. You could have lost control of the car and mounted the pavement. You might have killed somebody,' she stated.

'You've got to be kidding me,' said Sophia.

'No, I'm not *kidding* you,' she said, raising her voice a little more. Just then a white transit van slowed to a crawl and the two workmen rubbernecked when they saw the stunning young blond being hassled by the two police officers.

'Leave her alone,' shouted the driver of the van.

'Ok, move along gentleman, there's nothing to see here,' said the male officer. The two workmen in the white van muttered something offensive towards the police before building up speed and driving off.

Sophia looked back down the street towards the traffic lights where she had come from. It was quiet and there were no pedestrians in sight.

'But there's nobody there,' said Sophia.

'But you weren't to know that. There could have been a mother pushing a baby in a pram.'

'Oh for fuck's sake,' said Sophia.

'Swearing at a police officer madam?'

Sophia could see that she was dealing with a total jobsworth bitch. She could feel the anger building up inside her as the WPC gave her a glare of authority.

'Can I ask you a question, officer?' said Sophia, to the WPC.

'Of course,' she said.

'What would happen if I called you a cunt?'

'That's it, I've warned you about swearing at a police officer,' she said. 'One more remark like that and I'll arrest you.'

'I'm sorry, you misunderstood, I wasn't swearing at you, I was simply asking you a question. Would you like me to ask it again?' said Sophia.

'You can ask it again, but tread very carefully, you're walking on thin ice,' she said.

'The question was, what would happen if I called you a cunt?' she asked again.

'Madam, you'd be arrested and taken to the police station,' said the male officer, intervening.

'So what would you do if I merely thought you were a cunt?' Sophia asked the WPC.

'Ok, that's quite enough,' said the male officer.

'Madam, your thoughts are your own. You can think whatever you like,' said the WPC.

'In that case, I think you're a cunt,' said Sophia.

'That's it, I'm arresting you for–' before the WPC could finish her sentence, Sophia had removed the cover from her cardboard cup of black coffee and thrown its contents straight into the WPCs face. The scalding hot black coffee caused the WPC to let out a pained squeal as she cupped her face with her hands. With this, the male officer stepped forward to arrest and restrain Sophia. As he did so, Sophia turned and, uncharacteristically, kicked him hard in the groin. He doubled forward holding his privates in pain. The WPC – her face red and stinging like hell – lunged forward and rugby-tackled Sophia to the ground. She wrestled Sophia over onto her front and pulled one of her arms up behind her back and snapped her handcuffs onto her wrist. She wrestled Sophia's other arm around and handcuffed that one too. While Sophia was face down on the pavement being restrained, she could hear her mobile ringing in her handbag; it was her sister's ringtone.

'I'm arresting you for ABH, resisting arrest and using abusive language towards a police officer. You do not have to say anything. But it may harm your defence–'

'I need to answer my phone,' pleaded Sophia.

The WPC ignored her request and continued, '… if you do not mention when questioned something which you later rely on in court. Anything you do say may be given in evidence,' said the WPC, pulling Sophia to her feet. The male police officer had also got to his feet, but was in pain. The two of them managed to wrestle the reluctant Sophia into the back of their police car.

Chapter 17

The police car pulled up at the side of Kentish Town police station in north London. The two officers escorted the handcuffed Sophia from the car to the side entrance door. Just inside the door Sophia and the officers waited in a caged area until the custody sergeant buzzed them in. Sophia had calmed down a little during the ride to the station in the police car. She was told to sit on a wooden bench in the custody area while another prisoner was being processed.

Sophia looked around at the grim décor. The building was obviously old and the interior looked like it hadn't been modernised since the Victorian period. The chunky dark wooden bench and the bleak concrete rendering made it all the more depressing. This place was the polar opposite of stylish. It had a horrible funky smell, like thousands of drunks, drug addicts, psychopaths and general scumbags had passed through here over the years.

'What do we have here?' said the custody sergeant to the two officers who brought Sophia in. Sophia was ordered to step up to the tall counter, where the routine began. They booked her in and took her name and address. The officers explained to the custody sergeant

SOPHIA

why she'd been arrested. The custody sergeant gave Sophia a surprised look as if to say, 'but you look so innocent, like an angel'.

The custody sergeant filled out various forms on his computer and asked Sophia many questions. When the booking-in process was complete, Sophia had to sign an electronic pad. She was then searched and her possessions were bagged and tagged.

'Should I organise a cozart?' asked the male officer who brought her in.

'I don't think that will be necessary,' said the custody sergeant.

Cozart was a drug test the police often did on prisoners to check if there was any sign of class A drugs in their blood, such as crack cocaine and heroin. The custody sergeant assessed the situation and decided that Sophia did not fit this profile.

'She'll need to be assessed by the doctor,' said the WPC, gesturing towards Sophia's hands. Sophia had struggled with the handcuffs on which, in turn, had bruised both her wrists.

'Ok, I'll arrange that,' said the custody sergeant. 'In the meantime we'll need to get your face looked at straight away,' he said, directing his attention to the WPC with the scalded face. 'We'll get you checked out at the same time,' he said to the male officer.

Sophia was then taken through to be photographed and fingerprinted. This was about the most up-to-date part of the process. Her fingerprints were taken electronically, then immediately sent to Scotland Yard via computer.

When asked if she wanted to call a solicitor – or have one appointed – she declined. When everything had been processed, Sophia was taken to a cell. The officer closed and locked the heavy-duty cell door. He glanced at her through the small hammer-proof Perspex window before walking off.

The cell was just as grim as the rest of the building. It was small, about five by eight feet. There was a metal toilet at the end under a barred toughened glass window. There was a small concrete wall that was supposed to divide the toilet from the rest of the cell, but it offered little privacy. The bed was a concrete slab with a thin blue rubberised mattress that offered the bare minimum of comfort. And the stench of bleach wasn't enough to cover the smell of urine and vomit.

It wasn't long before somebody came to her cell and asked if she wanted to make a phone call. This, she would have to think about. In the meantime, she was taken to a small room containing a wooden table and four black plastic chairs. Mounted on the wall there was a small microphone and an old-fashioned tape cassette recorder with eject doors for two tapes. Still refusing the presence of a solicitor, Sophia was interviewed by two officers, plus a higher-ranking female officer.

Sophia could not see the point of having a solicitor. Now that she'd calmed down she knew she was on a sticky wicket, so she didn't kick up a fuss. She asked one of the officers if she could make her phone call. She phoned her father, who was shocked to say the least.

SOPHIA

He naturally wanted to get to her as soon as possible, as well as sort out her legal representation. But Sophia insisted that this was her mess and she would deal with it on her own. The news of Sophia being arrested and held in custody at Kentish Town police station sent shockwaves though her family. Andrew told Diana, who told Charlotte and Eleanor, who told Django …

Because of the aggressive nature of Sophia's crime, she was held in custody in the disgusting cell until her appearance at Highbury Magistrates Court in North London the next morning. She hardly slept and during the night she was aware of an officer checking on her through the small window every thirty minutes or so. *Where the hell do they think I'm going to go*, she thought. Or perhaps they just wanted to make sure she hadn't tried to harm herself, like so many of the previous crazy detainees had probably done before her.

The next morning Sophia was driven in a police van with three other prisoners to the courthouse, where she was escorted into the holding cells below. About an hour later somebody came to the cell to take her upstairs to the court. She was instructed to wait, alongside two other prisoners, for her case to be heard. Her mother and father were there in the public viewing area. How humiliating. Diana was sickened just to be in such a building. 'Just look at all these disgusting people,' she'd said. The courthouse was riddled with chavs and general low life scum who were there for breaking and entering, car theft, shoplifting, drug related offences, non-payment of fines, fraud, ABH. Talk about one extreme to the other. At one end of the spectrum were suited solicitors and smartly dressed magistrates and court staff and at the other end were low life petty criminals dressed in tracksuit bottoms, jeans, t-shirts and trainers. Most had facial and/or ear piercings and a collection of visible tattoos. The women criminals weren't much of an improvement either. All of them swore every other word and kept popping out for a smoke. Diana thought that there was probably a combined IQ of about six between the lot of them. These scumbags were as low as you could get. They could perform basic primitive tasks such as eating, shitting, spitting in the street and fucking to ensure a future generation of idiots who would grow up to be even thicker than their parents.

The first of the two in front of Sophia were Eastern European who spoke broken English. The first was a man in his twenties who was being charged with stealing copper pipes from a new housing development that was only half built. Security at the new homes development had caught him with a pipe cutter stealing all the copper plumbing that had been installed. *How desperate have you got to be*, thought Sophia.

The next was a woman who was there for a crack cocaine offence. She looked, and smelled homeless and dressed like a bargain-basement prostitute. She was about twenty years old, skinny with shoulder-length greasy hair that looked like it hadn't been washed in a month. Sophia assumed she'd had to have spent the night in a police cell, and lord knows what shithole the night before that. The magistrates had clearly lost patience with this young woman as she made excuse after excuse. 'It wasn't mine, I was just looking after it for somebody,' she said. One lie followed another. She sounded seriously undereducated. *Chav*, was a derogatory word that Sophia had heard in the past, and she suspected this young woman sat firmly in that social group. The magistrates told her that this was a very serious matter and that she would have to spend two weeks in prison, to give her time to think about her drug habits.

Then it was Sophia's turn. A court clerk instructed her to move forward and take a seat and when the Magistrates addressed her she should stand up.

'Miss Beckinsale,' said the magistrate in the middle. There were three magistrates in total: a tubby middle-aged balding man on the left, a rather stern looking woman of similar age on the right, and the lady who was addressing Sophia in the middle. This lady had a spindly build with mousy grey hair. Her eyes didn't look friendly, in fact they looked full of a lifetime of hate and bitterness. This woman looked like she had a permanent axe to grind and it was obvious that she had taken an instant dislike to Sophia. This aging woman had lost what looks she might have had a long time ago, and here, standing before her was a beautiful young blonde girl with a figure to die for.

'Looking over your papers I find it hard to believe that a young woman like you could be capable of such offences,' said the magistrate, while she continued to read the papers in front of her. 'I see you're of previous good character, but your offences are very serious indeed,' she continued. 'Miss Beckinsale, you've injured a female officer's eye by throwing scalding hot coffee into her face, and you also injured a male officer …' The magistrate flicked over to look at another sheet of paper. She then leaned to the left, then to the right to consult the other two magistrates, both were nodding and concurring. 'Miss Beckinsale, I know these are your first offences, but the seriousness of them simply can't be ignored. You could have blinded the WPC and caused permanent injury to the male officer. ABH is a serious offence young lady, and you've committed it twice, and to respectable officers of the law. Do you have anything to say for yourself?'

'Will it make any difference if I do?' said Sophia.

'Excuse me?' said the magistrate.

'Well, if this is the part where I'm supposed to weep and say how sorry I am, I really don't think I'll bother. You've already lectured me, and I suspect you've already made up your mind about my punishment. Let's face it lady you hate me and so do your two fucking minions.'

'I won't tolerate that kind of language in my court,' said the magistrate. 'Now, do you have anything constructive to say before sentencing?'

'I thought I just did,' said Sophia. Her parents looked on in disbelief at their daughter's attitude. This was not the Sophia they'd brought up.

There was a brief pause while the magistrate looked down at Sophia's papers one final time. She looked up at Sophia and said, 'I'm going to sentence you to thirty days in prison. This will hopefully give you time to think about the seriousness of your offences. And while you are in prison I'd try and do something about your attitude.'

Sophia looked over at her mother and father, who were shocked and speechless. Sophia was escorted back down to the cells below the courthouse where she would wait to be transported to prison.

Chapter 18

After waiting all afternoon in the court holding cells, Sophia was eventually escorted from the cell to the prison transportation vehicle, where she would be escorted to Holloway Women's Prison in North London. Although Sophia was one of three women being transferred to prison that day, she didn't really see or hear the other prisoners as the transportation vehicle had individual internal cells. These cells were *small*, ludicrously small. Luckily for Sophia the journey from Highbury Corner Magistrates Court to Holloway Prison was barely a mile and a half. So she only had to tolerate being cramped in the confined cell for a short time.

The prison transport vehicle drove through the large gates of the prison and pulled up outside the reception area. Sophia and the other prisoners were released from the van and taken into reception and shown into a holding room until the senior reception officer was ready to see them. Twenty minutes later a female officer came to fetch Sophia.

She was asked many questions, the usual full name and date of birth just to establish that they were checking in the right prisoner. They asked her various questions about illnesses and if she was on any medication or if she took any kind of recreational drugs.

Then she was taken to a private area and given a full strip search by two female officers. After this humiliating process she was taken to see a health care officer for a brief medical; emphasis on the word 'brief'. This consisted of measuring and weighing her and giving her a quick once over to establish her general state of health.

Then she was escorted to yet another holding room where she had to wait for somebody to take her to the reception wing. During this time she was given water to drink and a barely edible microwave dinner that she suspected was lasagne. Whatever it was, it had the taste and texture of boil-washed sackcloth.

Once on the reception wing, she was asked more questions – lots more questions. She was interviewed about her case and why she was in prison. They also explained to her how the prison system worked and how she was expected to behave while she carried out her sentence. Although the custody sergeant at the court holding cells had already told her, her heart lifted slightly when one of the prison officers confirmed that she would only have to serve half of her sentence. This meant she would be out of there fifteen days from now.

She also had several meetings with probation staff, social workers and the offenders management unit. Sophia could not believe the length of these procedures. And all because she'd lost it with a couple of police officers.

About two hours later, Sophia was taken to a cell on

what was called the first night induction wing. Here, she spent her first night in prison alone.

The cell was disgusting. It was painted in pale blue, which just didn't go with the pale sickly green paintwork in the corridors. The bed was an old style metal-framed affair, with metal slats to support a thin rubberised mattress. The only other furniture in her cell was a basic cupboard for her clothes.

Sophia felt like she would never get to sleep as she played back the events of the past few days. Eventually, she did get to sleep only to be woken by a loud metallic clang coming from the corridor outside. She opened her eyes and looked around the dark cell, and then she almost had a heart attack. In the darkest corner of her cell she saw Spencer. It was dark, but it was definitely him. She recognised his silhouetted outline. He was holding something. She squinted and rubbed her eyes to try and focus.

'Spencer,' she whispered. She was nervous and scared, knowing she could not escape the cell, and not knowing if it was going to be the *nice* Spencer, or the *evil* Spencer. Even though he was dead and little more than her imagination playing tricks on her, whenever he did turn up, he seemed to have some sort of dual personality thing going on. Was it a reflection of her own state of mind?

He stepped forward into a small pool of light. It was as if the pool of light had been put there just for him. Sophia screamed as Spencer stepped out of the shadow and into the light. He was covered head to toe in blood and was holding a bloody limp dead fox in his arms, its lame head and legs dangling below.

'Get out, leave me alone,' she screamed. Sophia heard the flap on her cell door open. She looked towards it as her cell light came on. An officer looked through to see what all the noise was about. Her cell door opened and a female prison guard entered. Sophia spun around and looked into the empty space where Spencer was standing moments earlier. The female guard was sympathetic, putting it down to a simple nightmare and first night anxiety.

The next morning Sophia was given a *shared cell risk assessment* to determine if she could share a cell with another prisoner, or prisoners. It turned out that she could, so they placed her in a cell with one other prisoner called Delphine. She was a 25-year old mixed race girl who had found herself serving a thirty-day sentence for a prostitution offence. Like Sophia, she only had to serve half her sentence. She had arrived four days before and had eleven days left to serve.

To begin with Sophia didn't really like Delphine; she thought she was common. Delphine wasn't too keen on Sophia either. She thought Sophia was a snob born with a silver spoon in her mouth and she didn't have the faintest clue about what a difficult and tough life was. But their friendship, or lack of it, was about to change – for the better.

Four days into her sentence Sophia was sitting in the enclosed garden area where prisoners could go outside at allocated times. She was reading a book and generally minding her own business. Most of the other prisoners were smoking cigarettes or talking with other inmates. Then it happened. As Delphine walked past, two other inmates started to give her trouble. The girl mouthing off at Delphine the most didn't have what you could call a *female* figure at all. She was in her early twenties and built more like an out-of-shape middle-aged male bricklayer. She had no waistline and had round shoulders, a flat barrel-chest and a deep voice to match. She had already eyed Sophia once or twice over the past few days. Sophia still couldn't quite make out why this brute of a woman and her sidekick were giving Delphine so much grief. But she could see that Delphine didn't like being hounded by them. Bricklayer girl looked across at Sophia.

'What the fuck are you looking at?' she said, in her best trailer park trash voice.

'I have absolutely no idea,' said Sophia, getting back to her book.

'Wot did you fuckin' say?' said bricklayer girl.

'Please, I'm trying to read my book, it's far more interesting,' said Sophia, as she winked a friendly wink at Delphine. Delphine smiled at Sophia and was happy that Sophia had taken her badgering fellow inmates' attention away from her, momentarily at least.

'I've seen you around … are you listening to me, bitch?' Sophia glanced up and looked bricklayer girl up and down with disgust, then got back to her book.

'Who the fuck do you think you are, looking at me like I'm shit. Listen bitch, I'm gonna be making some future plans for you.' Sophia giggled to herself then looked up from her book.

'*Future plans*? I've never heard such a ridiculous sentence. Isn't the very notion of advance preparation included in that little incy wincy four-letter word *plan*? As for future planning, well, aren't all plans for the future? What the hell good would a *retro plan* be?' said Sophia. Even Delphine couldn't help chucking to herself at this.

Bricklayer girl's tiny IQ failed to grasp what Sophia was talking about, but she knew Sophia had just made her look stupid. She turned her attention back to Delphine.

'Time for me to teach you a lesson you whore,' said bricklayer girl, making for Delphine. But before she got to Delphine, Sophia had run up behind her, grabbed a handful of her hair and pulled her backwards, causing her to stumble and fall down. She clumsily got up and swung for Sophia, but Sophia moved her head back to avoid her slow reckless swing. Within a few seconds three prison officers, one man and two women, were on the scene to break it up.

'I'm gonna get you bitch; and your whore girlfriend,' she said, while being restrained by the two female officers, who proceeded to take her away for reprimanding. Sophia had some explaining to do too but, all in all, the prison officials let it go, as they knew bricklayer girl had a reputation for causing trouble.

Sophia could not believe the sheer lack of intellect in the establishment. Most of the inmates had little to no education and seemed to be the lowest form of life imaginable. Sophia had never witnessed anything like it.

The level of conversation seemed so utterly futile and primitive to Sophia, who definitely did *not* belong here with the rest of these illiterate uneducated morons. Every other word she heard was an obscenity. These women were neanderthal plebs at best. Delphine, however, was an exception to the norm in here.

That evening Delphine warmed to Sophia and she made huge efforts to be friendly and to get to know her. After all, Sophia had come to her defence with the bricklayer girl incident. Seeing how much effort Delphine was putting in, Sophia decided to reciprocate. To Sophia's amazement, she found that the more she learned about Delphine the more she liked her. Within a few days they had become the best of friends. Sharing the same cell meant they practically lived in each other's pockets and they found that they were spending all their time together during the day as well. Apart from her younger sister, Sophia had never really had a female friend who she could talk to and confide in but, here she was, on the verge of developing a great friendship with a call girl.

Funny, after many hours of talking with Delphine, and there wasn't much else to do in prison, she really didn't mind about Delphine's profession either. In fact, she became rather fascinated by the world's oldest profession. Delphine wasn't just some low-life street hooker who was feeding a drug habit. She was a high-class call girl. She worked for a madam who had a regular client list of well-to-do businessmen. Delphine had built up a rapport with most of her clients and knew them well. Most of them were discerning gentlemen, city businessmen and the like. The madam put all new clients through her own unique vetting process which the client had to pay for. She ran a tight ship when it came to her girls' safety.

Delphine's profession aside, it turned out that she and Sophia had a lot in common. On the face of it, Delphine's dress sense and general demeanour would suggest she was not academic. But over the days and nights together, Sophia learned that Delphine did rather well at school and even went to university and had a degree in French. Delphine was tall, slim and attractive with long black straight hair. People have often likened Delphine's beautiful mixed race olive skin and good looks to the Vampire Diaries actress, Katerina Graham. Her father was a blues guitarist from Jamaica and her mother was French and ran her own florist shop in Paris. Her parents met while her father was touring Europe with his jazz/blues band – mainly small clubs. Delphine's mother named her after a flower called the Delphinium. Although it's a poisonous plant, it's also used in herbal medicine. So, like Delphine, it's deadly and healing at the same time. Well, perhaps 'deadly' is a bit strong, but Delphine's sensitive nature meant she could be a little volatile sometimes if somebody upset her.

As well as being a call girl, Delphine also worked part time in a jazz club in London called The Baltimore Oriole as one of the house jazz singers. There were three female singers who sang regularly at the club, one of whom was Delphine. Delphine always went down really well at the club. She had a sensual and syrupy voice to die for.

The club's owner named the club after the song, 'Baltimore Oriole' by Hoagy Carmichael. But he also loved the little orange, yellow and black North American birds. The club's logo had two of these colourful little birds either side of its name.

At closing time, the tradition at the club was for one of the girls to sing 'Baltimore Oriole' as the final song of the night, by way of subtly telling the regulars that it was closing time. Delphine's rendition of the song was remarkably like Sheila Jordan's 1962 recording. Delphine had similar vocal qualities and the accompanying double bass and brushes lightly stroking a snare drum made it all the more authentic. No matter how many times Delphine sang it, she never tired of it and always gave it the same emotion as if it were the first time.

Sophia liked the fact that they shared a deep love for music. Although Sophia was a classical musician, she owned many jazz and blues records on cd and vinyl. Delphine, though a jazz/blues singer, also appreciated classical music and had a soft spot for composers from the romantic period such as: Chopin, Grieg, Schumann, Rachmaninov, Elgar, and naturally, with her French heritage, Debussy.

Sophia and Delphine spent hours talking about music, discussing their favourite pieces and songs. They learned about each other's lives, their different backgrounds, and found a mutual respect for each other as their friendship deepened.

SOPHIA

Sophia had only known Delphine for ten days, but the night before Delphine's release date they both found quite emotional. How could this be, Sophia and Delphine came from quite different backgrounds, yet they had bonded like long-lost sisters. Sophia told Delphine that she was closer to her after just ten days than she had ever managed to be with her older sister, Eleanor, in twenty-two years.

The next morning Sophia and Delphine almost had to be prised apart by two prison officers as they hugged each other goodbye with tears in their eyes.

'I'll be back to pick you up in four days, ok. I'll be waiting right outside those gates. Just hang in there and keep to yourself,' said Delphine.

'Ok' said Sophia, wiping her wet nose.

The remaining four days of Sophia's sentence seemed long, cold and lonely. Because Sophia's new best friend was not there anymore, bricklayer girl tried to give Sophia some stick on a few occasions. But Sophia was not about to lose remission and have to stay in prison extra days for getting into a catfight. She realized that bricklayer girl was of seriously limited intelligence, so she kept to herself and read a lot during those long final days.

Chapter 19

A female prison officer escorted Sophia across the concrete courtyard. They arrived at the prison's exit gate, which was a very high electronically operated iron-barred affair. A male prison guard sat inside a small security room ready to open the gate.

'Take care of yourself, Sophia,' said the female prison officer, who didn't feel the need to say anything like 'let's not see you back here,' as she knew Sophia was not the usual jail bird type.

'I will,' said Sophia. The large electronic gate opened to reveal the world outside. As Sophia walked out of the gate and along the loading area road, she saw Delphine standing there, leaning against her aging green BMW 3-series. She looked genuinely happy to see Sophia again. They both had big beaming smiles on their faces as they ran up to each other and hugged.

'Oh my God, you came?' said Sophia.

'Hey, I said I would.'

'I know, but over the past few days some doubts started to creep into my mind.'

'Look, wild horses couldn't keep me away,' said Delphine, smiling. 'So, how were the last few days?'

Sophia

'Grim and lonely ... very lonely. I think you were the only person in there with a brain,' said Sophia.

'Why, thank you, dear,' said Delphine in her best mock-regal voice.

'I was only in there for two weeks, but it felt like three months.'

'Well, you're out now; we both are. Where do you want to go?' asked Delphine.

'Home. I need to take a long hot shower to wash the smell of prison out of my hair, and then I vote we go out to a nice restaurant – my treat. I'm desperate for some real cuisine.'

'Your wish is my command,' said Delphine, opening the passenger door for Sophia.

'I love your apartment,' said Delphine, as Sophia walked into the living room wearing a bathrobe with a towel tied around her wet hair. 'Have you lived here long?'

'About a year now.'

'Do you like it here?'

'Its ok I guess. I'm close to my family and its convenient for London recitals and the airports for international ones.'

'Hmm, doesn't sound like you really love it though?' asked Delphine.

'Yeah, you're right. When you've travelled around as much as I have doing recitals all over the UK, Europe and the rest of the world, it doesn't take long to realise that London isn't such a great place to live after all.'

'Oh?'

'Well, I guess you either love it or hate it … London that is,' said Sophia.

'And you hate it?'

'I wouldn't say I hate it; I just don't really feel it's for me anymore. It just feels too dirty and hectic. I don't know, its just lost its appeal. Maybe I'll move out of London, one day.'

'So out of all the exotic places you've visited, where would you like to live?'

'I'd still live here in England, just not London.'

'Ok, so where?'

'I'm not really sure. I kind of like Cambridge.'

'Hmmm, a university city.'

'Yeah, I've been there quite a lot and I just like the feel of the place. It's a city, but a small one so it's not so overwhelming. And people are much friendlier there.'

'Yeah, I'll agree with you on that one. There are some rude buggers in London that's for sure.'

'So how come you've been to Cambridge so much?'

'The man who made my cello is based there, so I go there when my instrument needs any adjustments. The man who re-hairs my bow is also in Cambridge.'

'And I guess you've given recitals there too?'

'Yes, many. It's also got its own city airport and Stansted's only half an hour down the M11.'

'So why don't you sell this place and buy somewhere in Cambridge. The money you'd get for this would probably buy you a five-bedroom house up there. Not that I want you to leave,' stressed Delphine.

'I know that, silly. You're probably right though. I'm

not sure the time's right just yet.'

Sophia and Delphine talked more about their lives, sharing more and more as their friendship continued to deepen. This pleased Sophia as she was a little worried that once she was out of prison their friendship might be different somehow. But it wasn't, it continued just where they'd left off in Holloway. The same thoughts had gone through Delphine's head, so she too was pleased and relieved.

Before they knew it the whole afternoon had passed, during which, Sophia had also made some important family phone calls. Her father desperately wanted to pick her up on her release date, but she insisted that her friend was picking her up and she'd be fine. Her mother wanted her to go around to see her straight away, but again, Sophia insisted she had catching up to do and that she was fine and just wanted to put it all behind her. When Sophia explained that she was with her new friend, Delphine, who she met in prison, it did not go down well with her mother. But Sophia was insistent that Delphine was a kind and decent person and very defensive of her.

That evening Sophia and Delphine got dressed up and went out to a classy restaurant in the West End. Delphine was tall and slim and the exact same dress size as Sophia, which meant they didn't have to stop by Delphine's place as Sophia let Delphine pick out one of her dresses to wear. By chance, they were also the same shoe size too. They were like two sisters, best of friends, as they both tried on different dresses and tossed them onto the bed before trying on the next. With several dresses on Sophia's bed, and several pairs of shoes scattered around her bedroom floor, they headed out to Delphine's car.

After the restaurant Delphine wanted to take Sophia to the Baltimore Oriole club where she worked part time a couple of evenings per week. Of the two jobs Delphine did, this was the one she was proud of, and the one she truly loved. Not so much the bar work, but the singing. But fortunately Delphine didn't spend too much time serving behind the bar, she spent the majority of it on stage singing.

Sophia was surprised at what a respectable establishment it was. She didn't really know what to expect. Not that she had any preconceived ideas. Although the lighting was dim, giving the place a slightly seamy look, once your eyes adjusted, it actually had a plush executive feel to it. It didn't attract any riff-raff or drunks tipping out of other clubs; classy jazz/blues music didn't really do it for those types anyway. The clientele were mostly suited, with a few artsy types and jazz evangelists.

Delphine introduced Sophia to her boss and the barman and, when she'd finished her short set, the singer who was on stage that night. Sophia was impressed and felt comfortable there. Sophia said she would come back on Friday night when Delphine was going to be on stage.

Chapter 20

Sophia phoned for a taxi and went to collect her Audi, which had been impounded. After the police took Sophia to the police station two weeks previously, her car had remained on a double yellow line. The male officer had put a POLICE AWARE sticker on the car with a twenty-four hour grace period for her to come back and move it. But, because she'd been remanded in custody and then sent straight to prison the next day, there was not much she could do about it. Her car had accumulated four parking tickets before it was eventually lifted onto a truck and towed away. Sophia was not happy. She had to pay for the four parking tickets at £65 each, plus a £200 removal fee, plus £40 per night storage for the fourteen nights her car had been impounded. So, she reluctantly paid the £1,020 with her debit card and was shown to her car. As she got in she expressed her annoyance by shouting some mild obscenities. She drove off in the direction of her parents' house.

'Mummy, I don't need a lecture. It's over and done with

so can you please let it go,' said Sophia. Things were starting to get a little heated.

'Let it go? How are we supposed to let it go? You–', started Diana, before Andrew cut in.

'Ok, ok,' he said. 'This isn't doing anybody any good. Look darling, I'm sure Sophia's learned her lesson.'

'Well I certainly hope so. I have absolutely no idea what I'm going to tell your poor grandmother. What will she think? You've disgraced this family young lady.'

'Mummy, please, I think you've lectured me enough now. And can you please change this damn channel,' said Sophia, gesturing towards the radio on the kitchen window sill.

'I most certainly will not. What's happened to you? You used to like Radio 4,' said Diana.

'No Mummy, *you* like Radio 4. I never liked it. It's for old people who like listening to people chirruping on about the bloody arts all day long.'

'How dare you. Calm your tongue, young lady. I can't believe what I'm hearing. What's happened to you? When did you become so ... shallow?' said Diana.

'Don't underestimate the depths of my shallowness, Mummy.'

Charlotte, who was standing in the kitchen doorway, could not suppress a short giggle.

'Sophia Beckinsale, I won't have you talk like that in this house,' said Diana. 'As for you, madam,' she said, turning her attentions to Charlotte, 'this isn't funny. If you're going to laugh, you can go to your room.'

'Diana, darling, she's twenty years old,' said Andrew,

defending his youngest daughter.

'Doesn't anybody have any respect anymore? Am I the only one in this house who's concerned about this? Andrew, talk to her, make her see sense.'

'Look, darling–'

'And just look at that hair, and those absurd skimpy outlandish clothes. Revealing yourself like that. You look like a ... cheap tart,' said Diana.

'That's it, Daddy. I'm leaving,' said Sophia, storming out of the kitchen. Charlotte chased after her.

'What?' said Diana, 'don't give me that look.'

'I'm saying nothing,' said Andrew.

'Well, that's the trouble. You never do say anything. I just don't understand it, Sophia can do no wrong in your eyes – none of them can.'

'Darling, Sophia's been though a lot. Are you forgetting that Spencer died and she lost a baby? She can't just get over that in five minutes.'

'Yes, I understand that. But dyeing her hair blonde and wearing those ridiculous outfits and getting herself arrested for acts of violence against the police. What on earth has gotten into her?'

'Well, we all have our own ways of dealing with grief.'

'Yes we do, but we don't all go around acting reckless and assaulting police officers.'

'Darling, I'm not happy about it either. But I think the best thing we can do right now is to give her a little space and try and cut her some slack. She needs our support. I'll call Jacques to let him know he can call her so she can get back to the sessions.'

Sophia hugged Charlotte goodbye outside the house then went back to her apartment to make some more phone calls.

First she called her agent, Meredith, to get her recitals back on track, but not before being given another lecture about how the media had got wind of her stint in prison and it was in some of the national papers.

Later that evening Sophia had arranged to go and see her older sister, Eleanor, who was keen to see Sophia and talk to her. Sophia suspected she was going to be lectured again, only this time by the most responsible of the sisters. But the way Sophia's mood had changed throughout the afternoon she really couldn't give two hoots. *What the hell. Let's see what the sensible Eleanor has to say about it*, she thought.

Sophia arrived at Eleanor's house in Primrose Hill at 7:30 p.m. Her boyfriend, Michael, answered the door. He explained that Eleanor was going to be late as she got called in to an emergency last minute meeting at work.

'She shouldn't be much more than about an hour,' said Michael.

'Oh well, it's just you and me then,' said Sophia.

'What can I get you to drink?' he said.

'After the day I've had, something strong.'

'Oh, I'm sorry to hear you've had a bad day. I'll see what we have.' Michael went out into the kitchen. Sophia followed him.

'We've got wine,' he said, taking a recently opened bottle of red out of the cupboard. He then opened the fridge and took out a bottle of Chablis. 'Or white?' he asked.

'That'll do,' she said, taking the bottle of Rioja from Michael's hand.

'Let me get you a glass,' he said.

'Don't worry, the bottle's fine,' she said, heading back to the living room. Michael followed after pouring himself a glass of Chablis and sat on the sofa. Sophia sauntered around the living room looking at the various pictures on the walls, as if at an art gallery.

'I recognise this one,' said Sophia.

'Yes, he's an Italian artist. You're mother showed some of his work earlier in the year at her gallery.'

'Do you like it?' said Sophia.

'Well ... Eleanor likes it. I don't really understand modern art. I prefer something a little more ... obvious.'

Sophia was making quick work of the Rioja. Of the two thirds that was there, there was now less than a third left. Sophia had not eaten all day and the alcohol was going to her head fast.

'Mind if I use the bathroom,' she said.

'Go ahead. You know where it is.' Sophia left the living room, taking the almost empty bottle of Rioja with her. After relieving herself of nearly two thirds of a bottle of wine, she stood in front of the bathroom cabinet and studied her face closely.

'Who are you?' she whispered, half closing her eyes to scrutinize the devilish woman staring back at her. Out of curiosity, she opened the cabinet to see what her sister kept in there; nothing too exciting, just the usual feminine bathroom cabinet occupants. She closed the cabinet door and almost jumped out of her skin. Right there in the mirror she saw Spencer's reflection. He was staring right at her. Blood dripped down the side of his face from a deep gash in his temple. More blood dripped into his eyes from yet another gash on the top of his head. In the stark white bathroom lighting Spencer was even whiter than death. She could only stand there, frozen to the spot. Then, he snapped his head first to the right, then to the left, the way a boxer might flex their neck muscles and ligaments moments before going out for the first round. Only when Spencer did it there was a distinct cracking sound. Not like a knuckle cracking, more like a bone snapping. Unable to straighten up his broken neck, he looked at her through his bloody eyes, and then he spoke.

'Tsk, tsk, tsk,' he said, wagging his finger at her in the mirror. 'I know what you're thinking you bad, bad girl.'

Sophia spun around but all she saw was an empty shower, no Spencer. She looked back into the cabinet mirror, but Spencer was not there. She pulled the shower curtain back, but there was just an empty bath. *What the hell?* She thought, letting out a sigh.

Feeling a little tipsy and wicked, she stopped by the bedroom on her way back from the bathroom for a curious snoop around. She had a sneaky look in the bedside drawers on both sides of the bed. There were absolutely no signs of a sex life here, not even a box of Kleenex by the side of the bed. *Doesn't look like much action goes on in here*, she thought, looking at the perfectly made up bed and decorative cushions.

'There you are,' said Michael. Sophia spun around,

slightly startled.

'I was beginning to wonder where you'd got to,' he said. The fact that he'd caught Sophia snooping around in their bedroom embarrassed him more than it did her. By now, the alcohol had put Sophia into a rather blasé mood.

'Tell me, Michael. When was the last time you fucked my sister?'

'Wh ... I ... I'm sorry,' he stammered.

'In fact, when was the last time you fucked anyone,' she said, before putting her finger into her mouth, licking it suggestively.

'Sophia, I think you've had a little too much to drink,' he said. She could see that Michael was embarrassed. He didn't know where to look or what to do. She walked over to him and grabbed him by his shoulders.

'Michael, have you ever had any excitement in your life. I seriously don't believe that you're as lame as you look,' she said, spinning him around and pushing him so he fell backwards onto the bed. She stepped forward and leapt on top of him, pinning him down by his wrists.

'Sophia, what are you doing?'

'Something that my sister should be doing,' she said, lowering her right hand and yanking open the button on his trousers.

'Sophia, I'm going to have to insist that you stop this at once,' he said, sounding like a prude Oxford college boy. But he wasn't putting up that much of a struggle.

'Oooo, or what? Are you going to spank me, sir?' she laughed, thrusting her hand into his boxer shorts and grabbing him, causing him to let out a panicked gasp.

'Oh God, Sophia, stop, let go, please,' he pleaded. He tried to get up, but Sophia squeezed it harder.

'Stop, why would I want to stop?' she said. 'I'm just getting started.' She stuck two fingers into his mouth to shut him up, while rubbing his cock, which now had a mind of its own. He tried to groan out something or another, but Sophia stuck her fingers deeper into his throat, making him gag and splutter, all the while things down below had absolutely no objections.

'I think this guy's just about ready,' she said, stroking him. 'Now, stay here and stop bitching,' she said, as she moved her head quickly down to his navel, keeping her fingers jammed in his mouth and her other hand gripping his balls in a threatening, *move and I'll squeeze hard*, sort of way. Then she pulled her fingers from his mouth, allowing her to move lower so she could take him in her mouth.

'Oh my God,' he said, half in pleasure and half in panic and disgust with himself while Sophia sucked and licked hungrily at his erect cock.

'Sophia, I can't,' he said, grabbing her hair and pulling at it feebly.

'But you are,' she said, coming up for air. 'Now you've started, you've got to finish,' she said, jumping up and pulling her dress up around her waist. She straddled over him and pulled her knickers to one side then grabbed his cock and guided it in.

'No, oh God, no,' gasped Michael who found that his hands had unwillingly ended up resting on Sophia's thighs.

SOPHIA

He looked down and noticed he'd disappeared completely into Sophia as she grinded back and forth on him, using him for her own sexual pleasure.

'Sophia, please, I can't, we shouldn't be doing this,' he said.

'Will you shut the fuck up, you're ruining this for me,' she said. Michael was shocked and startled by Sophia's language. He'd never heard her swear before. Seeing the angered look she shot him, he figured he'd better let her finish, in the same way you might let a very large and vicious Rottweiler finish humping your leg. Sophia continued to grind, faster, harder. She grabbed Michael's waist and squeezed really hard. He leg out a groan of pain as her short fingernails cut into his flesh. She continued to grip him like an eagle gripping a captured rabbit in its talons. As he looked at her, it was as if he wasn't there. Sure, she was there physically, but her mind was not. Sophia continued to grind fast and furious on top of him, her eyes closed and in her own world.

'Ah, Ah, Ahhhh, fuck yes,' she shouted. Michael, panicked, looked around the room, as if her loud noises might be disturbing somebody. He felt her body suddenly get very tense. Then, five hard grinds and a long shudder later, she came. She released her vice-like grip on Michael's waist, to his relief. He looked down - she'd drawn blood. There were five, small, red swollen marks either side of his waist where her fingernails had ripped into his skin.

'Oh fuck,' he said, wondering how the hell he was going to hide this from Eleanor. Sophia got off him and slumped onto the bed next to him and adjusted her knickers and pushed her dress back down to her knees.

'Wow, that really hit the spot,' she said.

'Sophia, you've got to get up, you've got to get out of the bedroom and go downstairs,' he said, looking at his watch. 'Oh Christ,' he said, looking at the mess the bed was in.

'Don't panic,' she said, getting up. Michael went about straightening up the quilt and pillows as fast as he could, while Sophia stood there giggling – cool as you like.

'Look, stop panicking and get a grip,' she said.

'Get a grip, after what we just did, how am–'

'Michael, shut up. If you carry on like this, she'll find you out straight away. If it makes you feel better, I used you, ok. You don't have to feel guilty. Now, get your shit together and come downstairs.'

After making the bed perfect again, Michael went to the bathroom. Not that he had any cleaning up to do, as he didn't actually get that far. But he didn't want to greet his girlfriend smelling of sex. Before he could get out of the bathroom, he heard the key in the front door as Eleanor let herself in.

'Hi sis,' said Sophia, as Eleanor entered the living room.

'Hey, where's Michael?' she said.

'Bathroom.'

'I'm sorry I'm late, they called a last minute meeting.'

'Don't worry, it's not a problem. Michael's been entertaining me.'

'That's good,' said Eleanor.

'Hi,' said Michael, entering the living room. 'Can I get

you a drink, darling' he said, avoiding their ritual kiss in fear of her smelling Sophia's perfume on him.

'Don't worry, honey. I'll get one myself in a minute. I'm just gonna nip upstairs to get changed. Back in a minute.'

Michael looked worried as Eleanor went up the stairs. Knowing how OCD she is about everything being in apple pie order, he worried that something in the bedroom might be out of place, that he might have forgotten to straighten something. But he worried more that she might smell the scent and aftermath of his sordid little sexual encounter with her younger sister.

'There's a strange smell in the bedroom,' she said, entering the living room with a glass of white wine.

Have you ever had sex, sis,' thought Sophia. Most women would recognise the pungent sickly sweet smell of sex anywhere, but Eleanor didn't seem to.

'Erm, I can't say I've noticed anything, honey,' said Michael.

'Hmmm. Well, I've opened the window in there. Anyway, who fancies a takeaway,' said Eleanor.

'Sounds good,' said Sophia.

'Chinese ok?' said Eleanor.

'Sounds great, honey,' said Michael.

'Chinese will be perfect,' said Sophia.

'Ok, I'll get the menu.'

Halfway though their meal, Sophia rubbed Michael's shin under the kitchen table, to wind him up a little. He pulled his leg away fast and nearly choked on the forkful of dangling chicken chow mein he was manipulating into his mouth with his chopsticks.

'Are you ok, honey?' said Eleanor.

'Hmm, hmm, he mumbled though a full mouth. Sophia giggled to herself, which earned her a *look* from Eleanor. Before she knew it, Sophia could not control herself and had fallen into a fit of hysterical laughter. She took a swig of wine to wash some trapped food away. Sophia looked at Michael, who didn't know where to look. Eleanor looked at them both and was not amused.

'What the hell's got into you,' said Eleanor.

'Wouldn't you like to know,' said Sophia, laughing louder now and looking at Michael, who's face had now turned a bright shade of crimson.

Eleanor shot Michael a look. Michael looked at Eleanor and shrugged his shoulders with an, *I don't know*, look on his face. Deep down, Michael had never been so scared in all his life. He was squirming and the panic was beginning to show via little beads of sweat forming on his brow. Sophia's drunken giggly behaviour was doing nothing to charm her sister, who was fast losing patience with her.

'I thought I might get chance to speak with you this evening, on an adult level, but I don't think that's going to happen is it?' said Eleanor.

'I've had all the adult entertainment I can take for one evening,' said Sophia, laughing while pushing a crispy aromatic duck pancake into her mouth.

'What *is* wrong with you?' said Eleanor. 'How much did she have to drink before I got here?' she said to Michael.

SOPHIA

'Erm, it wasn't my fault. She said she just wanted the bottle.'

'Couldn't you see when she'd had enough?' she said, giving him another *look*.

'I'm sorry,' he said, *sorry for the whole evening.*

After they finished their food, Eleanor called her sister a taxi as she was obviously in no fit state to drive home.

Chapter 21

Sophia arrived at her psychologist's office ten minutes late for her four thirty appointment.

'Good afternoon, Sophia,' said Jacques, entering the waiting area. 'Come on through,' he said. Sophia didn't like coming here. She didn't think she needed to see anybody, especially a psychologist. She only did it to please her parents. But her feelings of wanting to please her parents were dwindling. *What the fuck am I doing here?* she thought, as she sat down on the familiar, but uncomfortable leather armchair. It was very upright and made Sophia feel like she was sitting to attention. Also, the back was too low so she couldn't relax her neck and rest her head. The décor in Jacques de Beaumont's office was quite sparse. There were two large wooden windows on the outside wall, which had no wallpaper or paint, just treated brickwork. Sophia figured this was to remind him of home and whatever rustic French farm cottage he was brought up in. The wall to the left had a bookcase full of books and on the opposite wall hung a lone piece of contemporary art on canvas. It was an oil painting of an uneven, orange, oblong shape with a couple of awkwardly hand-daubed random black circles

Sophia

overlapping it. The whole thing looked like it could have been painted by a five year old. But the artist's signature – which was more artistic than the actual painting – at the bottom left suggested otherwise.

Between Sophia and Jacques stood a small mahogany table on which sat a stylish, brushed aluminium lamp and two coffee coasters. The lamp was dim, but this suited Sophia's mood. Around the skirting boards were some built-in led lights for added atmosphere. These were also dimmed to give the room a soft orange glow and add to the ambience. The mood in the room was relaxed, but the low-level lighting gave Jacques' pupils an enlarged look and actually made him look a little sinister.

'So, how have you been?' he asked.

'I've been the same as I was the last time you asked, and the time before that.'

'Ok, so tell me about your week.'

'There's nothing to tell.'

'Nothing? We haven't seen each other for more than two weeks. You must have something you want to talk to me about?'

'You mean prison?'

'If you like?'

'I really don't feel like it. Actually, I can't see the point in any of this. It's a waste of my time and yours.'

'You don't feel like we're making any headway?'

'With what? You dragging Spencer up every five minutes isn't going to change the fact that he's dead and I'm now stuck on this fucking planet alone. And trying to get me to talk about my miscarriage isn't going to make me pregnant with Spencer's child again is it? Can you fix those two little issues Jacques? Can you bring Spencer back?'

'No, no I can't do that.'

'Well then I have no use for you do I?'

'Are you still having nightmares?'

'About the accident?' she asked

'Yes,' he said.

'All the time. When I'm asleep, when I'm awake, when I'm at home, when I'm out. It's there all the time.'

'Please, Sophia, I'd like you to try and talk to me about them.'

'I don't know what to say. It's hard to explain.'

'Do you still have flashbacks?'

'All the time. Weird, strange, fucked up ones.'

'Please, I'd like you to describe them, if you can.'

'I can't and I don't want to. I don't want to be here. I'm going home,' she said, standing up.

'Sophia, please. I implore you to stay and talk to me about this. You've never gone into any detail about them during our previous sessions, you just skirt around the subject or you're vague. Please, Sophia, I'm ... fascinated.'

Sophia sighed, sat down and took a deep breath.

'What do you want first, the nightmares or the flashbacks?'

'I'll let you decide.'

'Ok, I dread falling asleep because Spencer appears in my dreams, just random stuff and not always relating to the accident. The last nightmare I had I was performing on stage and Spencer was in the front row. He was dead and covered in blood and he was showing signs of decomposition. The next thing I know he'd leapt forward and grabbed my ankle.'

'And then what?'

'He dragged me off my chair. It was so real I felt my backside hurt as it hit the wooden stage floor. Then he dragged me towards the audience and the front of the stage. Only the audience were no longer the audience. It was like something out of *Night Of The Living Dead*. They'd all become flesh-eating zombies. I was their meal and Spencer was personally serving me up to them.'

'What happened next?'

'He dragged me to the edge of the stage and pulled me over the edge, but just as I began to drop into the clutches of the dead, I woke up. So, what the fuck does that mean, Doctor?'

'Is Spencer always like this in your nightmares?'

'Most of the time, but not always. At the beginning it was fifty fifty, sometimes he was his nice usual self. But over the past few months he's got much worse.'

'Like you perhaps?'

'Meaning?'

'Sophia, I've seen a big change in your character and personality since we started these sessions and your father's expressed his concerns with the road you're going down.'

'I'm not going down any road, I'm just trying to move forward.'

'Ok, tell me about the flashbacks.'

'They're vivid.'

'Vivid?'

'Yes, they seem so real sometimes.'

'What time of day do they occur?'

'It varies. There's no pattern to them. Morning, afternoon, evening. They just pop up whenever they bloody well like.'

'Can you remember what you're doing or how you're feeling when a flashback occurs?'

'No. Well, I don't exactly keep any kind of record.'

'Can you tell me about one that happened recently?'

'Sure, only it wasn't really a flashback, more a hallucination.'

'Go on.'

'Well, I keep seeing this fox.'

'Like the fox Spencer skidded to avoid hitting in the accident?'

'Exactly. I just keep seeing the damn thing everywhere.'

'What is the fox doing?'

'Nothing in particular, it's just there. I can't make my mind up about the fox.'

'What do you mean?'

'Well, I can't decide if the fox is looking out for me and trying to help me in some strange way, or if it means something else.'

'Can you give me an example?'

'When I was in America I thought I saw Spencer across the street.'

'What time of day was this?'

'It was the middle of the day, lunchtime. Anyway, I went to cross the road to go to him and a car beeped at me. The next thing I knew I was having a flashback, right there in the middle of a busy road.'

'A flashback to the accident?'

'Yes, only it was different. Every time I have a flashback, the accident seems to vary, sometimes quite considerably. Anyway, the fox was there and it was looking at me intently.'

'Very interesting,' he said. 'Please, continue.'

'Sometimes I don't see the fox, I just hear it.'

'Barking?'

'Sometimes, but sometimes it sounds like it's screaming. It's horrible.'

'What about the hallucinations? Does the fox appear in those too?'

'Sometimes, but not all the time. When I was in prison I saw Spencer standing in my cell and he was holding it. But it was dead on that occasion.'

'Please, go on.'

'Sometimes it's with Spencer, like it's his faithful companion or something. But I don't understand that part because we never hit the fox and it never died. So why would it be with Spencer now, during my nightmares and hallucinations?'

'It could mean several things. Can you tell me how long you've been having hallucinations? It's just you've never mentioned them before.'

'They started soon after I left my parents' place after I came out of hospital.' Jacques jotted down some notes on his pad.

'Look, I have twisted fucked up flashbacks, weird

hallucinations and vivid nightmares. Sometimes when I wake up I can even smell the blood in my nostrils and it stays there until I've had a shower. I don't know what the hell is going on. It feels like something's got a hold on my mind and its grip is getting tighter. If Spencer's getting more sinister means I'm getting worse, then I guess I'm fucked,' she said, getting up and leaving without saying goodbye.

Maybe not, thought Jacques, taking more notes.

Chapter 22

Later that evening a taxi picked Sophia up from her apartment in Hampstead and headed for the West End. A couple of short twists and turns from Tottenham Court Road tube station and Sophia arrived at The Baltimore Oriole jazz club just after 10 p.m. After giving the taxi driver £25 and telling him to keep the change, she went inside to meet Delphine, as promised.

The lighting was dim enough to set the mood. Once Sophia's eyes had adjusted, she could see that it was quite a plush club. A small permanent raised stage was set in the corner, on which sat a five-foot baby grand piano, a small jazz/fusion drum kit and a large acoustic double bass on a stand. At this moment the only musician on the stage was a pianist playing a medley of Cole Porter songs.

Along the shorter wall was the bar, again nicely lit with additional led lights sunk into the under part of the bar, adding to the overall feel and laid-back mood. Around the remaining walls were plush leather seating booths with mahogany tables with neat little table lamps. All around the walls were framed photographs of famous jazz blues musicians and singers: Ella Fitzgerald,

Sarah Vaughan, Dinah Washington, Louis Armstrong, Chet Baker, Ray Charles, Nat King Cole, Frank Sinatra, Duke Ellington, Dave Brubeck, Charles Mingus, Oscar Peterson, Miles Davis, Norah Jones, Diana Krall, Natalie Cole. Picture upon picture lined the walls. On the floor area stood more plush mahogany tables to seat two, four or six people. Sophia suspected the carpets were deep wine red, but it was hard to tell in the dim light. Hanging from the ceilings were numerous circular lampshades, their dimmed bulbs revealing their deep red colour. There were low mahogany partitions mapping out the various walkways around the floor, which were nicely set off with brass bars running along their tops. The mahogany and brass theme continued along the bar. Sophia's eyes followed the glinting brass work along the length of the bar until she saw Delphine. She was sitting on a barstool at the stage end of the bar, talking to the barman.

'Hey you,' said Sophia. Delphine turned around and smiled when she saw Sophia.

'Hey, you came,' she said, hugging her.

'Wild horses couldn't keep me away,' said Sophia, smiling.

'Sophia, this is Glen,' she said, gesturing to the barman. Glen was in his mid thirties, reasonably tall, in good shape and quite handsome. 'Glen, this is Sophia.'

'Pleased to meet you,' said Glen, extending his hand. 'I've heard a lot about you,' he said.

'Nothing too bad I hope,' joked Sophia.

'On the contrary, Delphine has nothing but praise for

you. So, you're a classical concert cellist?' he said.

'Yes, ' she said, looking to Delphine.

'Don't worry, I didn't tell him that,' said Delphine.

'When Delphine told me your name and that you were a classical musician, I asked her what your surname was. I instantly knew who you were. In here I have no choice but to listen to jazz and blues, but at home I'm a classical man,' he said. 'I feel compelled to tell you that I've never heard a soloist play with such organic authenticity. When I listen to your recordings, it's like I'm being given a snapshot into the composers life,' he said.

'Wow, that's quite a compliment. Thank you.'

'May I ask you something?' he said.

'After a compliment like that, how could I say no.'

'There's something about Natalie Cleine's playing that just doesn't quite ring true for me. I mean, it just doesn't seem … heartfelt. Do you know what I mean?' he said.

'Yes, yes I do,' said Sophia.

'So, what's that all about? She's obviously a very talented cellist but there's something missing, her playing just doesn't seem to evoke any of my emotions; kind of sterile.'

'Well, music's a very subjective thing. Some people like the voice of Billie Holiday, while others prefer Nina Simone.'

'Ok, let me be more direct. What do you think of Natalie's playing?'

'Well, personally, I think she'd be a better musician if she concentrated more on the music and less on how she looks when she's playing.'

'Explain,' he said.

'You know, all those over-romanticised body movements are not necessary. They almost look choreographed. I think any music-goer with an ounce of musical intellect could see right through that façade. Tilting your head back and closing your eyes while playing doesn't make you a better musician,' she said.

'Yes, my sentiments exactly. I've seen videos of Natalie on YouTube and she does seem to use her looks and body movements rather a lot.'

'For women, there's the added pressure of relying on glamour to sell records. I have firm views on this; there are certain things that I won't do. Even since I got my record contract I've always been careful not to allow myself to be photographed in certain ways. I'm known for my playing and musical ability, not the way I look,' she said.

'Well, you're very lucky because you also happen to be a very attractive young woman,' he smiled.

'You're just full of compliments aren't you,' said Delphine.

'Well, it just so happens to be true,' he said, opening a fresh pack of napkins. 'Anyway, what can I get you to drink,' he said.

'Tia Maria and Coke, please,' said Sophia.

'Hmm, haven't had one of those for a while, I'll have one too, Glen,' said Delphine.

The double bassist gestured towards Delphine; it was time for her to get up on stage to sing.

SOPHIA

'Looks like my presence is required. Relax and enjoy. I'll be back in twenty for a break.' Delphine walked majestically across the floor and up onto the stage. Members of the club watched her as she walked. She wore a beautiful long flowing strapless midnight blue dress, with a silver necklace accentuating her exquisite neck.

The pianist and double bassist had been joined by the drummer.

'I'd like to dedicate this first song to my new best friend, Sophia. I've only known her for a few weeks, but it feels like I've known her all my life,' said Delphine, in her soft tones that matched the soft moody lighting. Sophia looked across the room at her and smiled. The pianist started to play, followed by a laid-back double bass line and some delicate brushwork on the snare drum. Then Delphine started to sing a beautiful jazz rendition of 'You've Got A Friend' by Carole King.

Sophia was overwhelmed, not only by the sentiments of the song, but also by Delphine's incredible voice. *She's amazing.* Delphine's incredible talent astounded Sophia. She had no idea she could sing like that.

Delphine finished the first half of her set, and then went to join Sophia at the bar.

'Wow, *you* are truly amazing,' said Sophia, giving Delphine a big hug. 'I had no idea you were so talented. You've got an incredible voice.'

'You really think so?' asked Delphine.

'Are you kidding me, you know you've got a serious talent there, right?'

'Well, I know I can sing in tune. I was a little nervous

singing in the presence of a professional concert cellist. You've probably heard lots of professional singers.'

'Yes, but I've never heard anybody sing the way you do. Where did you learn to sing like that?'

'The truth ... I've never had a lesson. Just spent hour after hour listening to other famous jazz singers. At first I tried to imitate them, then I stopped and developed my own style and just started to sing the way that felt right for me.'

'Well, you've certainly got a unique style. Really, I'm speechless, Delphine.'

'Oh my God, coming from you that means so much,' she said, grabbing Sophia and squeezing her tight.

'You really mean it? You're not just saying that?' said Delphine.

'No, I really mean it. Look, I know I'm a classical cellist, but you know I love jazz and blues as well. I've heard a lot of well known female jazz singers, and I'm telling you, Delphine, you're right there with them.' A tear of sheer happiness escaped Delphine's eye and settled on her cheekbone. Sophia took a napkin off the bar and blotted it away, taking care not to ruin her make-up.

Delphine sang the second half of her set while Sophia watched her from the bar. After sinking a few more Tia Maria's, Sophia had moved on to Vodka and Cokes. By the time Delphine got back to her after her set was over, Sophia was a little tipsy and was starting to get a little too flirtatious with Glen.

'Hey, is everything ok?' said Delphine.

'Everything's great,' said Sophia, slurring her words

SOPHIA

slightly. 'I've got to go to the ladies,' she said, and ambled off.

'How much has she had to drink?' said Delphine.

'I'm not sure. About three Tia Maria's and maybe another three Vodka and Cokes,' said Glen. Delphine gave him a *look*. 'I'm sorry, she seemed ok,' he said. Delphine went after her.

'Sophia, are you ok?' said Delphine. 'Glen told me you've had quite a lot to drink.'

'Well, I think I still need a few more. Just until the screaming stops in my head,' she joked.

'Are you ok, darling. Maybe we should just go home.'

'I'm great, really,' she said, tweaking her make up in the mirror. 'Dancing.'

'Sorry?'

'Let's go dancing,' said Sophia.

'Are you sure?'

'Yes, I've never been dancing in a nightclub before. Do you know anywhere we could go?'

'Yes, there's a nightclub just around the corner from here.'

'Good, let's go.'

'Are you sure?' asked Delphine.

'Never been more sure about anything in my life. Come on, it'll be fun.'

'Ok, let me change out of this and slip into something more suitable,' said Delphine.

Chapter 23

Sophia and Delphine arrived at a nightclub in Soho. Looking the way they did, they didn't have any trouble getting in. One of the men on the door recognised Delphine as she had been there before on a few occasions.

Inside, loud music pumped out across the dance floor. The deep bass thumped into Sophia's chest – she liked the sensation. It was dimly lit inside with red, green, blue and white lights flashing around the dance floor. Sophia grabbed Delphine's hand and dragged her through the crowd and into an empty space on the dance floor, which was made of tough clear Perspex tiles with white lights shining up from underneath.

Sophia grabbed Delphine's other hand and started to dance to the upbeat music. She swung her hips side to side and shook her head side to side. Her long blonde hair whipped across her face as she moved. She released Delphine and moved her hands above her head locking her fingers together. Her body swayed and moved to the beat. Delphine smiled at Sophia as they both danced. She could hardly believe what she was seeing. Delphine had watched a DVD that Sophia had given her where

SOPHIA

she was performing one of her recitals. She didn't think it would have been possible for such an elegantly dressed and graceful classical cellist such as Sophia, to turn into this frenetic goddess of the dance floor. She had to see it to believe it.

It wasn't long before Sophia was attracting a lot of male attention. One young man, fancying his chances, danced his way over and stepped between Delphine and Sophia, so he was facing Sophia. He put his hands above his head and tried to imitate Sophia's moves. Sophia was not impressed; she dropped her hands and pushed him out of the way, causing him to lose his balance and fall over. She grabbed Delphine's hands and continued to dance with her.

'Fucking dyke,' shouted the man, getting up and moving away in a desperate attempt to maintain his dignity.

Delphine leaned close to Sophia and shouted in her ear, 'I need the bathroom.'

'Ok, I'll come with you,' said Sophia.

As they walked down a crowded hallway to the bathroom, a man stepped into their path. 'Need a little something to give you energy? You can dance all night long.' he said, gesturing down to his hand. Sophia saw a couple of paper wraps in his hand.

'What's that?' said Sophia.

'Speed,' said Delphine, eying the man with caution.

'Ah, you've done this before,' he said.

'What does it do?' asked Sophia.

'It'll give you tons of energy. Out there on the dance

floor, you'll feel like an athlete,' he said.

'Fuck it, why not,' said Sophia.

'Are you sure about this?' said Delphine.

'I've spent my whole life playing the cello and being a bloody goody two shoes. For the first time in my life, I'm letting my hair down.'

Sophia paid the man £25 for the two wraps before continuing to the bathroom.

'So, how do you do this?' said Sophia.

'I'll show you,' said Delphine.

'You've done this before?' said Sophia.

'Yes.'

'Do you do it a lot?'

'Not anymore. Truth is, I don't really touch it these days.'

After waiting an age for a cubicle to come free, Delphine and Sophia locked themselves in and Delphine showed Sophia how to snort her first hit of speed. It didn't take long for the speed to kick in, and with Sophia it took effect pretty quickly. She developed verbal diarrhoea, and back out on the dance floor she had the energy of a frenzied gazelle. While dancing she felt a man's hand land hard on her shoulder from behind. In her frenetic state, she spun around and found herself face to face with Spencer. Only this time, the blood had dried up and he was showing definite signs of decomposition. His clothes were covered in earth. The smell was putrid. He looked at her from his black empty eye sockets. An earthworm slithered out of one of them and slid down his rotting face. Sophia screamed and slammed Spencer's corpse hard in the chest, sending

SOPHIA

it stumbling backwards. The corpse stumbled into a group of dancing girls before eventually falling to the floor. Sophia stood frozen to the spot momentarily before going into a fit of hysteria. Delphine grabbed Sophia and tried to calm her down, then she shouted at the man on the floor, 'What the hell do you think you're doing, grabbing her shoulder like that. She doesn't want to dance with you,' she shouted.

'Fuckin' bitch is crazy,' said the man, getting to his feet. 'I don't know what the hell she's on but you should take her home until she comes the hell down,' he said.

'Look, just go and find somebody else to annoy,' said Delphine.

Two hours, and several Vodkas later, they decided to leave. Once outside the fresh night air hit Sophia in the face like a cold slap.

'Well, if it isn't my old friend the high-class hooker?' said a smartly dressed, but obviously drunk, middle-aged man. Delphine turned around to see one of her ex clients, who she'd had to let go due to his obnoxious personality and violent tendencies in the bedroom. At first he'd simply given Delphine a couple of light friendly slaps, kind of role-play. But then he hit her and gave her a black eye. That was it. Delphine told her madam about it and she struck him off her client list.

Delphine ignored him and turned back to Sophia.

'Let's get a cab. I really need to get home to my bed. I need to sleep,' said Delphine.

'Funny, I didn't think your bed was anything more than a meat stand,' said the arsehole. There were a few onlookers hanging around outside the nightclub. Although Delphine was a high-class call girl, the comment actually hurt her, especially when said in public with onlookers listening.

'Orrr, wadamadda, little whore gonna cry?' He laughed as his stupid drunken arsehole friends egged him on. Sophia could see that Delphine was getting upset.

'Look, why don't you just fuck off,' shouted Sophia. She turned to the road and waved a taxi down.

'Hey, how about a threesome?' said one of his stupid drunken friends.

'I don't know who's got use of the family brain cell this week, but it obviously isn't you, you fucking loser,' said Sophia, opening the taxi door. They both climbed in as the arseholes continued to yell drunken crap at them. In the back of the taxi, Sophia could see that Delphine was crying a little.

'It's ok, let's get you home,' said Sophia, putting her arm around her friend.

Delphine told the taxi driver the address of her apartment in Camden Town. When they arrived, they were both as drunk as each other. The speed was starting to wear off as they helped each other out of the cab and into Delphine's apartment. It was now four in the morning and they were exhausted.

Sophia collapsed onto Delphine's sofa. 'I'm shattered,' she said.

'Look, it's four in the morning, you should spend the night here,' said Delphine.

Sophia looked at Delphine's rather small sofa, which

Sophia

it stumbling backwards. The corpse stumbled into a group of dancing girls before eventually falling to the floor. Sophia stood frozen to the spot momentarily before going into a fit of hysteria. Delphine grabbed Sophia and tried to calm her down, then she shouted at the man on the floor, 'What the hell do you think you're doing, grabbing her shoulder like that. She doesn't want to dance with you,' she shouted.

'Fuckin' bitch is crazy,' said the man, getting to his feet. 'I don't know what the hell she's on but you should take her home until she comes the hell down,' he said.

'Look, just go and find somebody else to annoy,' said Delphine.

Two hours, and several Vodkas later, they decided to leave. Once outside the fresh night air hit Sophia in the face like a cold slap.

'Well, if it isn't my old friend the high-class hooker?' said a smartly dressed, but obviously drunk, middle-aged man. Delphine turned around to see one of her ex clients, who she'd had to let go due to his obnoxious personality and violent tendencies in the bedroom. At first he'd simply given Delphine a couple of light friendly slaps, kind of role-play. But then he hit her and gave her a black eye. That was it. Delphine told her madam about it and she struck him off her client list.

Delphine ignored him and turned back to Sophia.

'Let's get a cab. I really need to get home to my bed. I need to sleep,' said Delphine.

'Funny, I didn't think your bed was anything more than a meat stand,' said the arsehole. There were a few onlookers hanging around outside the nightclub. Although Delphine was a high-class call girl, the comment actually hurt her, especially when said in public with onlookers listening.

'Orrr, wadamadda, little whore gonna cry?' He laughed as his stupid drunken arsehole friends egged him on. Sophia could see that Delphine was getting upset.

'Look, why don't you just fuck off,' shouted Sophia. She turned to the road and waved a taxi down.

'Hey, how about a threesome?' said one of his stupid drunken friends.

'I don't know who's got use of the family brain cell this week, but it obviously isn't you, you fucking loser,' said Sophia, opening the taxi door. They both climbed in as the arseholes continued to yell drunken crap at them. In the back of the taxi, Sophia could see that Delphine was crying a little.

'It's ok, let's get you home,' said Sophia, putting her arm around her friend.

Delphine told the taxi driver the address of her apartment in Camden Town. When they arrived, they were both as drunk as each other. The speed was starting to wear off as they helped each other out of the cab and into Delphine's apartment. It was now four in the morning and they were exhausted.

Sophia collapsed onto Delphine's sofa. 'I'm shattered,' she said.

'Look, it's four in the morning, you should spend the night here,' said Delphine.

Sophia looked at Delphine's rather small sofa, which

was too small for somebody of Sophia's height to sleep on comfortably.

'Look, why don't you take my bed. I'll sleep on the sofa,' she said.

'That's not fair. I'll be fine.'

'No you won't. I'll take the sofa and that's final,' said Delphine.

'Where's your bathroom?' said Sophia

'Just through that door,' said Delphine, pointing.

On her way back from the bathroom Sophia glanced into the bedroom and noticed that Delphine's bed was a huge king-size affair, it only just fitted in the room.

'Are you crazy?' said Sophia.

'What do you mean?' said Delphine, throwing a blanket across the sofa.

'You bed's fucking huge. We can both sleep in there,' she said.

'Well, are you sure?' said Delphine.

'Of course I'm sure, silly rabbit.'

They lay in bed next to each other, exhausted, in the almost pitch-black room. Delphine had curtains lined with blackout material as she often got back from The Baltimore Oriole club late and didn't like getting woken up by the early morning light. As they lay there perfectly still, Sophia felt the back of Delphine's hand lightly brush her leg as she turned to get comfortable. Sophia's mind was far from her own right now as her emotions ran riot. The images of Spencer's death were as present as ever and the strange haunting flashbacks, fuelled with tonight's alcohol and speed didn't help either.

Sophia felt around under the quilt until she found Delphine's hand, she took it in hers and held it for comfort. Delphine turned to face Sophia.

'Are you ok?' she whispered.

'I don't know, Delphi. I'm scared.'

'Hey, what is it?' Sophia, in her mixed up state of coming down from the speed, being drunk and generally messed up emotionally, started to sob.

'It feels like there's something going on inside me, Delphi, and I'm scared of it, really scared.'

'Come here,' said Delphine, wrapping her arms around Sophia in an attempt to comfort her. 'Look, I'm here for you, Sophia, I'll always be here for you. I'll help you get through it, no matter what.'

'I'm so glad I met you, Delphi. I feel like I can talk to you about anything.'

'I'm glad about that, because whatever it is that's scaring you, we'll beat it together. I won't let you go through it alone.'

Sophia squeezed Delphine tightly. 'Thank you,' said Sophia.

'I feel like I need to explain something to you,' said Delphine.

'Sure.'

'I just want you to know that I'm not proud of what I do, and I don't enjoy it. I'm talking about my other job as a call girl. The thing is, the money's really good and I only see two clients a week,' she said.

'It's ok, Delphi, I understand.'

'The cost of living in London's outrageous and I'm

trying to make it as a jazz singer. If I did a regular job I wouldn't be able to afford to live here. I really want to stop being a call girl, but I can't afford to just yet.'

'Delphine, it's ok. I understand, and I really don't mind,' said Sophia, kissing Delphine on the cheek. The high-energy night was catching up with them and the effects of the speed had worn off, sapping their final reserves of energy in the process. Delphine placed her hand over Sophia's and held it gently. They both slumped back, fingers entwined, and within minutes they were asleep.

Chapter 24

The next morning Sophia woke up in an empty bed. She got up and put on Delphine's bathrobe, which was hanging on the back of the bedroom door, before venturing into to the kitchen. Delphine was sitting at her small breakfast table drinking tea and eating toast.

'Hey,' said Sophia.

'Good morning, sleepy head,' said Delphine. 'You want something to eat?'

'Toast looks good,' she said, rubbing her forehead.

'Tea or coffee?' said Delphine, getting up.

'Oh, tea would be great. My mouth's as dry as the Atacama Desert.'

'Come over here and sit down.' Sophia took the second chair at the table.

'You have a headache?' asked Delphine, noticing Sophia nursing her forehead with the palm of her hand.

'Something like that. I think I drunk a little too much last night.'

'I've got some Panadol Extra,' she said, reaching into one of the cupboards above the kettle. She put a mug of tea and two white oval tablets on the table in front of Sophia. 'Here you go.'

'Thanks,' she said, scooping them up and swallowing them with a mouthful of tea.

'Delphine, I've got some very hazy and distorted memories from last night.'

'Yeah, me too. We got pretty wrecked, and throwing that speed into the mix didn't help either. I couldn't believe what you were like on that dance floor,' said Delphine, smiling away.

'I don't mean that, I mean when we got back here … in bed. I didn't say or do anything to embarrass myself did I?'

'No, you didn't,' said Delphine. 'You just opened up to me a little … I was upset and emotional too.'

'Thank God for that. When I woke up and you weren't there, I was worried I might have offended you.'

'Now who's being a silly rabbit,' said Delphine.

'I'm so glad we found each other. You're like a sister to me,' said Sophia.

'I know, I feel exactly the same way about you. Though I don't relish the thought of having to tell people how and when we first met,' said Delphine, laughing.

'Yes, that might be a little awkward,' said Sophia, smiling. 'Remind me never to have a night out like that again,' said Sophia, still trying to nurse her headache away with a closed fist.

'How's your head?' said Delphine.

'Terrible. It feels like something's in there trying to burst out.'

'Don't fret, the Panadol will take effect soon.'

'What a night,' said Sophia.

'You can say that again.'

Although they promised each other there would be no more crazy nights out like that, there were. Over the next few weeks Sophia's behaviour became more reckless and dysfunctional.

When Delphine was not carrying out her call girl duties, or singing in The Baltimore Oriole, she spent every waking hour with Sophia. They went out clubbing, they got drunk and they took more speed. But the speed wasn't doing it for Sophia anymore. She told a dealer at one of the nightclubs they visited that she wanted to try something else, something more intense. So now she'd moved up from speed and was snorting line after line of cocaine. Well, she was an international concert cellist with a major record deal and she could afford it. And after all, cocaine is the preferred drug of rock stars and rich actresses.

Although Sophia loved the instant euphoric high she got from coke, unusually, she didn't become addicted. Whether or not she snorted coke depended purely on her state of mind, which right now was a jumbled chaotic mess. When she didn't have coke or speed, she seemed to be on her own kind of high.

One evening Sophia and Delphine were enjoying a quiet drink in a bar, happily chatting with two harmless guys when Sophia, out of the blue, became quite volatile. After getting upset with one of the guys and slapping his face, over nothing in particular, the guy had said to Sophia, 'You know what, your amygdala is seriously over stimulated – you need help.'

SOPHIA

Sophia hadn't been in touch with her parents much after her mother said she looked like a cheap tart. She wasn't really in touch with anybody, let alone herself. In fact, she wasn't really in touch with reality. Sophia seemed to be on her own special blend of self-destruction and other crazy shenanigans. Django was especially concerned. He could see that Sophia had become somebody else, he barely recognised her these days. She turned up late for their Beethoven rehearsals and sometimes she played like she was possessed – this just wasn't the Sophia that Django knew. He was distraught. He loved her like a sister. Maybe it was time he said something and really tried to get to the bottom of it. But then he thought of Spencer, still not that long buried. Maybe she was just going through the grieving process and this was her way of dealing with her loss.

Django and Sophia had always had a brilliant working relationship and a great friendship. But these days, Sophia got angry with him, shouted at him, and even swore at him whenever he brought up Spencer's death. All he tried to do was be a good friend to her, to help her and, most importantly, to stop her career going down the toilet. But no matter what he said, or how he said it, she shot him down in flames. Django was perplexed and confused beyond belief. He could see that Sophia was getting worse, much worse.

Sophia's agent, Meredith, had her own concerns. Sophia had instructed her to cancel the less important upcoming recitals, keeping only her high profile engagements.

As for her record company, she was under contract and obligated to do the Beethoven recordings with Django. Cracks were starting to appear both in her life, and in her career as an international artist – and she didn't seem to care. She was on a dangerous path of self-destruction and there was no stopping her.

She was spending money like there was no tomorrow. She went to expensive restaurants with Delphine and always insisted on paying. She bought expensive and extravagant clothes and shoes and generally lived it up. She even spent £14,000 on a ladies Cartier watch as a present for Delphine who became seriously concerned and insisted that it was too much and that she take it back to the shop. But Sophia wouldn't hear of it. When Delphine insisted, Sophia snapped at her and snatched the watch box back out of her hand and stormed off. This was the first time Sophia had snapped at Delphine. Of course, the next evening Sophia went to The Baltimore Oriole and apologised to her for being such a bitch.

Sophia continued to spend money though. On Wednesday night Delphine had an appointment with one of her clients. She had to meet him at The Carrington Tower Hotel on Park Lane, where she would spend the night with him and in exchange for £250 per hour she would fulfil all of his desires.

Sophia was feeling lonely and didn't want to be alone. She begged Delphine to let her go along with her. It wasn't ideal, but at least she wouldn't be alone. But if truth be told, Sophia was a little curious about Delphine's fascinating job as a call girl. Obviously she could not spend the night with Delphine and her client in the same room. But, because Delphine trusted Sophia, she told Sophia what room they were going to be in and Sophia phoned the hotel and paid £300 for the room next door. They both got dressed up as if going out on a classy date. Sophia got to the hotel first and seated herself on one of the plush green upholstered chairs and waited. Delphine had described her client to Sophia and told her that she could sit in the lobby and watch Delphine come in and meet him but on the condition that she was discreet. After that, they would meet up in the morning for breakfast in the hotel. Sophia secretly watched the wealthy-looking middle-aged English man as he paced up and down in the lobby waiting area. It was 11 p.m. when Delphine entered the hotel. She walked with grace and elegance to greet the gentleman. After brief hellos they took the stairs to his room. Delphine looked really classy in her black dress. She looked like a true *lady*. Sophia followed, discreetly, and let herself into her room next door.

Delphine had explained to Sophia how a typical night with a client would play out. Out of morbid fascination and curiosity Sophia put a glass up to the wall and pressed her ear against it, but she heard little to nothing. Delphine had told Sophia that he was a quiet type. He was even quiet and non-vocal during his climax. Although some clients liked Delphine to moan and groan with pleasure, even if she had to pretend, this particular client wasn't fussed either way. He was there to receive pleasure, not give it. So Delphine kept her moaning sound-effects to a minimum.

Sophia lay in the plush king-size bed imagining the goings on in the next room. Delphine had told her that – knowing she was spending the whole night with him –she typically began very slowly with conversation and foreplay. Then she would work towards the girlfriend experience when the time felt right. They would kiss intimately and have sex. Sometimes, depending on the client, he would have multiple climaxes during the long session, but not this client. After the foreplay, kissing and groping, they had sex, then he fell asleep and didn't wake up until the morning. He liked to fall asleep in Delphine's arms. The next morning he also took a shower with her. Delphine washed his back and body with soap. But he didn't want sex again, just her physical company in the shower. He got dressed, paid Delphine £2,250 for her time, plus another £250 tip – all in cash. Then they both left the room together. Delphine would typically get a cab home at this stage, but as Sophia had stayed in the next room, they'd arranged to meet and have breakfast.

Over breakfast, Delphine explained that she gave thirty percent of her earnings to her madam.

'Still, a pretty good payday,' said Sophia.

'Yes, that's how I manage to do it. I just switch my mind off, think of the money and don't get emotionally involved,' said Delphine.

'Thanks for letting me come along. I just didn't want to be alone last night, and I guess I wanted to see what your other job involved. Or perhaps it was just my ... perverted curiosity,' she said, smiling and taking another sip of coffee.

'Well, you didn't actually see anything, apart from me walking across the lobby and meeting him.'

'I know, but I enjoyed spending the night here. The room was great. I love spending time away in hotels. I stay in hotels a lot when I'm doing recitals further afield, but never anything quite this nice – I could get used to hotels like this.'

'Well, I wasn't sure whether to ask you, but how would you like to come out with me this Friday, for some fun with a difference?' said Delphine.

'What time? I have an appointment with my psychologist at four thirty,' said Sophia.

'You have a psychologist?' said Delphine.

'Yes. It wasn't my idea. After Spencer died my parents thought it might help me come to terms with what happened.'

'Has it?'

'Not really. He spends most of his time trying to figure me out.'

'What do you mean?'

'I don't know. He thinks I've developed some sort of personality disorder. He thinks the way I'm carrying on isn't normal and that I've developed an unhealthy dark side to my character. He also thinks I've become sexually promiscuous.'

'Wow, what do you think about that, the promiscuous thing I mean?'

'I don't really know. I'm not sure I understand it myself. Soon after Spencer died I felt something change inside me, well, in my head at least. It's like I've become addicted to it. I find myself daydreaming about weird sexual fantasies.'

'Maybe it's just because you're out of your teenage years and you feel more adventurous now?'

'Maybe. I don't really understand it. My psychologist and parents think its wrong, but to me it just seems perfectly normal. Is it?'

'Sophia, if it feels right to you, it is right.'

'Maybe. So tell me about Friday evening. Is it in a hotel?'

'No. One of my clients has invited me to a dinner party at a rather splendid stately home in Virginia Water in Surrey.'

'I don't understand. A client's invited you to a dinner party?'

'I know, it's an unusual situation. He's a regular of mine. I see him once a month at a hotel in London. But, get this; his friend said he would give him £50,000 if he invited his favourite call girl to their next cosy dinner party. They're always inviting groups of friends around, and they often want their friends to bring new friends.'

'Are you serious?' said Sophia, putting her hand up to her mouth.

'Oh yes.'

'Wow, if I was a man and I saw a call girl on a regular basis I don't think I'd want to share that with any of my friends.'

'They've been friends for years; they share everything and trust each other with even their deepest secrets. He told him about me a while back and he was fascinated. Then as a joke he dared him to invite me along. Then my client asked him how much money he would give him to carry out the dare.'

'Is this client married?'

'Yes, well it wouldn't be much of a dare if he wasn't. And this is where it gets interesting.'

'Wow, will his wife be there?'

'Naturally, sitting right there at the dining table next to her husband.'

'And you'll be sitting at the same table?'

'Yes,' said Delphine, smiling.

'Wait a minute, you just agreed to take part in this fiasco?'

'He said he'd give me ten per cent of his winnings. That's what I'd earn from him in four of our usual meetings. And, I don't have to take my clothes off for it. So for me, it's just an extension of our client relationship anyway. Only with a much better pay day.'

'I still don't get it. If he's happily married and living in a large house with his wife, why does he use the services of a high class call girl?'

'Because he's married to Mrs Frigid. Trust me, it's more common than you might think – especially in the upper and upper middle classes.'

'What do you mean?'

'Well, they're happily married with children and a big house and loads of money. But their wives just won't open their legs anymore. For the husbands it's easier and far cheaper to call upon my services than it is to get a divorce and wreck the family.'

'Does this goes on a lot?'

'All the time.'

'So how's it going to work, and where do I fit in?'

'He's told his wife I'm a dancer with the English National Ballet Company. He asked me if I had a friend I could bring along, just to take some of the attention off me to lessen the chances of his wife finding out and everything going tits up.'

'The English National Ballet Company?'

'Yes, he's a huge fan, goes to the ballet all the time.'

'But if they're regular ballet goers, we could get caught out by her?' said Sophia.

'It'll never happen, she hates ballet, he goes on his own, sometimes with work colleagues. She has no interest in ballet and knows nothing about it. That's why he's using the ballet dancer theme to win his £50,000 bet.'

'Will he be ok with me going?'

'Oh yes, like I said, him and his wife are expecting two of us. Besides, when he sees you he'll see it as a bonus,' she said.

'A bonus?'

'Once you meet his wife, you'll know what I mean,' she said.

'How many people will be there?'

'My client and his wife, his friend and his wife, plus two other couples. So ten including me and you.'

Sophia thought about this for a moment. The idea of going along to a dinner party pretending to be a dancer

SOPHIA

with the English National Ballet Company was quite appealing, in a weird sort of way she could relate to it in her current state of mind. *Could I keep up the façade all evening?* thought Sophia. Well, it would be fun and entertaining trying.

'What the hell, let's do it,' said Sophia.

Chapter 25

Sophia had booked a taxi for what would have been a thirty-mile journey from her apartment in Hampstead to the house in Virginia Water. But she had the taxi driver go via Camden Town to pick up Delphine en route, adding another two. They arrived at the house in Virginia Water at seven thirty five. As the taxi drove along the sweeping driveway, the house came into view. Although the architecture was suggestive of the Edwardian period, it was actually built in the nineteen eighties. It was tastefully done in light red brick and was in keeping with the immaculately maintained stately grounds. Delphine insisted on paying for the taxi. She rang the bell and they stood and waited between the two concrete pillars either side of the black wooden door.

'Hello,' said the lady of the house, opening the door. 'Now let me guess, you must be Zoë, she said to Delphine. 'And you must be Christine,' she said to Sophia. Delphine's client had insisted they didn't use their own names, not for any reason other than to make the evening a little more challenging. He liked to take risks. Delphine and Sophia had chosen names they thought they would remember easily. Sophia liked

Phantom of the Opera when she was a teenager and wanted to be just like Christine, so that was the obvious choice for her. Delphine chose Zoë after Zoë Kravitz, the American actress and daughter of the singer, Lenny Kravitz. She had seen her in a couple of movies but knew her more for her association with her musician father, Lenny. But mostly, she just liked the name, Zoë.

'Please come on in,' she said.

This must be Delphine's client's wife, thought Sophia, as the woman led them through into the lounge. It was very modern inside and stylishly decorated in a minimalist sort of way. There were no pictures or paintings hanging on the eggshell-white painted walls. The carpets were light beige with a large black and grey rug in the center. Black cloth upholstered sofas and matching armchairs were strategically positioned around the spacious room. On one of the walls there was a modern white fireplace with a large chrome-bezel mirror above it. And in one of the corners stood a tall plant that looked so vibrantly green and immaculate Sophia wondered if it was fake.

'Ah, Zoë, have a seat, this must be your friend, Christine?' said Thomas. Delphine gave Sophia a sneaky wink to let her know that this was her client. He was a handsome middle-aged man who looked in pretty good shape. After noticing how attractive his wife was, and how handsome he was, Sophie was still surprised that he would need the services of a call girl. And what did Delphine mean with her 'Once you meet his wife, you'll know what I mean' comment. *She looks great to me,* thought Sophia.

But it didn't take long for Sophia to realise that Delphine had said '*meet* his wife' and not '*see* his wife.' Yes, she looked like a fifty-year-old version of Joan Collins; immaculately dressed, very attractive and incredibly slim – what's not to like. But, when she spoke she became very unattractive with her constant sarcasm and belittling of her husband and her snobby remarks about the working classes. She was cold and calculating and Sophia had to wonder if she actually had a heart beating in that soulless chest. She looked down her nose and spited pretty much everybody. *Bloody hell, I know what Delphine means; this woman's a she-devil.* Sophia believed that this woman would eat her own young.

The pre-dinner conversations went well enough. With Sophia's background and upbringing she was used to the etiquette of dinner parties like these. Keeping up the façade of being a ballet dancer called Christine was proving shockingly easy. The other guests didn't suspect a thing and they didn't ask any challenging questions about ballet that would give them away. After several drinks Thomas's wife didn't care one way or another. She definitely liked a drink and the more she drank the more irritating she became. Sophia caught Thomas's eye and gave him a, *I can totally understand why you see Delphine,* look of approval. He seemed to read her mind and smiled back at her.

The dining room was tastefully lit, primarily by candlelight. By the time they were half way through dinner most of the guests were rather tipsy and, by the time they'd finished, they were all quite boisterous.

SOPHIA

Somehow, the gentlemen all ended up going into the lounge, while all the ladies ended up in the kitchen. As everybody had lost their inhibitions, the ladies found that they were suddenly talking about their sex lives and their sexual fantasies. Not your typical classy dinner party conversation piece, but the ladies were alone and it was all fairly light-hearted, in that slightly tipsy kind of way. They were all fairly broad-minded and even though the host was a little frigid, even she got in on the conversation. They all took turns explaining their deepest most intimate sexual fantasy. Some were quite lame with one lady saying she would like to do it outside in the snow, while some of the other ladies were a little more daring with what they revealed. When it got to Sophia's turn, her fantasy got mixed reactions. She'd had her fair share of wine and didn't have any problem opening up to these strangers. Delphine was a little worried that, in her slightly drunken state, Sophia might slip up and give the game away, but she didn't.

'Me,' said Sophia, who'd had time to think about it while waiting for her turn. 'I've always wanted a man to eat my pussy …' she said.

'Oh come on sister, that's hardly a fantasy, that should be a regular routine,' said one of the women.

'… while I'm driving a car at 100mph,' she said, with a wicked smile on her face. 'Of course, it would have to have cruise control because with my legs apart and my feet on the dashboard I wouldn't be able to use the accelerator.' One of the women almost choked on her wine, while the others tried to picture Sophia's fantasy.

'Bravo,' shouted one of the women. 'Let's toast,' she said, raising her glass. 'To Christine, may your fantasy come true.' The ladies raised their glasses. Just then one of the men came in to find his wife.

'Hey, you coming through to join us?' he said.

'We'll be right there,' said his wife.

Steven gave Sophia a quick smile before heading back to the lounge.

Sophia excused herself to use the bathroom. While she was checking her make-up in the mirror she heard a voice behind her.

'What are you doing, Sophia?' said Spencer. She spun around, but Spencer was not there. His voice sounded calm and soothing, unlike the other nightmarish flashbacks she'd recently had. She stood there in silence waiting for his voice again – but it didn't come. Sophia was pleased that it was only his voice, and a friendly one at that.

Apart from the momentary blip in the bathroom, the evening went quite well. As Thomas's friend was leaving, Thomas held his hand up and drew a little squiggle in the air to suggest he wanted his cheque for £50,000. His friend smiled back with a look that suggested it was worth every penny.

Outside, one of the couples who lived in Bushey offered to drop Sophia and Delphine off on their way home. Or at least the wife had volunteered her husband, Steven, for the taxi duties. He didn't mind, why would he? Most men would jump at the chance to drive two stunning girls home in their car. Steven's wife suggested that he drop her home in Bushey first so she could go inside and get changed, while Steven continued on with the girls to Camden Town, then back to Hampstead, then back home to Bushey.

After they dropped Steven's wife off in Bushey their conversation opened up a little and became more relaxed. Steven had come into his own now his wife was no longer in the car and he'd become quite talkative. After Delphine was dropped off, Steven suggested that Sophia jump in the front for the short drive to Hampstead. His new BMW 5-series was plush and warm – and roomy. Once Delphine was out of the car and they were driving, Steven quickly changed the topic of conversation and told Sophia that he'd overheard her talking about her sexual fantasy in the kitchen with the women. And before she knew it the snake had offered to fulfil her fantasy, if she liked. Sophia was ahead of him and had already decided what she was going to say.

They pulled over to the side of the road. Sophia jumped into the driver's seat while Steve got comfortable in the passenger side. They belted up and headed for the nearest stretch of motorway where she could get up to speed, which happened to be the M1 about four miles away. It was twelve thirty in the morning and the streets of London were deserted. Ten minutes later they were at Brent Cross joining the M1. Sophia hadn't worked out exactly how this was going to play out. She figured she would improvise. The M1 was relatively quiet; just the usual trucks and lorries and a broken stream of cars. But the fast lane was totally free. Steven's BMW was silky smooth and it pretty much drove itself. It was automatic with cruise control buttons on the steering wheel so Sophia didn't have to worry about using her feet. After a mile or so the M1 turned into three lanes, plus the hard shoulder. It was dark and quiet and the front windows of the BMW were lightly tinted so it would be difficult for other drivers to see into their car. Sophia accelerated up to the legal motorway limit of 70mph then pressed the cruise control button to maintain the speed. She removed her seatbelt and reached down to pull her shoes off and threw them into the passenger side footwell out of the way. Then she hitched up her dress with her left hand while steering with her right and keeping an eye on the road. She lifted her bottom off the seat and used her left hand to pull her knickers down, kicking them off into the footwell. To say that Steven was enjoying the show would have been the understatement of the year. His eyes were practically popping out of his head at the sight of Sophia's naked thighs.

She pulled her right leg back and put her right foot up onto the driver's door armrest with her heel resting precariously near the electric window switch. After taking a moment to get accustomed to the car propelling forward by itself, she lifted her left leg and jammed her heel against the GPS screen in the middle of the dashboard. She looked across at Steven, who was practically drooling.

'I think I'm ready,' she said, with a devilish look in her eyes.

Steven quickly removed his tie and opened the top

button of his shirt. He leaned over the centre console, manoeuvring himself into a comfortable position so the automatic gear lever was not digging into his side. Then he fine-tuned his position so his head was between Sophia's legs. Her smell excited him; he inhaled deeply before pushing his tongue hard against her pussy. Sophia kept her eyes on the road while enjoying the sensations of Steven's tongue working on her, which made it quite difficult to keep the car between the lane markings on the motorway. Steven's tongue was all over the place, up down, in out. As he built up speed, so did Sophia. She pressed the accelerate button on the steering wheel with her thumb. 75mph, 80mph, as Steven continued to build up momentum and pressure against Sophia's now soaking wet clit. Sophia accelerated more; 85, 90 as both the car and Steven got faster. The car inadvertently crossed the lane lines as the muscles in Sophia's arms and legs started to tense and spasm out of control. 95, 96, 97, 98, 'Oh my God, don't stop,' she moaned as her behind continued to writhe around on the seat. The powerful engine of the BMW reached 100mph as Steven's powerful tongue pressed harder and faster. 'I'm coming, I'm coming,' she cried, as her legs and arms tensed up hard. She felt a burst of pleasure explode down below. As she writhed with her orgasm, her right heel inadvertently pressed hard into the door armrest and triggered the electric window button. The driver's window came down and the cold motorway wind hit her face as she continued to moan out loud with pleasure. Her long blonde hair whipped across her face in the

100mph wind and the temperature in the car dropped from toasty warm to freezing cold in an instant as the car veered hard over to the left. Sophia had lost control of every muscle in her body, and in turn, she'd also lost control of the steering wheel. She grabbed Steven's hair with her left hand and pushed his head away as her sensitivity down there was unbearable. She hit the electric window button and closed the window.

Just as Steven was manoeuvring himself back into his own seat he heard a very distinct rumbling sound coming from under the car tyres. He looked out of the windscreen just in time to see the car shoot across the hard shoulder, causing another driver on the inside lane to swerve out of their way.

'LOOK OUT!' he shouted, as the car went straight off the hard shoulder and onto the grass verge. Sophia dragged her hair out of her eyes and slammed her foot down hard on the brake, causing the BMW to spin sideways onto the wet grass and skid along at 90mph. The car continued to spin and skid along the wet grassy verge. Steven and Sophia saw the world outside the car going round and around like an adrenalin rush fairground ride.

Lucky for them the car mounted the grass verge on a clear stretch and there were no immediate trees or other obstacles for their car to hit. But just as the car started to straighten up, Steven noticed that they were careering directly towards an orange emergency SOS motorway telephone – mounted on top of a solid metal post.

It was too late for either of them to put their seatbelts

back on. All they could do was hold their breath and pray as the orange SOS box got closer and closer until they could read its unique identity number. They both let out a sigh of relief as the car came to a halt about five feet from the metal telephone post. Steven looked out of the window and realised, to his great relief, that they hadn't actually hit anything. They sat there for a minute, catching their breath and composing themselves.

'Oh fuck,' said Steven, as a police car cruised past them and pulled over onto the hard shoulder. On came the blue flashing lights and hazards and two policemen got out of the car and came rushing towards the BMW, which sat stationary on the grass verge at an awkward angle with a very long muddy skid mark behind it in the damp grass.

'Fuck, fuck, fuck,' he said.

Sophia said nothing. The craziness she'd been feeling for the past few hours started to subdue. But it was fast being replaced by a strange surreal feeling as a cold chill ran down her spine.

'Sophia?' said a voice coming from the back seat. Sophia took a sharp intake of breath as she heard the clear and distinct sound of Spencer's voice. She looked in the rear view mirror and there he was, sitting perfectly still. He looked different; quite normal. He was dressed in one of his smart suits. His hair was neat and his face was as handsome as ever.

'Are you ok?' said Steven.

'What are you doing?' said Spencer.

'I don't know,' said Sophia.

'Look, it'll be ok. Just stay calm and don't say any more than you have to,' said Steven, noticing Sophia's fixed gaze on the rear view mirror.

'This isn't you, Sophia, your mind's not your own,' said Spencer.

'I know, it feels like that sometimes, but I can't control it. I just can't stop myself. It takes over and there's nothing I can do,' she said.

'I'm sorry?' said Steven.

'You've got a dark passenger and it's hijacked your mind like a parasite. Its gonna make you worse, Sophia – much worse. You've got to get rid of it, Sophia. If you don't it will eventually drive you insane and it will finally kill you.' said Spencer.

'But when it drives, I feel good – it's like a drug. I don't know how to get rid of it, and I don't know if I want to,' she said.

'What are you talking about? Are you ok?' said Steven, confused by Sophia's words.

Sophia was so fixed on Spencer in the rear view mirror that she didn't notice one of the police officers run up to her door. He knocked on the window. Sophia was startled. She spun her head to the right and noticed the officer gesturing for her to open the window. She looked back in the rear view mirror, but Spencer had vanished. She spun around and looked across the back seat. But he was not there.

Rap, rap, rap. The policeman shouted, 'Madam, are you ok? Can you open your window?'

She obliged and flicked the electronic window button.

SOPHIA

'Is everyone ok?' asked the policeman.

'Yes, we're fine, officer,' said Steven.

The other officer looked back up the grass verge and noticed the very long muddy skid marks in the grass. While the officers were quickly trying to assess the situation, Sophia noticed a fox on the hard shoulder between the BMW and the police car. It was just standing there looking right at her. Then, it abruptly turned and ran up the grass verge. Sophia watched it run up the verge to the top. Then, she saw Spencer again, standing with his back to the moon. The fox arrived at his side and stood next to him, like an obedient dog. The two of them silhouetted against the moon. *Is this real?* thought Sophia.

'Can you tell us what happened?' asked the officer, startling Sophia. She turned to the officer who was standing right by her window.

'I ... I swerved ... to avoid something.'

'To avoid what, madam?'

'A fox, a fox ran across the motorway in front of the car. I swerved to avoid hitting it and lost control in the wet.' As she spoke the officer noticed a pair of knickers in the driver's footwell.

'Can you explain those?' said the officer, pointing to her discarded knickers.

'Oh, yes, they were cutting into me and were getting uncomfortable, so I took them off.'

'Well you shouldn't leave them lying in the driver's footwell. They could get tangled in the pedals and cause an accident,' he stated.

'I'm sorry officer, it won't happen again,' she said, still coming down from her orgasm and trying to get her head around the surreal experience with Spencer and the fox. Meanwhile, the other officer was walking around the car and assessing it for damage. 'Well, it would appear you've been very lucky,' he said. Both officers had a brief chat, and then they made sure Sophia could drive off the slippery grass and back onto the hard shoulder safely. Then one of the officers instructed them to wait on the hard shoulder until they moved their police car out of their path. The police car pulled out onto the motorway and drove off. Steven took over the driving and dropped Sophia home. He'd lost his appetite for sex, not that Sophia cared. She'd got what she wanted out of this little venture.

Chapter 26

Sophia was woken by the telephone on her bedside table. In her hung-over and sleepy state, she reached over to answer it while glancing at the digital clock at the same time: 12:35 p.m. *Oh God.*

'Hello,' she said.

'Oh dear, somebody doesn't sound good. Are you still in bed?' said Delphine.

'Yeah, I just woke up.'

'Oh, sorry, did I wake you?'

'It's ok, I should get up and try and salvage something from the rest of the day.'

'Are you hungry?' asked Delphine.

'I will be just as soon as I've had a shower and my taste buds have woken up.'

'Do you want to meet up for lunch. I know a good little place on Haverstock Hill.'

'Ok, what time?'

'How about two o'clock? Will that give you enough time?'

'Yeah, that should be ok.'

Delphine gave Sophia the name of the restaurant and told her it was a couple of doors up from Belsize

Park tube. Sophia struggled out of bed with yet another headache from hell. *Oooh, too much wine.*

Sophia scanned the restaurant then saw Delphine waving to get her attention. 'Hey, here she is,' said Delphine, standing up.

'Hi,' said Sophia, hugging Delphine and giving her a friendly kiss on the cheek. They sat down and got comfortable. Delphine pushed a menu across the table to Sophia. Just then, an over-enthusiastic waiter appeared.

'Hello, ladies. Can I get you any drinks while you look at the menu?'

'Yes, could I have an Americano with a double-shot, please?' said Sophia.

'Certainly,' he said.

'I'll have a Chai Latte, please,' said Delphine.

'Very good, I'll be right back,' he said, with a huge smile on his face.

Delphine caught Sophia checking out his cute butt in his smart tight black trousers as he walked away.

'I agree,' said Delphine, smiling at Sophia.

'Well, a girl can look can't she?' she said, smiling.

'So, have you considered getting back into it?' said Delphine.

'Into what?'

'The dating game, silly.'

'Oh. Well, if I'm honest, I've never done the dating game. Besides, I don't really have anything to offer right now.'

SOPHIA

'Look, Sophia. I know you're suffering,' she said, taking Sophia's hand in hers.

'Spencer was my world, Delphi. There was nobody like him on the planet. We were about to get engaged,' she said.

'I know, honey, I know,' she said, squeezing Sophia's hand.

'I even lost his baby, Delphi. I shouldn't have even got pregnant. I was on the pill for crying out loud. Then I go and have a miscarriage and lose Spencer's child. What sort of fucking message is that?'

'I really wish I knew the answer to that, honey, I really do,' said Delphine.

'Our relationship was beyond deep, Delphi. We were meant to be together from the day we were born.'

'Sophia, I know you don't believe it now, but you'll find love again. It'll take time, but eventually it will come up behind you and grab you right when you least expect it.'

'I know you mean well, Delphi, but I doubt that will ever happen. A beautiful relationship is a once in a lifetime thing, and I've already had mine.'

'Oh, you poor darling,' said Delphine, shedding a tear at Sophia's last sentence.

'Anyway, I'm a little fucked up right now. You can't tell me you haven't noticed?'

'Erm, well, I've noticed you act a little *strange* sometimes,' she said, trying to be polite, but deep down, knowing full well that Sophia has done some crazy shit recently and does have a tendency to be a tad volatile.

Delphine was thankful that she never really found herself on the receiving end of any of Sophia's sudden mood swings.

'Strange, that's a polite way of putting it. But let's face it Delphi, it goes a little deeper than strange. One minute I'm jogging along ok, then the next this darkness washes over me and takes over.'

'Sophia, you just need more time. Everything will be ok eventually; you'll see.'

'Maybe. Anyway, I don't have anything to offer in a relationship at the moment, and maybe I never will.'

'Well, you might think you don't have anything to offer. But where does it say in the book of rules that you can't have a bit of fun,' said Delphine. 'Just a couple of casual dates perhaps, what harm could that do?'

'What, as in actually talking to somebody and getting to know them?' said Sophia.

'Why not? You don't have to get to know them that well. Just a casual date over a few drinks or a coffee.'

'I don't know, Delphi.'

The waiter appeared at their table. 'Here you go,' he said, placing the drinks on the table. 'Have you decided what you'd like to eat?' he asked.

'Not yet, can you give us a few minutes,' said Delphine.

'Certainly,' he said.

'I'm not talking about anything exclusive,' said Delphine, getting back to the topic in hand. 'You could sign up on a dating site.'

'I don't know how the whole dating thing works.'

'Well it's not like there are rules. You just be yourself.'

SOPHIA

Sophia thought about it while sipping at her Americano.

'I don't know. I don't really like the idea of joining a dating site. I'd rather just go out and meet somebody.'

'What, like at a night club?'

'No, I thought maybe a hotel.'

'What do you mean?'

'The other night when I was waiting in the lobby of the Carrington Tower a few classy looking gentlemen glanced in my direction and smiled. One man even came over and tried to strike up a conversation. I told him I was meeting somebody.'

'So, you want to hang around the lobby of a hotel in the hope of finding a date?'

'Why not?' said Sophia. Delphine studied her serious expression.

'Ok. I have an idea. In a couple of days I have to meet a client at a hotel near Green Park. It's not an all-nighter. Why don't you come with me, like before? Only while I'm entertaining my client you can sit in the bar downstairs and have a drink and see what happens.'

'How long are you going to be there?' asked Sophia.

'He wants me for four hours from eight to midnight.'

'Great, it's a date.'

Sophia did her hair and make-up and put on a classy black cocktail dress and matching shoes. She chose a deep wine-red satin look trench coat to wear over the top. She drove to Delphine's place to pick her up, and then they went on to the hotel. After parking in the hotel car park, they went inside. Sophia got comfortable on a bar stool while Delphine went upstairs to her client's room.

Even though there were plenty of people drinking in the bar, Sophia felt a little exposed there, so she moved to a small table in the darkest far corner she could find and sat there people-watching with her drink. She looked incredible. The dress clung to her body revealing its perfect slender form. She'd used some large heated curlers in her hair to give it a sensual, sultry, and ravishing look. The soft, loose and dishevelled blonde curls flowed over her shoulders while the center parting and split fringe screamed sex goddess.

She took out her mobile phone to look busy more than anything else. *Might as well catch up on a few emails and text messages,* she thought. After about forty minutes, just as she was tapping away on her iPhone, somebody approached her table.

'Hello,' said a polite male voice in a fairly neutral tone. She looked up to see a relatively average looking man in his mid thirties.

'Hello,' she said back, matching his neutral tone, suggesting nothing more than politeness. He studied her for a moment.

'I don't want to appear forward, but if you're not waiting for anybody, I'd love to join you,' he said. His tone wasn't overly polite, or rude; just matter-of-fact. He wasn't really her type, going by his age and general deportment. *What the hell, it'll be good practice.*

'Sure,' she said.

SOPHIA

'Can I get you another drink?'

'Southern Comfort and lemonade, please,' she said.

Before she knew it, two hours had passed, along with several more Southern Comforts. The more time she spent talking to him the more attractive he became – or maybe that was just the effects of the drink kicking in. Either way, it soon became obvious that he kept himself in shape and spent time at the gym. At first glance he looked average, but on closer inspection Sophia could see that he was physically strong under his suit, in a slim and lean way. He wasn't tall, but he had an air of confidence about him that suggested he knew what he wanted and how to get it.

Sophia's dark side was starting to put in an appearance and it had her mind in a vice-like grip. Once this short transition had taken place she found herself wanting, but what? She didn't really know, nor fully understand. But she had an urge deep inside that needed feeding.

'You know, I have a room here,' he said, in what seemed like a cold uninviting tone. In Sophia's present state of mind, this suited her just fine.

'Well, I guess you'd better take me there,' she said, with a sinister *look* in her eyes.

Once they got to his room, Sophia didn't pussy foot around, she barely gave him a chance to close the door before she pushed him up against the wall, grabbed his head and kissed him passionately.

'Whoa, take it easy, we have all the time in the world,' he said.

'Maybe I don't want to take it easy,' she said, undoing

his tie and whipping it from his neck. She tossed it onto the floor then tried to open his top shirt button, but his shirt felt like it was half a neck size too small and she couldn't get enough purchase to open it. She pinched his neck with her fingers in frustration.

'Ouch, I'll do it,' he said. Before he could undo his top button, Sophia had dropped her hands to his waist and pulled his shirt out of his trousers and ripped it open from the bottom, sending the bottom three buttons flying across the floor.

'Fuck it,' he said, and ripped the shirt open from the top. Sophia grabbed his chest and pulled him close, kissing him hard while thrusting her tongue into his mouth. He moaned into her mouth in response to her enthusiasm. They stumbled over to the bed and Sophia shoved him backwards onto it while kicking her shoes off.

'Wow, this is new and unusual,' he said, ' I like it.'

'It's not about what you like,' she said, pulling her knickers off and jumping on top of him so her knees were either side of his chest. She slid forward and started to move her hips back and forth, rubbing her vagina along his naked chest. She kept going until the friction against his chest excited her so much it eventually turned into a pleasurable wet glide.

She moved up higher and pressed her vagina down onto his mouth. She continued to grind hard against his mouth and face. He struggled for breath unable to breathe under Sophia's continued pressure. He grabbed her by her waist and pushed her back, gasping for air.

SOPHIA

Sophia yanked his belt from his trousers and pulled them down to his knees. Then she pulled his stiff cock through the slit at the front of his boxer shorts and sat on him. She guided him in and started to grind back and forth and thrust up and down. She sped up, turning the act into a manic episode of frenetic sexual pleasure.

It was an hour later by the time Sophia had finished with him. She was sweating under her cocktail dress, which she hadn't bothered to remove, and her fringe was soaking wet. His chest and forehead glistened with sweat. He felt like he'd been at the gym for an hour doing some seriously hard cardiovascular circuit training. They both lay there, sweating and panting, too exhausted to speak or move.

Sophia heard the message alert sound on her mobile. *I'm fucked if I'm getting up to read that.* Eventually, he got up to take a shower. By the time he got back, Sophia had taken her dress off, got into bed and fallen asleep.

The next morning, Sophia woke up in an empty bed. She looked around the room at the evidence of the night before. Her dress was flung on the floor on one side of the bed, her knickers on the floor on the other, and her two shoes scattered eight feet apart on the other side of the room. Then she noticed a small wad of twenty-pound notes on the bedside table, with a note next to them. She was about to call out his name to see if he was in the bathroom, then she realized she didn't actually know his name, and hadn't bothered to ask. Come to think of it, he hadn't bothered to ask hers either.

'Thank you, that was quite different and not the typical service I've come to expect from a lobby mistress – but it was great fun just the same. I hope this covers it. Make sure you are out of the hotel room before twelve.'

She picked up the wad of twenty pound notes. 'Oh my God, he thought I was a prostitute,' she said, fanning the notes.

Chapter 27

'Hello,' said Delphine, answering her mobile.

'Are you home?' said Sophia.

'What happened? I've been worried about you.'

'I'm sorry, I was too exhausted to check my messages last night.'

'Are you ok, what happened to you last night?'

'If you're around, how about I stop by for a coffee and tell you.'

'Sure, how long will you be?'

'I'll be leaving the hotel in about fifteen minutes.'

'What, you're still there?'

'Yeah, I'll tell you all about it when I see you.'

Delphine let Sophia in and they went into the living room. Sophia casually tossed a wad of twenty pound notes onto Delphine's coffee table.

'What's that?' asked Delphine.

'Apparently, that's what I'm worth.'

'What?'

'£2,000.'

'Erm, you're going to have to explain, honey.'

'Well, it's quite simple really. A wealthy gentleman

chatted me up in the bar last night. We chatted for a while and things were going well. Then I had one drink too many and ended up going to his room. The rest is a bit of a blur. But this morning I woke up alone in his hotel room with that pile of cash and this note by the bed.' Sophia handed Delphine the note.

'I don't believe it,' she said, 'you told him you were a call girl?'

'I certainly did not. I just thought he was some guy chatting me up. Just two people who met in a hotel bar.'

'And you never mentioned money?'

'No.'

'Did he?'

'No, not that I remember anyway. We just ended up going to his room. We had sex and then I fell asleep.'

'Wow, so he mistook you for a high-class hooker,' said Delphine.

'It would appear so,' said Sophia.

Delphine could not hold back a short laugh. Then she composed herself and tried to look serious, but then Sophia started to laugh too, so Delphine joined in again. But beneath Sophia's laugh her dark demon was still lingering. It didn't have the vice-like grip on her like the night before, but it was definitely poised in her subconscious.

'So, now that I've had unofficial experience as a call girl, you can set me up for a date with one of your clients?'

'Whoa, where did that come from?' said Delphine, shocked.

Sophia

'Just a one off. Like you said, it'll be non-exclusive and at least I won't have to form any emotional attachment, not that I'm capable of that right now. It'll be good dating practice for me, for when I'm ready to form something more meaningful,' she said, with a *dark* glint still in her eyes from the night before. Delphine had got to know this *look* and she was aware that Sophia had a dark side that she couldn't get under control. Still, against her better judgment, she actually gave it some thought.

'I can't just set you up for a date with one of my clients. They're *my* clients for a reason and they request me for a whole set of different reasons.'

'Well, can't you just loan me one for an evening? Look, I don't want to make a career out of it. I just want to do it the once, to see what it's like,' she said.

'Sophia, it's not my call. I have a boss you know, she takes care of my client list and the diary. Look, you don't want to get into this. Hell, I'd get out of it myself if I could afford to.'

'What's her name?' asked Sophia.

'Please, Sophia, don't do this.'

'Just tell me her name,' she insisted.

'Martina.'

'Well, can't you talk to Martina? I'm sure she has other clients on her books.'

'You're missing the point. Even if I did and even if she agreed, which I doubt she would, these are paying clients and they pay for a specific service; not a date — they're two totally different things.'

'The words *yesterday* and *born* spring to mind,' said

Sophia. Delphine studied Sophia's face. *Of course she knows what's involved,'* thought Delphine. *Hell, I've told her enough intimate details about what I do with my clients.*

'And what do you propose I say exactly? "My friend wants to be a call girl for a night while she tries to figure out how to shake her dark morbid obsession with sex." It'll never happen, Sophia. Martina will never agree to set you up for a one-off. '

'Well don't word it like that. Ask her to interview me at least, to give me a trial period. Then, after my first client I'll just tell her sorry, but it's not for me.'

'Why don't we just fix you up with a regular date via a dating site? It'll be more … normal.'

'No,' said Sophia, sternly. 'I want to do this. I want to see what it's like, please, Delphi?' said Sophia. Delphine could see that Sophia was not going to drop it. She wasn't happy about the situation, but reluctantly, she agreed to talk to Martina.

'Ok, let me talk to her; but I'm not promising anything. And, if she says no, you promise me you'll drop this whole stupid idea?'

'I promise,' said Sophia, with a big beaming smile on her face.

Chapter 28

Sophia arrived at Martina's house in Edgware just after 8 p.m.

'You must be Sophia,' said Martina, opening the door.

'Yes.' Sophia didn't have any idea how this was going to pan out. But, as she was feeling confident and even a little bit arrogant right now, she really didn't care. She had nothing to be nervous about. In her current state-of-mind she could take it or leave it.

'Won't you come in,' said Martina, leading the way into the living room. Martina was in her late forties, but still wore her make up and hair in the manner of somebody half her age. She was dressed smartly, like a businesswoman. Even though it was eight in the evening she was still wearing the power suit she'd probably been wearing during the day. Sophia couldn't imagine that she'd put it on just for her benefit. She had an air of a very confident woman and her eyes and expression said, *don't fuck with me*. Sophia figured that Martina had put on this expression so many times in the past that it had set permanently.

'Can I get you something to drink?'

'No, I'm fine, thank you.'

'Ok, first things first, let's get the essential part out of the way shall we?'

'Ok, what would that be?' asked Sophia.

'Strip,' she ordered, matter-of-fact.

'Excuse me?'

'Your clothes, take them off.'

'Oh.'

'Look, I have a lot of businessmen, executives and important people on my client list. For the high prices they pay they expect perfection. If they wanted just any old Eastern European whore they could walk into their nearest massage parlour and pay a fraction of the price. My clients pay £250 to £300 per hour, so they expect a lot more. I need to see your body to make sure you're up to scratch. So, if you could be so kind,' she said, waving her hand and gesturing down Sophia's body.

'What, right here?'

'Yes right here. If you can't even strip in front of me, how can I expect you to be able to get undressed in front of a paying client? Trust me, a client won't be happy with you nipping off the bathroom and coming back in a robe,' she said, with a sarcastic laugh.

'Ok.' Sophia kicked her shoes off and proceeded to unbutton her blouse. Then she removed her trousers and stood there in her knickers and bra.

Martina sighed. 'Are those two remaining garments glued to your body?'

'No.'

'Well, take them off,' she demanded. She seemed to be losing her patience with Sophia. She undid her bra and

SOPHIA

tossed it onto Martina's sofa, and then she removed her knickers and stood there, arms by her sides, waiting for Martina's approval. Sophia was just as stunning naked, as she was dressed. Her breasts were pert and perfectly formed and lower down she was groomed to perfection. Sophia looked at Martina confidently, as she knew she had a good body.

'Ok, get dressed,' she said, mildly annoyed. Martina let out a sigh as she looked out of the window. Sophia finished dressing and went to sit on the chair opposite Martina.

'Don't sit down. I want you to get undressed.'

'But, I just did.'

'Yes you did, but you did it in the manner of somebody who was getting undressed before going to bed. This time, I want you to do it with a little more grace and elegance. Take your time. I'm not asking you to put on a striptease show for me honey, but I expect you to look sexy when you're doing it. Like I said, my clients expect a little bit more from my girls.' She gestured to Sophia's body again, in a manner that said, *and ... action.*

Sophia started to get undressed again. This time she really didn't give a fuck so she decided to give the *madam* a show. Sophia locked her eyes on Martina's and didn't take them off her until she was totally naked. She took her time, making her fingers and hands work sensually on her blouse buttons. She let her blouse drop naturally off her shoulders, stopping at her wrists. She continued, very slowly, to remove her trousers, this time, turning away from Martina. She leaned forward so the cow could get a good view of her backside as she bent down to slip her trouser legs over her ankles and feet. She stood up and started to remove her bra, slowly, while her body still faced away, but with her head looking over her shoulder at Martina. She flung her bra over her other shoulder so it landed on Martina's lap. She turned around, with her arms crossed over her breasts, keeping them hidden. Then she lowered both her hands, slowly, revealing them. Her hands continued down to her knickers. She toyed with the thin straps on her hips, sliding her fingers under them and moving them from the sides to the front a few times before leisurely sliding them down her thighs to her knees. She stood up and wriggled her hips until her knickers fell to her ankles. She lifted one foot free of them so they were still hooked over the toes of her other. She looked directly at Martina, and then flicked them up with her foot so they landed on the sofa next to her.

'Ok, so you've got the body, the looks, and apparently you've got the moves. Now let's see if you have the right attitude.'

'Do I have to be naked for this part?' she said, sarcastically.

'No, dear, you don't.'

Sophia got dressed and sat down. Apparently her body was ok. Lord knows what Martina was looking for. Hideous scars or unsightly birthmarks perhaps, or maybe cellulite, stretchmarks, flabby love handles or a plain old fat backside. Whatever her criteria, Sophia passed. For the next forty minutes, Martina told Sophia what was involved, sometimes in detail. She seemed to be happy with Sophia. She could see that Sophia could hold her own and was not lame. Based on her questions, and the answers Sophia gave, Martina told her that there were a number of clients that she thought she'd work well with.

'Ok, I have a client in mind who I can try you out with. He's not too demanding and he's pretty easy going. He doesn't require anything special or out of the ordinary. He typically wants a good old-fashioned girlfriend experience. He'll be a good client for you to start with. I'll tell him you're new and I'll ask him for his feedback afterwards. Depending on how it goes, will depend on whether or not I decide to keep you on.'

'Sounds good to me. When do you want me to see him?'

'Is nine o'clock tomorrow evening too soon? He phoned me this afternoon and asked if I had anybody who could see him at short notice. No pressure. He'll understand if it doesn't happen. He usually calls three or four days before to book an appointment.'

'Tomorrow night's fine. Where does he live?'

'Just around the corner from Marble Arch. I'll give you his full details once I've spoken to him on the phone tomorrow afternoon.'

'That's great.'

'And don't forget to think up a name that you'll be happy to use all the time; a name you won't forget. It's not a good idea to use your real name.'

'I already have a name in mind.'

'What?' asked Martina?
'Christine.'

Chapter 29

As Sophia took her morning shower she noticed, for the first time in weeks, that she didn't have a throbbing headache. And she felt reasonably normal. *What the hell was I thinking*, she thought, as she lathered her body. *Delphine was right; it was a bloody crazy idea. I'll call her and cancel it.* Out of the shower, she went through her usual routine of fixing her hair, getting dressed and making a cup of tea. Sophia typically didn't wear make-up, or very little. Only when she was performing did she apply a little more, but even then it was minimal and tasteful. She looked over at her cello case and began to wonder when she'd last taken it out of its case and practised.

'Hello, you.' She took her cello out of its case and held it lovingly for a moment before extending the spike and setting it on the floor. She positioned the cello between her knees, and then she put some rosin on her bow and played the first five bars from Elgar's Cello Concerto. Then she stopped and imagined the delicate sound of the clarinets coming in. She lowered her bow and sat there thinking. The musical world had been screaming for Sophia to perform the Elgar in public for about four years now. But Sophia had never entertained playing it in public for several reasons. One of which was that she didn't want the inevitable comparisons with a certain Jacqueline du Pré. Although she had nothing against the Elgar, it was not one of her favourite concertos either. And, like Jackie, Sophia actually preferred the Schumann A minor Concerto. In fact, there were three or four Concertos Sophia would choose over the Elgar. Rostropovich's signature piece, the Dvorak Concerto for example, or Haydn's D major Concerto. Then there's Boccherini, Georg Matthias Monn – take your pick. Even the emotionally lacking Saint-Saens Concerto or Tchaikovsky's Rococo variations would be higher on Sophia's list of preferred works. Or maybe it was just because the Elgar had a stigma attached to it; especially for female cellists. All Sophia knew was when she played those opening five bars of the Elgar, she found herself lost in her blissful musical world again. A place her mind had not allowed her to go to for some weeks now. Sophia was yanked out of her blissful thoughts by her doorbell ringing.

'DJ?' she said, surprised.

'Sorry to come around unannounced like this,' he said.

'It's ok, come on in.'

'Was that the Elgar I just heard you playing?'

'Yes, yes it was.'

'I tried calling you several times. You never seem to be here and I haven't had any success getting you on your mobile either.'

'DJ, I'm sorry, I haven't been myself lately.'

'What about now?'

'Erm, right now ... I feel fine.'

'So are you ready to get back on track with the Beethoven rehearsals?'

'Of course, I guess so.'

'Good, I'll phone Steinway Hall and give you some fresh dates.'

'DJ, I'm sorry, I'm ... I won't let you down again.'

'Don't worry. I'm just concerned about you that's all. I have been for a while now.'

'And I appreciate that – I really do.'

'Would you like a drink?'

'As much as I'd love to, it's only a flying visit. I'm on my way to try a couple of pianos out.'

'You're finally replacing the Yamaha?'

'Hopefully, yes.'

'That's good; I never did like the C3. It just sounds too ... Japanese.'

'I know, it's too harsh. Anyway, I've just been so busy I've hardly had a chance to look around and try anything else.'

'So what are you going to look at now?'

'A Bösendorfer 185 and a Steingraeber & Söhne B-192.'

'Very nice. But how will Steinway feel about you owning a piano that isn't one of theirs? I mean, with you being a Steinway artist?'

'Well, I won't be making any public appearances with it. It's purely for practice at my place. I don't think the Steinway police are going to find out anytime soon. Besides, if I'm honest, I don't really like the idea of

Steinway having a monopoly on the concert world platform. The next thing you know they'll be the Microsoft of pianos.'

'What will you do with the Yamaha?'

'The professor will move it back into his main house. Anyway, I gotta dash. I'll call you tomorrow with the new dates ok.'

'Ok, good luck with the pianos.'

Sophia went back into her living room, took out the sheet music for the Beethoven Cello Sonatas and got stuck into some serious practice, forgetting that she had to call Martina to cancel her call girl appointment later that evening.

She'd been practising well into the afternoon when she was interrupted by the doorbell for the second time that day.

'Yes?' she said, opening the door and seeing a woman in her thirties standing there.

'Oh, I'm so sorry to disturb you, but I haven't seen my cat for two days now so I'm checking with all the neighbours. She's a little tabby cat with a cute face. I don't suppose you've seen her, or know where she is?'

'Well how the fuck would I know!' said Sophia, slamming the door in the woman's face. 'Jesus Fucking Christ', she said, walking through into the kitchen. She opened one of the kitchen cupboards and took out a bottle of Smirnoff. She filled a glass one third and topped it up with Coke then grabbed a couple of ice cubes from the freezer and dropped them in. By the time she'd done the short walk from the kitchen to the living room she'd managed to gulp half of it down. The moment that alcoholics referred to as a *moment of clarity* had left Sophia. While she was practising, her dark side had quietly crept up on her and had seized her mind. Just as she sat down with her drink her mobile rang.

'Hello,' she said, before putting the glass to her mouth and taking another large gulp.

'Ok, I have the gentleman's name and address for tonight. Do you have a pen?' said Martina.

Sophia swallowed and slammed her drink down on the coffee table. Just a few hours ago she was happily practising and felt almost normal. But as the afternoon had progressed, something had happened. That *thing* had reared its ugly head again and its dark shadow had washed over her while she was playing. It had slowly enveloped her conscious mind without her being aware of the transition. At least not until cat woman rang on her doorbell, then it leapt right out to say hello.

Fuck it; this is gonna be fun, thought Sophia as she picked up a pen and turned over a junk mail letter from that morning's post. 'Yes, I have a pen,' she said.

'His name's Mark Nicholas and he's expecting you at nine.' Sophia scribbled the name on the back of the envelope. Martina gave Sophia the address and some final instructions. After she put the phone down, she walked across the room and caught her reflection in the mirror. She studied her face and pondered for a moment. She walked over to the mirror and leaned forward and looked deep into the eyes that were staring back at her, but whose eyes were they? *Who the fuck are you?* said a distant voice deep in her subconscious.

Chapter 30

Sophia had just driven past Lord's Cricket Ground in St John's Wood when Martina called her mobile. She pressed the Bluetooth answer button on the dash.

'Hello.'

'Sophia, it's Martina. Where are you?'

'St. John's Wood. I'll be there in ten minutes.'

'I need you to forget that client and to go to the Royal International Hotel in Piccadilly instead.'

'What do you mean, I'm almost there?'

'One of my girls has been involved in a car accident. She can't get to her client and I can't afford to let him down. So I've cancelled your scheduled appointment with Mr Nicholas and I need you to go and fill in for another girl.'

'What about Mr Nicholas?'

'I told him I'd double-booked. He's a good client; he was fine about it. Look, Sophia, the gentleman I'm sending you to now is one of my best clients, but he has very specific requirements.'

'What sort of requirements?'

'He likes role play. I don't have time to explain it right now, but just go with it ok. If you do, everything will be fine' said Martina. She knew she was taking a big risk sending a new girl to Mr Mancini. 'You're going to meet one of his bodyguards outside the main entrance. What are you wearing?'

'What difference does that make?'

'I need to describe what you're wearing so his bodyguard can recognise you?'

'A dark grey satin cocktail dress and a deep red satin trench coat.'

'Ok, I'll call him now and let him know you'll be there within half an hour.'

After parking in the Royal International Hotel car park, Sophia made her way to the main entrance where one of Mr Mancini's bodyguards spotted Sophia straight away.

'Christine?' said the man, with an Italian accent. He didn't look like your typical bodyguard. Sure, he was six feet tall and looked like he could handle himself, but his face had a gentle expression and his eyes smiled.

'Yes.'

'Please, this way.'

Sophia followed him through the hotel to Mr Mancini's suite.

'Ah, you must be Christine,' said Mr Mancini, in a strong Italian accent. 'Please, come in, make yourself comfortable.' There was another bodyguard in the room with him.

'Do you want us to wait outside?' asked one of the bodyguards?

'I don't think that will be necessary. Why don't you go

down to the casino and relax.'

'Yes, Mr Mancini.'

'Alone at last,' he said. 'Well, Martina was right. You really are a pleasant surprise,' he said, as he walked around Sophia and studied her from top to bottom. 'Let me take your coat for you,' he said, standing behind her. Sophia gracefully let her trench coat slide down her shoulders and arms for Mr Mancini to catch. He took a hanger out of the wardrobe and hung Sophia's coat. 'Now, what can I get you to drink?'

'I'll have what you're having,' she said.

'Daring, I like that,' he said, picking up the phone for room service. 'It's Mr Mancini. Could I have a bottle of Louis Roederer Cristal sent up right away,' he said, while studying the shape of Sophia's body through her clinging satin dress. He hung up the phone and went back over to her. He walked around Sophia, running the tips of his fingers over her shoulders, lower back, then around her waist until he was standing in front of her again. He slipped both his index fingers under the thin shoulder straps of her dress and slid them down until they came to rest just above her breasts. 'Martina has certainly served me up a special treat with you,' he said. He leaned forward and kissed her sensually with his lips ever so slightly parted. Mancini spent the next three or four minutes feasting his eyes on Sophia's stunning body while lightly running his fingers over her satin dress. There was a knock at the door.

'Excuse me,' he said, going to answer it. He came back, followed by a waiter pushing a small silver trolley with a bottle of champagne on ice and some glasses.

'Would you like me to open the champagne sir?'

'Please.'

Mr Mancini's penetrating dark brown eyes held Sophia's intently, while the waiter filled two flutes.

'Will that be all, Mr Mancini?' said the waiter.

'Yes, thank you.' The waiter left and Mr Mancini gave Sophia one of the flutes of champagne then held his own up in front of her. 'To an interesting evening ahead,' he said, clinking Sophia's glass. After a couple of sips each, he took Sophia's glass and placed it on the coffee table in the middle of the room. Then he turned his attentions back to her. He lightly brushed her breasts through her satin dress, pausing momentarily over her nipples. Then he leaned forward and kissed her, this time with a little tongue. As per instructions from Martina, Sophia went with it. She placed her hands on his hips. *Well, this is going to be easy,* she thought. He suddenly pushed his tongue deeper into Sophia's mouth and reached down and grabbed her behind with both hands. 'Hmmm,' he moaned into her mouth. Then he pulled his face away, and out of the blue, he smiled wickedly and gave Sophia a friendly slap on the face. She was slightly taken back. *Is this part of his role-play?* Sophia reciprocated by giving him a gentle slap back. The smile instantly dropped from Mr Mancini's face. His idea of dominant role-play was one-way and he fully expected Sophia to be submissive. He slapped Sophia hard across the face. She let out a squeal of pain this time and stood there, startled, looking at Mr Mancini, whose smile had now returned. Sophia saw red

SOPHIA

and with all her strength, she swung hard and slapped his face with all the power she could muster up.

'You fuckin' bitch,' he said, grabbing Sophia's hair with his left hand. He coiled his right arm back and let it fly, hitting Sophia hard in the face with his fist – sending her flying to the floor. She squealed in agonizing pain, holding her face. 'You wanna play rough with me? I'll give you rough,' he said, getting down on the floor and reaching up Sophia's dress between her legs.

'No,' she screamed. She kicked and scuffled along the floor, trying to get away from him. But he leant down and grabbed her left ankle and pulled her backwards towards him. Sophia kicked him in the chest with her right heel. She was free of his grip again and tried to scramble on her hands and knees towards the door. But he caught up with her and before she could get fully to her feet he'd pushed her in the back, sending her crashing forward into the silver trolley. The trolley, ice bucket and champagne went crashing to the ground, with Sophia landing on top of it. Mancini got on top of her and turned her over so she was facing him. Her arms and legs thrashed about under his dead weight. She could not get out from under him as he grabbed her dress and ripped it open, revealing her bra. 'No,' she screamed again.

She turned her head to the side and saw a fox run across the room. She turned her head to the other side and looked across the room to where the fox ran. Then she saw Spencer sitting in one of the comfy armchairs. His black sinister eyes looked out from his pale bloody face, and straight into her soul.

'Where's the nice Spencer?' she shouted.

'Trust me, you don't need him right now. Right now, I'm the one you need,' said the dead Spencer. His voice was deep and dark like a demon.

Mancini grabbed Sophia's hair in his left hand and straightened up her head to face him. Then he pressed his lips hard against hers. She mumbled and tried to scream, but his mouth pressed hard up against hers muted her calls for help. He lowered his right hand and jammed it between her legs, groping her through her knickers.

Sophia's arms thrashed around on the carpet as she desperately searched for something to hit him with. Then the back of her hand struck the champagne bottle, which was pouring its contents all over the carpet.

'What are you waiting for,' said Spencer. 'Hit the fucker,' he shouted.

Sophia struggled to spin the bottle around with her fingertips, but eventually managed and grabbed it by the neck.

WHACK! She struck Mr Mancini across the side of his temple, sending him sideways onto the floor. The bottle didn't break, but it made one hell of a clunking sound as it struck the side of his skull. Sophia got to her feet and looked across at the chair where Spencer had been sitting, but he wasn't there. She dropped the bottle and tried to put the straps of her dress over her shoulders, but one of them had snapped during her tussle with Mancini. She ran to the wardrobe and got

Sophia

her trench coat. As she struggled to put it on, she looked at Mr Mancini on the floor holding his bleeding head in pain while trying to come back to earth after just being knocked almost unconscious. As Sophia ran for the door he looked up, moaning, blood streaming down the side of his head and face. He called after her.

'You bitch, do you know who I am?' Sophia opened the door and ran out into the hallway. 'You're fucking dead,' he shouted. Sophia slammed the door and as she ran down the corridor she could still hear him shouting. 'Do you hear me? You're dead.'

Chapter 31

That's just fucking great, thought Sophia, looking at her new shiner of a black eye in the mirror, courtesy of Mr Mancini's fist. It was sensitive to the touch, but nowhere near as sensitive as her pounding headache, which was amplified by her throbbing black eye. It was so bad it had woken her a few hours previously. She'd taken two Nurofen Plus, but they'd done nothing to relieve the pressure she felt behind her eyes. She applied some foundation to try and cover up the bruising around her eye. Foundation was something she only used in emergencies, such as covering up a pimple that had come up during the night. But this was a bit more than a pimple. The foundation covered the bruising but it could not hide the swelling under her eye. After calling Delphine's landline and not getting an answer, she tried her mobile.

'Hey you,' said Delphine, seeing Sophia's name come up on her mobile.

'Where are you?' asked Sophia.

'I'm out getting some shopping. I'm almost done so I'll be home in about half an hour. Hey, how did it go with your client last night?'

SOPHIA

'I'll be at your place in half an hour to tell you all about it.'

'Jesus, what happened to your eye?' said Delphine, opening the door. Sophia barged straight past Delphine and into her kitchen.

'Martina cancelled my allocated appointment at the last minute and sent me to see some fucking Italian arsehole,' she said, looking through Delphine's cupboards for something alcoholic.

'What are you looking for?' asked Delphine.

'A drink,' she said, frantically opening and slamming kitchen cupboards.

'Sophia, it's only lunchtime. Sit down, I'll make you some tea.'

'I don't want any fucking tea,' she said, continuing her frenzied hunt around the kitchen.

'Sophia, I'm not letting you drink yourself into a hole in the middle of the day. I want you to tell me what happened with a clear head. Will you stop tearing my kitchen apart and sit the fuck down.' Sophia stopped in her tracks and threw herself into a chair at Delphine's breakfast table and folded her arms.

'Now, tell me what happened,' said Delphine, flicking the switch on the kettle.

'I was ten minutes away from Mr Nicholas' house–'

'Mark Nicolas?' said Delphine, interrupting.

'Yes. But then Martina phoned and told me to go to the Royal International Hotel in Piccadilly instead.'

'Why?'

'I'm not sure, something about one of her regular girls being in a car accident. Apparently this Italian arsehole's an important client and she didn't want to let him down. So she pulled me from my appointment and sent me to take her place.'

'You said Italian, was it Mancini?'

'Yes, you know him?'

'Yes, he was one of my clients once … once. I told Martina I wouldn't see him anymore. He pays a lot more than the other clients because of his specific requirements. Even so, there are only a few girls who are prepared to take his shit in exchange for the extra money.'

'What kind of requirements?'

'He likes to dominate. He wouldn't harm anyone, well, not really. But he likes to role play rape scenes and sometimes he can get a little bit rough.'

'What do you mean?'

'Well, he might put his hands around the girl's throat and squeeze, not to stop them breathing or anything, just enough to make it seem real. He's also been known to slap girls around the face, again, not hard, but just hard enough to get a reaction. He'll pin the girl down and stuff like that. He doesn't go too far, but some girls can't handle it. Some think it's a little too close for comfort and they get quite scared. Some girls, on the other hand, will put up with it because they get a lot more money and he tips well.'

'Well, the fucker didn't stop at slapping me; he punched me and nearly knocked me out. I saw stars in front of my eyes for fuck's sake.'

'That's unusual, I've never heard of him badly hurting any of Martina's girls before. How did it come about?' she said, pouring the tea.

'It started off fine, and then he slapped me, not hard. So I joined in the game and gave him a gentle slap back. Then he went fucking crazy and slapped me really hard. It felt like the side of my face had exploded. So I slapped him back, only this time I slapped him really hard; it even hurt the palm of my hand.'

'Oh my God,' said Delphine, putting a cup of tea in front of Sophia.

'It was a reflex reaction more than anything.'

'Mancini likes to dominate, he doesn't like to be dominated.'

'Well it would have been bloody nice to have known that before I got there.'

Just then Sophia's mobile rang. She looked at the screen. 'Great, it's Martina.'

'You should take it,' said Delphine.

'Hello,' said Sophia.

'You fucking stupid bitch. Do you have any fucking idea what you've done?'

'Yeah, I know what I've done. I escaped the clutches of a stupid fucking Italian maniac, that's what I've done.'

'And do you have any idea who that stupid fucking Italian maniac is?'

'No, and I don't care because I'm not going to see him, or you, ever again.'

'Well, you should fucking care because he's not just some rich Italian businessman.'

'Oh really? Why should I care? I've got news for you,

I only wanted to try it the once anyway, and now I'm through.'

'Well I've got news for you too because Mr Mancini doesn't make his millions by legal means. He knows some very unpleasant people.'

'Like I said, why should I care?'

'Because he's standing right next to me with a bandage around his head covering up ten stitches.'

'Good, he asked for it. Maybe now he won't treat women that way anymore.'

'Wrong, what I asked for was a woman who can do as she's fucking told and give me what I wanted,' said Mancini, who'd relieved Martina of the phone.

'Fuck you,' said Sophia, hanging up. Within a few seconds it rang again, and again, Martina's name came up.

'What?' said Sophia.

'I can't even begin to imagine how difficult it would be to play the cello with no fucking fingers on your left hand,' threatened Mancini.

'Go to hell, I'm not scared of you, or your fucking goons,' she said.

'Maybe not, but your little sister will be when I find her and make her bleed. What's her name? Oh yes, Charlotte,' he said, laughing. Sophia fell silent. 'Oh, what's the matter, cat got your tongue?' he said.

'Don't you dare fucking touch my sister.'

'If you weren't a woman, you'd be dead by now. How they say, oh yes, swimming with the fishes.' Sophia could hear him sniggering to himself. 'Now, there's something I want you to do for me. To make amends so to speak.'

SOPHIA

'I'm not going to do *anything* for you.'

'Well that's where you're wrong. We'll talk again when you get back from Paris,' he said, hanging up the phone. Sophia hung up too.

'What the hell did you do last night?' asked Delphine.

'How does he know about my Paris recital?'

'We're talking about Corrado Mancini here. He can find out whatever the hell he wants, about *whoever* he wants. If he wants to know how much milk you put on your cornflakes in the morning, he can find out before you've finished eating them. He's connected, and to people you don't want to know, Sophia. Now, what exactly did you do?'

'I hit him over the head with a bottle of champagne.'

'Holy fucking shit. Do you have any idea who he is?'

'Apparently not.'

'Well, I don't have time to go into detail. But he's basically a gangster, a nasty one. Not somebody you want to cross or get on the wrong side of.'

'Well now he's threatening my family … unless I do something for him.'

'What does he want you to do?'

'I don't know. He said we'd talk when I get back from Paris.'

'Sophia, I'm really sorry.'

'It's not your fault. I'm the one who insisted on being a damn call girl for a night.'

'I know, but I shouldn't have entertained the idea. I should have put my foot down and just said no.'

'Hey, don't beat yourself up about it. I hardly left you

a choice.'

'Look, we're in this together. So we'll figure out what to do together.'

'Are you sure?'

'Yes, I'm sure. So when's your Paris recital?'

'I'm taking the Eurostar from St Pancras the day after tomorrow.'

'How long are you out there for?'

'Just two nights.'

'Christ, Sophia. You should have asked him what he wanted you to do.'

'Well, I wasn't thinking straight. Look, I've got to go. I have an appointment with my agent in an hour.'

'Ok. I'll call you later.'

Chapter 32

Sophia had been practising for two hours when her doorbell rang. After her meeting with her agent Meredith, she'd decided to focus on her playing and the up-coming Paris recital.

Sophia opened her apartment door and saw her older sister Eleanor standing there with an angry look on her face.

'Hey, s–'

'Don't you dare sis me,' she shouted, slapping Sophia hard across the face before barging past and stampeding into her living room.

'What the hell's wrong with you?' asked Sophia, holding her throbbing cheek.

'You know damn well what's up. Michael decided to come clean about your dirty little secret this morning.'

'Oh, that.'

'Yes, that. I knew there was something wrong. The way he's been acting lately, walking around with his head down and unable to look me in the eyes. He's been acting like a guilty puppy every since you came over for dinner,' she said, giving Sophia an evil look of contempt.

'What did he say?'

'He came clean. He said he couldn't carry the burden

of guilt anymore so he told me what happened; how you seduced him in *my* bedroom. Anyway, I ended it. I told him to pack his things and get out.'

'I'm sorry.'

'No you're not. You're not sorry about anything. What the hell's happened to you, Sophia? Running around acting like a total bloody lunatic. You've cut yourself off from the world. You don't contact Mummy and Daddy anymore. Grandmother's worried about you and poor little Charlotte's confused as hell and can't understand why you don't call her anymore. I suppose you got that black eye after getting caught screwing somebody else's boyfriend?'

'Not exactly,' said Sophia, touching the purple and yellow bruising with her fingertips.

'Well I don't care; I hope it hurts like hell. I can't believe you did this to me – my own sister.'

'You're not seeing the bigger picture, sis. You're overreacting,' said Sophia.

'Overreacting, how dare you.'

'Well, at least you're rid of him now. It wasn't my fault your boyfriend couldn't keep it in his pants,' said Sophia.

'You … are a complete bitch.'

'Oh come on, I did you a favour. If he loved you or gave a shit about you, he wouldn't have let me suck his dick.'

'That's it, you've gone, you've totally flipped, Sophia. You're totally off your head and I want nothing more to do with you – ever. You're not my sister anymore. Goodbye,' she said, storming off out of the apartment and slamming the door.

SOPHIA

Almost the instant that Eleanor left, Sophia went to the kitchen and fixed herself something to eat and drink and then got back to her cello practice as if nothing had happened. She spent the whole afternoon practising but didn't recall any of it. As she played she was on autopilot, oblivious to what she was actually playing. Her fingers moved up and down the fingerboard and her bow moved across the strings and sounds were produced. But the sounds were distant echoes, echoes of a previous life that was eluding her more and more with each passing day.

At eight thirty that evening Sophia's parents arrived at her apartment, unannounced.

'I think we need to talk, darling,' said her father as Sophia opened the door just a few inches, just enough to see who was there.

'Come in,' she said, leading them into the living room. Sophia turned to face her father.

'Oh my God, what happened to you,' said Andrew, stepping closer to her and inspecting her black eye.

'It's ok, Daddy, it's nothing.'

'Well, it doesn't look like nothing,' said Diana.

'I suppose you're here because of what happened with Eleanor this morning?' said Sophia.

'Or to be a little more precise, what happened with you and Michael,' said Diana. 'How could you, Sophia. How could you do such a thing to your own sister?'

'I've already had all this from Eleanor, I don't need another lecture.'

'Well you're going to jolly well get one young lady. You cut yourself off from the world, you don't speak to us anymore, you get into trouble with the police and you're out until the early hours of the morning.' Sophia gave her mother a look. 'That's right, I spoke with one of your neighbours.' *No doubt the nosey cat woman.*

'Sophia, darling, we're concerned about you that's all,' said Andrew. We never see you during the day anymore. You just sit in your apartment with the curtains drawn and the lights low and you only go out after dark?'

'Well, you can't see your dark shadow when you live in the dark,' said Sophia

'This isn't good enough, Sophia,' said Diana. 'You're destroying your life and now you're destroying the lives of everybody around you in the process. You've certainly ruined Eleanor's life. Do you have any idea how upset she is? She's thrown Michael out of her house. She's devastated. What's going on with you? What's happened … don't just sit there in silence young lady, you've got some serious explaining to do,' said Diana.

Sophia just looked at her mother as she felt her inner darkness wash over her; running through her veins, reaching the far corners of her mind, body and soul.

'Well?' said Diana, 'don't you have anything to say?'

'No, Mummy, I don't.'

Andrew observed from the touchline, trying to figure out what was going on with his precious daughter. What Andrew saw wasn't his daughter; she was a shadow of her former self. He could barely recognise her. Sure, she looked like his daughter, well, except for the blond hair and eccentric clothes. But the real Sophia that he knew and loved was simply not there.

'Darling, I'd like to get you some help,' said Andrew.

'You mean the psychologist, Jacques. I've stopped seeing him. He didn't help, he just wanted to keep dragging up the car accident and Spencer all the time.'

'Listen, darling, there's something wrong, you've changed, everyone can see it except you.'

'Daddy, there's nothing wrong with me, it's everybody else who has the problem.'

'How dare you?' said Diana. 'Just look at you, sitting there as if everything's perfectly ok. Meredith knows something's wrong, your sisters know it, your father and I know it; even Django can see that you've changed.'

'When did you speak to DJ?' asked Sophia.

'Last night. He's just as concerned as we are, but he doesn't know what to do. Like the rest of us, he can't really understand what's going on with you, Sophia. He said he can't seem to reach you.'

'Well, maybe I don't want to be reached. Maybe I just want everybody to get off my case and leave me alone.'

'You know something, I barely recognise you, Sophia. You simply can't carry on like th–'

'Like what, Mummy, like what?' shouted Sophia.

'Like this, your volatile nature. You weren't like this before. Spencer's dead, darling and you've got to accept it and move on.'

'I want you to leave,' said Sophia, glaring at Diana.

'I'm not going anywhere. We need to sort this out.'

'Get out,' said Sophia, standing up. 'GET OUT, GET

OUT, GET OUT!' Sophia ran over to her hi-fi, pressed play on the CD player and turned the volume up high. 'GET OUT' she shouted, just as the guitar riff and drums of Motorhead's 'The Ace Of Spades' blasted out of her hi-fi speakers. She turned away from her parents, faced the window and folded her arms. Diana put her hands over her ears and screwed up her face in disgust at the music.

Andrew took Diana by her arm and gestured for her to leave the apartment with him. He knew that this was not going anywhere. Diana would continue lecturing and Sophia would continue to be on the defensive. Diana agreed with Andrew, anything to get away from that ghastly noise. They left, leaving Sophia alone with Motorhead.

Chapter 33

The two hour and fifteen minute Eurostar journey from London to Paris was effortless. The boarding process at St Pancras was painless enough and everything was relatively straightforward. Even taking her cello onto the train didn't create any problems. But once she arrived at Gare du Nord railway station in Paris, things didn't go quite so swimmingly. Things were no longer easy or straightforward. Negotiating her way through the station and finding a cab wasn't easy and the Parisians she'd encountered so far had proved unhelpful and downright rude.

When she did eventually find a taxi, the unfriendly theme continued. After hearing Sophia's English accent the taxi driver decided to just stand there and watch her struggle to put her cello case into the car; offering no help whatsoever. Sophia finally arrived at her hotel and, as before, struggled to get her cello case out of the taxi by herself. After paying the driver, without a tip, she went into the hotel and hoped she might receive a little more civility there. The hotel staff were helpful enough, in a minimalist sort of way, but they hardly went out of their way to make Sophia feel welcome or comfortable either. *Does everybody in Paris hate the English?*

After dumping her things in her room and making sure her cello was safe, she went out to find a café where she could relax with a coffee and perhaps something to eat. After walking around the busy streets of Paris she found a nice looking restaurant on Boulevard des Capucines. Sophia sat at one of the tables on the pavement at the front of the restaurant and looked at the menu, which was in French.

It was a busy street with lots of cars and vans driving up and down in a continuous steady stream. Hardly the peaceful environment she craved right now. A quaint little quiet café overlooking a small park in a less busy part of the city would have suited her better, but she wasn't prepared to trudge around Paris all afternoon looking for such a place, so this would just have to do.

'Madame, vous désirez déjeuner?' said a waitress.

'I'm sorry, I don't speak French,' said Sophia.

'Are you here to eat?' repeated the waitress, in pretty good English.

'No, just a grand crème, please.'

'Of course. A croissant perhaps?'

'Maybe later, thank you.'

The waitress disappeared inside the restaurant. In the meantime some of Sophia's fellow diners had heard her English accent and were looking at her. The fact that Sophia had bleached blonde hair and was dressed somewhat provocatively gave them reason to talk amongst themselves – in French. One old lady sitting next but one table away mumbled something in her husband's ear while looking at Sophia. *Was that a disapproving look on her face, or is that how she always looked?*

'Is there something I can help you with?' said Sophia, shooting her a *look*. The old woman mumbled to herself again as she cut off a large corner of her croque madame and put it into her mouth. *At least you can't mumble anymore while you stuff your stupid face with food.*

Sophia looked at her watch, more for something to do than anything else. She was getting impatient sitting here with no coffee and feeling self-conscious with Parisian eyes on her. *Christ, how long does it take to make a cup of coffee?* She got up to go into the restaurant to find out what the delay was, just as her waitress made her way out with her grand crème.

'Un café crème – voilà,' she said, deliberately in French, as she rudely slammed the grand crème on the table. She quickly turned on her heels and went back inside. *How rude.*

'What did you have to do, roast the bloody beans yourself?' shouted Sophia after her, giving her fellow diners even more ammunition.

'Is she giving you a hard time?' said a young French man, helping himself to the other chair at Sophia's table, uninvited. She was just about to tell him to get lost and leave her alone when he spoke again. 'Not all French people are quite so rude,' he said, trying to convince Sophia.

'Really, because I was beginning to think it was a Hate-The-Fucking-English national holiday around here,' she said, putting sugar in her coffee, not even bothering to look up at her uninvited coffee guest.

'I couldn't help noticing from back there that some of the other diners were giving you dirty looks. So, I thought I'd come over and try and make you feel a little more ... comfortable,' he said. Sophia glanced up from her coffee just long enough to catch his friendly smile. 'I'm Sébastien. Do you mind if I join you?' he asked.

'It looks like you already have ... Sébastien,' she said, looking up at him with a wry smile.

'There, I knew there was a little smile hidden under there somewhere,' he said.

'Well it's difficult to smile when you're surrounded by rude people who don't smile back at you,' she said. Now that there was a French man sitting with Sophia, the other diners got back to their own business.

'Parisians can be a strange bunch. They generally don't smile unless they mean it. And they like foreigners to make an effort to speak French,' he said.

'Well I guess I'm screwed. I never got on with French at school. It's such a difficult language to learn, I don't even know how French people can speak it,' she said.

'Well, just try and ignore the locals and don't take it personally. Parisians can be especially rude to English people who don't speak any French. And many were just born rude, self-centered and ignorant,' he said, smiling. Sophia let out a little laugh.

'So, you're not from Paris then?' she asked.

'Do I appear rude to you?' he said, laughing again.

'No, not at all,' she said.

'I am not from Paris. I come from further south. So,

Sophia

where in England are you from?' he asked.

'Really? Is that the best you can come up with? I'm sure you really don't care where I'm from,' she said, expecting a more sophisticated chat-up line.

'I'm serious. My parents are both English, I was born there,' he said.

'You're kidding me?'

'No, they bought a house about fifty kilometers north of Toulouse and moved there when I was one. That's why I have a strong French accent.'

'So how did you end up in Paris?'

'I study here.'

'What do you study?'

'Art.'

'Are you serious?' she said, laughing.

'Oui, my father was a painter and there's a history of painters in my family. I'm told I have a great talent too. So, I'm here to fine tune my gift and hopefully become a famous artist.'

'What do you paint? Not contemporary nonsense I hope.'

'Oh no, I prefer landscapes with cottages, horses and rivers and trees. I'm more of a Constable than a Pollock,' he said, smiling.

'Well, Sébastien, I'm relieved to hear it. The last thing the art world needs is another bloody contemporary painter.' He smiled at her.

'Would you like another coffee,' he said, his eyes hopeful.

'I'd love one, thank you.' Just then, the old croque

madame eating woman's husband approached Sophia's table.

'I'm sorry to bother you. Just my wife does not speak English. But she is a huge fan. She says your playing unlocks many musical mysteries and speaks to her like no other. We have tickets to come and see you tomorrow night. But, in the meantime, would you be so kind as to autograph this for my wife,' he said, handing Sophia his wife's diary, open at today's date. Sophia looked over to where the old woman was sitting; she now had a smile on her face. Sophia took the diary off her husband and asked for her name.

'Isabelle,' he said. Sophia signed the diary to Isabelle. The old man looked at what Sophia had written and smiled.

'She also told me to tell you she likes your new hair colour,' he said. He then returned to his wife at their table. Isabelle took the diary off her husband and read it, then smiled and held it like it was some sort of precious artifact to be cherished.

'You're a famous musician?' asked Sébastien. Sophia just smiled at him. 'What do you play?'

'I'm a concert cellist.'

'And you are playing here, in Paris … tomorrow evening?'

'Yes.'

'Wow, this is incredible. You must tell me where, I'll come and see you play.'

The waitress arrived with a fresh grand crème and something or another in a glass for Sébastien. 'You know, when I first glanced over and saw you, I thought of Pamela Courson – you look just like her, except you have much lighter hair.'

'Pamela who?' she asked.

'Courson. She was Jim Morrison's girlfriend.'

'As in The Doors Jim Morrison.'

'The one and only,' he said.

'So, you're a Doors fan?' she asked.

'Oui, very much. I like a lot of rock music from the sixties and seventies. But I especially like The Doors. How about you?'

'You mean do I like The Doors?'

'Oui.'

'I can't say I do. I know some of their songs. Light My Fire, L.A. Woman … oh yes, Riders On The Storm. That's about it though.'

'Well you're missing out. You must buy two of their albums. The first one, simply called The Doors, and Strange Days.'

'Do either of those albums include Riders On The Storm?'

'No, that's from the album L.A. Woman.'

'Ok, so maybe when I get back to England I'll buy those three.'

'Very good,' he said. 'You know, he's buried right here in Paris.'

'Who?'

'Why Jim Morrison of course.'

'Is that a fact?'

'Oui,' he said.' For some reason, Sébastien seemed to

slip back into French when it came to saying "yes"'. I could take you to see his gravesite if you like – I mean, if you are not too busy. He's buried in Père Lachaise Cemetery; it's a huge tourist attraction,' he said, with enthusiasm.

'Sébastien, you really know how to show a girl a good time,' she said, smiling. 'I don't think a man's ever asked me to go to a cemetery before.'

'Well, it's an incredible place. You really must see it while you're here,' he said.

Sophia found his enthusiasm infectious. His French accent had gone up an octave in pitch as he enthusiastically told Sophia about the cemetery.

'Is it far from here?'

'No, about fifteen minutes in my car.'

'*Your* car?'

'Oui, it's parked just around the corner.' *Well, he seems harmless enough.*

'Ok, why not,' she said, not having much else to do that afternoon.

'Great. I'll go and get my car. I'll be back in five minutes,' he said, dashing off. Moments later he pulled up outside the restaurant in a bright yellow classic Mercedes 450 SL convertible – **not what she was expecting.**

'Wow, this is different,' she said.

'Isn't it,' he said, with a big proud smile on his face. She climbed into the passenger seat and they drove off.

'How old is this?' she said, noting the lack of airbags and other modern day comforts.

'She was made in 1979.'

'She? Please tell me you haven't given your car a name?'

'No, I just see cars as feminine. Just like in French, *une voiture*,' he said.

'Why don't you drive a modern car, it would be safer?'

'Modern cars have no character – they all look the same. This car, it has history, a story to tell. She has done many miles and has travelled to many places.'

'I bet she has. Look, is there anywhere we can stop to buy some bananas?' asked Sophia.

'You want to eat bananas, right now?' asked Sébastien?

'Not right now. But I need one for my recital tomorrow evening.'

'You need a banana for your recital?' he questioned.

'I always eat a banana in the green room, about half an hour before I go on stage.'

'Why?'

'It's just a habit I picked up from music college. Banana's contain potassium and it not only gives you energy, but it also acts as a beta-blocker too.'

'A beta-blocker?'

'Yes, it calms your nerves and helps you relax.'

'Well, I'm educated,' he said, smiling. 'There's a place not far from the cemetery where you can buy some,' he said.

'Thank you.'

Sébastien parked up on Rue de la Roquette opposite the main entrance to Père Lachaise Cemetery. He decided they didn't need a guidebook or map. He also explained that the tour was useless and took away any actual meaningfulness from the experience.

'It looks huge, do you know where to go?' she asked.

'Oui,' he said. 'I've been here many times. I often come here when it's quiet, it helps me relax – like a beta-blocker,' he said, smiling.

They walked along the main walkway and then deviated onto a small winding pathway. As Sophia soaked up the sights she found herself in awe of the wonder of the place. It was beautiful and serene, yet kind of creepy all at the same time.

'You know, there are many famous people buried here.'

'Really, like who?' she asked.

'Chopin, Rossini, Edith Piaf, Moliere, Bernard Shaw, Oscar Wilde,' he said, as they ambled along the winding pathways. Sophia was saddened by the obvious signs of vandalism that had taken place over the years. *Why would anybody want to come into a beautiful cemetery to destroy tombstones and spray graffiti?* she thought.

'You're right, this is better than the tour,' she said, after previously spotting a group of Japanese tourists being ushered along by a young tour guide. 'I much prefer taking things at my own pace,' she said. As they walked along she became aware that they were holding hands. *How did that happen?* she thought. But his warm hand felt nice holding hers. Before she knew it, two hours had passed. She'd seen the burial places of Chopin, Edith Piaf, Oscar Wilde and of course, Jim Morrison. At Morrison's grave Sébastien educated her with another of his useless snippets of information.

'Did you know that it was Jim's wish to be buried in this cemetery. But after his death when his friends approached the cemetery about burying him here, the director refused to admit him. But when they mentioned that Jim was a writer, the director said "A writer?" and promptly found a spot for him.'

'Is that a fact?' she said.

'Oui, it's absolutely true.'

As they walked and Sébastien talked, hand-in-hand, Sophia felt a familiar uncontrollable urge rising inside her; or rather the urge of her new dark side. She freed her hand from his and put her arm around his waist instead – more intimate. He reciprocated. As they passed a tightly packed cluster of small tombs she found herself navigating him between them.

'You want to look in here?' he asked.

'Why not,' she said, continuing to navigate deeper into the cluster of tombs until they were hidden away in the middle of them – nobody else around. She stopped and pushed him backwards into a seven-foot high tomb and kissed him. Once he took in the taste of her lips and her scent it was impossible for him to refuse. He kissed her back, wanting to taste her again. Her soft lips, her sweet taste, her warm breath. His senses had been so busy taking her in, he didn't realize she'd undone his trousers and her hand was in his pants. Here she was again. For the second time she found herself in a cemetery about to have sex with a total stranger. But it felt good, really good. She grabbed his cock and massaged it, moaning into his mouth in anticipation. Impatient, she went down on him, to fully prepare him for her. He moaned as Sophia expertly encouraged a rock-hard erection.

Then she came up and whispered in his ear. 'Your turn,' she said, pushing him down onto his knees. While he undid her trousers she kicked off her shoes.

'Do you think I should use a dental dam or something?' he said, questioning Sophia's cleanliness and suspecting she might be promiscuous.

'A what?' she said.

'A dental dam, it's for protec—'

'I know what they're for. Did I ask you to put a condom on before sucking your cock? I don't think so. I want to feel your tongue, not a piece of fucking latex,' she said, pushing his face closer. He obliged, cautiously at first, and then he got into the moment. *What the hell*, he thought, as he went for it. When she was ready she pulled him up by his hair. They were both worked up and at a sexual high. She turned away from him and leaned forward against the tomb. He didn't need any instruction or encouragement. He penetrated her from behind and within seconds he was fucking her hard and fast.

When it was over they made themselves respectable and sneaked out from between the tombs and back onto the winding pathway. It would appear that a quick fuck was a good cure for Sébastien's verbal diarrhea. He didn't say much as they walked through the cemetery back to his car. Sophia bought three bananas then Sébastien dropped her back at her hotel.

'Can I see you again?' he said.

'Look, Sébastien, it's been fun. But boyfriends are for Christmas, not for life. I'm not the girl you think I am.'

'What do you mean?' he enquired.

SOPHIA

'My mind isn't my own right now. Take it easy ok,' she said, getting out of his car and vanishing from his life.

Chapter 34

The following morning Sophia decided to go to the concert hall venue early to do a quick recce and practise there before the recital that evening. As she sat in the stationary taxi at a junction she noticed a tattoo parlour. In the window she saw a striking black, red and white butterfly.

'I'm sorry, can you let me out here,' she said. The taxi driver pulled over and let Sophia out. After paying the driver she stood on the pavement next to her cello case browsing the various tattoo designs in the window. The one that appealed was the one that caught her eye from the taxi. Underneath the striking illustration of the butterfly was a caption reading, *Crimson Rose (Pachliopta hector)*. It was predominantly black in colour. Its fore wings had two white detached irregular broad streaks, while its hind wings had a curved series of crimson spots, which looked striking against the black wings. *It's so beautiful*, she thought.

'Do you speak English?' she said to the lone heavily tattooed woman in the shop.

'Yes,' she said. She was in her early thirties, thin, with long black hair, goth make-up and tattoos all over her arms, neck, navel, and probably other parts of her anatomy that weren't visible. Sophia had never been in a tattoo parlour before, and she had never seen a female tattooist. But, if she had to guess what one looked like before today, she probably would have pictured a woman just like this.

'I'm interested in the black, red and white butterfly in the window,' she said. There were only a few butterfly designs in the window, this being the only black, red and white one.

'The Crimson Rose?' said the woman, taking the cardboard display out of the window. She pointed it out on the design chart.

'That's the one,' said Sophia.

'Would you like me to do it for you now?'

'Could you? I mean, don't I need to book an appointment?'

'Normally you would, but I'm quiet and have a few hours before my next booking.'

'Will it take long?'

'No, about an hour.'

'Ok, but when you do it, I'd like you to leave out the red and white markings.'

'So you want it all black?'

'Not exactly, I only want you to do the black parts of the butterfly, leaving the red and white parts empty.'

'So where the red and white colours should go you just want to see your skin?'

'Yes.'

'Ok, where would you like it?'

'On my right shoulder blade, so it's hidden under my clothing.

The woman got Sophia comfortable on an appropriate chair, prepared the area and stencilled on the outline then got to work.

'Out of curiosity, why no colour?' said the tattooist, as her needle buzzed away.

'Let's just say I'm having a strange relationship with my dark side right now. I'm not ready for any colour in my life.'

Forty minutes later she'd finished the butterfly tattoo, about two inches in diameter and minus the vibrant colours. She put a dressing on the area and explained to Sophia about hygiene and how she should look after the area until it heals.

Sophia took a taxi from the tattoo parlour to the venue. After being shown around the concert hall and the green room, Sophia got her cello out and played through a few pieces on the stage to get a feel for the acoustics. After about forty minutes she started to feel a little nauseous. She went to the bathroom, thinking she might actually vomit, but she did not. Perhaps this was how a person felt after having a foreign body injected into the skin via a tattooist electric needle. She went back to her hotel, had an extra sweet cup of tea then lay down to rest for the afternoon.

While Sophia sat eating her banana in the greenroom,

SOPHIA

she could hear people arriving and the auditorium rapidly filling up. There was a knock at her door.

'Come in?' she said.

'Fifteen minutes, Ms Beckinsale,' said the backstage usher peering around the door.

'Thank you,' she said, catching him glimpse at her exposed thigh as she sat there cross-legged. He closed the door and Sophia was alone again. Even though she'd done this hundreds of times Sophia always found the solitariness of her profession a little difficult to come to terms with. Being a soloist is not like any other profession. It's not like you have work colleagues around to give you moral support, or people to hug you or pat you on the shoulder and tell you that everything is going to be ok. Being a concert cellist is a lonely occupation that requires endless hours in isolation. Sophia studies alone, she practises alone, she visits venues alone, she sits in the green room before a recital alone, and if she is playing solo works, she even performs on stage alone. She does get some relief when rehearsing with Django or her other accompanists for those recitals that require it. She also gets some interaction when she works with orchestras for concertos in larger venues. But for the most part, she is alone in her world.

But today something was different. As she sat in the green room she didn't feel the usual lonely isolation associated with a solo cello recital with no accompanist. Strangely, she felt relieved to be alone. In fact she felt positively comfortable in her own company – well, her and her new-found dark side.

In the auditorium she could hear the house manager making an announcement on stage. 'Mesdames et Messieurs,' he began. She could only pick out the odd word here and there. '… téléphone,' he continued. He was obviously telling the audience to turn off their mobile phones. Sophia gave her bow one final coat of rosin and checked her tuning once more. As there was no accompanist for this recital there was no piano to tune up to, so tuning up on stage wouldn't be necessary. The backstage usher knocked on Sophia's door to tell her it was time. He instructed Sophia to wait, momentarily, at the bottom of four wooden steps that led up onto the stage. 'Mesdames et Messieurs Veuillez accueillir, Sophia Beckinsale,' announced the house manager, to the loud applause of the audience. The co-ordination between the usher and the house manager was timed to perfection. The house manager left the stage via the other side. The usher then gestured for Sophia to go onto the stage. As she walked onto the stage from the right the audience applause increased.

But within seconds, the audience noticed her clothing and the applause quickly started to fade.

While in Paris, Sophia had visited some rather unique and unusual ladies clothing shops and had stocked up on some rather unorthodox garments. As she went through her ritual curtsey routine – to a much quieter applause than usual – the audience got the full extent of Sophia's outrageous outfit. Even this broad-minded Parisian crowd were a little shocked by her choice of attire for this evening's recital. As usual, Sophia made a big deal out of her curtsey, taking her time over it. Only this time she had to make a few subtle changes as she was not wearing a typical long dress so she didn't have anything to hold with her right hand as she took her curtsey. Instead, she simply held her right palm out to her right as she slid her left foot across the stage floor, positioning it behind her right. She slowly knelt down to the floor; various leather straps attached around her waist and on her knee length leather boots creaked as she did so. As she lowered and bowed her head, the audience nearer the front observed her outfit, which was made up of long leather boots with a multitude of straps and buckles, a white Victorian style blouse covered with a deep reddish brown corset. Her right forearm was covered with an elongated dark brown leather strap, while her left arm had three wide leather wrist bands in black, deep red and dark brown from wrist to just below her elbow. Her dress barely covered her thighs revealing a few inches of flesh before her black and brown woollen stockings started, held up by two tan coloured leather and lace garters. On both hands she wore fingerless black fishnet gloves with her fingernails painted black and purple. The bulk of her hair had been bunched up high on top of her head with long strands that had worked themselves free and trailed down her face and neck. She'd piled on foundation, a lighter shade than she typically wore at recitals and had piled dark shadowy make up around her eyes. Although Sophia was not familiar with the *Steampunk* look, she had managed to inadvertently pull it off spectacularly.

She finished her curtsey ritual and sat down. As she

adjusted her rubber spike strip and positioned her cello she heard a few mute mumbles coming from the front two rows. But as soon as she started to play the mumbles dissolved into silence.

Her bow glided elegantly across the strings; the vibration of the strings producing the sweetest of sounds. The beautiful surreal tones that Sophia produced quickly reminded the audience why they were there. They soon forgot about Sophia's costume and warmed to her as they were taken on a musical journey like no other. All except one lady sitting in the front row just to the right. Sophia was half way through the Prelude from Bach's Cello Suite number four when she noticed her. This woman wasn't paying any attention to Sophia; she wasn't even listening. Instead, she was reading a book. Sophia, with her acute musical ear, had heard the lady turn a page. The woman was about forty years old and going by her dress and general deportment, she was obviously quite wealthy.

Sophia could not believe the arrogance of this woman. *Why is she even here?* She thought. Sophia abruptly stopped playing, mid-bar, mid-note and mid-bow stroke. She sat perfectly still with her bow still pressed up against the D string and her fingers still holding down the note. Sophia glared at the woman, who was still oblivious to what was going on, or what wasn't going on. Other members of the immediate audience followed Sophia's eyes to the woman in the front row. It was only when she turned the page of the book she was reading that she realised the auditorium was silent. Her page turn was deafening in the eerie silence. She looked around her and noticed people in the audience looking at her, then she looked onto the stage and saw Sophia glaring down at her with a look that was halfway between sinister and pure evil; if looks could kill. Embarrassed, the woman closed her book and placed it on the floor between her feet and gave Sophia her undivided attention. With this, Sophia continued to play exactly where she left off. Her bow continued its stroke, playing the last half of the very same note where she'd paused. It was as if a pause button had been pressed in Sophia's mind, then pressed again to continue twenty five seconds later. Most musicians would have gone back to the beginning of the bar, or phrase, or even piece. Actually, most musicians would have continued playing, ignoring the woman; but not Sophia, and not today. She demanded the undivided attention of her audience's ears.

When the recital was over, as usual, the audience demanded an encore; this is where things got very interesting. Sophia would typically come back onto the stage to perform a short three-minute piece. And sometimes she would come back again to perform another short piece. But this time, she came back out onto the stage and played the first Popper Etude. After she performed it, the audience applauded, but Sophia did not stand to curtsey, nor did she leave the stage. Instead, while the audience were still applauding, she started to play the second Popper Etude, then the third, then the fourth, and so on and so forth. Until, eventually, she played the fortieth and final Etude. At a total of

85-minutes, this crazy stunt would almost certainly go down in history as one of the longest encores ever performed.

All over the world, the media got hold of it and jumped on it. One English music critic had written a piece for a national newspaper, which included:

Playing all forty of the Popper Etudes back-to-back must have been an exhausting feat as they are all pretty relentless. What was even more amazing was that not a single member of the audience left the auditorium during her strange choice of encore. Miss Beckinsale took 85-minutes to complete the forty etudes, but the audience was totally captivated for the duration. Miss Beckinsale's lengthy encore reminds me of a story about the famous concert pianist, Rudolf Serkin, who, when he was just 17-years old, played the Bach Goldberg Variations as an encore. This came about by mistake after his German violinist friend, Adolf Busch, pushed Mr Serkin back out onto the stage after his recital was over, saying he should play an encore. "What shall I play?" asked Mr Serkin. "The Goldberg Variations," replied Busch, as a joke. Serkin took him seriously and went out and played them for the next 35-minutes. The key difference between that encore and Sophia's 85-minute encore last night was that at the end of Mr Serkin's endeavour there were only four people left in the auditorium –himself, Adolf Busch, Arthur Schnabel and the musicologist, Alfred Einstein. How Miss Beckinsale kept every member of the audience rooted firmly in their seats during a set of forty etudes is beyond me and I doubt anybody will ever witness such a strange musical phenomenon ever again.

Apart from the brief pause because of the book-reading woman, the recital had been a huge success. As usual, Sophia had the audience in the palm of her hand. The fact that her practising had taken a back seat in recent weeks did not show at all. She was as musical and virtuosic as ever. The audience were mesmerised by her formidable playing and the sheer purity of her interpretation. For the most part, the media had concentrated on Sophia's incredibly long encore, and not her outrageous outfit.

Chapter 35

Sophia had barely been back in England five minutes when her mobile rang.

'Hello?' she said, seeing Martina's name come up on the display.

'Well it's about bloody time. Where've you been and why haven't you returned any of my calls?' she said. Sophia knew a rant was coming as she'd ignored all Martina's calls and messages while she was in Paris.

'Look, I don't work for you and I don't want anything to do with you. In a nutshell, there's no reason for you to ever phone me again.'

'I'm afraid things aren't quite that simple. You complicated things when you decided to play *It's A Knockout* with a champagne bottle and Corrado Mancini's head. While you were gallivanting around in Paris, Mr Mancini paid me a visit and in not so many words told me there's only one way for me to keep my business and for you to keep your fingers.' *Mancini must have told her I was in Paris.*

'Look, I've told him, and now I'm telling you. Go to hell and don't ever call me again,' she said, pressing the *End* call button on her mobile. Naturally, Martina

SOPHIA

called back within seconds, but Sophia turned her phone to silent and ignored her calls. Several calls and three messages later, Martina eventually gave up.

Sophia's mind was not her own and she just couldn't get any kind of routine together. She didn't feel like doing anything and she certainly didn't have any motivation to practise right now.

She spent the entire afternoon pacing up and down in her apartment. She wandered aimlessly from her living room, to her bedroom, to her kitchen. Her brain felt like it was all tied up in knots and she just couldn't focus or think straight. She fixed herself another Vodka and Coke in the kitchen and then went back into her living room. Hours had passed yet her thoughts had shown no sign of clearing. *Maybe I should call DJ? ... or perhaps Delphine?* She thought. Then she looked at her reflection in the mirror on her living room wall. *Who the hell are you?* she thought, trying to figure out exactly what she had become. She stared at her reflection and looked straight into those unrecognisable eyes. Whose eyes were they that looked back at her so intently? She just stood there and stared right into them without blinking. It was as if she was trying to psych out the girl in the mirror. Sophia continued to stare right through those eyes in the mirror, as if trying to understand them and learn about the person looking back at her. Then her imagination ran wild as her focused staring induced a hallucination. The face in the mirror started to contort, taking on a monster-like demonic appearance. Its eyes changed colour and became deep red with large black pupils. The demon's mouth opened revealing row upon row of elongated razor sharp teeth. Then it smiled briefly at her before letting out a deafening roar. Sophia, startled, threw her glass of drink at the mirror, shattering the demon into hundreds of tiny shards of glass. She stood there looking at the pieces of broken mirror all over the floor and the remains of her Vodka and Coke dripping down the wall. Then she was yanked out of the surreal moment and back to reality by the sound of her doorbell. She'd be happy to see anyone right about now; anything to help pull her back to reality. She ran to the front door and without checking the spy-hole, flung it open. Standing there were two middle-aged men in suits. One was quite stocky and his ill-fitting suit jacket looked two sizes too small. The other was of average build with a slightly better fitting suit, but with a gaudy vibrant green tie. Both looked equally menacing.

'Our boss wants us to have a little chat with you,' said green tie. Sophia went to slam the door.

'Oh, nu, nu, nu, nu, no,' said the stocky one, jamming his foot in the door before pushing it open with such force it knocked Sophia backwards into her hallway. The two men invited themselves in, closing the door behind them.

'It seems you have some unfinished business with Mr Mancini,' said green tie. Sophia was now firmly back in reality.

'Get out, before I call the police.' With this, the stocky one grabbed Sophia by the throat and pinned her hard up against the wall with his large meat hook of a hand.

SOPHIA

'I don't think you fully understand,' said stocky, with his face just inches away from Sophia's. She could smell his disgusting breath. She spat in his face.

'Fuck you,' she said, under the grip of his podgy hand. Green tie sighed and moved closer to Sophia, taking something out of his pocket.

'You know, I really don't want to have to go down this road, but if you don't start co-operating I'm afraid you'll leave me no choice,' said green tie.

'Go to hell,' she said.

'Ok, have it your way,' said green tie, gesturing for stocky to turn her around. Stocky grabbed Sophia's hair with his other hand. The next thing she knew, she'd been spun around, her right arm was twisted up her back and her right cheek was pressed up hard against the wall. Stocky held her arm so far up her back it felt like it would break if he moved it up another centimetre. She squealed in agonising pain. Green tie held a pair of secateurs against the wall in front of her face. 'I hear you play the cello ... not for long,' he said, grabbing Sophia's left hand and prising open her middle finger.

'No!' she screamed as she felt the cold steel blades of the secateurs close around her finger. The blades pinched into her skin. 'Please, no,' she pleaded. The pain of her right arm was excruciating and the secateurs blades were cutting into her finger.

'Do I have your attention?' said green tie.

'Yes, yes,' she pleaded.

'Mr Mancini wants you to do something for him. If you don't, you're going to start losing fingers. And then when you run out of digits, we'll move onto your little sister, Charlotte, and then who knows what next,' he said. He sounded angry, pissed off and serious all at the same time. He put his mouth right up against Sophia's ear. 'Now, in my pocket I have an envelope, and in that envelope is a very specific set of instructions, instructions which you're going to follow. And if you don't complete this little task, well, I think you know what's going to happen,' he said, tightening the grip on the secateurs further still, causing the blades to cut deeper into the skin around her finger. Green tie released the secateurs, leaving her finger intact, then looked at stocky and gestured for him to release her. Sophia's arm fell down to her side; she could hardly feel it. She held up her left hand and noticed blood coming from the two small cuts either side of her finger. Green tie grabbed her hand and slapped the envelope into it. Then stocky took out a tiny bottle with a little rubber air plunger on top. It looked like one of those small eyedropper bottles you buy at the pharmacy.

'You'll need this as well,' said stocky, grabbing her other hand and putting the tiny bottle into her palm.

'What's this?'

'Everything you need to know is in that envelope, I suggest you read it without delay' said green tie.

'We'll be back the day after tomorrow to pick it up; nice and early,' said stocky.

'You have a nice evening,' said green tie. They left, not giving Sophia a chance to ask any more questions. When her apartment door slammed, she looked at her finger and was thankful it was only two small cuts. After fixing a plaster around it she examined the tiny bottle, then opened the envelope and started to read.

Chapter 36

The envelope contained details and instructions for Sophia. A businessman was going to be staying at Le Grand Hotel in Piccadilly the following night. In his possession he was going to have a small aluminium briefcase, the contents of which were worth a lot to Mr Mancini. Knowing that this businessman, a Mr Dino Vacanti, likes his women and also likes a drink or two, Mancini had instructed Sophia to pick him up in the hotel bar, where he would probably be from about 8 p.m. Because Mancini knows Sophia has had her little dabble with being a call girl, he knows that she shouldn't have too much trouble seducing Vacanti, getting him back to his room and relieving him of said briefcase. That's where the small bottle comes in. She suspected it contained some sort of tranquiliser as the written instructions said it would take effect pretty much straight away, and then he would be out cold for hours. All she had to do was squeeze a dropper full into his drink once they were in his room. *Great*, she thought. But as she pondered she knew she had no choice because they'd made it crystal clear that they would not stop at Sophia, they would move onto her younger sister and there was no way she was ever going to let that happen.

The next morning Meredith called Sophia and told her to check her email then call her right back. The email contained a PDF attachment of a page out of *Le Figaro*, one of France's largest national daily newspapers. There was a three-quarter-page photo of Sophia with the headline:

VIOLONCELLISTE ANGLAISE CHOQUE SON PUBLIC AVEC SON LOOK STEAMPUNK PROVOCATEUR

Which roughly translates, *English Concert Cellist Shocks Audience With Sexy Steampunk Look*. Naturally Sophia could not read the article as it was in French. But going by the revealing angle of the photograph, she suspected it was not going to be a complimentary article.

'Hello, Meredith. I've just looked at the attachment.'

'So, do you want to explain it to me?' she said.

'Well, I can hardly do that. I can't read French.'

'Well, my daughter can, and I can tell you, it doesn't look good.'

'What does it say?'

'Well, right at the end of the article there's a short paragraph saying what a brilliant musician you are. But the other ninety percent of it concentrates on your provocative and outrageous choice of clothing. My daughter tells me your outfit was steampunk. Can you explain exactly what that is and why you chose to wear such an outfit?'

'Not really, there was no design to it, I just threw some garments together that I'd bought in Paris. I've never heard of steampunk either.'

'Well, my daughter thinks it's cool, but I certainly don't. And it's hardly fitting attire for a respectable concert cellist.'

'I'm not really sure why it makes such a difference what I wear at my recitals?'

'Sophia, offending the French, broadminded as they are, is quite a difficult thing to do, but somehow you managed it.'

'Why would they be offended? I wasn't naked for crying out loud.'

'Well from what I understand of the article, you might as well have been. A picture speaks a thousand words, Sophia. Your thighs are naked and I can practically see your underwear.' Sophia couldn't help laughing to herself. For a moment Meredith sounded like her headmistress telling her off.

'It's no laughing matter. Sophia, you can't carry on like this or your career's going to be seriously damaged.'

'Meredith, I'm sorry, but now really isn't a good time.'

'Why has your life turned into such a crisis, Sophia? You need to get whatever it is you've got in your system out – once and for all,' said Meredith.

'Well, you can't spell catharsis, without crisis,' said Sophia.

'Darling, what's happening? I wish you'd talk to me. I'm deeply concerned about you.'

'I'm just going through something right now.'

'Darling, you know I'm here if you need to talk?'

'I know, Meredith. But I really must get off the phone. I'll speak to you soon,' she said, then hung up the phone. Sophia didn't actually need to get off the phone for any reason other than she could feel her dark side rising inside her and she wanted to try to shield Meredith from it. Kicking off and being abusive towards Meredith would not be good for her working relationship with her. Instead, she set about coming up with a master plan for relieving Mr Dino Vacanti of his briefcase that evening.

She arrived at the NCP car park in Brewer Street at 7:30 p.m. After checking the tariff she figured if it took her until midnight to achieve her goal it was going to cost her £25. She'd rather it didn't take that long, not to save money on the car parking fees, she just wanted this to be over and done with as soon as possible. She made the short five-minute walk to Le Grand Hotel and ordered herself a drink and tried not to look too conspicuous. She'd tried to dress down a little, nothing too bright or vibrant or revealing, but sexy enough to get Vacanti's attention. She wanted to appeal to this guy, but she didn't want to draw too much attention to herself either.

She'd studied the instructions in the envelope as well as memorizing the included photograph. Vacanti looked in his early forties. He had short black hair, cut neatly and wore an expensive looking tailor-made suit. Mr Mancini said the picture was only taken a few weeks previously, but that was no assurance that he'd be wearing the same suit tonight; so she forgot that part in her mental picture as she studied everybody who came into the bar. Wanting to keep a clear mind, as clear as was possible considering her internal somewhat volatile dark friend, she stuck to drinking Apple and Mango J2O. She'd drunk three bottles of the stuff, been to the toilet twice and was about to start her fourth when, there he was, and in he walked. Bold as brass, he just walked right in as if he owned the place. *Well, aren't you the confident bastard*, she thought. Sophia had positioned herself at the opposite far corner to the entrance to the bar. She'd picked a spot hidden away in the corner, where she wouldn't stand out, but had a good view of the entrance and everybody who came in. However, before Mr Vacanti even got to the bar, he spotted her watching him. '*Shit*,' she thought, quickly looking down at her glass. She wondered if it was her vibrant blond hair that caught his eye. She could hardly dress that down and wasn't about to go all 007 by cutting it short and dyeing it dark brown.

The next thing she knew, his shadow had fallen across her table and he was standing right in front of her. She looked up at him. He didn't look like a gangster. *What's the connection between this guy and Mancini? And more importantly, where's his aluminium briefcase?* She thought. It certainly wasn't with him.

'May I join you,' he said, delicately caressing the stem of his glass, 'if you don't already have company that is?' Sophia considered this for a moment, though she knew

SOPHIA

damn well that she was going to let him, but she wasn't going to make it easy, or obvious. 'I'm sorry, how rude of me. I expect you get this a lot. Forgive me,' he said, turning to walk back to the bar.' *Shit*.

'Wait,' she said. Vacanti turned around, 'You're Italian?' she asked, still trying to keep just enough distance not to be obvious.

'Yes, yes I am. Is my accent that obvious?' he said.

'You speak very good English, but the Italian's still quite prominent.'

'Have you ever been?' he said, still not sitting down or placing his drink on the table. He was obviously a gentleman and was not going to settle at the table until he was invited.

'To Italy?' she said.

'Yes.'

'A few times,' she said.

'Whereabouts?'

'Well, if you'd care to sit down I'll tell you.' He smiled and placed his drink on a placemat on the table.

'My name's Dino,' he said, extending his hand.

'Christine,' she said, almost as a reflex. She felt strangely comfortable lying about her name, perhaps because she'd had a little experience using this fake name at the dinner party with Delphine. She shook his hand. He sat down and got comfortable.

'So, where did you visit?' he asked.

'Florence,' she said.

'Ah yes, a very beautiful city. I've been there many times. Do you know people there?'

'Yes. A friend of mine moved out there a few years ago, we stay in touch and I go and visit her sometimes,' she said. She was surprised at how easy the lie came. She'd never lied to anybody about anything right up until the accident and Spencer's death. She couldn't tell a lie if her life depended on it. But her new dark side had schooled her well in her new ways, of which lying was one of them. Sophia had been to Italy a few times to give recitals, once to Florence, but she was not about to divulge any personal information to Mr Vacanti.

It soon became apparent that Vacanti was something of a Casanova and she could see why. He was charming and had dark, handsome, Mediterranean good looks. They talked for the next three hours, during which time Dino consumed more and more alcohol while Sophia's mind was a jumbled mess of emotions as her dark side fought it out with her rational side. *I really want to fuck this guy, but I also need to get that briefcase. Or maybe I could just do both?* she thought.

Dino had drunk enough to put any other man under the table, but he didn't seem too phased by it and still managed to speak articulately and without slurring his words. *I suppose if you drink a lot, your body gets used to it?* Sophia stuck with her J2O, but her last drink had been a Margarita, to be sociable. She drank the final mouthful, then it came, the moment she'd been waiting for.

'How about I order us two more of these ... from the telephone next to my bed in my room,' he said, standing up with a confident smile on his face.

'Why not,' said Sophia. *You really are a confident bastard aren't you?* she thought. He extended his hand. Sophia took it and was led through the hotel bar, across the lobby and into the elevator. They exited at the forth floor and went to his room. It was incredibly luxurious and very spacious. There was a huge king-size bed against the wall to the right, and straight ahead were large floor-to-ceiling windows with burgundy velvet curtains. There was a mahogany desk with chairs and a couple of comfy armchairs as well. The walls were painted tastefully in a colour that could possibly be described as daffodil white. There was a door to her left, which she suspected led through to the ensuite.

Vacanti walked across to the telephone to call room service. While he was ordering two Margaritas, Sophia put her handbag over one of the chairs next to the desk. She scanned the room, pretending to be taking in the décor, when she was really looking for this aluminium briefcase. *Where the hell is it?*

'Make yourself comfortable, I'm going to take a quick shower,' he said, heading through the door to the ensuite. He closed the door and within minutes she heard the sound of water jetting from the shower. Then there was a knock at the door.

'Room service,' said a male voice. Sophia opened the door and a young waiter came into the room with the two Margaritas on a silver tray. He placed them on the desk.

'Thank you,' she said.

'You're welcome,' he said, heading out. This is going to be easy,' she thought, taking the small bottle out of her handbag. She looked over to the closed ensuite door, from behind which still came the sound of jetting water. She squeezed the rubber teat and released it, allowing the contents of the bottle to be sucked into the transparent tube. Then she squeezed it into the Margarita on the left. *Now, where's that briefcase*, she thought, putting the bottle back in her handbag and zipping it up. She checked under the bed, nothing. Then she looked around the room for any other nooks and crannies where it could be, but it was nowhere to be seen. *The wardrobe, that's the only place left.* She walked over to it and slid one of the two large doors open and scanned on the shelf at eye-level, then on the floor, but it was not there. *Shit,'* she thought, as she closed the door and moved left to open the other one. She was so wrapped up searching that she didn't notice the sound of water stopping. She slid the door open and right there on the floor was a small aluminium briefcase. Then a hand landed on her shoulder. 'Looking for something,' said Vacanti. Startled, she jumped with fright.

'Just somewhere to put my shoes,' she said, kicking the left one off and dropping it with her big toe into the wardrobe floor area next to the case. 'You made me jump,' she said, repeating the procedure with her other shoe.

'Come and have a drink, that will calm you down,' he said, sliding the wardrobe door closed and leading the way over to the drinks on the table. He picked up the two Margaritas and turned to Sophia. She noticed that the drink on the left, the drink she'd spiked, had been picked up by his left hand. That was *his* drink. Sophia's drink was the one in his right hand. *Shit, what if*

SOPHIA

he offers me the spiked one? she thought, as he walked over to her. To throw her concentration even more, he only had a small white towel wrapped around his waist. Even though, judging by his face, she suspected he might be forty, his body was that of someone ten years younger; it was firm and well toned. His olive skin, strong biceps and toned pecs excited her beyond belief. She wanted nothing more than for this guy to grab her up in those strong arms and carry her over to the bed, but first, she had to stay focused on those two drinks. What a dilemma. Her dark urges were in overdrive. She secretly prayed that whatever it was she'd put in his drink would take an hour to kick in.

'Here you go,' he said, extending his right arm with the *correct* Margarita. *Thank fuck for that.* 'To pleasures yet unforeseen,' he said, raising his glass. Sophia raised hers and gave a gentle clink. Then she took a large gulp, in the hope that this gesture would encourage him to do the same, which he did. She then downed the rest in one go. 'Wow, steady on,' he said.

'I'm just trying to loosen up and get in the mood,' she said smiling. Vacanti went to take another drink and gently sipped. Just when he was about to move the glass away from his lips, Sophia gently placed two fingers on the bottom of his glass and tilted it back up towards his lips, encouraging him to drink more and giving him her best sexy seductress smile as she did so. He obliged by drinking. She continued to push up with her two fingers until he finished it all. *That should do it.* He took her glass and placed them both back onto the silver tray before taking Sophia's hand and leading her over to the bed. She was backed up to it with her calf muscles pressed against the soft mattress. He stood back and observed her body with a look of pure delight on his face.

'I need to use the bathroom,' she said, heading for the ensuite and leaving him standing there half naked in just his towel. Walking away from him took serious will power as she battled with her thoughts. She had to fight off her dark urges and concentrate on getting that case, and getting away from him into the ensuite was the only way she stood any chance of doing that. Once inside, she closed the door and looked at her watch. *Come on, come on, take effect,*' she thought. While she was in the ensuite she made use of the toilet, not that she really needed to, but anything to pass an extra minute away from him without the temptation of his half-naked body. While she was washing her hands she caught her reflection in the mirror and saw a devilish girl staring back at her. *Fuck it,*' she thought, prettying up her hair with her fingers as she prepared to be fucked by the hunk of a Mediterranean god that awaited her. She could feel urges shouting at her from in her mind, as well as deep down below. Without further ado, she flung the ensuite door open and took up her previous position between him and the bed. Now that she didn't have the spiked Margarita to worry about she could concentrate on his strong naked body pressed against hers. He stepped forward and put his hands on Sophia's hips, sliding them gently down the outside of her thighs. He leaned forward and kissed her lips. She kissed him back pressing her lips harder against his before grabbing his waist and pulling his body into hers. Then she felt him, hard, pressing against her belly.

He knelt down and slid his hands up the outside of Sophia's legs and under her dress until his fingertips made contact with her knickers. He pulled them down, taking his time about it, while looking up into her eyes. His hands moved back up her legs, on the inside this time. Sophia tilted her head back and looked at the ceiling, giving out a gasp as his tongue came into contact with her inner thigh. His tongue drew a slow line up the inside of her right leg. Then, when it was literally half an inch away from *there*, his hands released their soft grip on her legs, and then she heard a thump as he slumped to the floor. She looked down and saw him slumped across the floor, eyes closed and out cold. '*Shit*,' she said, frustrated as hell. *Fuck*,' she thought, heading to the wardrobe. She slid the left side door open and while bending down to take out her shoes she looked over at Vacanti, who was still out cold on the floor. She put her shoes on then walked over and took her handbag off the chair. She then grabbed the aluminium briefcase on her way out the door.

Chapter 37

Sophia woke up in a hospital bed; she was alone on a large ward. The bright heavenly sunlight was slightly diffused by the white opaque net curtains covering the twelve windows down the long wall. The walls were clinically white and fresh looking, same for the ceiling. Everything was pristine and spotless and it smelt fresh. *But why is it so quiet, where is everybody?* she thought, as she lay there with her head and shoulders propped up on three plump white pillows while taking in her strange new surroundings. She looked down the bed at her arms, which were resting on top of the white sheet. Sophia noticed that her left hand was bound in bandages. She carefully lifted her left arm to study the thick dressing of bandages. She took a sharp intake of breath as she noticed the only fingers that remained were her thumb and little finger. As she held her hand out she could clearly see the bandage dressing pressed up against the remnants of three stumps. Perfectly formed little blotted circles of blood about the size of a ten pence piece sat on each one, with just a naked pinkie and thumb poking through the dressing either side. She wiggled her fingers and although she only saw her pinkie and thumb move, she felt all five fingers move. *How can this be, I can feel all my fingers right to their tips?* she thought, not quite understanding that what she was seeing and what she was feeling were two completely different things. Her brain could not grasp this strange medical phenomenon. *What happened, how did I get here?* Then she remembered green tie man threatening her with a pair of secateurs and panic set in as it dawned on her that she would never play the cello again.

'NOOOOOOOOOO,' she screamed. She continued to shout and scream and whip herself up into a state of frenzied panic. Her screams echoed through the ward and spilled out into the empty corridors. Strange, but she thought she heard her screams continuing down the corridors in the hospital with a surreal, yet somehow insidious delay. Her echoed screams sounded different somehow. Sophia silenced herself and leaned forward, propping herself up on her right elbow. Then she heard the screams again, in the distance, echoing from the far end of the corridor outside the ward. But it wasn't her screams echoing back at her; it was a sound she'd heard before. It was the familiar high-pitched bark-like screaming of a fox – *her* fox. She sat upright on her bed, frozen, looking over at the only doorway into her ward, about fifty feet away in the far right corner. The fox's screams were not like typical fox barks or mating calls, these were quite painful and horrific, and they were getting closer and louder until it was deafening and just outside her ward door. Then they stopped. Sophia was motionless, she couldn't move. Her eyes were fixed on the door as she held her breath. She felt faint, as her brain had not received oxygen for nearly a minute as she continued to hold her breath in fear of making a sound. She tried to breathe out quietly, before sucking in a quiet gasp of air. Somebody was standing right outside the door in that corridor; she could feel it as strong as the hot sun outside. She dare not speak as she sat there in a state of sheer terror. Then, it entered the ward.

It looked like Spencer, holding a fox in his arms, but it wasn't Spencer. Whatever it was, it wasn't human. As he started to walk towards Sophia, the fox struggled in his arms, but his grip was too tight. As the fox thrashed and wriggled and tried to get free, it looked perfectly normal, unlike the thing gripping it. As he approached, Sophia could see Spencer's features behind the demonic mask that had engulfed his face like an unsightly tumour. It used to be Spencer, until he was taken over and possessed by this ... *thing*. The fox looked at her with sympathy, unlike its evil captor whose fierce eyes looked straight into her soul. Then he was right there, at the foot of her bed. She pulled her knees and feet up to the middle of the bed away from him. Still, she felt physically weak and could not move any more than this. He leaned forward over her bed; the swollen demonic lesions on his face oozed and dripped blood and grey matter on to the pristine white bed sheet. He lifted his left hand up to reveal three missing fingers. With only one arm around the fox, it managed to free itself from his grip and leapt from his arm and on to the bed then down on to the floor. The fox ran across the ward and out of the

SOPHIA

door. Sophia looked back at the *thing*, still holding up its hand. There was no bandage, just bloody stumps. Blood started to jet out of the holes where his fingers used to be, showering onto the white sheet on her bed. The deep red blood went everywhere, there was so much of it. It soaked into the white sheet and was creeping up the bed towards her. She could still hardly move, as if this thing had seized control of her muscles. She tried to pull her feet up into her body further still to escape the rivers of blood, which were creeping faster up the sheet towards her. She looked at the blood, then up at the thing and started to writhe and struggle and panic. But it was no good, the sheet felt like lead and she could hardly move. The flowing blood soaked deeper into the sheet and just kept on coming, it was almost half way up the bed now and just inches from her body. She got it into her head that if the blood soaking its way up the sheet touched her body, she too would end up being possessed by this thing. She started to scream for help, but nobody came. The blood was just a few millimetres from her flesh under the sheet now; she could feel the warm heat of it as it drew closer. The metallic smell of slightly decaying blood filled her nostrils. She looked past the thing and saw a flashing fire alarm on the wall directly over its shoulder. It rang and rang and rang, getting louder and clearer with each ring. Then, she shot bold upright.

'Holy fucking shit!' she said, as she sat there panting, in her own bed, in her own apartment. Her doorbell continued to ring and ring. 'Ok, I'm coming,' she shouted, as she dragged her sweat-soaked body out from under her quilt.

As she grabbed her bathrobe off the back of her bedroom door she glanced at the clock. It was six thirty in the morning. She checked the spy-hole and saw the two men who were there two nights previously. Green tie, was wearing the same green tie. In her sleepy state she opened the door. The briefcase sat on her hallway floor. Out of curiosity, she'd tried to look inside, but the combination lock on the case prevented her from doing so. Instead she'd shaken the case, it sounded like it only contained papers. Green tie looked past Sophia at the case on the floor. He barged past without saying anything, picked up the case and examined it, paying particular attention to the two combination locks.

'Nice doing business with you,' he said, barging past Sophia with the briefcase. Then they were gone. Sophia closed the door and ambled to the kitchen, relieved not only because her dream was, a dream, but also because the ghastly business with Mancini and his unpleasant friends was over.

Chapter 38

Sophia had spent the whole day avoiding people by not answering her landline or mobile phone. DJ had been calling non-stop about the Beethoven rehearsals. Charlotte had called twice wanting to know why she hadn't called her for nearly a week. Her parents had called dozens of times, not only throughout the day, but pretty much every day. Sophia didn't even want to speak with Grandma Lizzie; instead, she let her answering machine deal with her call from the day before. The only person who was not being persistent with phone calls was Eleanor, which was understandable, all things considered. The only person she answered the phone to these days was Delphine, perhaps because Delphine didn't lecture her. Instead, she just let Sophia be herself, listened to her, accepted her for who she was, and tried to understand what she was going through. Delphine knew Sophia was going through something, and even though she didn't quite understand why she sometimes carried on the way she did, she understood it was a *process* and she had to go through it in her own way and in her own time. Delphine was quite intelligent that way. She understood that sometimes, even though you could see that somebody was about to make a big mistake, you had to let them learn and do things their own way and find out for themselves.

Out of her parents, Andrew had the better understanding of what Sophia was going though. Diana had got to the point where she felt frustrated with Sophia; like she was banging her head against a brick wall. Diana had lost most of her patience with Sophia's outrageous goings on; she simply could not understand it anymore.

It was 8 p.m. when Sophia's parents came around to her apartment to see her. When she opened the door she could see straight away that something was wrong.

'Darling, we need to talk,' said Andrew.

'What's wrong?' said Sophia, letting them in and closing the door.

'We've been calling you at home and on your mobile all day, I've left a dozen messages for you to call us right away,' said Diana, unable to hold back her tears.

'I just want to be left alone. I'm getting sick and tired of you lecturing me all the time, Mummy. That's why I don't come around anymore, and that's why I don't answer the phone when you call.'

'Darling, sit down, this is serious. It's about—'

'No, Daddy, she always does this. She doesn't have any fucking idea what's going on in my head, nobody does. How can you when I don't even understand it myself?' Sophia was shouting now and was positively wound up and emotional.

'Where on God's earth did you get that foul tongue

SOPHIA

and where did this nasty side to your character come from?' said Diana, equally angry and now crying hysterically.

'Sophia, sit down,' ordered Andrew.

'Why should I?' she shouted back.

'Because your grandmother's dead,' shouted Diana. Silence fell upon the room. Sophia stood there frozen while it felt like the ground had been yanked from under her.

'What, when? She only called me yesterday.'

'Eight o'clock this morning,' said Andrew.

'But, I don't understand, she was doing so well and showing signs of improvement.'

'I know, honey,' he said. Before the sombre moment could continue, Diana butted in.

'Ok, tell her the other thing,' she said. Again, there was silence as Andrew tried to summon his prepared speech to the front of his mind.

'What other thing?' said Sophia, looking at her father.

'Honey, your mother and I ... well, the whole family, we've had a long conversation and we think it would be a good idea for you to go to hospital.'

'Hospital, why would I need to go to a hospital?'

'To help you get better, honey. It wouldn't be for long, just a month.'

'But I'm not ill or si–' the penny dropped. Andrew looked at Diana as if to say, *There, I've said it, are you happy now?* Sophia suspected this wasn't her father's idea.

'You want to have me sectioned?' said Sophia.

'It will only be for a short while and it will be for you

own good,' said Diana.

'We've found an excellent private hospital. It's not how you might imagine it to be. You'll receive the very best attention and treatment,' said Andrew.

'I can't believe you've even looked into this,' she said.

'Obviously we'll wait until after Grandma's funeral,' said Andrew. Sophia didn't know what to say. With everything that had been going on recently, and now two huge bombshells had been dropped on her. *I won't go along with this*, she thought.

'I want you to go,' said Sophia. Soon afterwards, they did, leaving Sophia to take everything in.

It got to 10 p.m. and Sophia's head felt like a pressure cooker about to explode. Everything seemed surreal and she was finding it very hard to deal with her emotions, which were all over the place. She felt everything all at once: anger, depression, frustration, tearful and sad. Her mind would not sit still and focus, it zipped all over the place. There was only one thing for it. Sophia picked up her mobile and called Delphine.

'Hello,' said Delphine.

'What are you doing right now?' said Sophia.

'Not much, I've just got in.'

'Well, how would you like to go straight back out again? If I don't get out of this apartment I'm going to go crazy.'

'You want to come over?' said Delphine.

'I want to go out. How about we hit that West End club again?'

'Sure. Is everything alright?'

Sophia

'It will be just as soon as I've had a few drinks. I'll just throw something on and I'll be at yours in about forty minutes.'

'Ok, see you soon.'

Sophia arrived at Delphine's at ten forty in a taxi, and then they headed straight for the nightclub. During the short journey, Sophia briefly told Delphine about her grandmother dying that morning and her parents wanting her to spend some time in a psychiatric hospital; well, her mother at least.

Once inside the nightclub, Sophia wasted no time ordering herself a double Vodka and Coke. They noticed some people leaving over in the far corner so they ran over and snared their table. The nightclub was heaving and heavy dance music blared out over the PA. The thumping drums and deep bass radiated through Sophia's chair and into her spine. They'd only been seated a few minutes when Sophia went back to the bar for another double Vodka and Coke. Delphine could see that Sophia was hell-bent on getting wasted. She wanted to talk to Sophia, but the loud music made conversation impossible. Instead, Delphine worked it so she went to the bar to get the drinks, making sure the barman only put in the smallest dash of Vodka into Sophia's drinks.

Sophia leaned over and shouted into Delphine's ear. 'I'm going to the bathroom, don't let anybody take our table.'

Sophia had to queue for ages, and then a cubicle eventually became free. While she was drying her hands she noticed a young woman sniffing hard and wiping traces of white powder from her nostrils.

'Do you have any more of that?' she asked.

'Excuse me?' said the woman. Instead of repeating the question, Sophia gestured by brushing her nostrils with her finger.

'Oh,' said the woman. No, I only bought the one,' she said.

'Did you get it here?'

'Yes.'

'Can you show me who?'

'Sure.' They left the bathroom and went back into the club.

'The guy with the black hair and black shirt,' she said, gesturing towards a sleazy looking character sitting on one of the comfy sofas in between two bimbos. 'His name's Dritan,' she said, walking away. Sophia walked over to his sofa in one of the alcoves. He was in his early thirties and looked like the kind of guy who had his fingers in all sorts of illegal and sordid pies. He wore a black silk shirt open to the naval, revealing his hairy chest and thick silver curb chain. His hair and eyes were as black as his shirt.

'Are you Dritan?' she asked.

'Who wants to know?' he said. The two bimbos either side of him looked Sophia up and down and gave her a synchronised look of contempt. One of them had her hands all over Dritan's leg, close to his crotch, while the other leaned against him while leering at Sophia.

'Somebody told me I could buy something off you.'

'Oh, and who would this somebody be?' he said, the two bimbos found this amusing and laughed.

SOPHIA

'Nobody special, just an undercover policewoman I met in the bathroom.' The smiles dropped from the bimbos' faces.

'Ha, you're really funny,' he said, smiling. He turned to face the bimbo to his right, 'Why don't you go and get me another drink,' he said, not phrasing it like a question, more an order. Like a good little bimbo, she kissed his cheek, 'Sure, honey,' and scurried off to the bar. Dritan patted the sofa next to him.

'Come, sit down,' he said, his accent clearly Albanian.

'I'd rather not, can you help me or do I have to go to someone else?' she said.

'Ooo, what's the matter, am I not pretty enough for you?' he said, stroking a long scar down the right side of his face.

'It's not that, I just don't like you,' she said, turning to walk away.

Dritan jumped to his feet and grabbed Sophia's hand, placing something in it. 'This one's for free,' he said, leaning closer to her face, ' because I like you. Now, if you want any more of that, you just give me a call.' Sophia looked down into her hand and saw a wrap of speed and a card with a mobile number on it.

'Tell me, why's a clean-looking girl like you taking drugs? You don't seem the type,' he said.

'You know, needs must when the devil drives,' she said.

'What?' said Dritan, with a gormless expression on his face.

'It's an old English proverb, aren't you familiar with it?'

'Obviously not,' said the confused Dritan.

'Don't worry. You wouldn't understand, you're Albanian,' she said, turning to walk away. Dritan grabbed her arm and pulled her back.

'Well, why don't you explain it to me anyway?' he said, getting slightly flustered.

'Shakespeare explained it best in All's Well That Ends Well. "My poor body, madam, requires it: I am driven on by the flesh; and he must needs go that the devil drives."'

'What the fuck are you talking about you crazy bitch?'

'I would have thought that the Shakespearean wording would have clarified the proverb for you - obviously not. Don't worry, it's really not that important.'

'Ok, I'm getting sick of this game, why don't you just tell me what the fuck it means? – in English.'

'It means, if the devil drives you, you have no fucking choice but to go. Or in my case, for some reason I can't quite fathom, events often compel me to do things I'd much rather not. Such as buy drugs from somebody like you.'

'Needs must when the devil drives ... I like that,' he said, releasing her arm. She looked at him briefly, then turned and walked back to her table dropping Dritan's card and the wrap of speed into her handbag on the way.

'Everything ok? I was about to send out a search party,' said Delphine.

'The queue in the ladies was a mile long,' she said, sitting down and taking out the speed.

'Where did you get that?'

'Just some guy,' she said, preparing to snort it.

'Shit, girl, you can't do that here,' said Delphine,

looking around frantically. But before she knew it Sophia had snorted the speed off the table and was knocking back the remainder of her drink.

'Let's dance,' said Sophia, grabbing Delphine's hand.

'I don't really feel like it,' said Delphine, hoping that Sophia would stay with her, and stay out of trouble.

'Please,' she insisted, pulling Delphine up by her hand.

'Ok, but just for ten minutes.' Sophia smiled and dragged Delphine onto the dance floor. Sophia danced frenetically. With her vibrant blonde hair and dressed the way she was, she was getting a lot of looks from pretty much every guy in there. Dritan had walked over to the edge of the dance floor, leaving his bimbos to keep his sofa warm. He watched as Sophia's dance became more flirty and tease-like as she wound the guys up around her. She kept this up for ages. Delphine's attempts to get Sophia off the dance floor and back to their table were futile. Sophia just wanted to dance, drink and snort more speed, which Dritan was happy to supply. Sophia was falling; spiralling down and out of control. Deeper and deeper she went, into her dark bottomless nightmare.

Chapter 39

The funeral service was held close to Lizzie's home in rural Kent. Sophia turned up at Grandma Lizzie's house just seconds before the procession was about to leave. She had driven down in her own car because Eleanor refused to be in the same car as her for the forty-mile journey. When Sophia arrived she found herself being the unwanted centre of attention and was getting some questionable looks. Diana rushed over to her, looking at her watch as she did so.

'Well you couldn't have left it any later if you'd tried,' she said. Andrew spotted her, and having noticed her chosen outfit for the day he decided to make a swift beeline to them before Diana caused a scene right there on the driveway. 'And what do you call that?' she said, in disgust, gesturing to Sophia's outfit, which looked like something Amy Winehouse might have worn on stage. It was a black satin cocktail dress that stopped just above the knee. From the waist down was a wash of black sequins sparkling away in the morning light. And to the sides and behind there were layers of black satin and netting material cascading down the back. 'That's hardly an appropriate dress for a funeral service,' she said. But it

SOPHIA

was when her father arrived and Sophia turned sideways to greet him that caused Diana to have a fit right there on the spot.

'Oh Lord, what on earth have you done?' said Diana, grabbing Sophia's arm and dragging her away from the house to have a stern word with her. Sophia's sleeveless dress only had two thin straps over her shoulders and she was no longer wearing the dressing over her all-new black butterfly tattoo. Sophia hadn't realised, well, it was on her shoulder blade after all.

'What is it? What's going on?' said Andrew, trotting after them.

'This, this is what's going on,' said Diana, spinning Sophia around like a mannequin and pointing out her tattoo.

'Sophia, you're going to have to cover yourself up. We can't have you sitting though the service with that on display,' said Andrew.

'Is that all you've got to say?' said Diana, furious with Andrew for not reprimanding their daughter for her lack of respect.

'Honey, what do you want me to do, put her over my knee. She's a bit old for that and this is hardly the time or the place to get into this. So, let's just get her covered up, people are starting to look,' he said.

'Do you have a jacket in your car?' asked Diana.

'No, Mummy.'

'Well, why didn't you bring one?' asked Diana.

'I forgot, I haven't been myself lately.'

'You can damn well say that again, young lady,' said

Diana. Andrew took off his suit jacket and put it around Sophia's shoulders. Charlotte came running over when she saw her sister. Eleanor was keeping her distance, doing her best to ignore Sophia.

'Sis, are you ok? I've missed you so much,' said Charlotte, hugging her.

'Ok, let's get ready to go. The cars are waiting,' said Andrew.

'Why are you wearing Daddy's jacket?' asked Charlotte.

'Because your sister decided to get a tattoo on her shoulder,' said Diana.

'Oh,' said Charlotte, a little shocked, but also a little curious to know what it was. 'You can wear my jacket if you like,' said Charlotte, taking it off.

'Thanks, sis,' said Sophia, taking her father's jacket off and handing it back to him. Charlotte didn't see the tattoo as Sophia put her jacket on, and she wasn't going to insist on seeing it at this delicate moment; it would have to wait until later. With Sophia covered up with Charlotte's respectable jacket the procession got underway.

Eleanor had insisted she sit as far away as possible from Sophia in the car to the church, but a car is a car and even the black Jaguar limousine didn't allow Eleanor to be seated that far from Sophia. Although Eleanor tried, for the sake of Lizzie, there was tension in the air.

Eleanor was relieved when they arrived at the church and wasted no time getting out of the car and away from Sophia. Eleanor kept this up during the service, making sure Andrew, Diana and Charlotte occupied the three seats between her and Sophia. Eleanor also made sure that her parents were standing between her and Sophia at the graveside.

They all drove back to Lizzie's house, where the caterers had prepared and laid out food. Again, Eleanor wanted nothing to do with Sophia, and Sophia knew it. Their eyes never met throughout the entire day.

Then it was all over. Everybody said goodbye and although Andrew and Diana were not about to get into anything with Sophia right after Lizzie's funeral, they did give her a look that suggested things had come to a head with her behaviour, and action had to be taken. Throughout the entire duration of the funeral, Sophia hadn't felt emotional or shed a single tear. She'd also had a *couldn't-care-less* attitude about her older sister, Eleanor. Her sensitive emotional side seemed to be well and truly under wraps; or at least something was keeping it there. But right now, even her darkest demons could not suppress her emotions, which had been simmering away in the background and were now brimming closer to the surface.

When Sophia found herself alone in the solitary confinement of her own car, it hit her all at once. She sat there in silence thinking about Grandma Lizzie, and how she never got the chance to speak with her properly, to say goodbye. But she'd had chances to say goodbye; she'd had lots of chances. But that *thing* in Sophia's head prevented her from taking them. She sat in her car on Grandma Lizzie's driveway and burst out crying. But no matter how hard she cried, the thoughts, the feelings, the flashbacks and the nightmares, none of them were going to go away; not today anyway. And now, poor Lizzie was in her head, along with all the other disorderly mess, adding to the pressure that was already on her mind. She could feel her blood pressure rising and the tension in her head was starting to pulsate behind her eyes and forehead. She heard conversations, voices, the screaming barks of the fox, Spencer's voice, and now Lizzie was jostling for space too.

She started her car and turned on the stereo and scrolled through the artists on the iPod hidden away in the glove compartment. Motorhead was the last band playing. She scrolled backwards a few artists until she got to Max Raptor, another band recommended to her by the skinny young trendy salesman at HMV. 'Mother's Ruin was definitely the most awesome album to come out in 2013. They're a loud, fresh, aggressive punk-tinged alternative rock band with raw guitar riffs that transcend genres. You've just gotta buy this album. And they're British, from the Midlands', is how the young salesman had described them. *That should do the trick*, thought Sophia, wanting to disperse the onslaught going on inside her head. She pressed play and turned up the volume, loud. She pulled off Lizzie's drive and out on to the main road. She accelerated up to speed as 'Back Of A Barrel Wave' blasted out over the car stereo, filling every crevice in the car. The loud music certainly made the forty-mile journey back around the outskirts of London to Hampstead more bearable. It took two complete plays, loud plays, of the album to get Sophia

SOPHIA

the sixty-five minute journey.

Chapter 40

The day after the funeral Sophia received a phone call from her father, insisting that she go to visit them so they could talk. Well, she knew exactly what talking would entail. There was no way on earth she was going to spend any time in a psychiatric hospital. So, instead of going to visit her parents, she packed some bare essentials and went to Delphine's apartment to stay with her for a while.

'I really appreciate this, Delphi, it'll only be for a few weeks,' she said, lugging her overnight bag into Delphine's apartment.

'Hey, you can stay as long as you like,' she said.

'Look, I'll sleep on the sofa ok. Crashing out in your bed after a drunken night out is one thing, but I won't invade your bedroom as well as your living room,' said Sophia.

'Look, we'll work something out ok. I was about to make a stir-fry, would you like some?'

'That sounds great, thank you.'

Over the next few days Sophia rarely left Delphine's apartment. When she did, it was usually to visit the shop around the corner for comfort food. However, on the

SOPHIA

first day, after noticing that Delphine had a fifty-five inch HD television and a Blu-ray player, she did visit HMV in Gower Street to buy some DVD movies for escapism. She'd taken her mobile phone with her, but had not switched it on since she arrived at Delphine's place. If Delphine wanted to call her while she was out, she'd call the landline number in her apartment, knowing that Sophia would probably be there.

After four days, Delphine could clearly see that Sophia was definitely not right. She knew that she was still going through a difficult time since Spencer's death, and she was not showing any signs of pulling through. In fact, she was getting worse, much worse. Delphine could see that Sophia was sinking into a deep state of depression, even though she was putting on a brave face when Delphine was around. The only relief for Sophia was when the evening came around. She would dim the lights and watch a movie; sometimes with Delphine when she was not singing at the club or entertaining a client.

Delphine ambled out of bed at 11:30 a.m. having got back late from the club the previous night. She found Sophia sitting in the living room staring into space. Sophia didn't even notice Delphine standing in the doorway.

'Hey, are you ok?' asked Delphine, rubbing her eyes.

'Oh, yes, fine. I didn't notice you there. I must have been miles away.'

'I'm going to make a coffee, you want one?' she asked.

'No, I'm ok,' said Sophia, getting up and following

Delphine into the kitchen.

'So, how are you?' said Delphine, opening the fridge.

'I'm fine,' said Sophia, sitting down at the breakfast table.

'No, really. I mean ... how are you, Sophia?' she said, in soft gentle tones.

Sophia sighed and rubbed her temple. 'I miss him, Delphi, I miss him so much.' Delphine could see that Sophia was about to cry so she put her arm around her shoulder and kissed her on top of her head.

Sophia had spent the previous few hours trying to push the darkness out of her mind, so she could try and remember some of the good times she'd had with Spencer. She didn't want the demonic Spencer screaming away in her head, or the fox barking in pain, or any of the other thoughts that had dominated her mind recently. Instead, she longed for nice thoughts, thoughts of making love with Spencer, the tender loving moments they had together, the warm fuzzy feelings she felt whenever she was near him, the longing she felt when he was not there. She battled with whatever it was she had to fight in her mind, but struggled to seek out moments of clarity.

The state of being alone, without Spencer, didn't hurt quite as much now as it did at the beginning. The sharpness of Sophia's pain had muted into a permanent dull ache. But the feelings were still there; the loneliness, the loss, the aching, the longing, the emptiness. It would always be there, running in the background. These feelings were going to be the underpinnings of her life.

SOPHIA

'I think I'm going crazy, Delphi. Really, I feel like I don't own my own mind anymore. Maybe I do need help, maybe there's something really wrong with me. I've been stuck in here for the past few days trying to figure it out, but I can't. My mind's a bloody emotional junkyard and God knows what else is going on in there. I don't feel right, Delphi; there's something strange happening to me.'

'Look, you've been stuck in here for days. I think you need to get out. So how would you like to go out and see a band tonight?' asked Delphine.

'I really don't know if I'm in the mood.'

'I think it will do you good.'

'I don't know, Delphi.'

'It's close, the Electric Ballroom just around the corner. They're a really great band and my friend's the bass player. And I'm already down on the guest list, plus one.'

'Ok.'

'Great,' said Delphine. 'Look, I've got to get ready, I have to see a client this afternoon but I'll be back by about seven, ok?'

'Sure.'

After Delphine had left, Sophia grabbed her handbag for her lip balm and while searching for it she stumbled upon Dritan's card with his mobile number on it. Dealing with an unsavoury Albanian drug dealer was not something Sophia relished, but, *needs must when the devil drives*, she thought, as she powered up her iPhone to call him.

Later that evening when Delphine got home she found Sophia extraordinarily upbeat and raring to go.

'Ok, whatever it is you're on, can you share some with me?' joked Delphine. But before long she suspected Sophia really was on something as she was acting like a woman who had just scored the winning goal in the ladies FA cup final.

Delphine got changed and while she fixed herself a drink she continued to analyse Sophia, who was getting louder and starting to act like an annoying bitch with her incessant gibbering.

'Ok, what did you take, Sophia? You're obviously on some sort of high. You're acting a little crazy right now.'

'I just needed a little something to pick me up,' she said, heading into the living room. Delphine noticed several paper wraps on her coffee table.

'What the hell are they and where did you get them?' asked Delphine.

'It's nothing, just a little cocaine that's all. I bought them off Dritan.'

'Who the hell's Dritan, and please tell me he didn't come here to my apartment?' Delphine gave Sophia a stern *look*.

'He's a drug dealer I met the last time we were at that nightclub. And no, he didn't come here, silly. I went to him.'

'Wait a minute. I don't remember you meeting anyone that night.'

'It was when I was coming back from the bathroom.'

'What, and you just happened to bump into him?'

'No, there was a girl taking speed in the bathroom

and I asked her where she got it, and she pointed him out to me in the club.'

'What kind of name's Dritan?'

'I think he's Albanian.'

'Sophia, I'm worried. I don't want you mixing with people like that.'

'Yes, Mummy,' she said, laughing away on a high. Delphine walked over to her and grabbed her shoulders.

'Sophia, I'm deadly serious. Please, promise me you won't do this again ... promise,' she said, shaking her shoulders.

'Ok, ok. Can we go out now?'

Sophia grabbed her coat and, while Delphine was not looking, she slipped one more wrap of cocaine into her handbag.

It only took five minutes to walk to the Electric Ballroom from Delphine's apartment. When they got there the queue was non-existent, as Delphine was not too fussed about seeing the support act. Once inside they managed to squeeze their way to the front, where the crowd were quite rowdy. After ten crazy minutes and three loud rock songs later, Sophia could feel the effects of her cocaine wearing off so she left Delphine and went to the bathroom for another hit. When she returned she was positively frenetic, as she grabbed guys around her, trying to force them to dance, to the annoyance of some of their girlfriends. Then the inevitable happened.

'Hey, take your fucking hands off my boyfriend you bitch,' shouted a young woman, pushing Sophia in the chest.

'Don't you fucking touch me,' said Sophia, pushing the woman back. The woman slapped Sophia in the face so hard she lost her balance and fell to the floor amongst the many dancing bodies. The woman's boyfriend restrained her and managed to calm her down while Delphine helped Sophia back to her feet. Delphine, being very protective of Sophia, gave the woman a look and shouted, 'Touch her again and I'll fucking kill you.' The woman read the look on Delphine's face and understood it loud and clear. She stepped to the other side of her boyfriend and got back to enjoying the band. Sophia was too high to let the mishap spoil her fun and before long a willing young man was indulging Sophia with her crazy dance moves and flirty antics. The band's set was almost over. Delphine shouted into Sophia's ear that she was going to the bathroom. But when Delphine got back, Sophia was not there. Delphine looked all around, but she was nowhere to be seen.

Outside, Sophia was crossing the road with Liam, the guy she'd spent the last five minutes dancing and flirting with. His car was parked just a few streets away. Sophia was still high and talking a lot. Liam wasn't paying too much attention to her constant gibbering. They got into his car and drove off towards his place.

'So, how far away is your place, Liam?' asked Sophia, giggling away and being seriously over the top.

'Not that far. At this time of night we'll be there in five minutes.' They soon arrived at Liam's ground floor one bedroom flat, which was just the other side of Hornsey Lane Bridge. He led Sophia into his flat, the effects of

SOPHIA

cocaine still working it's magic on her. She was positively excited and full of energy. She was high on cocaine and she found this young Irishman insanely attractive. All she could think about was ripping his clothes off to see those toned pecs under his tight t-shirt. She wasted no time. His bedroom was off the hallway and the door was half open. Liam was heading for the living room, until Sophia grabbed his arm, pulled him back and pushed him through the half-open door into the bedroom. She bundled in after him and pushed him onto the bed. Sophia was insatiable and rampant as she grabbed at his t-shirt and tore it along the seam with her impatience to get it off.

'Hey, take it eas–' but Sophia grabbed his head and started to French kiss him before he could finish his sentence. She was like a crazed sexual lunatic – out of control. The sex was manic, and unprotected. First Liam was on top, but Sophia felt too energetic so she jumped on top and rode him non-stop for the next fifteen minutes. Her body was glistening with sweat as she thrust herself back and forth until she'd had all the pleasure and orgasms she could take.

'Jesus, I've never experienced anything like that before,' said Liam, lying next to the motionless Sophia. 'Hey, you want a drink?' he said, getting up and heading to the kitchen.

'Yeah, anything cold.'

Liam returned with two cold cans of Sprite and handed one to Sophia. 'Do you have anything else, I think the coke's worn off.'

'I don't have any coke, but I can roll a joint if you like?'

'Sure,' said Sophia, not entirely sure what the effects of a joint would be as she'd never smoked one before. But there's a first time for everything. Liam went back to the living room and came back a few minutes later with an extra large joint. He lit it up, took a few drags, put an ashtray next to the bed and handed the joint to Sophia. Inhaling the first drag caused her to cough, but she soon got used to it. As she drank her Sprite and smoked the joint she could feel a dark wave of depression washing over her and engulfing her soul. The cocaine had worn off and she was on a serious downer and the joint wasn't helping. After about thirty minutes Sophia felt like she was in a dark dungeon and the overwhelming feelings of depression were closing in from all sides. Liam's bedroom was getting smaller and everything was starting to turn in that slow nauseous sort of way.

'I've got to get out of here,' she said, struggling to get up and get dressed in her stoned condition.

'Are you ok? Do you want me to call you a cab?' he said, genuinely concerned.

'No, I need the fresh air,' she said, finally managing to put her shoes on.

'Well, will I see you again? Can I give you my number?' he said. But Sophia was ambling out of the bedroom and making her way to the front door, holding onto the corridor wall as she did so.

'Please, let me call you a cab,' said Liam.

'No, really, I'm fine. I just want to walk in the night air to clear my head. I'll be ok, really,' she said, just wanting

SOPHIA

to walk. She grabbed the handle of the door and pulled it closed, leaving Liam inside.

She ambled along Hornsey Lane. The night air felt good, but she felt sick and her head was spinning from the joint. As she got to Hornsey Lane Bridge she looked up at the night sky. It was dark, everything around her was dark, inside and out. Then she started to think about Grandma Lizzie and how she didn't get to say goodbye while she was still alive. Then everything dawned on her all at once. She didn't have Spencer anymore, Eleanor hated her and didn't want to know her, and her parents wanted to have her sectioned. The thoughts, the guilt, the depression, the dark *thing,* it was all too much. Before she knew it, she'd kicked off her shoes and had climbed six feet up onto the central concrete post on the bridge, cutting one of her hands on the spiked railing in the process. She looked down onto Archway Road, it was a long way down onto the dual carriageway below. It was nearly two o'clock in the morning and there was hardly any traffic, just the occasional car, truck and taxi. Holding onto the metal streetlamp post she balanced herself on the concrete pillar. Although it was a sixty-foot drop, it looked a lot more than that from where Sophia was standing. She looked down at the grey asphalt below. It was lit by streetlamps and looked strangely welcoming like a warm, deep, blue outdoor swimming pool. The night air was perfectly still, even from up there high on the bridge. She let go of the small metal streetlamp that was fixed into the concrete pillar and, balancing tentatively for a moment, she let herself fall forward.

She felt the wind rush against her face and body as she plummeted down towards the concrete below. Her stomach rose up into the back of her throat. The impact of the asphalt below was just a fraction of a second away. She opened her eyes wide then in an instant, she saw a white flash. Then – nothing.

Chapter 41

'Oh my God!!! Did you see that?' said a young woman, looking towards the point on the bridge where Sophia had just jumped.

'Yes,' said her boyfriend. The young couple were about fifty yards from the bridge and even though it was two o'clock in the morning there was enough moonlight and street lighting for them to clearly see a young blonde-haired woman jump off the bridge. They ran as fast as they could along the bridge to the spot where Sophia jumped. They looked down, but saw nothing. The man heaved himself up onto the concrete pillar, so he could lean over a little to get a better view straight down below, but there was no body on the road.

'I'm going to call the police,' said the woman.

'Good idea.'

Within minutes a police car arrived and two male officers jumped out of the car. The couple explained that they had just witnessed a woman jump off the bridge.

'You say she jumped from this point right here?' said one of the officers, patting the concrete pillar. The other officer was relaying information over his walkie-talkie while walking across the bridge and looking down towards the road for any sign of a body.

'Yes, right here,' said the woman.

'And where were you at the time?' asked the officer.

'We were back there, we hadn't reached the bridge yet,' said her boyfriend. The officer gave them a questioning look.

'Look, officer, we're telling you, a woman definitely jumped. I know it's dark, but we know what we saw. She was tall and slim with long blonde hair,' she said. The other officer came over to them. 'There's no sign of a body, not on the road or caught up under the bridge,' he said.

'What are you both doing out at two in the morning?' asked the first officer.

'We're on our way home. We've been to a friend's party,' he said.

'I see,' said the officer.

'Officer, my boyfriend and I are teetotal. We know what we saw.'

'Ok, but I must warn you, if this is some kind of sick hoax you'll both be prosecuted for wasting police time,' said the officer.

'We don't care,' said the woman. 'All we care about is what happened to the woman we just saw jump off the bridge.' The officers assessed the situation and decided they were telling the truth. The second officer got back onto his walkie-talkie and reinforcements were called in.

Sophia

Ten minutes later at ten past two in the morning a large lorry pulled into its depot just off Holloway Road. It reversed up to the loading bay where it was met by warehouse staff. The back of the lorry was opened and the warehouse staff proceeded to unload its contents, which consisted of various materials such as rolls of leather, cloth, wadding and thick padding to make sofas, armchairs and cushions. They were about a quarter of the way through the unloading process when one of the warehouse staff noticed a large tear in the vinyl roof with a gaping hole in it.

'Well, how do you suppose that happened?' he said to his work colleague, who in turn studied the inside of the lorry scrupulously.

'Look,' he said, pointing to a pale limp arm that was poking out from between two very large rolls of white wadding material. They both scrambled to unload the contents of the lorry, which prevented them from getting to the person who lay deep in the middle of the lorry's load. They eventually got close enough to see a female body lying motionless. She was on top of a large industrial size roll of white sofa wadding, with two more rolls jammed either side of her. One of the guys started to pull a roll away, which was holding Sophia's body firmly in place, balanced precariously on top of another large roll of wadding.

'Wait,' shouted the other guy, as he noticed that his colleague moving the roll was causing Sophia to slowly slip off the roll she was sprawled across. The rolls were about seven foot high each and Sophia was starting to slide off. As she slid down the side of the roll, the man closest ran between the gap that had formed and managed to catch Sophia in his arms before she hit the hard wooden floor. He gently lay her down.

'She's alive,' he shouted. 'Call an ambulance now.' His colleague pulled his mobile out of his pocket and dialled 999. By the time the ambulance and the police arrived, Sophia was awake, but dazed and confused and still with traces of cocaine, alcohol and cannabis in her system. She was taken to Whittington Hospital off Highgate Hill, where she was treated for her numerous superficial scrapes and bruises.

The white flash that Sophia had seen just before hitting the road wasn't one of those final white flashes that people are supposed to see right before they die, but the bright white vinyl roof of the long, large lorry that had passed under the bridge, and under Sophia, just a fraction of a second before she would have hit the road. Sophia had plunged through the tough vinyl roof and into several large industrial rolls of furniture padding. She was not knocked unconscious, at least not by the impact, but she did catch the left side of her chest on the edge of an industrial size cardboard box, which was enough to leave her with a nasty elongated graze.

The police put two and two together. After questioning the driver about his route and the exact time he passed under the bridge on Archway Road, they concluded that Sophia had fallen through the roof of his lorry, saving her life in the process. The driver explained to the police that he thought he heard a thump, but he assumed he'd hit a pothole in the road. His lorry was huge and the cab was well and truly isolated from the large storage section of the lorry behind. He was shaken up, but relieved to find out that the girl was ok with only minor injuries. He told the police that he was familiar with Suicide Bridge, which is what the locals call it, and he would never take that route again. But after the police explained that if he'd taken another route that night the young woman would be dead, he decided to stick to that route in future after all.

Chapter 42

The doctor had told the police that Sophia was in no fit state to talk to them and they would have to come back. The police accepted this and, as they felt Sophia was in good hands, they didn't feel the need to leave an officer with her at the hospital, but they would be back later to speak with her.

Sophia's parents arrived at the hospital and were told to wait in the relative's room. Shortly afterwards a doctor and a policeman arrived. Andrew and Diana stood up when they entered.

'Mr and Mrs Beckinsale?' asked the doctor, entering the relative's room.

'Yes. What happened, is she ok?' said Andrew.

'She's going to be fine. She's incredibly lucky,' said the doctor.

'It's a miracle that lorry passed under the bridge when it did,' said the policeman.

'Your daughter's been taken upstairs onto one of the wards. She's been treated for a few superficial cuts and bruises, but nothing serious. She just needs to rest, but she's going to be just fine,' said the doctor.

'What lorry? What bridge?' asked Diana.

SOPHIA

'Well, we haven't spoken to your daughter yet, but it looks like she might have tried to kill herself,' said the officer.

'I'm sorry, you're going to have to explain, officer,' said Andrew.

'Two witnesses saw her jump off sui–' the officer quickly corrected himself from saying "suicide bridge", 'Hornsey Lane Bridge. But just as she did a lorry passed underneath and she went straight through the vinyl roof and landed on some sort of soft furnishings. It's a miracle,' said the officer.

'Oh dear Lord,' said Diana.

'Can we see her?' said Andrew.

'Of course, she's a little dazed, and ... she's a little drunk and we think she might have taken something,' said the doctor.

'Taken something?' said Andrew.

'Does your daughter take drugs?' asked the doctor, 'I mean, the recreational type?'

'No, no she doesn't,' said Diana.

'We're going to have to speak with your daughter about this. One of my colleagues will be back at about eight thirty,' said the officer, leaving the doctor to escort them up to the ward.

Sophia was in a hospital bed propped up with three pillows under her head and shoulders. She had a small bruise under her eye, but that was from where the woman's ring had caught her when she slapped Sophia in the face at the Electric Ballroom the night before. There was also a nasty graze about two inches wide starting at her collarbone going down the side of her body from where she collided with a strong cardboard box in the lorry.

'Oh darling, what have you done?' said Diana, sympathetically as she gave her daughter a gentle hug. Andrew kissed her forehead, tears in his eyes.

'Darling, please tell us you didn't try to kill yourself?' asked Andrew, tears running down his cheeks.

'Daddy, I'm not happy. I don't know who I am anymore,' she said. The effects of the cocaine had almost worn off. So too had the joint she'd smoked.

Suddenly, Delphine came running across the ward. 'I got here as soon as I could. What happened?' she said. Andrew and Diana looked at Delphine, and then at Sophia.

'I'm sorry, who are you?' asked Diana, looking at her suspiciously.

'Mummy this is my friend Delphine. She's been really good to me.' This was all Andrew needed to hear.

'It's a pleasure to meet you, Delphine,' he said, extending his hand. As usual, Diana gave him a *look*. As soon as Sophia had been able to make a phone call from the hospital Delphine was the first person she called, then she called her parents. But she was not about to reveal the order in which she'd phoned them.

The hospital staff told Sophia's parents and Delphine that they had to leave and let Sophia get some rest. They did, but after Delphine had said goodbye to Sophia's parents in the car park, she went back in and sweet-talked one of the male night staff into letting her sit on

SOPHIA

the chair next to Sophia's bed for a while. He reluctantly agreed, and only on the condition that she didn't speak to her and let her rest. Back on the ward, Delphine sat next to Sophia and held her hand until she fell asleep.

Early in the morning two police officers, a man and a woman arrived back at the hospital to question Sophia about what had happened. Shortly afterwards Andrew and Diana arrived. They had both discussed the situation in depth and had decided that they should take Sophia home to their house to take care of her and help her get through whatever it was she was going through, once and for all. Diana had cancelled an important client who was due to come to her gallery that morning and had made the decision to really try and understand what Sophia was going though. Andrew had also cancelled his appointments for the day.

The police were not entirely happy after speaking with Sophia, but when they found out her father was a doctor they were happy for Sophia to be released into her parents' care, with the caveat that they seek help for their daughter without delay.

'Darling, your father and I have talked and we really want you to come home with us.' Sophia looked at them and considered what her mother had just said. 'Look, honey, I know I haven't been very supportive or sympathetic recently, but I really want to try and understand what you're going through now ok. I promise, if you come home with us I'll be there for you; we all will,' she said. Andrew held Diana's hand in support and gave Sophia an encouraging smile.

'Ok,' said Sophia. They had to wait until the doctor came around to assess Sophia, but once he did, and he'd given her permission to go home, Sophia left the hospital with her parents.

Chapter 43

Sophia's parents got Sophia settled into her old room and made her feel comfortable. Charlotte, keen to spend time with Sophia, had arranged to study at home for the next few days. Andrew had arranged for Jacques the psychologist, to come over that afternoon at short notice. And after speaking with some of his medical peers, he'd managed to find a suitable carer who could be with Sophia during the day while he and Diana were not there. Unlike the carer they'd hired after the car accident, this new one had a lot of experience with post-traumatic stress, depression and personality disorders.

Andrew and Diana had pulled out all the stops. As well as calling in Jacques and an experienced carer, they were both going to spend a lot of time listening to Sophia so they could really try and understand what she was going through and hopefully find a solution that would get her off her current path of self-destruction.

Sophia had insisted that a day carer was not necessary and she could look after herself just fine. But her parents had suggested that the carer would be good company for Sophia when they were at work and Charlotte was at university.

'Honey, Rachel's an excellent carer; she'll be very good for you. She's got a lot of experience and she might be able to help you get through this,' said Andrew.

'Honey, we're really trying to help, but we need you to try and work with us,' said Diana.

She reluctantly agreed. 'Ok, Mummy.'

What Andrew had said about the carer was true. Rachel was supposed to be excellent and came highly recommended and, by chance, she was available to help them for the coming weeks at short notice. But Andrew was also relieved that there would be somebody there to keep a close eye on Sophia. Andrew and Diana were worried she might try to kill herself again and they were leaving nothing to chance. They were going to be there as much as possible, so was Charlotte. Andrew had given Rachel all the details and stressed how important it was that she knew every move Sophia made and to watch her like a hawk when there was no family around.

Jacques arrived at three o'clock sharp and after a brief talk with Andrew and Diana, he went upstairs to Sophia's room. He tapped lightly on her bedroom door.

'Come in,' she said.

Jacques entered and saw Sophia sitting upright on the bed reading a book. 'Hello, Sophia.'

'Hi,' she said, briefly glancing up from her book. Jacques detected a lack of enthusiasm in her voice, so decided to make small talk instead of diving right to the crux of the issue. 'What are you reading?' he asked. Sophia angled the book slightly so the cover was facing him. *Me Before You,* read the cover. 'Jojo Moyes, I can't

SOPHIA

say I've read any of her books. Is it any good?' he asked.

'Well, it allows me to escape,' she said, still not looking up from the pages.

'What's it about?' he enquired.

'It's about a man who's in a worse position than I am, apparently,' she said, followed by a sigh, obviously not wanting to engage in this futile small talk.

'Sophia, I know you haven't relished our sessions recently, but your parents are very concerned about you, and so am I,' he said.

'Did they tell you what happened? Is that why you've come rushing over?'

'Well, they told me you'd been involved in an accident,' he said, not wanting to mention the word *suicide*.

'An accident, that's one way of putting it. Just cut the crap, Jacques. I see what you're trying to do. At least have the professional courtesy to be straight with me. They told you I tried to kill myself by jumping off a bridge, didn't they?' she said. This time she looked up from her book and straight at him.

'Well, they didn't exactly word it like that. They're not really sure what happened. Why don't you explain it to me?'

'I don't think so. I just want to be left alone to read,' she said. Jacques just looked at her. Sophia could feel his eyes on her and could no longer concentrate on her reading. She knew she was going to have to say something to get rid of him.

'Sophia, please,' he said.

'Look, I really don't remember what happened and I

don't know how I ended up on that bridge and I don't remember jumping off. All I can remember was waking up with a blazing headache in the back of a lorry.'

'You don't recall anything at all?'

'No, I remember going to see a band in Camden Town with Delphine. I think I might have picked some guy up and gone back to his place. It was all very hazy and surreal. But then I'd had a few drinks and was out of my head on coke,' she said.

'Cocaine?' he asked.

'Well it would be pretty bloody difficult to get out of your head on Coca Cola now wouldn't it?'

'Did you take anything else?'

'I think I might have smoked a joint.'

'Like marijuana?' he asked.

'Yes.'

After their session was over Jacques could clearly see that Sophia was getting worse. She was well on her way to being out of control and her path of self-destruction was showing no signs of letting up. He knew that if she carried on with the drink, the drugs and the sleeping around, things were not going to end well for her. And if it was a suicide attempt, she might try it again; and maybe succeed.

Jacques went downstairs and spoke to Andrew and Diana before leaving, outlining his concerns and suggesting a new course of action – a drastic one. The first part of this plan of action involved Andrew phoning Sophia's GP, Dr Cheung, and making a home appointment.

SOPHIA

The afternoon passed and the evening came and went without event. Sophia's parents weren't giving her any lectures and were trying really hard. Even though she could sense their constant presence, they were not putting her under any undue pressure. However, dinner felt a little awkward. Even though she was sitting at a familiar family dining table with her parents and younger sister, Charlotte, she somehow felt like she didn't fit in. Her parents and Charlotte barely recognised her. She wasn't interested in their usual dinner conversations about classical music, Mummy's art gallery, Daddy's work at Harley Street or Charlotte's dental studies and the like. Even when Charlotte was alone with Sophia, she could see that Sophia had some sort of façade going on and was not her usual open, loving sisterly self.

That night she had an undisturbed night and slept right through until 10 a.m. She ambled down to the kitchen to get herself a drink and found her father sitting at the kitchen table with a middle-aged woman. The woman looked at Sophia and smiled.

'Good morning, darling. How did you sleep?' said Andrew, getting up and kissing his daughter on the cheek.

'Good,' she said, rubbing her forehead with her eyes still half closed.

'There's tea in the pot, would you like some?'

'Please, and something for my headache if you have anything.'

'Sure, honey,' he said, pouring a cup of tea. 'Have a seat,' he said. 'Sophia, this is Rachel,' he said.

'Hello, Sophia,' she said.

'You're the carer?' she asked.

'Well, I'm a little more than that, but yes. I'm going to be around during the day to help you in any way I can. So if you need anything, anything at all, I want you to know I'm here for you,' she said. *Wow, where did Daddy find you?* She thought.

'Thank you,' she said.

Rachel was in her mid forties and could definitely benefit from going on a diet. She looked like one of those cuddly country farmer's wives. Her slightly ginger coloured curly hair matched her plump rosy cheeks.

'Here you go, darling,' said Andrew, putting a packet of Panadol Extra in front of her. She popped two of the tablets onto the palm of her hand and swallowed them with some tea.

'Darling, I have to go out, but I'll be back soon, ok?'

'Are you going to Harley Street?'

'No darling, I've cancelled my appointments for today.'

'So where are you going?' she asked. This was awkward. Andrew would never lie to his daughter so he had to answer this question carefully.

'I just have to go and see some people for an hour or so, I'll be as quick as I can though,' he said, hoping she wouldn't press him for more information.

'Where's Mummy?'

'She had to go to the gallery early to see an important client. But she'll be back at lunchtime.'

'Ok,' she said.

'Ok, I'll see you soon, honey,' he said, giving her a kiss on the forehead while giving Rachel a knowing glance.

SOPHIA

Great, now I'm going to be stuck here with the happy smiley elephant woman,' she thought. The first twenty minutes alone in the house with Rachel were awkward for Sophia. She didn't want her there and she didn't need her there, flapping around her like old mother hen.

'I'm going back to my room to read,' announced Sophia, topping up her cup of tea.

'Ok, dear. I'm here if you need me. I'll come up and see you shortly.'

'Sure,' said Sophia, heading out the kitchen door.

In her room she phoned Delphine.

'Hey, how are you?' asked Delphine, seeing Sophia's name come up on her mobile.

'I'm ok, I guess.'

'Are you still at the hospital?'

'No, I'm at my parents house. I'm going to stay here for a few days.'

'That's probably not a bad thing,' she said, sensing in Sophia's voice that she was not overly thrilled about it.

'Well, I'm not thrilled about it.'

'Do you want me to come over and see you later?'

'That would be nice. What time?'

'Early evening, about seven?' said Delphine.

'Great. Do you have a pen, I'll give you the address.'

Barely ten minutes had passed when there was a light knock on Sophia's bedroom door. Before she could answer, Rachel opened it and stuck her head around the corner.

'Just checking to see if you're ok, dear?' she said.

'I'm fine,' said Sophia. 'And if you have to come and

check on me every five minutes can you at least let me answer before just opening the door like that?'

'Of course, dear.' She closed the door and went back downstairs.

As the morning gave way to the afternoon, Sophia started to feel depressed and emotional. The fact that Rachel constantly interrupted her every ten minutes didn't help the situation either. Her depression was worse than the day before when she'd smoked a joint and was coming down from the cocaine. She wasn't really having withdrawal symptoms from the drugs as she hadn't been taking them long enough to form any serious kind of addiction. This was a different kind of addiction altogether, an addiction she still didn't understand.

Her car was still parked at Delphine's apartment in Camden Town so going out would mean calling a taxi and although her parents had not instructed her to stay in the house, reading between the lines, she knew that was exactly what they wanted her to do. Besides, if she did wander off anywhere, elephant woman would notice and report back to her parents. She suddenly had a craving for something sweet, so she went to the kitchen to look for some chocolate, biscuits, cake, anything. Rachel was sitting at the kitchen table with a drink.

'How are you feeling, dear?' asked Rachel.

'I don't feel like talking,' she said, grabbing a plate and opening the fridge. She prayed that Rachel would not try to strike up a mundane conversation. *God, I hate it when she calls me dear.*

'How's that scrape on your chest?' she asked, 'It looks

pretty sore.'

'Well how do you think it feels after falling off a sixty foot bridge,' she said. Rachel looked at her as if to question the *falling* part. Sophia really didn't like the way this woman was analysing her and watching her every move. She could feel her eyes on her as she took a slice of cheesecake out of the fridge and put it onto her plate. When she closed the fridge door and turned around, Rachel was giving her an analytical *look*. Sophia lost it and tossed her plate six feet across the kitchen, sending it skidding along the work surface and smashing into the tiled wall. The cheesecake made a mess up the backsplash and pieces of broken plate ended up on the side, in the sink and on the floor.

'Did I say something wrong?' said Sophia, giving Rachel a hard look. 'If you've got something to say to me, just fucking say it,' she demanded.

Rachel was shocked and didn't know what to say. She looked to her left and noticed Charlotte standing in the doorway. With all that was going on nobody had noticed her standing there. Sophia looked to her right to see what Rachel was looking at. Charlotte looked shocked at what she had just witnessed. In the background, the radio on the kitchen side played 'Where Is My Mind' by the Pixies. *How ironic*, thought Rachel.

'I don't need you here and I don't want you here. Why doesn't anybody understand?' said Sophia, turning to get another plate. She rushed around the kitchen and took another slice of cheesecake, a piece of homemade flapjack and some chocolate biscuits. 'I'm sorry you had to see that,' said Sophia as she walked past Charlotte and back upstairs. Charlotte followed her up to her room, knocked on her door and cautiously entered. Sophia was sitting on her bed, perfectly calm as if nothing had just happened.

'Are you ok?' asked Charlotte.

'Hey, sis. I'm fine, come on in and help me eat some of this.'

'Sophia, I'm really scared,' she said, sitting on the end of the bed.

Sophia looked at her sister, mid-bite of cheesecake. 'What are you scared about?'

'You,' she said, looking down at her hands, unable to look her in the eyes.

Rachel opened the door and entered, she didn't even knock this time. Sophia shot her a look.

'I'm just here to help. Your parents are concerned about you and they've asked me to come here to help you,' said Rachel.

'Watch me you mean. To make sure I don't do anything stupid like jump off a bridge. Just leave me alone. I want to spend some time with my sister.' Rachel could see that Sophia needed time to calm down, and she was satisfied that she would not do anything stupid with her sister in the room. She closed the door and left them alone.

Sophia turned back to Charlotte. 'You don't have to worry about me, sis, I'm ok.' Tears were starting to well in Charlotte's eyes.

'Did you jump off that bridge on purpose?' asked Charlotte.

SOPHIA

'Look, I wasn't in my right mind, I really don't remember what happened.'

'Are you in your right mind now?' Sophia looked at her and pondered for a moment.

'If I'm honest, I really don't know what my right mind is anymore. All I can say is that even though I'm not behaving rationally, it feels right to me. Most of the time anyway.'

'What do you mean?'

'I know I've changed and I've been acting a little crazy lately, but it doesn't feel crazy to me, it feels normal.'

'So if it feels normal, how do you know you're acting crazy?'

'I don't, other people tell me after the event and when I look back at it I can't really see or understand what the big deal was.'

'Sis, you're not the same anymore, everybody can see it except you.'

'Can you see it?' said Sophia.

'Yes, yes I can, and that's what scares me.'

'What do you see?'

'Well, I don't see my sister anymore, not the Sophia I knew before … well, you know.'

'Before Spencer died?'

'Yes.'

'Go on.'

'At first you were emotionally traumatised by what happened, which was totally understandable. But then …'

'But then what?'

'Then you started to change; it was like witnessing some kind of strange transformation. You became somebody else ...' Charlotte trailed off and started to cry.

'Don't cry,' said Sophia, putting her hand on Charlotte's shoulder.

'I just want my sister back,' she said, sobbing. 'I don't want anything to happen to you.'

'Hey, nothing's going to happen to me. Everything's going to be ok,' she said, not entirely sure what that meant, but she knew it might at least make her younger sister feel somewhat comforted; but it didn't.

When Andrew and Diana got home they were relieved to find Sophia well and reading a book in her bedroom. She seemed well, considering her recent volatile behaviour and her tendency to go from one extreme to the other – even throughout the course of a morning.

But then Rachel filled them in on the morning's events and the episode in the kitchen. Andrew and Diana tried to talk to Sophia, but she clearly didn't want to talk to them. Not about the kitchen fiasco or anything else. Then she was irritable and snapped at them every time they tried to talk to her. Whenever Sophia came out of her room to use the bathroom or go to the kitchen for a drink, she sensed that she was interrupting a private conversation. Her parents would suddenly stop talking or change the subject whenever Sophia appeared. *Something's going on,'* she thought.

Chapter 44

Delphine arrived at 7 p.m. as promised. She pressed the intercom buzzer at the main gate of Sophia's parents' house. After telling Diana who she was, the electric gate opened.

'That young woman from the hospital's here to see Sophia,' said Diana to Andrew.

'Which young woman?' he asked.

'The one who was at the hospital visiting her, Delphine.'

'Oh,' he said. Diana opened the front door, Andrew standing behind her. Delphine pulled up outside the house in her tatty sixteen-year-old green BMW, which attracted a *look* from Diana.

'Hello,' said Delphine.

'Hello,' said Diana.

'Nice to see you again,' said Andrew.

Sophia had heard the door and came down to greet Delphine.

'Well don't just leave her outside, Mummy, invite her in,' said Sophia.

'I'm sorry, please, come in,' said Diana.

'Hey you,' said Sophia, hugging Delphine. Diana

looked at Andrew, who was smiling, happy to see Sophia acting normal with her new friend.

'So, Delphine, what do you do?' asked Diana.

'For crying out loud, Mummy, can you stop it,' said Sophia, shooting her mother a *look*.

'What, I'm only making polite conversation.'

'No you're not, you know damn well what you're doing. Delphine's only been in the door two fucking seconds and already you're vetting her.' Diana inhaled sharply and put her hand over her mouth in shock at the way Sophia spoke to her.

'Let's just give Sophia and Delphine some space shall we,' said Andrew, putting his arm around Diana's shoulder and leading her away from a potentially explosive situation.

'Come on, let's go upstairs,' said Sophia. Delphine, slightly embarrassed, took her shoes off and followed Sophia up to her room.

'So this is your old bedroom, huh?' said Delphine, looking around.

'The very one. I've got a lot of fond memories of this bedroom.'

'You mean you managed to sneak boys in, past your mother?' she said, joking.

'Stop it,' said Sophia, throwing a cushion at Delphine. 'You want a drink?' asked Sophia.

'I'm ok for now. So, how are you doing?'

'Bored. I don't know how much more of this I can take. I'm going crazy stuck here all day. Well, everybody thinks I really am crazy anyway,' she laughed. 'All I've got

SOPHIA

to look forward to is my bloody psychologist coming to the house every day.'

They continued to talk for the next few hours. Delphine got the whole story about Suicide Bridge and the lorry; what little Sophia could remember of it anyway. On the whole, Delphine was more help to Sophia during those few hours than Jacques, the psychologist, had been during all their sessions together. But now Delphine was just as concerned as Sophia's family were.

'Look, I'm going to help you get through this. Whatever it takes, I'm here for you, twenty-four seven,' said Delphine. Even she knew that this was crunch time and something had to be done to get Sophia's life back on an even keel.

The following morning didn't start well at all. Sophia's parents were definitely up to something as they clearly were not themselves and they'd both taken the day off work again. Having had the company of Delphine for a few hours the evening before, Sophia now felt isolated and depressed. And to add insult to injury, she had yet another headache from hell that was making her irritable beyond belief. Her skin was crawling with invisible insects and the escapism of her Jojo Moyes novel had come to a rather austere end and she didn't have anything else to read; not here anyway. She didn't even have her iPod with her so she couldn't even escape with her music.

Diana was in the kitchen pacing up and down and Andrew was in the living room looking out of the window towards the main gate to the house.

'Expecting somebody?' said Sophia. Andrew spun around.

'Oh, hi Honey, I didn't hear you come in,' he said. *This isn't right,* thought Sophia. She could see that Andrew was on edge and fidgety.

'Daddy, what's going on?' she demanded.

'Honey, you know that we all love you very much and–'

'Daddy?' she interrupted.

Just then the intercom buzzer went.

'Who's that?' asked Sophia.

'It's our GP,' said Andrew, going to buzz him in. Sophia followed Andrew out into the hall.

'Why's Dr Cheung coming to the house?' she said.

'Darling, we thought it would be a good idea if he came to see you, to see if he can help,' he said, opening the front door.

'Dr Cheung. Thank you for creating an opening in your busy schedule,' said Andrew, shaking his hand.

'It's quite alright,' he said. 'Hello, Sophia,' he said, looking past Andrew.

'Come though to the lounge,' said Andrew.

Diana came into the lounge to join them. 'Would you like a drink doctor?' she asked.

'I'm quite alright, thank you,' he said.

The four of them got comfortable. At first, Sophia wasn't thrilled about Dr Cheung's visit. After all, she'd just come out of hospital and her GP was well aware that her personality had changed significantly since Spencer's death. Andrew had told Dr Cheung about everything that had been happening with Sophia over the past few months and how she'd changed. He told him about her brush with the law and her spell in Holloway Women's Prison and the path of self-destruction she'd been on ever since. But Sophia jumping off Hornsey Road Bridge was the last straw. Dr Cheung agreed that things were very serious and measures had to be taken. He'd only seen Sophia once after Spencer's death and he'd recommended some medication for her to take, which she didn't. But, until now, he wasn't aware of all the other things that had been going on.

Dr Cheung was there for an hour. He asked how Sophia was in herself, how she was coping since Spencer's death; the usual stuff. Then the questions became a little more probing and Sophia started to get irritable with him. Dr Cheung could clearly see that Sophia's personality had changed, considerably. He'd been the family GP for fifteen years now and had seen Sophia grow up. This was not the same Sophia he'd known since she was seven years old, this was a different person altogether.

Eventually, Sophia lost control right there in the living room. Dr Cheung, who spoke in soft tones and whom Sophia really liked because he was understanding and compassionate, suddenly became public enemy number one. At first he seemed concerned for Sophia, but then he started talking about hospitals and professional help, which did not go down well at all. Sophia stormed out of the living room, kicking the wastepaper basket across the floor as she went. They felt the house shake as Sophia slammed her bedroom door.

Dr Cheung talked with Andrew and Diana in depth.

Afterwards they all agreed that there was enough cause for concern over Sophia's safety. With Andrew and Diana's approval, he said he would make the first recommendation for Sophia to be sectioned under Section Two of the Mental Health Act, which meant she would be detained in a psychiatric hospital for up to twenty-eight days. He explained that he would contact the emergency standby Social Work Team so one of their approved mental health practitioners could come back to the house with a section twelve doctor to assess Sophia and make the second recommendation and complete the section arrangements.

It was mid afternoon when the approved mental health practitioner and the section twelve doctor arrived at the house. Sophia had not left her room since Dr Cheung left a few hours previously. She was upset, depressed, angry and irritable all at the same time. She'd simply gone to her room, closed her eyes and tried to empty her head of all that was going on in there. But whatever it was that had a grip on Sophia's mind, it was not going to leave of its own accord.

Andrew went to Sophia's room and asked her to come downstairs to the lounge, which was when she saw the two doctors.

'Now what? Who the hell are they?' she asked.

'Sophia, this is Dr Ross and Lisa Crabtree,' said Andrew.

'Hello, Sophia,' said Dr Ross, with a broad Scottish accent. He extended his hand for Sophia to shake.

SOPHIA

Sophia ignored his gesture. She didn't like the look of him. He was well over six feet tall and quite thin and his lip curled up on one side when he smiled, giving him a horrible sinister look. Dr Ross was the section twelve doctor who was there to assess Sophia and do the second recommendation if necessary.

'Darling, please, the doctor is here to talk to you, to try and help,' said Diana.

'Hello, Sophia,' said Lisa. Sophia looked at her, but did not answer. She just studied the strange looking woman. She was in her early fifties, thickset with wiry silver hair that she obviously couldn't do anything with.

'Would either of you like a drink?' said Diana.

'No thank you,' said Lisa. She spoke loudly and her voice was shrill as it cut through the air. She had the kind of voice that would have a class of primary school children sitting bolt upright to attention and frozen in their chairs. *Crabby by name, crabby by nature*, thought Sophia. Lisa Crabtree was the approved mental health practitioner. She basically made up the trio of people required by law to have Sophia sectioned under the Mental Health Act.

The meeting didn't go well at all. Sophia realised that these people were there to assess her and she could well be sectioned. At first she tried to answer their questions with answers she thought would be the correct ones to keep her out of a psychiatric hospital. But it didn't take long before their questions started to irritate her and get under her skin, so she gave up the façade and started to let rip.

'I can't believe you've done this to me,' she said to her parents.

'Darling, we really didn't know what else to do, it's for your own safety,' said Andrew.

'So you decided to have me sectioned. I told you, I don't need to go to a fucking psychiatric hospital,' she said.

'I'm sorry we had to do it this way, darling, truly we are,' said Andrew.

'You left us no choice, darling,' said Diana.

'No choice? Well I do have a choice, I'm not going to any damn psychiatric hospital and that's that,' she said, running up to her room. Andrew looked at the two doctors.

'Give me a minute,' he said.

The next twenty minutes were fraught with difficulties. Andrew and Diana managed to get her to come back into the lounge twice. The last time, Sophia lost control altogether. From the interrupted conversations they'd had with her, Dr Ross and Lisa could clearly see that Sophia had serious issues that she needed help with; and fast. They all agreed that she should be detained under section two and completed the necessary paper work to go with the form Dr Cheung had already completed and left with Andrew and Diana.

'If it's going to be difficult I can call for assistance,' said Lisa, reassuringly.

'Just let me talk to her for a minute,' said Andrew. He went upstairs and entered Sophia's room. She was sitting on the bed, hugging her knees and rocking back and forth.

'Darling please, it's only for twenty eight days, maybe less,' he said.

'A mental hospital? How could you, Daddy, how could you?'

'Sophia, it's not a mental hospital, it's a specialist psychiatric hospital.'

'It's the same thing, Daddy, and you of all people know that.'

'Darling, it's a private hospital. I've done a lot of research into this and I'm sparing no expense.'

'Research, how long have you been planning this, Daddy?'

'Look, honey, they have a team of professionals, you're going to get the very best help and treatment possible. This place, it's one of the best hospitals in the country.'

'And that's supposed to make me feel better? I can't believe you've done this behind my back. It was that bloody psychologist wasn't it? This was all his idea?'

'He'd mentioned it as a possibility. Your mother and I talked about it and decided it would be best for you.'

'What about Charlotte, did she know about this?'

'No, no she didn't. We arranged it for today because we knew she was in class and we didn't want her to be here when …' he didn't know how to finish.

'Well I'm not going. I don't have to go and you can't force me to. I'm not a teenager anymore, I'm twenty two years old.'

'Look, darling, Mr Cheung and his colleagues have

decided. Please, it'll be better if you just try and see the positive side to this and go along to the hospital without a fuss.'

'Or what, they'll take me away by force?' Andrew looked down at his hands.

'I don't believe it,' she said, shaking her head at him. 'I'm going, and not to a mental hospital. I'm going home,' she said, barging past her father and down the stairs.

'Sophia, please, wait,' he said, chasing downstairs after her. Sophia grabbed the telephone in the kitchen and called for a taxi. But Lisa Crabtree had wasted no time and had called the police for their assistance. They had tried to get Sophia to see reason, but she wasn't having any of it.

'Sophia, please,' said Andrew.

'Hello, I need a taxi right away,' said Sophia into the phone. She proceeded to give the taxi office the address of her parents' house. Andrew stood at the kitchen door and did nothing to stop Sophia calling a taxi. She continued to shout and scream at her mother and father while Dr Ross and Lisa waited patiently in the lounge for the police to arrive, which they seemed to do almost right away.

The buzzer on the intercom sounded. Sophia barged out of the kitchen and past her father to buzz the taxi in. But when she opened the front door it wasn't her taxi coming up the drive, it was the police car. Two male police officers got out and came up to the front door to assist.

SOPHIA

'Darling, please. Don't make a scene,' pleaded Diana.

'How could you do this to me?' she said.

'Miss Beckinsale, it will be easier for everyone if you get into the car and come of your own accord,' said one of the officers. Sophia knew what the alternative would involve if she didn't. She looked at her parents in anger.

'The only place I'm going is home. You can't do this,' said Sophia, running up to her room.

'Sophia, please,' Andrew shouted after her.

Sophia grabbed her handbag and ran back down the stairs with every intention of walking right out of the front door, down the driveway and away from there.

'I'm going home,' she stated, barging past her parents and out the front door. But she didn't get far. Crabtree gave the officers a *look*.

'Miss Beckinsale, we can't let you leave,' said one of the officers. Sophia ignored him, but as she went to walk past the officers they both stepped in and grabbed her.

'Let go, let go of me,' she demanded. But the two officers restrained her. She struggled to free herself but the officers were having none of it as they started to manhandle her towards the police car. She managed to yank one arm free from the officer on her left. She then swung it hard in the direction of his face, but her lashing out didn't make contact as he blocked her swing and grabbed her arm again. This time he reached for his handcuffs on his belt and before Sophia knew what had happened, the officer had efficiently clamped them around her wrists.

'Take those off me, you can't do this,' she protested.

She continued to thrash and scream as they manhandled her to the police car. The whole scene caused much upset for her parents.

The officers managed to get Sophia into the back of the police car. One of them sat in the back with her while the other went over to speak with Dr Ross, Lisa Crabtree and Sophia's parents. The police officer made arrangements to follow Lisa to the hospital in the police car. Although Sophia was starting to calm down, they suspected her volatile nature could kick in at any time so they didn't take any chances. Andrew and Diana followed behind in Andrew's car. Dr Ross had done his part so he headed off in a different direction.

Chapter 45

The psychiatric hospital was a large private affair secluded in its own grounds in Cuffley, Hertfordshire. Lisa Crabtree's car arrived at the private gate first. She reached out of the window and pressed the intercom. The electronic gates opened and she drove through, followed by the police car and finally Andrew and Diana. Sophia looked out of the window of the police car as they drove along the private gravel drive and up to the house. The grounds were magnificent and the large redbrick house resembled the kind of place where a lord of the manor might live. *How could this place possibly be a psychiatric hospital*, thought Sophia.

'Well, it looks like you've hit the jackpot,' said the officer in the passenger seat.

'I'm sorry?' said Sophia, still handcuffed, but somewhat calmer.

'It could be a lot worse. You could have ended up in one of those NHS places. This place looks like a country club,' he said.

Lisa's car pulled up right outside the main entrance just as a middle-aged well-dressed woman came out to welcome them. The police car and Andrew's car pulled into two free parking spaces. The officer in the passenger seat got out and opened the door for Sophia. Lisa went to greet the lady while Sophia and her parents waited alongside the police car.

'It's going to be ok, darling,' said Andrew. 'Please, give it a chance.'

'Are the handcuffs really necessary, officer?' said Diana.

The officer assessed Sophia. 'Ok, if I remove them, you've got to stay calm. Or they'll go right back on again,' he said, removing the handcuffs.

The lady and Lisa came over to greet them.

'Hello, I'm Pamela, I'm the hospital manager,' she said, in a cheery voice. Brief pleasantries were exchanged between them, except for Sophia, who was rubbing her wrists and not really feeling like being pleasant right now. They all went inside and the police, seeing that their assistance was no longer required, made the short journey back to north London.

'Ok, if you just want to wait in here,' said Pamela, showing them into the visitors' room, 'I'll go and get Stephanie. She's going to be your allocated key,' she said. Sophia looked at her blankly. 'Don't worry; I'll explain what that means in more detail in good time. It basically means she's there for you whenever you want anything, have any concerns or just need to talk. I'll be right back, then we'll get your property checked in and give you all the grand tour,' she said, trotting off.

When Pamela returned she introduced Sophia and her parents to Stephanie. Stephanie was tall and slim and in her mid thirties. She was wearing a beige trouser suit and wore her dark blonde hair in a ponytail. She looked more like a hotel receptionist than a psychiatric worker – perhaps not quite as smart though. When she spoke she had an annoying habit of interlinking her fingers and pushing her palms together hard as if she was trying to do that trick where somebody gives you an egg to place in between your palms lengthways and asks you to try and crush it, only for you to find it won't break; only Stephanie's egg was invisible.

'If you have any concerns or need anything at all, I'm *here* for you,' she said, pressing her palms together to emphasise the word "here".

The large Victorian house had eight single-sex wards and all the individual private bedrooms had ensuite facilities. Andrew and Diana were delighted with the facilities. Sophia's room was beautifully decorated and a generous size. It had a decent size single bed, a two-seater sofa, a desk and chair, a dressing table and mirror, a wardrobe and a 32-inch LED television mounted on the wall. There was even a nightstand table with a telephone on it. In fact, it looked just like a decent quality hotel room; only the minibar was absent.

'Well, this is very nice isn't it, darling,' said Diana, who was genuinely impressed with what was going to be Sophia's room for the next twenty-eight days. Although Sophia didn't say anything, she was obviously relieved it wasn't like the picture she had painted in her mind. The communal lounge was just as impressive. Everything was spotless. There were large comfy sofas and armchairs and numerous coffee tables. Mounted on the wall at the far end was a large 55-inch plasma television that even had additional surround sound loudspeakers mounted around the walls. There was definitely a lot more to do here than play Scrabble with an old game with several of the letters missing. Andrew had obviously spared no expense. Not only was this private hospital well facilitated with all mod cons, but also the medical staff here were second to none.

After the grand tour was over, Sophia's parents took care of the hand-over and gave the staff a brief history of what had been going on with their daughter from Spencer's death right up to her suicide attempt – if in fact it was a genuine suicide attempt. Nobody really knew for sure; not even Sophia. They discussed what part they would play. Andrew was designated the *nearest relative*, which, considering his medical experience made the most sense.

Andrew and Diana left so that Sophia could be checked in and seen by the team. They both drove over to Sophia's apartment with the key she'd given them so they could collect a list of things for her, which they would bring back later on. In the meantime, Sophia was checked in by the team and put on one-to-one enhanced observation, which basically meant suicide watch.

She was told that within the next few days she would see a psychologist to be assessed. They also discussed what they could help with, and talked about the various daily activities and sessions. She would also be seeing a social worker to discuss family matters and who was going to be there for her when she eventually left.

SOPHIA

She was given a brief once over by a doctor to make sure she was physically ok, which she was. She was also put on two-milligram Lorazepam tablets, or what they like to call "the blue tablet". Lorazepam are typically used for their sedative, anxiety-relieving and muscle-relaxing effects. But in a nutshell they are used to calm and sedate patients, in turn decreasing the likelihood of agitation with those who have a history of volatile or aggressive behaviour.

Over the next few days Sophia struggled with the structured daily routine and what she thought were rather dull and futile activities. And she certainly didn't have anything in common with the other patients, one of whom was Melissa who was in her forties and as nutty as a fruitcake. She was a quintessential 60s throwback. If she'd been born twenty years earlier she'd have been one of those women who went on CND marches pushing her baby along in a pram through the streets of London. She dressed like a hippy and was a vegetarian. Her theories on world peace and how everybody should be living their lives were endless. She'd swallowed all the animal rights, green issues, rain forest and anti-war books and was following all the clichéd rules in them. She only saw one side of any given coin, her side. Seriously, this woman was missing the bloody point and not seeing the bigger picture.

Then there was Malcolm. Oh my God. He can't have been a day over forty, but he looked twenty years older. He was skinny with beer glass bottoms for glasses, a comb over hairstyle that made him look like Bobby

Charlton. Sophia had no idea what his issue was and didn't want to know. Malcolm was happy to just wander around the hospital shoe-gazing and muttering to himself. Although he seemed harmless enough, every now and then he would suddenly start screaming for no apparent reason, shouting abuse at some imaginary thing in front of him; it was freaky as hell to see. Whenever Sophia saw him, she always gave him a wide berth and avoided eye contact.

Angel, if that was her real name, was a fat dumpy young woman about the same age as Sophia. She really did have a figure like one of those 1970s Weeble Wobble toys. Only Angel really did fall down, constantly. She was the clumsiest person Sophia had ever come across. If there was a coffee table in the middle of the room, she'd walk right into it and crack her shin on the edge. She dropped her knife and fork at mealtimes and was constantly spilling her drinks. She bumped into other patients, sometimes with serious consequences. Hell, she couldn't even walk through an open door without slamming her shoulder into the side of it on her way though. Once she did this so hard she actually dislocated it. Sophia almost found it amusing to watch her, as she knew that sooner or later she would bump into something. To pass time, Sophia would sit there and count how many accidents Angel would have in the course of an hour – nine was her record.

As for Brenda, what a total and utter fuck-up she was. Aged about sixty-five years old. She was your typical crazy-arse bag woman. She seemed to speak in some sort of demented back slang. Sophia could not quite decide if she was harmless, or downright dangerous. So, like with the other patients, she steered well clear.

There were other patients at the hospital, but Sophia didn't know them by name, as there was nothing about them that made them stand out. She only knew Melissa, Malcolm, Angel and Brenda by name as the nursing staff were constantly calling out their names, as they were the ones who were usually doing or saying something stupid. 'Melissa, I don't think Natalie's really interested in hearing about the cruelty to dogs in clinical testing facilities.' Or 'Angel, did you bump your head again, oh dear.' Or 'Malcolm, if you don't stop screaming you'll have to go into isolation again.'

Phyllis was probably the sanest person in there. Although she never gave the nursing staff any trouble, Sophia she was intrigued as to why she was actually in there at all. She was a mixed race woman about thirty years old. She was obviously a very attractive woman, if only she'd do something about that massive Afro. She looked like a female version of T.C. out of the 70s movie, Carwash. She had an air of intelligence about her. Phyllis kept to herself; she just sat there and read most of the time. She didn't bother anybody, and nobody bothered her. Every now and then she'd look up from her book and give Sophia a brief smile before getting back to her reading. It was kind of an acknowledgement – one woman to another, on the same wavelength. Sophia wondered why any parent would call their daughter Phyllis, she wasn't that old. Although

Sophia was gagging for some stimulating conversation, she did not approach Phyllis, but she watched her from time to time, hoping that she would approach her for a chat – but she never did. So, for the most part, Sophia just kept to herself.

Sophia had undergone a lengthy assessment with a psychiatrist and a psychologist, an occupational therapist and various nursing staff, so they could all decide on the diagnosis and the best course of action, treatment and medication.

The medication they had put her on was doing nothing more than mildly numbing the effects of her, yet to be diagnosed, unusual personality disorder and new-found volatile nature. Her newly-appointed psychologist was at a loss and unable to put a name to what Sophia was suffering from. Post-traumatic stress disorder doesn't typically evoke such extreme behaviour, and before the death of her boyfriend, Sophia had never acted so out of character and there was no family history of schizophrenia, psychosis, bipolar or depression. The psychologist said that Sophia seemed to have undergone a serious personality change with a strange mix of bipolar-like manic episodes mixed with psychosis. But there was something abnormal and very different about Sophia's case, which needed deeper investigation.

As the days slowly progressed Sophia got more and more irritated with the constant one-to-one shadowing and hourly checks. She'd done nothing to suggest she was a danger to herself, or anybody else, and she certainly hadn't given anybody the impression that she was going

SOPHIA

to try and kill herself, or so she thought. Perhaps they saw things differently, or could see something she couldn't. As for the various activity programmes and group sessions, Sophia really didn't want to be part of any of them. She'd vented her frustrations on more than one occasion and had been quite volatile, with serious mood swings and changes in personality. In the morning she was one person, then by the afternoon she was somebody else entirely.

Her frustrations were taking over from the inside out. She missed the effects of the speed and cocaine she'd taken. And she was certainly missing sex, which she hadn't had since Liam the Irishman. How and why Sophia had become so sexually promiscuous nobody knew, not even her. Before Spencer died she would have been disgusted at the very thought of promiscuity. But here she was, seeking it out whenever and wherever she could. All she knew was that she enjoyed the way it felt and she liked the danger. During her moments of orgasm, she was on a high, much more so than ever before. There was nothing else for it, she needed a sexual fix and she needed it now.

James was one of the Orderlies at the hospital. He came in three days a week to help out with general duties. He was always pleasant and smiling. James was about thirty years old and wasn't a bad looking man, all things considered. Sophia didn't have much choice around here and James was certainly the pick of the bunch of the male staff. He seemed like a bit of a pushover so Sophia figured seducing him somewhere quiet wouldn't be too difficult.

It was early evening; everyone had had dinner and had settled down. All was quiet. There were several patients and a few members of staff watching a movie in the lounge. The lights had been dimmed slightly and James was sitting near the door. Sophia, quiet as a mouse, sneaked into the lounge and tapped James on the shoulder and whispered in his ear.

'I'm out of toilet roll,' she said.

'Ok, I'll get some for you,' he said, getting up. He left the lounge and Sophia followed close behind. He got to the storeroom, punched in the code to unlock the door and went inside. Sophia went in behind him. Inside it was quite small with wall-to-wall shelves filled with toiletries and other supplies. Sophia closed the door behind her while James reached up onto a shelf and took down a large industrial pack of toilet rolls and started to rip it open. He removed a roll and turned to hand it to Sophia.

'Here you are,' he said.

'You know I don't really need that. Well, we'll probably need it in about ten minutes,' she said, advancing towards him.

'Sophia, you told me you needed a toilet roll.'

'I will need it, but first I need you,' she said, grabbing his face and going straight in for an open mouthed snog.

'Sophia, what are you doing?' he said, pushing her away.

'Don't you find me attractive?' she said.

'That's not the point. You're a patient here and I'm an orderly,' he said, trying to be authoritative, but failing miserably. Sophia laughed at his attempts at being a disciplinarian.

'Look, the door's locked. Don't you want to fuck me?' she said, unzipping her trousers.

'Sophia, stop this right now. I could lose my job. You've got to leave,' he demanded. Sophia was hearing none of it and started to pull her trousers down.

'Sophia, if you don't pull your trousers back up right now I'm hitting this button,' he said, hovering his finger over his panic alarm. She moved close to him and grabbed his hand and tried to force him to touch her down below. The altercation turned into a struggle, during which James pressed his panic alarm. Sophia heard a distant alarm. She stepped back and looked down at his panic alarm, which was flashing red. She gave him a *look*, huffed and pulled her trousers back up.

'I don't fucking believe you,' she shouted, storming out of the storeroom. James ran out out after her, just in time to see back up running along the corridor towards them.

'It's ok,' shouted James. 'It was an accident,' he said. The two orderlies looked at Sophia, then at James.

'Are you sure?' said one of them.

'Quite sure,' he said. He turned to Sophia, 'Here's your toilet roll,' he said, handing it to her. Sophia snatched it off him and went back to her room, leaving James to explain what happened.

'It was an accident. A box fell off the shelf in the storeroom and caught my panic alarm button as I tried to catch it,' he said.

The two orderlies watched Sophia disappear around the corner then turned their attentions back to the flustered James. One of them smiled, 'Ok, you be careful, James,' he said.

'You got it,' he said.

James went back to the lounge, somewhat relieved; while Sophia went to her room to make sure she was relieved – solo.

Sophia's parents and Charlotte had visited twice during the past ten days and Sophia knew that they had spoken to the staff before seeing her to be brought up to speed and given all the details of the preceding days since their last visit. They kept saying things like, 'You really must try, darling,' or, 'Being more open during your sessions will help them better understand what you're going through,' or, 'Please, honey, these people want to help you get better.'

But Sophia didn't try harder, and she didn't try to fit in or be co-operative and open during her various sessions with her psychologist and allocated key. If anything, she was getting worse, only it wasn't as obvious because of the numbing effects of the medication she was on. If anything, the medication was making her headaches worse. However, even her daily dose of Lorazepam could not hold back what was about to happen next.

Sophia was about half way through a scheduled one-hour Art & Craft activity slot. Out of all the activities, this was the one that she could tolerate the most as she could sit and paint at her easel and pretty much get on with what she was doing and keep to herself; she didn't have to interact with anyone. Phyllis always sat next to Sophia in this class, which was comforting. Apart from

Sophia, there were four other patients in this class; Phyllis, Malcolm, and two others who she did not know by name, but had seen around often enough. From what she had seen, none of them posed any serious threat to her. Then again, psychiatric patients could be quite volatile and unpredictable at times. The only downside to the arts class was that watercolours required a certain skill to prevent the colours running down the paper mounted on the vertical easel. *What the hell, I'll go for an impressionistic look,'* she thought, as she made sweeping strokes of light tan with her brush. *This was a bad idea*, she thought, *self-portraits are not easy.* Mixing the paints to achieve the correct skin tone was proving difficult, and as for her blonde hair, *what the hell colours do you have to mix to get blonde?* Her vibrant red blouse proved much easier. Primary colours don't kick up such a stink, they just do what you want them to and are very agreeable. Phyllis, on the other hand, seemed to make it look incredibly easy.

As Sophia leaned back to view her handiwork, the colours in the painting started to take on a surreal effect. Sophia stared long and hard at her self-portrait and even though the impressionistic style made it difficult to make it out, it became even more difficult as the painting started to morph right in front of her eyes. *Is this the effects of my medications?* she thought, as she continued to stare at the painting, which now looked like one of those stereogram posters that you had to stare at for ages to see a hidden 3D image appear within another scrambled picture. As Sophia continued to gaze at the painting it became a mosaic of snowy multi-coloured noise, like that of an un-tuned television channel; only this was becoming seriously psychedelic. Then, like a stereogram poster, an image started to emerge from the mass of snowy noise. It was hard to make it out against the optical illusion that made up the background, but it was definitely somebody's face. Sophia continued to look deep into the picture, as if she was looking through it. As her eyes fell slightly out of focus, the face became clearer, turning into a three-dimensional head. It was Sophia, but not the Sophia she had painted. This Sophia was dark and frightening. Sophia leaned to her left and her darker self in the picture moved to its right, not taking its eyes off Sophia for a moment, not even to blink. As Sophia regarded the stereogram head looking back at her, she tried to make sense of the many thoughts that fired through her mind. She was now frozen in her seat, transfixed on the face staring out of the picture at her. In her mesmerized state, all she could do was stare right back. Then, it spoke.

'Soooooon,' it said in a whisper. Sophia flinched and took a sharp intake of breath, startled. Then the face in the image lifted an index finger up to its lips and said, 'Shhh.'

Sophia was hypnotized by the three-dimensional head looking back at her. She could not take her eyes off it as she sat there perfectly motionless. The head had her under some sort of spell. Phyllis had stopped painting and was aware that something was not right with Sophia.

There were two supervising staff in the class. One was the assistant occupational therapist and the other was a health care assistant, both female. The health care assistant noticed that Sophia didn't look right and ambled over to see if she was ok.

The Sophia in the image dropped her finger from her lips then moved closer to the front of the image, much closer. Her head was now projecting out of the painting and invading Sophia's immediate space, so much so that it caused Sophia to lean back in her chair in fear of coming into contact with her other self. She could see the face so clearly now. It reminded her of some sort of evil twin sister that she didn't have. It's nose started to bleed; dark blood, almost black. Then it started to haemorrhage blood from its ears, sending deep red watercolour running down the paper and onto the floor. Sophia looked down at her feet and saw the blood pooling around them. She pulled her feet back under her chair to avoid the running blood coming into contact with her shoes. The bleeding image of Sophia smiled, and then broke out into a quiet, yet sinister laugh.

'SOON!' it said, as it thrust its three-dimensional arm out of the painting, reaching for the mesmerized Sophia.

'Are you ok, Sophia?' asked the health care assistant, placing her hand on Sophia's shoulder. Sophia, half in reality and half in another world almost jumped out of her skin. Her manic psychotic reflex reaction caused her to jump to her feet, grab the easel and slam it around the health care assistant's head; all in one swift movement. The health care assistant's large body slumped to the floor, unconscious.

The assistant occupational therapist raised the alarm

by hitting the button on her personal attack alarm. By the time reinforcements arrived, Sophia was in a state of frenetic panic, tearing up the classroom and upsetting the other patients. Malcolm got on to his hands and knees and put his hands over his ears, scrunched his eyes closed and tried to jam his head between his knees. He started to scream hysterically, 'I AM AN OSTRICH, I AM AN OSTRICH, I AM AN OSTRICH.' over and over again.

Two male orderlies restrained Sophia and dragged her away. A combination of the picture hallucination, her scrambled emotions and the medication she was on was a bad mix. She felt trapped in this strange surreal place, surrounded by strange people, in a strange world. She could not be reasoned with, she saw everyone as the enemy. The staff tried to talk to Sophia to calm her down – to no avail. She was still frenetic and wild. There was nothing else for it. They took her to the emergency medication room where they would restrain her and give her an Achuphase injection. The medication room had various locked medicine cabinets fixed to the walls and a white metal waist-level hospital bed on wheels in the centre of the room. With some struggling and objections, they managed to give Sophia the injection, and then they took her to an isolation room.

The isolation room was empty, except for a single rubber mattress on the floor. It was ligature-free, not even an electrical light flex hanging from the ceiling; nothing. A rather nasty side effect of the injection left Sophia standing motionless for hours on end like

SOPHIA

a statue with drool hanging from her mouth. Hospital staff checked on her via the small Perspex window twice an hour, but in her drugged up state, she didn't even know they were there. The zuclopenthixol acetate stayed in her system for the next three days.

Chapter 46

Two days after they'd given Sophia the Achuphase injection, Delphine visited her. She was disgusted and upset at the lobotomised state the medication had put her best friend in. Delphine was livid and complained to the hospital manager. She told her that she was going to come back to visit Sophia in two days, and if she wasn't in a state of full awareness with the ability to communicate sharply, she would contact a major national newspaper about the barbaric methods that they practised there. She emphasised the threat by telling Pamela that her sister was a journalist, which was a lie of course. However, it seemed to do the trick, as Pamela's over-confident corporate smile suddenly looked a little ragged around the edges. Delphine figured that no psychiatric hospital would want to be accused of treating its patients like they did back in the Victorian days; especially a privately owned one.

Later in the afternoon, Django came to visit Sophia, and although the effects of the zuclopenthixol acetate were diminishing, she was clearly still in a docile state. Although, on the face of it, Sophia could communicate with DJ, she explained to him that everything seemed

Sophia

strangely surreal and for the past few days she'd had no idea where she really was. DJ had the same thoughts and feelings that Delphine had had earlier in the day. DJ had been growing more and more concerned and worried about Sophia, but this was too much for him to handle. Seeing her like this pained him and he wondered how she had arrived here, or if there was anything he could have done to prevent it getting this far. He felt emotionally overwhelmed and deeply saddened for this girl who he cared so much for and loved like a sister.

It was 11 p.m. when Sophia's mobile rang, and this was the first time in three days that she'd been in any physical or mental state to actually answer it.

'Hello,' she said, not recognising the number coming up on the screen.

'Miss Beckinsale, how lovely to hear your voice again,' said the vaguely familiar voice. With her musical ear, Sophia recognised the voice, but couldn't quite place it.

'Who is this?'

'Oh, come on now. It hasn't been that long. Have you forgotten about us already?' he said. 'Let me refresh your memory. Hotel room, champagne bottle, head. Is it coming back to you yet?'

Then it did come back to her, sending an uncomfortably cold feeling through her body. 'What do you want?'

'Our employer, Mr Mancini, feels that you still owe him.'

'Oh, how so? I did what he asked. I don't owe him anything anymore.'

'Well, you see, that's where you're wrong. He feels

that the crack on the head and concussion you gave him is worth two jobs, and as he was *so* pleased with the good work you did for him last time, he feels somewhat compelled to call upon your services again.'

Although the Achuphase injection had pretty much worn off, Sophia was still feeling a little docile due to the Lorazepam they were making her take. But she was sharp-minded enough to know that if she agreed to do whatever favour they were going to ask for a second time, it would probably never stop.

'Well, Mr Mancini can feel as compelled as he likes. I'm not doing any more of his dirty work, not now, or ever. Goodbye,' she said, pressing the *End* call button.

Less than a minute later the *new text* alert sounded on her phone. She picked it up and clicked on her *Messages* icon. At the top of her messages sat a new one from an unknown caller. She tapped it with her thumb and saw a message with a little thumbnail picture below it. She couldn't quite make out the tiny picture so she tapped it so it filled the screen; then all became clear. It was a photograph of her cello. It was leaning upright against a wooden crate next to its case. But it was not in her apartment where it should be. It was in a small room that resembled an abandoned warehouse, and sitting on the floor next to it was a green 5 litre plastic canister with the word PETROL written on its side. She tapped back to the message, which read: If you don't want this little beauty to burn you should call us back on this number without delay.

'I thought that would get your attention,' he said,

answering his mobile.

'How dare you break into my apartment and take my things.'

'Miss Beckinsale, please, we're not burglars, we're professionals. We don't need to *break* in. We have a key,' he said.

'How the hell did you get my key?'

'Not *your* key, *a* key. Now, stop concerning yourself with the inconsequentials and start taking us seriously. Mr Mancini's calling in another favour and, one way or another, you will oblige him.'

'And if I don't?'

'Well, I think you know the answer to that question, and it ends with the words *expensive* and *fire*.'

'If I do this, you'll just keep coming back and making me do more crap for you, it'll never end.'

'Mr Mancini told us you'd say that. So, he told me to tell you that you have his word. If you do this one last thing for him, he'll release you from your obligations to him and he'll never bother you again.'

'And I'm supposed to believe that?' she said.

'I really don't give a flying fuck what you believe. You don't have any choice in the matter. Well, you do, but the alternative won't stop at the burning of a cello, and it really is a very nice cello.'

'What does he want me to do?' said Sophia, knowing that they might hurt Charlotte if she didn't agree. All she could do was hope that Mr Mancini was a man of his word.

'Nothing you can't handle. But time is of the essence.

Meet us outside Bond Street tube station at nine o'clock tomorrow night.'

'I can't do that. I'm …'

'We know where you are, Miss Beckinsale. When you weren't answering your mobile, we tried your apartment a few times. Then we had an acquaintance of ours trace the whereabouts of your phone. Well, we were quite surprised to see the GPS location of it. But don't worry, your little psychiatric holiday secret's safe with us.'

'I can't get out of here, it's locked down.'

'It's hardly a fucking prison. Find a way, get out, and be outside Bond Street tube for nine o'clock tomorrow night.'

'Which exit?'

'Whichever one takes your pretty little fancy. We'll find you. Oh, and be sure to dress to kill,' he said. The phone went dead.

Knowing their reputation, Sophia thought he could have worded that last request a little differently.

The next morning one of the nurses gave Sophia her *blue tablet*, and as usual, she checked under her tongue to make sure she'd swallowed it. Sophia needed to think. She needed to figure out how she was going to escape from the hospital, and for this, and whatever it was Mancini was going to have her do tonight, she had to stay sharp and focused. She could not afford to be on any kind of sedative, no matter how mild. So, the Lorazepam tablet had to come up – one way or another. Sneaking a quarter of a glass of salt out of the kitchen didn't prove too difficult. Then, in the privacy of her room, she filled the glass with water and downed it in one. This made her gag and she almost threw up right there and then; two fingers jammed down her throat did the trick. Up came the undigested little blue tablet, along with the poached egg on toast she'd had for breakfast.

She spent the rest of the day on her best behaviour, trying to be as inconspicuous as possible to avoid the attention of the orderlies, various doctors, nurses, psychiatrists and other staff members. She went about her morning routine as usual. Thank God there was nothing heavy scheduled for the day. No psychologist or other one-to-one sessions. Just dull old activities so she had plenty of opportunity to wander around and figure out how to get out.

One thing she had resigned herself to was the fact that she probably wouldn't be able to sneak back in undetected, even if they didn't notice she was missing, which was a virtual impossibility considering she was on suicide watch with hourly checks. What the hell, she would cross that bridge when she came to it. For now, she had to prioritise saving her cello, but more importantly, saving her younger sister from whatever they might go on to do to her.

She had to plan and time her escape to perfection. Most of the exit doors and some of the internal ones were only locked down at night, but Sophia could not just walk out the front door as the lady on reception would see her and raise the alarm. There was a side door, a back door and a delivery entrance, but these were usually locked via coded keypads. Most of the windows had lockable internal white grills, which were always locked. However, Pamela's office was one room that didn't seem to have a lockable sliding metal grill. Sophia had noticed this during the one time she was in there when she first arrived. However, Pamela was as sharp as a tack and didn't miss a trick. When she was not in her office, she kept it locked, and Pamela's office was one of the few rooms in the place that used a key instead of an electronic keypad. Getting the key would be next to impossible, so she was going to have to think of how else she could get into Pamela's office so she could climb out of the window and make her escape.

She didn't quite know how she was going to get in there, and one thing she had to take into account was the fact that Pamela might actually be in there when she made her move, which would kill that plan dead in its tracks.

There was not time to come up with any real plan of action, this was going to have to be improvised on the spot because even if she did get out, she was still miles from anywhere here in rural Hertfordshire. Lord knows how she was going to get from there to her apartment in Hampstead with no car or money. This was another bridge that would have to be crossed at the time, as Sophia didn't have time to come up with a well thought out plan and she was still feeling a little subdued due to her prescribed Lorazepam over the past few weeks.

Sophia went back to her room having done a recce and figured out her escape route. Now all she had to do

SOPHIA

was wait for her hourly check, which was due in about twenty minutes.

Like clockwork, there was a knock at her door and a nurse stuck her head around the corner and asked if Sophia was feeling ok and if everything was fine.

'I'm just peachy,' said Sophia. The nurse studied her for a moment before closing her door. Sophia waited long enough for the nurse to get to the end of the corridor and around the corner. She grabbed her iPhone and jacket, then cautiously made her way along the corridor in the opposite direction to the nurse. She went down the flight of stairs then peaked around the corner to make sure there were no members of staff lurking in the corridor. There weren't. She looked down the corridor to the second door on the right, Pamela's office door. She let out a nervous sigh. *Christ, this feels like The Great Escape,'* she thought, as she trotted quietly towards Pamela's door. She paused outside and listened for any sounds from within. She tapped quietly on the door and prayed nobody would say, 'come in'. They didn't, all was quiet, which meant the door would be locked. Sophia eyed the fire extinguisher hanging on the wall a few feet away. She pictured a movie where somebody grabbed such a fire extinguisher and used it as a battering ram to break down a door. *Too noisy. Shit.* She reached down to try the door handle anyway. She grabbed the brass doorknob and slowly turned it clockwise until it stopped, then she held her breath and gently pushed the door slightly. To her utter disbelief it actually opened an inch. Then panic hit her. What if Pamela was inside? Why else would it be open? Her nerves were a wreck and her legs were shaking. She pushed the door further still, slowly, trying not to make it creak. She put her head around the door and scanned the office; empty. She went inside and closed the door behind her then ran to the other side of the desk, opened the window and climbed out. She pushed the window closed from the outside then made her way across the back yard and through the rubbish bin area. It was a good fifty yards to the lightly wooded area of cover. Until then she kept looking back, scanning the various ground floor and upstairs windows in case anybody was looking out and saw her. There wasn't and they didn't. She reached the woodland area, but didn't stop until she was a half a dozen or so trees in and well and truly under cover.

She knew that Cuffley railway station was not too far away as she remembered passing it in the police car. She arrived at the boundary fence. Luckily it was only about ten feet tall and there was no barbed wire along the top. She could just about manage to fit the toes of her shoes into the strong mesh rectangular openings to climb it. Once outside the grounds it took her about twenty minutes to get to the station, after stopping to ask for directions twice.

The station was quiet and it was easy for Sophia to hop over the ticket barrier and get to the platform. She called Delphine from her mobile.

'Sophia,' she said, seeing her name on her phone's display.

'Thank God you picked up. Please tell me you're free.'

Sophia

'Sure, what's going on?'

'Look, I need a huge favour.'

'Anything.'

'I need you to come and pick me up from Highbury & Islington station.'

'Sophia, what's going on, what are you doing there?'

'I'm not there yet, but I'll be arriving in about forty minutes. I don't have any money so I need you to come inside and meet me at the ticket barrier to pay for my ticket. Please, Delphi.'

'Sure, honey, don't worry; I'll be there.'

Chapter 47

After explaining that it was rather unorthodox, an understanding ticket officer at Highbury & Islington station took Delphine's money for Sophia's journey from Cuffley.

'Thanks so much, Delphi,' said Sophia, as they made their way to Delphine's car.

'So, you wanna tell me what's going on?' said Delphine.

'One of Mancini's men called me last night.'

'Oh shit, what did they want?'

'Mancini wants me to do another favour for him. He reckons my belting him over the head with a bottle is worth two favours. So he's cashing in his second stamp.'

'What does he want you to do?'

'I have no idea. I've got to meet two of his men at Bond Street tube at nine tonight.'

'And you have no idea what they're going to ask you to do?'

'No, all I know is the man I spoke to told me to dress to kill, whatever the hell that means.'

'Sounds like he might want you to rip somebody off, like last time?' said Delphine.

'I don't know, all I know is they're going to set fire to

my cello if I don't do it,' said Sophia, showing Delphine the picture they texted to her phone.

'Oh my God,' said Delphine.

'And last time they threatened to hurt my sister, Charlotte. So, I guess I don't have any choice.'

'What can I do to help?'

'Well, the hospital staff will have noticed I'm missing by now so I can't go back to my place. Any chance I could borrow one of your 'dress to kill' outfits?'

'Sure,' she said, unlocking her car door.

'Let me come with you, to cover your back.'

'Delphi, I really appreciate that, but I'm not going to drag you into this. I created this mess, so I'll end it. I will need some cash though; for taxis and drinks and, well, I'm not sure.'

'No problem,' said Delphine, pulling out onto the main road.

At Delphine's apartment, Delphine pulled some of her dresses and shoes out of her wardrobe for Sophia to choose from. While Sophia picked out and tried on a dress, Delphine slipped into a dress that looked fancy enough, but was comfortable and practical. She also picked out some shoes that looked equally fancy, but were relatively easy to run in.

'I'm coming with you,' said Delphine, slipping her shoes on.

'Delphi, no. This is my problem.'

'Yeah well, you're my best friend so now it's my problem too. A problem shared and all that,' she said, standing up to straighten her dress.

'Delphi, you've no idea how comforted I feel knowing I have your support. But, there's nothing you can do to help me.'

'Look, I'm just gonna come along to watch your back, from a distance.'

'Delphi–'

'Sophia, I'm coming with you. No arguments.'

Sophia stood up wearing just one shoe and hugged Delphine.

'Ok, put that other shoe on and let's get this over with,' said Delphine.

They changed at Tottenham Court Road and hopped onto the Central Line to Bond Street. There weren't many people waiting on the platform. A couple of well turned out Japanese businessmen, a young couple, and a middle-aged woman with a large suitcase littered with airline tags. Sophia and Delphine looked at a suspiciously dirty bench and decided to stand while waiting for the train.

'How much charge is on your mobile?' asked Delphine.

Sophia took out her phone, 'Eighty percent,' she said.

'Good. Ok, here's the plan. When we get there I'll go up the escalator first. I need you to wait a few minutes before coming up.

'Why do you need to go up first? Where are you going to go?' asked Sophia.

SOPHIA

'I need to get out on to the street first so my mobile can get a signal in advance.'

'In advance of what?'

'I'll get to that in a minute. Once I'm outside I'll find suitable cover in a shop doorway nearby and I'll wait and watch.'

'Then what?'

'Well, we don't know what they have planned or where they're going to take you or how they're going to get you there. They could be on foot or they could be in a car. If they're in a car it's important that you find out where they're taking you. So I can jump in a taxi.'

'How am I supposed to let you know? I won't be able to say, "Hey guys, can I just phone my friend to let her know where I'm going to be".'

'Hence me needing to get out of the station first,' she said. Sophia gave her a puzzled look. 'Don't worry; you'll see when we get there.

There was a gust of warm wind and a discarded cover page of the Metro newspaper blew down the tracks. Then the sound of metal wheels screeching on metal tracks sounded and lights appeared in the tunnel. Sophia always thought it was a little eerie how you could sense the train coming before you could actually hear it. Sophia straightened her windswept hair as they boarded the tube. It was only two stops to Bond Street so they decided to stand.

They exited the tube and made their way through the various walkways before finally arriving at the foot of the escalator. Delphine grabbed Sophia's arm to prevent her stepping onto the escalator.

'What?' she said.

'Take your mobile out,' said Delphine. 'Do you have a signal?'

'No. Not yet'

'Me neither. As soon as we get to the top we'll get a signal again. I need you to constantly check your phone as you go up this escalator and the second you have a signal call me.'

'I don't understand?'

'I'll answer, but I won't speak. Then leave your phone on the call and keep it near the top of your bag with your bag open so I can hear what's being said. Ask them where you're going so I know. But in case I can't hear what they say, I'll need you to repeat it by saying something like, "Why are we going to Harrods?" or whatever. Then I can jump in a taxi and get to where you are.'

'Jesus, have you done this before?' said Sophia, surprised at Delphine's detailed plan.

'No,' she laughed. 'After that we'll just have to play it by ear. Ok, so remember. When I get on the escalator wait for two minutes before coming up.'

'Ok,' said Sophia. Delphine stepped onto the escalator. Sophia checked the time on her phone.

Sophia stepped onto the escalator and stared at the NO SIGNAL indicator on her phone, willing some signal bars to appear. She was almost at the top. 'Come on, come on,' she whispered. Still no signal. The shoes of a man thirty steps up from Sophia disappeared as the escalator under his feet levelled out at the top. Then

SOPHIA

his lower body, and a second later, his head disappeared from Sophia's view.

She looked from the top of the escalator to her phone several times in a few seconds. Then a bar appeared, quickly followed by another two. *Thank God*. She already had Delphine cued up on her *favourites* list. Relieved, she tapped Delphine's name on the screen. *Calling*, showed on the screen. She dropped her phone into the top of her handbag just as she approached the top of the escalator. As more of the station came into view, she looked around, but didn't see either of the men who'd visited her apartment.

She left the station and waited at the Oxford Street entrance. She looked around, but didn't see either of the men, or Delphine. She looked to her right and the two men that had been to her apartment, Mr Green Tie and Mr Stocky, suddenly came into view as they came around the corner and walked past Dorothy Perkins. And low and behold, green tie was actually wearing the same green gaudy tie he'd worn last time she'd seen him.

'Come with us, we're parked just around the corner,' said green tie.

'Where are we going?' she asked.

'You'll see when we get there,' said stocky guy.

Green tie opened the back door of a black Audi S8 and gestured for Sophia to get in. 'Love ya dress,' he said, as Sophia climbed in. He closed the door and got in the front passenger seat as stocky took up position in the driver's seat and started the car.

Sophia placed her handbag on her lap. She had a brief

moment to check through the slight opening to make sure the call was still active, but the phone had slipped down the side of her bag and she didn't have time to rummage for it before green tie got in and looked over his shoulder at her.

'So, you wanna tell me what you want me to do?' she asked. Green tie paused and studied her for a moment before speaking.

'We're going to a bar just off the Strand.'

'The Strand?' said Sophia, loud, but not obviously loud.

'This is the man you're looking for,' he said, tossing a brown envelope onto the back seat. Sophia took a photograph out and studied the man. There was nothing distinct about him. He wore a dark pinstripe suit, white shirt and a striped tie. He was in his late fifties with thinning mousy brown short hair. That was about it. He looked like your average politician.

'Who is he?'

'That's of no importance. What he has on his person, however, is of *great* importance.'

'What would that be?' said Sophia, wondering if Delphine had heard 'The Strand'.

'A flash memory stick,' he said.

'A flash memory stick?' she asked.

'Yeah, you know, the small USB type.

'I know what they are,' she said.

'Good, so you'll know what you're looking for.'

'So what's on it?'

'What's on it doesn't matter. What does matter is that you shut up and stop asking questions. Now, give me

Sophia

your mobile,' he demanded.

'What? What for?'

'I'm gonna put a number in it for you to call when you're done,' he said, reaching out his open hand. Sophia reached into her bag and turned the phone over and pressed the *End* call button before taking it out and handing it to him. He pressed the Phone icon and dialled a mobile number and pressed Call. A mobile in his jacket pocked rang. He hung up Sophia's phone and handed it back to her.

'When you've got the memory stick, hit that last dialled number straight away and we'll come and get it.'

'How am I supposed to get it?'

'You figure it out; not my problem.'

'But I'll have to lie to him, and maybe sleep with him. I don't know if I can do that,' she said.

'Of course you can do that. Trust me, you're a *woman*, lying and sleeping with men is the most natural thing in the world to you.'

'But he's quite old. I can't just pick him up. He might be happily married. I don't have any of that drug stuff that you gave me last time, what if—'

'*If* you don't succeed, I think you know what happens next. Fire, fire, and then who knows what next,' shouted green tie, interrupting.

They turned off the Strand and pulled over to the side of the road.

'Just around that corner,' said green tie, pointing, 'there's a bar called The Looking Glass Music Lounge.'

'What if he isn't in there?'

'He'll be there.'

'What's his name?'

'It's better you don't know. You've never met him before remember; I don't want you slipping up. Now go.'

Sophia got out of the car and crossed the street towards the corner. The Audi sped past her as she turned into the street and walked towards the bar. The second the car was out of sight she took her mobile out and called Delphine.

'Hello,' answered Delphine, with caution in her voice.

'Hey, did you hear anything?' asked Sophia.

'All I heard was you say "The Strand". I'll be there in a minute. Where are you exactly? Asked Delphine.

Sophia looked up at the street name, and gave it, and the name of the bar, to Delphine.

'I'm going inside,' said Sophia.

'Ok, I'll be there in a few minutes. Be careful and don't do anything until you see me arrive.'

Inside, it was larger than expected. The lighting was not overly bright, but it wasn't dingy either. The large elongated bar had twelve low back bar stools lined along its width. Down the centre of the room were low tables with comfy two-seater lounge chairs either side, with several more similar arrangements around the walls. At the far end there was a small stage for when musicians performed. A young woman was on the stage plugging an electro acoustic guitar into a small amplifier and setting up her microphone.

Sophia ordered an apple and mango J2O and scanned the establishment for her man while the barman went to the fridge. She spotted him at a table along the wall opposite the bar. There were two younger men seated opposite him; all engaged in conversation. Sophia settled on a bar stool at the end of the bar where she was almost in his direct line of sight. *This is going to be tough,'* she thought. Then she saw Delphine walk in. Delphine glanced at her, and then looked away. Sophia did the same but she was aware of Delphine ordering a drink at the other end of the bar near the entrance.

Halfway though her second J2O the two young men who'd been talking to her memory stick man got up and said their goodbyes and left. Memory stick man caught Sophia's glance and gave her a brief smile. The man was now sitting on his own and still had two thirds of his drink left and showed no sign of leaving; thank God. But, he was probably close to three times Sophia's age and she had no idea how to go about getting that memory stick off him, if he actually had it on him at all that is. She tested the water by making a big deal of draping her jacket, at least Delphine's jacket, over her barstool while she walked over to the bathroom, which meant walking right past him. As she walked past, he glanced up at her. She glanced back at him and smiled, he smiled back, but he immediately looked back down at the papers he was thumbing through.

She'd only been in the bathroom a moment when Delphine came in after her.

'Well?' asked Delphine.

'There's a man in here. He's sitting at one of the tables along the wall. Apparently he's got a USB memory stick on him and they want me to get it somehow.'

'Shit. How the hell are you gonna do that?'

'I don't know, I'm working on it.'

'Shame he's not younger,' said Delphine.

'That's what I thought. I don't think he's the type who would go for a much younger woman. He just seems too straight and old-fashioned for that sort of thing. Look, I'd better get back out there. As long as I'm there and he can see me there's maybe a slim chance of striking up a conversation.'

'Ok. If I think of anything I'll text you,' said Delphine.

Sophia exited the ladies and as she walked along she noticed his briefcase on the floor jutting out a little. This time, his back was to her. As she walked past she accidently on purpose stubbed her toe into his case and faked a slight trip.

'I'm so sorry,' she said, bending down to put his case upright.

'No, I'm the one who should be apologising. I shouldn't have left my case sticking out like that. Are you ok?' he said.

'Yes, I'm fine, thank you.'

'Why don't I pay for your next drink as a token of my apology?' he said.

'Only if you let me join you to drink it,' she said.

'Well–'

'I've been stood up by my date and I'd really appreciate a little company before heading off home.'

He thought about it, then said, 'I guess that will be ok.'

Sophia went to get her coat and a drink, then went

back to join him.

'Looks like you've got your hands full there?' said Sophia, gesturing to the large pile of papers in front of him.

'Yes. It's been a busy month,' he said, not willing to elaborate.

'Do you mind if I ask what you do?' she said.

'I'm a politician ... but not a well-known one,' he said, smiling.

'And what about you?' he asked.

Not wanting to say what she really did for a living in fear of leaving him with facts, she lied. 'I'm an accountant's assistant,' she said. 'All very dull really.'

'Well, here's to our dull jobs,' he said, raising his glass.

After taking a drink he took out his wallet, removed a photograph and handed it to Sophia. 'What do you think?' he asked.

Sophia looked at the small black and white photograph. It was a young woman in her early twenties; tall and slim with long light hair.

'Wow, she looks just like me. Who is she?'

'My wife,' he said.

'Oh,' said Sophia. *This just gets harder.*

'It was taken when she was twenty one.'

'How old is she now?'

'She died two years ago. She was fifty-five,' he said, taking the photo back and gazing at it adoringly.

'I'm so sorry,' said Sophia. Talk about stuck between a rock and a hard place. How could she possibly steal a memory stick from such an endearing and kind gentleman? But if she didn't ...

'It's ok. I have a large family and they've been very supportive. Just looking at you reminded me of what she looked like when I first met her all those years ago. You even sound a little like her.' He put the photo back in his wallet and slipped it back into his jacket pocket on the seat next to him. 'Would you mind watching my things while I visit the gents?' he asked.

'Of course, go ahead.' Trusting as well. Leaving his case, papers, and jacket behind he disappeared into the gents. She just sat there thinking. She couldn't do it. The dark Sophia wasn't coming through for her; where the hell was she when she needed her. What if the contents of the memory stick are important to him, and by her taking it, it ruins his life somehow? He was just too nice a man to hurt. *What the hell's going on*, she thought. The dark Sophia had been fairly constant during the past weeks, and now she decides to take a break and give Sophia a moment of clarity.

Delphine appeared at her table like a bat out of hell.

'Well?' she said.

'I can't do this. He's too nice.'

Delphine looked towards the bar. The barman was preoccupied with customers and nobody else was paying any attention to her. She jumped into his vacant seat and rifled through his jacket pockets. 'You know what they'll do if you don't do this. Think about Charlotte. Nice doesn't come into it,' she said as she looked inside the breast pockets. 'Bingo!' she said, taking out a small red and black Sandisk memory stick. 'Let's go,' said Delphine. Sophia grabbed her jacket and bag and they both left in a hurry. Once outside they ran down the street and onto the Strand and flagged down a taxi.

Chapter 48

They'd only been in the taxi for a few minutes when Sophia asked the driver to pull over.

'What are you doing?' said Delphine. 'Let's just get home.'

'No, I can't. They said I've got to call them straight away. They might be in the area waiting.'

The taxi pulled over.

'Ok, I'll wait with you. Like before,' she said before turning to the taxi driver. 'I'm really sorry, how much do I owe you?'

The driver tutted and told Delphine how much. They both got out and Sophia dialled the number that green tie had dialled in earlier.

'Hello,' said the recognisable voice of green tie.

'It's me. I've got what you want.'

'Good. Where are you?'

'I'm standing outside the Adelphi Theatre on the Strand.'

'Stay there. We'll come and get you.' He hung up.

'They're coming,' said Sophia, putting her phone in her bag.

'How long?' asked Delphine.

SOPHIA

'They didn't say. And he hung up before I could ask. But I can't imagine it'll be that long. They only dropped me here half an hour ago so it could be a few minutes or it could be thirty. You can't be here though.'

'I know. Ok, we passed a pub fifty yards back up the road. I'll wait in there. As soon as they've been and collected the memory stick call to let me know then come to meet me,' she said, looking around then walking back up the Strand to the pub.

It was exactly twenty minutes later when the black Audi pulled up outside the theatre. The passenger side window opened and green tie looked out.

'Jump in,' he ordered. Sophia climbed in the back. She'd hardly had a chance to slam the door when stocky sped off. 'Ok, let's have it,' said green tie, reaching into the back with his hand open, palm up. Sophia took the memory stick out and handed it to him. He examined it, and then he studied Sophia. 'Did you look at this?' he said.

'What do you mean, did I look at it? Of course I looked at it, I'm looking at it right now,' she said.

'Don't get smart. I'm talking about what's on it?'

'Do you see a laptop on me?'

'Nonetheless. Mr Mancini wants to see you,' said green tie.

'You've got to be fucking kidding me,' she said. 'I've done what you wanted me to do. That bastard gave me his word.'

'Maybe he just wants to thank you personally,' said green tie.

'Well, that's all very nice. But no thanks required so if you could just pull over and let me out,' she said.

'Not possible I'm afraid. Mr Mancini was quite insistent,' said green tie. The car pulled up at a set of traffic lights. Sophia grabbed the door handle and yanked it, but the door didn't open.

'Nice try. Child locks do come in handy don't they,' said stocky, laughing and amused.

'Why don't you just sit back and relax,' said green tie.

While they drove across London towards Holborn green tie checked the memory card on his laptop. He'd adjusted his seating position and angled the screen away so Sophia could not see it. He smiled, then removed the memory stick and closed the laptop. Then he got busy texting. They drove through Farringdon and the Angel then along Upper Street to Highbury & Islington then eventually along Blackstock Road. The car turned right into Seven Sisters Road and drove alongside Finsbury Park. At the junction with Green lanes at Manor House they turned left. Then a few twists and turns later they were driving into an industrial estate that had seen better days. The car came to a halt right outside a small lock-up unit.

Green tie and stocky got out of the car. While green tie opened the back door for Sophia, stocky went and banged his large meat hook of a hand on the warehouse door.

'Ok, let's go,' said green tie. Sophia got out of the car. 'What the hell is this place?' she said.

'You'll find out. Just move,' he said, grabbing her arm.

Sophia

'Ouch,' she squealed as green tie's fingers dug hard into her arm as he dragged her through the door.

Stocky slammed it behind them.

What an absolute shithole,' thought Sophia. The place obviously hadn't been used for a while. The concrete floor was dusty with lumps missing out of it. There was one of those mini JCB excavators sitting next to a mound of rubble. Then she saw it. Her cello. Leaning against an old wooden crate. Mancini plucked a string.

'Nice,' he said, as he walked over.

Green tie took the memory stick out of his pocket and handed it to Mancini.

'Am I going to be happy?' Mancini asked.

'I haven't looked at all of it, but the bit I did see looked very juicy,' said green tie, smiling.

'Good,' said Mancini. 'How about her, do you know for sure that she didn't see the contents?'

'I'm pretty sure. She was in and out of there in less than thirty minutes and there's nowhere nearby where she could have checked,' said green tie.

'Look, I don't care what's on it. I just wanna get out of here and never see any of you again.' Mancini looked at Sophia and raised his eyebrow. 'Look, you gave me your word that you wouldn't bother me again after this. You said this would be the last time,' she said.

'Are you saying I'm not a man of my word?' he said, getting up close to her.

'Are you?' she said.

'Absolutely. But maybe I should ask you to finish what you started when we were alone in that hotel room together,' he said, smiling. Stocky sniggered to himself in amusement. 'Let's see, where did we get up to that night. Oh yes, just about here,' he said, grabbing her inner thigh and jamming his hand up hard between her legs.

Sophia slapped him, really hard. Mancini removed his hand, stunned and shocked by how hard she'd slapped his face. He stood back and gently touched the inside of his lip with his thumb. There was a tiny drip of blood where his inner lip had caught his tooth. His laid-back demeanour was suddenly replaced by anger.

'That's the second time you've drawn blood from me,' he said. He turned to stocky and said, 'hold her.' Stocky stepped forward and grabbed her, putting her into a tight bear hug from behind. Her arms were pinned to her sides and she couldn't free herself from stocky's python-like grip.

'You've never seen us before and you won't be seeing us again. Do you understand what I'm saying?'

'Yes,' she said, still unable to move.

'Good,' said Mancini, walking over to Sophia's cello. He bent down and picked up the petrol canister and proceeded to pour petrol all over her cello.

'No, no please,' she screamed. 'I did what you wanted,' she pleaded. Her emotions were all over the place. She cried in frustration and anger at the very thought of her beloved cello going up in flames.

Mancini removed a small pack of book matches from his inner jacket pocket and tore one off.

'Please … please, you don't have to do this. I beg you,

Sophia

you've got what you wanted,' she pleaded, tears now flowing down her face. Mancini just stood there with the book match and packet at the ready as he watched Sophia, who was now crying hysterically as her struggles to free herself from stocky's bear hug proved useless.

'You bastard,' she screamed. Mancini put his finger up to his mouth and said, 'Shhh.'

'You fucking bastard. I hope you all burn in–' Before she could finish, stocky slammed his large meaty hand over her mouth to shut her up.

'This is for drawing blood from me a second time,' he said, striking the match and holding it up in front of his face, making his expression look even more sinister.

Sophia mumbled and struggled, but stocky held her tighter than ever, tears streaming down her face.

'If you tell anybody about us or what you've done for us, this is what will happen to your little sister,' he said. Mancini flicked the lit match onto the body of Sophia's cello, which went up in flames in a matter of seconds. Sophia's legs turned to jelly as Mancini walked past her towards the door.

'Let's go,' he said to his two thugs.

Green tie followed him out the door while stocky kissed Sophia on the cheek and released his grip. Sophia dropped to her knees crying. All she could do was watch her cello burn. Mancini paused at the door momentarily.

'Now we're even. Go back to your life and stay out of my world and I'll stay out of yours,' he said, slamming the door behind him leaving Sophia in a sobbing heap on the floor next to her burning cello.

Chapter 49

Sophia stumbled out of the warehouse and called Delphine from her mobile.

'Hey, where are you, what's happening?' asked Delphine. Sophia could hardly speak for sobbing. 'Sophia, what's wrong? What's happened?' she asked.

'He burned my cello. The bastard burned my cello,' she said, still choking on her tears.

'Where are you, honey. I'll come and get you.'

'I don't know, somewhere near Manor House station,' she said.

'Ok, can you get to the station?'

'I'll try,' said Sophia, sobbing.

'I'm getting a taxi now. Get to the station and wait. I'll be there as fast as I can to pick you up.'

Delphine arrived at Manor House tube station, but Sophia was not there. She tried calling her mobile, but she didn't answer.

In her emotional state, Sophia was not thinking straight and was confused. Instead of waiting for Delphine, she'd misinterpreted what she had told her about waiting and instead had flagged down a taxi and gone back to her apartment in Hampstead. Knowing that her apartment keys were securely locked away in an office at the psychiatric hospital in Cuffley, she'd dialled 118118 and got the phone number of an out-of-hours locksmith, who'd advised her that he would be at her apartment in about an hour. She arrived back at her place, paid the driver and waited for the locksmith to arrive.

When he arrived he explained that he was not supposed to open the door without first seeing identification. But seeing the state she was in, and that she'd promised him that she had identification in the cupboard drawer in the living room, he took pity on her and within two minutes he'd opened the door and let her in. She showed him her ID and paid him with some of the emergency cash that she kept stashed away in the bottom of her drawer.

She went to the kitchen and filled a glass a third full with Vodka and topped it up with half a can of Coke. She took a large mouthful then went to one of the kitchen drawers and took the card with Dritan's mobile number on it. Right now she didn't want to be in the real world. She wanted this nightmare to go away even if only temporarily.

'Hello,' said Dritan.

'I need something,' she said.

'Oh really, who might this be?'

'You gave me your card and mobile number at a club near Soho. You sold me some speed.'

'Well, if you say I did, I guess I must have. So, what do you want?'

'Something to relax me and make me feel like all my problems don't exist anymore.'

'I've got something that can do that.'

'Can you send it over to my apartment?'

Dritan laughed, then said, 'What do you think I am, a taxi service?'

'Please.'

'Where do you live?' he asked.

'Hampstead.'

'Very nice. Let me see what I can do. I'll call you back in five minutes.' He hung up.

Sophia knocked back half her drink then went to the living room. As she sat on her sofa, thoughts of Spencer started to invade her mind: the crash, the fox, the blood, his twisted body in the wreckage. Then came the inevitable voice, his voice, echoing around and around in her mind. Then came Grandma Lizzie. They were all in her mind, going round and around like a verbal merry-go-round getting louder and louder. Then she thought about Mancini, his goons, her burning cello. So many voices, so many sounds. She didn't know what was real and what wasn't. She put her hands over her ears, but the voices and the fox continued to scream and bark. It was no good, she couldn't shut them out.

She got up and thumbed through the new pile of rock CDs, kindly picked out by the friendly young man at HMV. She picked out a band called *Heaven's Basement*, basing her choice purely on the look of the artwork on the cover - an extreme close up of a burning match head with a burning city forming part of the black and red smouldering hot match head. She put the CD in the player, pressed play and cranked up the volume.

SOPHIA

Drums, bass and electric guitar sent a wall of sound to her ears and directly into her brain. The screams of the singer during the intro to 'Welcome Home' were preferable to the screams in her head. She turned the music up louder still and decided the main light in the living room was too damn bright. She turned the lamp on in the corner, and then killed the main light. But it was still way too bright and her over-sensitive eyes could hardly focus. It was as if the light was shooting straight through her pupils directly into her brain, inducing the worse kind of migraine. The music probably wasn't helping, but at least it had taken care of the screaming voices in her head. She grabbed a pillowcase from the airing cupboard and draped it over the lamp. She slumped back onto the sofa, took another gulp of her drink and pushed the base of her palm hard into her forehead and closed her eyes.

Her mobile rang and she recognised Dritan's number on the display.

'Hello,' she said, turning the volume down on the hi-fi.

'It'll cost you £40 for the merchandise and another £50 for my friend to drive it over to you.'

'Fine,' she said.

'What's your address?'

Sophia gave it to him, and then got back to nursing her migraine with her palm. Her mobile rang again. This time it was Delphine, for the fifth time in the past hour.

'Hello,' she said.

'Hey, where are you?'

'I'm at my apartment.'

'I thought you were going to meet me at Manor House tube station. I looked everywhere for you. I've been really worried. Are you ok?'

'Not yet. But soon I'll be just peachy.' Delphine could hear that Sophia wasn't right.

'I'm coming over, ok,' said Delphine.

'No, don't. I want to be alone. I'm just going to take a bath and wash the smell of that hospital out of my hair.'

'Ok, I'm gonna take a taxi home to get changed. Then I'm getting in my car and I'm coming over whether you like it or not.'

'Ok,' said Sophia, taking another drink. She turned the music back up, and then settled on the sofa.

Dritan's buddy was fast. Thirty minutes after she'd spoken to him her doorbell went, which only just managed to cut through the loud rock music. She opened the door and saw a skinny man aged somewhere in his mid-thirties; but it was hard to tell. He'd totally gone to the dogs through years of drug abuse. His hair was shoulder-length and greasy and his eye sockets were set well back in his skull.

'These are from Dritan. It'll be a hundred and twenty quid,' he said.

'I thought it was a ninety?' she said, not that she gave a crap at this stage.

'Look, do you want it or not?'

'Wait a minute,' she said, closing the door and getting some extra cash from her drawer.

'Here,' she said, handing him the money. He handed her a small packet.

SOPHIA

'What is it?' she asked.

'LSD.'

'Wasn't that popular during the nineties?' she asked

'That's right. But our mutual friend can still get his hands on it. Besides, this is a little different and it works a lot faster; his own special blend. You wanna feel like all your problems have gone away? Just pop this under your tongue and let it dissolve for ten minutes. Then in about fifteen minutes you'll go on a trip you'll never forget. You won't want to come back,' he said, as he turned to go back to his car. Sophia closed the door and went to the kitchen and topped her glass up with a copious amount of Vodka. Back in the living room, she opened the small packet and found a couple of small pieces of paper about a quarter of an inch square. *Fuck it*, she thought, as she placed one of them under her tongue. Not only did she want her problems to go away, she wanted them well and truly buried. Whatever was blotted into the paper would hopefully achieve this.

She sat there for ten minutes listening to the music before getting up and taking her drink to the bathroom and put it on the side of the bath. She stuck the plug in and ran the hot tap, with a little cold mixed in. Then she lit three cinnamon spice scented candles, turned off the bathroom light and went to the bedroom to get undressed. As she walked, naked, back to the bathroom, the strangest feeling started to wash over her. Her head suddenly felt like it was filled with helium and was about to float away off her shoulders. She closed the bathroom door and stood there in the candle-lit room and waited for the bath to fill. The candles flickered, causing little shadows to dance across the white tiles. The scent of cinnamon spice filled Sophia's nostrils, while the sound of the water blasting into the bath filled her ears.

She leaned forward and poured some bubble bath under the stream of water, then stood on the bathroom mat for a moment and watched as the water gave birth to a large family of bubbles. She watched intently as they brimmed and frothed. Everything was perfect. Her acute musical ears heard the candles make the occasional flickering 'fffttt' sound as the wick burned and sizzled. The tiled walls were alive with eerie little rippling shadows dancing across them from left to right. The water looked heavenly and inviting, while vibrant purple and blue rainbows shimmered across the bubbles. She was encapsulated in her own personal utopia. Right now it felt like she could climb into that bath and lay there forever. She lifted her left leg over the side of the bath and lowered her foot slowly into the water, testing the temperature. She let out a satisfied sigh as her foot came into contact with the warm acrylic floor of the bath. The warm water felt good engulfing her foot and wrapping around her calf. Her head was very light, but in a good way. She closed her eyes and lifted her right leg to get in, but suddenly everything went very fuzzy, then she fainted. Her left foot slipped out from under her. She spun sideways and flipped backwards, cracking her head on the porcelain sink. She hit the floor, unconscious – blood pouring from her head, taps still running.

Chapter 50

Delphine rang and rang on Sophia's doorbell, but there was no answer. Standing outside her apartment door, she tried calling her mobile, but she didn't answer. Then the music stopped as the CD came to the end. She rang the doorbell again, thinking she might not have heard it because of the music. But there was still no answer. She opened the letterbox and shouted, 'SOPHIA. SOPHIA, ARE YOU IN THERE?' She leaned down a little more and looked through the letterbox. She could just about make out flickering light coming from under the bathroom door at the end of the corridor and she could hear running water.

'SOPHIA,' she shouted again, but she didn't answer. She stepped back and prepared to shoulder-charge the door and bust it open. But she had a change of heart in fear of dislocating her shoulder or injuring herself. She stepped forward and tried the handle on the door and pushed. 'Thank God,' she said, as the door opened. The locksmith had left the latch of the Yale lock down with the latch mechanism in.

'Sophia, it's only me. Where are you?' she said, glancing into the living room on her way down the corridor towards the bathroom. She also glanced in the kitchen, but Sophia was not there either.

'Sophia, are you in there?' she said, knocking on the bathroom door. 'Sophia,' she said, opening the door. 'Oh no, Sophia!' Delphine stooped down. 'Sophia, wake up,' she said, gently slapping her face. 'Oh no, Sophia, please, wake up,' she said. Then she felt her knee getting warm and noticed it was in a pool of blood, coming from Sophia's head. 'Oh no, please,' she said, taking her mobile out and dialling 999.

'Emergency services, which service do you require?' asked the woman on the other end of the phone.

'Ambulance, I need an ambulance, fast!' said Delphine, holding a flannel to Sophia's head to try and stop the bleeding.

And they were fast, really fast. It can't have been more than three minutes when Delphine heard the sirens coming down the street. She ran out of the front door waving frantically at the ambulance driver.

The paramedics were efficient, fast and totally professional. Within minutes they had a neck brace on Sophia, had stopped her head bleeding and had her stretchered out of there. Delphine followed them, grabbing Sophia's iPhone on her way out the door. The ambulance sped down Rosslyn Hill towards the Royal Free Hospital with blue lights flashing and sirens sounding.

Delphine spent the first two minutes of the journey seeking reassurance from the paramedic in the back. But he was more concerned with Delphine telling him how

Sophia

long she thought Sophia had been lying on the bathroom floor, unconscious.

At the hospital, Sophia was rushed into the A&E entrance, where doctors were on standby. All Delphine could do was stand and watch as the doctors rushed around. Delphine was anxious, but a doctor insisted she stand clear and let them do their job. A nurse showed Delphine to the waiting area and told her they would come and find her when they had some news. While she waited, she called Sophia's parents. Thank God Sophia didn't have her passcode lock activated on her iPhone.

Sophia started to come around within a few minutes of arriving at the hospital. The gash on her head was stitched up and arrangements were made for Sophia to have an x-ray to check her skull and neck. Also, because she'd been knocked unconscious, a routine CT scan was organised.

Sophia's parents arrived and were asked to wait until the doctor could see them. Forty minutes had passed when a doctor eventually came to give them news of their daughter.

'Mr and Mrs Beckinsale, I'm sorry you've had to wait so long. I'm Doctor Faulkner.'

'What happened? Is our daughter all right?' asked Diana.

'Yes, she's fine. Your daughter was brought in with a serious head injury. She was unconscious when she arrived, but she's since come around. She's had stitches to fix the deep cut on her head, but she's going to be fine.'

'Thank goodness,' said Diana, 'Can we see her?'

'Not just yet. She's been taken to the x-ray department to have her neck and skull checked for fractures, and then after that she's going to have a CT scan.'

'How long before we can see her, Doctor?' asked Andrew.

'About an hour, maybe a little longer. Somebody will come and find you when she's ready. I just wanted to reassure you in the meantime.'

'Thank you, Doctor,' said Andrew.

It was a relatively quiet evening at the hospital and it was just over an hour later when another doctor came to speak with Andrew and Diana.

'Mr and Mrs Beckinsale, I'm sorry you've had to wait. I'm Doctor Cheadle; I'm one of the neurologists here at the hospital. Please, follow me,' he said, leading the way to the relatives' room.

'This is a little unorthodox. The patient would usually be the first person to be informed of any results and findings, but Sophia isn't in a position to do that at present.'

'I'm sorry, I don't understand?' said Diana, looking at her husband, 'What do you mean she isn't in a position?' asked Diana.

'We found traces of Lysergic acid diethylamide in her blood, as well as large volumes of alcohol.'

'Wait a minute, Lysergic what?' asked Diana.

'LSD,' said Andrew.

'The drug? Oh no,' said Diana.

'Yes,' said the doctor, 'She's still feeling the effects

of it, so she's not really herself at the moment and isn't very communicative. It'll take until the morning before it's worn off.'

'Doctor, what are the results of the x-ray and CT scan?' asked Andrew.

'The x-ray's were fine; nothing's fractured or broken. But I'm afraid the CT scan revealed a tumour on the frontal lobe of her brain.

'Oh Lord,' said Diana, putting her hand up to her mouth.

'Oh dear Lord, no,' said Andrew, trying to compose himself.

'Look, if it's what we think it is, it might not be that bad.'

'What type of tumour do you think it is, Doctor?' he asked, hoping for the best case scenario.

'It has all the characteristics of a grade one meningioma. Its position and size would mean it could be operated on and removed using endonasal techniques,' said Doctor Cheadle. Andrew let out a small sigh of relief.

'What does that mean honey?' asked Diana.

'About eighty percent of meningiomas are benign and if they can remove it there won't be any long-term effects,' said Andrew.

'You're husband's right, Mrs Beckinsale. Look, we'll have the full picture in the morning. We're going to keep her in overnight for observation, then first thing tomorrow we're going to give her an MRI.'

'Can we see her now?' asked Diana, anxious for several reasons.

'Of course, but only for a few minutes. She's about to be taken up to a ward and it's way past visiting hours. Remember, she's not in any fit state to communicate. She's feeling strong effects from the LSD and has a lot of alcohol in her system.'

Doctor Cheadle took them through to see Sophia briefly before she was taken to the ward. On the way Doctor Cheadle explained that Sophia's friend, Delphine, had found her and was still sitting in the waiting area.

Sophia was lying down in bed with a bandage around her head. She wasn't very communicative and was gazing at the ceiling with a blank, but strangely eccentric expression on her face.

'Oh, my poor darling,' said Diana, taking Sophia's hand in hers. Andrew held her other hand while stroking her hair. Doctor Cheadle was right, Sophia barely knew they were there and was not very communicative.

Two orderlies came to take Sophia up to the ward. Andrew and Diana decided to go and find Delphine in the waiting area on their way out.

'Delphine?' said Andrew, recognising her.

'Mr Beckinsale,' she said, standing up.

'I understand you phoned for the ambulance. Can you tell us what happened?' he said.

'I'm not really sure. I went over to her apartment and couldn't get any answer, but I knew she was in. The front door was unlocked so I went inside, and that's when I found her lying unconscious on the bathroom floor.'

'She was supposed to be in hospital in Cuffley. Did you know she'd run away?' asked Diana.

SOPHIA

'She phoned me from Cuffley station and told me she was getting on a train. She asked me to pick her up from Highbury & Islington.'

'And you didn't think to call the hospital and tell them of her whereabouts?' said Diana.

'She's my friend. She needed my help. She sounded desperate; I was trying to help her.'

'Yes, and look what a great job you've done. And can you explain why she's taking LSD?' said Diana, accusingly.

'Look, Sophia's going through something right now. I'm trying to help her the best I can. I'm not happy that she's drinking and taking drugs; I've been trying to stop her. I'm trying to understand what Sophia's going through so I can help her. She's my friend,' she argued.

'Well, I wish you'd start acting like one. Our daughter's lying up there–'

'Look, this isn't getting us anywhere,' said Andrew, interrupting. 'Delphine, I know you've been looking out for Sophia, and we really do appreciate that. But do you have any idea how she ended up unconscious on the bathroom floor?' he asked.

'No. I spoke to her on the phone half an hour before I got there. She said she was going to take a bath. Because I was concerned for her, I decided to go over to her apartment anyway. When I went into the bathroom, the taps were still running and water was running over the edge of the bath. Sophia was lying on the floor naked with blood pouring out of her head. It looked like she'd slipped while getting into the bath and hit her head.

'You said she needed your help. What was so pressing that she had to run away from the hospital?' asked Diana.

'She was in trouble,' said Delphine.

'What kind of trouble?' asked Andrew.

'Look, it's probably best if you speak to Sophia about it. But from what I can gather, it's all ok now. Look, can you at least tell me how she is?'

'The CT scan revealed that she has a brain tumour,' said Andrew.

'Oh dear God, no,' said Delphine, dropping back into her seat as her legs turned to jelly.

'It might not be as bad as it sounds. It's what's called a grade one meningioma. They're mostly benign and it can easily be removed with surgery via her nostrils. We'll know more tomorrow when they've done the MRI scan,' he said.

'Can I give you my mobile number, so you can call me with news – please? Sophia's my best friend and I need to know she's ok,' said Delphine.

'Of course,' said Andrew, taking out his mobile.

Delphine gave him her number then they wrapped up the conversation and left the hospital.

Chapter 51

Sophia had an MRI scan first thing the following day and was then taken back to the ward. She was half way through eating the hospital breakfast when the neurologist came up to see her.

'Hello, Sophia. I'm Doctor Hutchinson. So, how are you feeling this morning?' he said, pulling the privacy curtain across.

'Apart from a splitting headache, a mouth that feels like the bottom of a birdcage and being starving hungry, I'm fine,' said Sophia.

'Well, I'm confident we can do something about your headache, but I'm not sure if that little breakfast will satisfy your hunger,' he joked. Just then, Andrew and Diana appeared.

'My baby,' said Diana, taking Sophia's hand and kissing her on the cheek. 'How are you feeling?' she asked.

'I'm ok, Mummy.'

'We thought you might need some clothes,' said Andrew, holding up a small overnight bag. He went to the other side of the bed and kissed her on the forehead.

'Darling, it's going to be alright,' he said.

'I know Daddy, it was only a bump on the head,' she

said, smiling.

Andrew looked at the doctor with a question in his eyes.

'I'm Doctor Hutchinson, the head neurologist,' he said, extending his hand to Andrew.

'Have you done the MRI yet?' he asked.

'Yes.'

'Have you spoken to our daughter about the results?' he asked.

'Not yet, we felt it would be better if we waited until you got here.'

'Daddy, what's going on?' asked Sophia.

'Look, why don't we all go down to my office,' he said, 'where we can have some privacy.' Sophia looked at the doctor, then at her parents.

'What's going on?' she asked.

'Darling, let's go to the doctor's office and talk about it there,' said Diana.

'Here you go, honey. Why don't you get dressed,' said Andrew, placing the overnight bag on the bottom of the bed. 'We'll wait,' he said. They stepped outside the privacy curtain and let Sophia get dressed.

Sophia was anxious and couldn't get dressed quickly enough. It took her all of forty seconds to put her trousers, shirt, socks and shoes on and draw the privacy curtain across.

On the way down to his office, the doctor apologised for the distance and amount of corridors they had to negotiate.

'Please, come in, have a seat,' he said, taking a seat behind his large plush leather-bound desk – fitting for a

Sophia

head neurologist.

'Ok, you were very lucky regarding the crack on your head. There were no fractures so that's good. However, the CT scan flagged something up, which needed further investigation. Now that we've done the MRI scan I can confirm that you have what's called a frontal meningioma brain tumour,' he said.

'Daddy,' said Sophia, grabbing her father's hand. In an instant she went into a state of utter panic as thoughts of, *malignant* and *how long do I have?* entered her mind. Andrew squeezed her hand and tried to reassure her, but Sophia started to tremble, dreading the next words to come out of the neurologist's mouth. She prayed that the word 'malignant' wouldn't be in there and the words, 'you're going to be fine' would be.

'Sophia, I know it sounds scary, but the good news is that your tumour is what's known as a grade one benign meningioma – that's the lowest grade you can get. In fact, medically speaking, it's not strictly a tumour. I've studied both the CT scan and the MRI and its very good news. It's going to be very easy to remove it.'

'You see darling,' said Diana, holding Sophia's other hand.

'Meningiomas are more common in people aged forty and fifty; you'd be surprised how many people get them. You don't often see them in people your age though,' he said.

'What does the operation involve, doctor?' asked Diana, looking for the doctor to reassure her daughter.

'It's a fairly routine procedure. The neurosurgeon will

go in through the nostrils using endonasal techniques. The tumour will be de-bunged and then it will be removed. The good news is that your tumour's near the surface and hasn't invaded any deep structures or major blood vessels so it should be relatively straightforward to deal with.'

'How long does the procedure take?' asked Diana.

'About three hours. After surgery you'll have to wear packs in your nostrils for about five days.'

'Packs?' asked Sophia.

'Don't worry, they're just like small tampons,' he explained.

'What about any long-term effects; I mean, will it affect my life and will it come back?' asked Sophia.

'I'd fully expect the neurosurgeon to be able to remove one hundred percent of the tumour. For this type of meningioma, the recurrence rate is little to none. You'll be given a clean bill of health and you can go on to live a long and happy life,' he said, smiling.

'Is this why I've been suffering from headaches over the past few months?' asked Sophia.

'Yes, the oedema around the tumour has been causing a lot of swelling and pressure on the frontal lobe of your brain.'

'Doctor, I'm correct in assuming that frontal lobe tumours such as these can cause personality changes?' said Andrew. Diana looked at her husband, questioningly.

'Is that true?' she asked.

'Yes it is,' said the doctor.

'What kind of personality changes?' asked Diana.

'Well, they can vary from one patient to the next and affect people in different ways. Some people show signs of aggressive behaviour or irritability. I had a lady patient a couple of years back who suddenly became very short-tempered and really quite volatile. Her husband told me that before the tumour she wouldn't say boo to a goose, then the next minute she was acting aggressively towards him and cursing every other word. He said he'd never heard such language come out of her mouth.'

'Could it cause somebody to start drinking and taking drugs; the recreational kind that is?' asked Sophia.

'Definitely. A tumour like this can cause one's personality and character to change drastically. It's like your whole world suddenly goes off axis. One minute everything is perfectly level and on an even keel, and the next everything's changed.'

'This explains everything,' said Diana.

'Explains what?' asked Doctor Hutchinson.

'Well, at first we thought it was post-traumatic stress disorder after Spencer died,' said Diana.

'Spencer?' asked the doctor.

'Spencer was Sophia's boyfriend. He died not too long ago,' she said.

'I'm sorry to hear that,' said the doctor, looking at Sophia.

'Anyway, shortly afterwards Sophia changed. Her personality I mean. It was like she became a different person.'

'Do go on,' said the doctor.

'Well, we noticed more aggression and volatility in

her behaviour. She started swearing, which she never did before. She's basically been on a path of self-destruction and she's all but totally alienated herself. Not to mention her career, which has slowly been coming apart at the seams,' said Diana.

'Well, what you're describing is a typical trait of this kind of frontal lobe tumour.'

'So this, meni …'

'Meningioma,' said the doctor.

'So this meningioma has been the cause of her change in personality?' asked Diana.

'I suspect so, yes, or rather the surrounding oedema, which has been putting considerable pressure on the frontal lobe of Sophia's brain, which essentially would change her view of the world.'

'Does this mean once you've removed it she'll return to normal?' asked Diana.

'I'd certainly expect you to notice a big difference once the oedema's gone and the pressure's been relieved. This should start to happen within a few days of the procedure. Then, after about three months she'll have made a full recovery and her personality should have returned back to normal.'

'Oh, thank God,' said Diana.

'Doctor, what would have been the cause of the tumour in somebody so young? Sophia's only twenty-two,' asked Andrew.

'Meningioma's are quite sporadic, they appear randomly and their causes are not that well understood. They're the most common primary type of brain tumour and as I've already mentioned, you generally find them in older people. That's not to say young people don't get them, they do, but it's rare.'

'How long do you think I've had it?' asked Sophia, who was not trembling quite so much now and was able to speak.

'It's difficult to pin down exactly as some grow more rapidly than others. But going by the size, I'd say three, maybe four months, and it would have grown quite a lot over the past eight to ten weeks, causing a lot more pressure.'

'The very same period that your personality's changed, darling,' said Diana.

'When will you schedule the operation?' asked Andrew.

'It won't be done here. I'll refer you to the National Hospital for Neurology and Neurosurgery in Queen Square. You'll need to have steroids pre-operatively for about forty-eight hours. But the operation will be approximately two weeks from now.'

Diana and Andrew held Sophia's hand and forced a light smile. But the next few weeks were going to be nerve-wracking for all of them.

'Mummy, Daddy. Would you mind if I spoke with Doctor Hutchinson in private for a minute?'

'Of course, darling. We'll wait outside,' said Andrew, leading Diana outside into the corridor.

'I don't really know how to put this, it's quite embarrassing.'

'Sophia, I'm well aware that frontal lobe tumours can make people do things they ordinarily wouldn't. It's quite ok; you don't have to be embarrassed.'

'Over the past few months I've been a little careless. I don't really know why, but I've become quite promiscuous, sexually. I've been sleeping around a lot and quite often unprotected. It all seemed perfectly normal to me. I know I was never like that before. Is this due to the tumour in my head?'

'Almost certainly. Look. I've been a neurologist for a long time now and over the years I've heard some quite shocking stories about how tumours like this have affected people and their families. There was one patient, she was in her early forties and had been happily married for nearly twenty years. She had a loving husband and three children. Then one day she changed. Out of the blue she demanded a divorce and left her husband and children. She went off and had several affairs over the next three or four months and didn't want anything to do with her family again. Then the pressure caused by the tumour got so great she eventually fainted and collapsed. After the tumour was removed, her sexual behaviour went into remission and her personality eventually returned to how it was previously.'

'Wow, did she go back to her husband and family?'

'I believe she did.'

Chapter 52

🎻 4 weeks post operation 🎻

Django pulled up outside Sophia's parents' house. Just as he parked up, blocking in another car, Diana came to the door to greet him.

'Django, how are you?' she asked.

'I'm good. Am I ok parked there?'

'Yes, that's fine. I didn't think it was possible to fit so many cars on one driveway,' she joked. 'Anyway, come on in, everyone's in the lounge.'

'Django, it's great to see you,' said Andrew, extending his hand.

'Hey you,' said Sophia.

'Hey, how are you?' said DJ.

'I'm great, just great. Thank you so much for coming.'

'I wouldn't want to be anywhere else,' he said.

The lounge was a congregation of family and friends, all engaged in conversation with a flute of champagne each and little plates of buffet food.

'Everyone,' said Sophia, clinking a fork against her half empty champagne glass. 'I just want to say a few words. First I'd like to thank you all for taking the time to be with me this evening to celebrate the success of my operation and a new start in life,' she said, glancing across the room at all the familiar faces. 'Now, I know that I haven't quite been myself lately,' she said, causing a few chuckles amongst her audience. 'And for this, I want to make a sincere and public apology – to everyone. Although I didn't feel like I was behaving out of character, I now know that I put my family though hell. Mum, Dad, Charlotte, Eleanor,' she said, looking at them all in turn, 'I'm so sorry for the trouble and stress I've caused you. Eleanor, what I did to you was unforgivable. I don't know how I'll ever make it up to you. I love you so much and although we didn't always see eye-to-eye, you have no idea how much you've inspired me over the years. Not only do I love you, but I've got so much respect for you and I've never told you this before but, I hold you up so high. I hope one day you can forgive me, I–'

'Shut up, just shut up,' said Eleanor, tears running down her face as she ran over to her sister and hugged her. 'I forgive you ... I forgive you,' she said, to rapturous applause.

'Thank you. I love you so much, sis.'

'I know, and I love you too,' she said, standing back so Sophia could see the sincerity on her face. 'I've got to tell you, I'm so glad you dyed your hair back to auburn. That whole blonde thing just didn't work,' joked Eleanor. Sophia laughed through her tears of joy.

'Now, get back to your speech,' said Eleanor, stepping to the side.

'Meredith, you've always been there for me, since I

SOPHIA

was just fourteen. I know that without you my career could have been ruined before it even got started. You shielded me and guided me along the right path. I feel like I've let you down recently. You've had to cancel concerts left, right and centre because of my outrageous behaviour. Meredith, I'm truly sorry that I've caused you so much trouble,' she said.

'Darling, it's in the past now. Lets move forward and look to the future,' said Meredith, raising her glass.

'Hear! hear!' somebody shouted.

'Anyway, most of you know already, but for those who don't, the operation was a complete success. The surgeon removed one hundred percent of the tumour and he's given me a clean bill of health,' she said, tears of joy running down her face. Andrew and Diana came to stand by her. Diana handed Sophia a napkin to blot up her tears.

'I'd like to raise a toast,' said Andrew, 'To the return of our daughter, Sophia.'

There were shouts of 'hear! hear!' and 'to Sophia!' as champagne glasses clinked around the room.

People started to leave shortly afterwards as it was a weekday, and many had to be up early for work the next morning.

'Mummy, Daddy, I have to go,' said Sophia.

'So soon?' said Diana.

'I need to go and see my friend, Delphine. I need to talk to her.'

'That's ok, darling. You go and talk to her,' said Andrew.

Sophia hugged and kissed her two sisters goodbye,

promising Eleanor that they would spend more time together from now on.

Sophia knocked on Delphine's door. She stood there, hoping she would be home. She hadn't called in advance, as she wanted to surprise her.

The door opened, Delphine took a step back and studied Sophia for a moment. Sure, she looked different now her hair had been dyed back to her natural auburn colour, but her whole deportment was different; her demeanour, her facial expression, the look in her eyes. This was a different person entirely.

'Hello, I'm Sophia Beckinsale,' she said, smiling and extending her hand.

'Hello, I'm Delphine Patterson, I'm so pleased to meet you,' she said, shaking Sophia's hand. 'Would you like to come in?'

'I'd love to.'

Delphine made a coffee for herself, and tea for Sophia.

'Your father called me to tell me the operation was a success' said Delphine. 'Look, I didn't want to disturb you after the operation and when I found out that the tumour was responsible for your behaviour, well, I figured that it might also have been responsible for your new choice of friend. So, I guess I just wanted to leave the ball in your court and if you called me, great, if not ...'

'You silly rabbit. You're a wonderful person, Delphi. You're my best friend,' she said.

'I'm so relieved,' said Delphine, hugging Sophia. 'So, are you going to be ok?' she asked.

'Yes. I've been given a clean bill of health. The surgeon told me I can move forward and live a long and normal life.'

'And the personality issues?'

'Well, it's only been four weeks since the operation but already I'm pretty much back to normal. It'll be a few more weeks before I make a full recovery, but psychologically speaking, I've recovered and I feel like my old self again.'

'That's great, Sophia. I'm so pleased.'

'Me too.'

'So, how does this work, I mean, your memory of events. Can you remember how you were, or what you did?'

'Oh yes, very clearly. It's really quite strange. I remember everything I did and how I'd been behaving, but at the time it all seemed perfectly normal. My actions, what I did and what I said, it all seemed perfectly reasonable to me. But now, when I look back, I can see just how destructive and dysfunctional I was.'

'Well, you had your moments. You even shocked me on a few occasions,' said Delphine, smiling.

'Look, I know we met under a strange set of circumstances, but you've been there for me, you've been a rock and I really do consider you to be my best friend,' she said. Delphine looked up at her and could not hold back the tear that escaped her eye.

'I'm so glad, I was worried you might not want to know me anymore.'

'Why on earth would you ever think such a thing? You're a wonderful person … Delphine Patterson,' she said. They both laughed.

'You know, when your father told me that your behaviour was down to the tumour and that they were going to remove it, I decided to change a few things in my own life.'

'Oh?'

'Yes, I'm not a call girl anymore.'

'Are you serious?'

'Yes. I know the money was good, but I'm doing a few more days at the club. A bit more bar work, but I'm also doing an extra night singing too. Anyway, I did some calculations and I can manage. I'm going to concentrate on my singing and give it my best shot,' she said, clearly excited.

'That's great news, Delphine. I'm so happy for you. And you know, with your voice, I know you'll make it. Oh, I almost forgot; I have something for you,' said Sophia, taking a small box out of her handbag and handing it to her. Delphine opened the box and saw a Cartier watch.

'The first time I gave you this I wasn't in my right mind. Now I am, and I genuinely want you to have it.' Delphine smiled and put the watch onto her wrist.

Chapter 53

🎻 **10 weeks post operation** 🎻

'Hi, come in,' said Sophia.

'So, what's the big surprise then? I've been on tenterhooks all day,' said Delphine, taking her boots off in Sophia's hallway.

'All in good time, come on through to the kitchen, we're celebrating,' said Sophia.

'Celebrating what? Just tell me, the suspense is unbearable.'

In the kitchen Sophia poured two flutes of champagne, but before giving Delphine hers, she first handed her a business card, and then a concert ticket.

'What are these?' asked Delphine, studying the record company business card.

'Well, as you know, I'm a signed up artist with that record company. And the man named on that card wants to hear you sing.'

'I don't understand,' said Delphine.

'Well, I was in his office yesterday discussing my long overdue Beethoven recording and I mentioned that I just happen to know the best jazz/blues singer in the world. I told him she's young and beautiful and she also happens to have the most incredible voice I've ever heard. So, he wants you to call him and let him know when you're next performing at The Baltomore Oriole so he can come and hear you sing.'

'Oh my God, I don't know what to say,' said Delphine, looking at the card, then at Sophia, 'I'm overwhelmed.'

'He's been scouting for an artist just like you for quite a while now. If he likes what he hears … ok, I'm going to come clean. He's already heard and seen you.'

'What?' said Delphine, puzzled.

'Remember the first time you sang 'You've Got A Friend' for me in the club?'

'Yes.'

'Well, I actually recorded a minute of it on my iPhone,' she said, smiling. He likes you, Delphi; I mean he *really* likes you. This is going to be very big for you, you're going to be a star.' Delphine hugged Sophia and didn't stop squeezing her.

'Thank you, thank you so much.'

'You're welcome. You're a great singer, Delphi. You deserve to be heard and why should the world be deprived of such a huge talent any longer.'

Delphine then looked at the ticket Sophia had handed her, which read:

SOPHIA

Royal Festival Hall
Presents
Edward Elgar Cello Concerto in E minor,
Op. 85
With the BBC Symphony Orchestra
Soloist: Sophia Beckinsale

'Oh wow. I didn't think you ever wanted to perform the Elgar in public?'

'Well, Meredith thought it would be a good idea to help me get back in favour with the public. I've had a bit of bad press in recent months. Not turning up for concerts, dressing inappropriately and even shocking audiences with improvised cadenzas. Anyway, I agreed. It will put me back in the limelight and it will give the public and music press something to talk about.'

'But how do you feel about actually performing it?'

'You know, I'm actually really looking forward to it. You could say I've changed my lifetime's tune,' she said.

'Well, I can't wait to hear you play,' said Delphine, noticing a white medical dressing poking out from under Sophia's dress strap. 'What's that,' she said, gesturing towards her shoulder.

'Yeah. Remember the tattoo I got in Paris?'

'The butterfly, of course.'

'Well, I had it coloured in with red and white.'

'So it's not black anymore?'

'No, and neither am I. I've morphed back to my

colourful self and all the darkness has gone away,' she said, smiling.

Chapter 54

'Welcome to the Royal Festival Hall for tonight's live performance of Elgar's Cello Concerto with the BBC Symphony Orchestra and soloist, Sophia Beckinsale,' announced the BBC radio presenter.

'Martin, Sophia Beckinsale's had a bit of negative press in recent months, but I've got a feeling that after this evening's performance she'll be back in favour with the public,' he continued.

'Well, I think she already is, David. Once it hit the news that she'd recently had an operation to remove a brain tumour, the classical music world were always going to be right behind her,' said Martin.

'Yes, and for the listeners who weren't aware, Sophia was diagnosed with a benign brain tumour, but she made a full recovery and she's here tonight to perform live, for the first time in her career, the Elgar Cello Concerto.'

'It's great news all round, David. Even the French have forgiven her for her somewhat unorthodox dress sense at a recital in Paris not long ago,' said Martin, humorously.

'Martin, why do you think Sophia's decided to perform the Elgar now? I mean, it's common knowledge that she never wanted to perform the Elgar in public.'

'Who knows, David. I can understand that many female cellists probably feel a little uncomfortable performing the Elgar. Comparisons to Jacqueline du Pré are always going to be inevitable. But I think Sophia's been worrying for nothing, and I'm sure she's going to hold her own this evening,' he said.

'It's interesting that she's playing a Montagnana cello that's being loaned to her for this evening's concert. Although Domenico Montagnana made violins, violas, cellos and double basses, he's best known for his cellos and many people say they're particularly suited to concertos.'

'That's right, David. Her preferred cello was a modern instrument made by a Cambridge-based luthier called Jonathan Woolston, but I understand it was destroyed recently in a fire.'

'Yes, absolutely tragic, Martin. But I understand Jonathan's in the middle of building her an identical replacement as we speak.'

'That's right, though they'll be a playing-in period before Sophia will be happy to perform with it in public,' said Martin.

'Absolutely, and of course it's not only the instrument that has to be played in, but the musician has to be played in as well. She'll have to find the instrument's tone and colour, and then the settling-in period will take a little time.'

'Yes, that settling-in period generally happens during the first year, and during this time the instrument's sound will also mellow and improve.'

The audience started to applaud loudly.

'I'm sure we won't have to wait too long to hear it, Martin. Well, it looks like the conductor's making his way onto the stage,' said David.

Delphine was seated in the front row next to Django, with Sophia's parents and two sisters next to him. Meredith was also there, along with some of Sophia's other friends and relatives.

Sophia walked out onto the stage, to a standing ovation. She looked incredible with her long auburn hair and full-length black silk dress. After shaking hands with the conductor and the first violin, she took a brief curtsey then sat down and located the spike of her cello into the rubber strip coming from the foot of the chair leg. She acknowledged to the conductor that she was ready. The capacity audience at the Festival Hall fell silent. Nobody coughed and nobody fidgeted in their seat. Absolutely everybody in the audience held their breath and waited in anticipation for Sophia to play, for the first time in her playing career, the Elgar Cello Concerto.

Then, with the taste of a recently eaten banana still lingering on her tongue, Sophia Beckinsale lifted her cello bow and struck the opening G and E of the famous first movement. The audience listened intently as Sophia played; spellbound by her musical genius and her pure untainted interpretation of the work. Each note, just as the composer had intended, each phrase was pure Elgarian perfection. As the conductor turned the pages of the score and the first movement progressed, the audience fell in love, all over again, in a way that they hadn't for more than fifty years. Sophia Beckinsale was captivating the public in a way that no other musician had since Jacqueline du Pré first performed this very concerto at this very venue back in 1962. If the audience loved Sophia before, they were *totally* in love with her now.

After the adagio at the end of the fourth and final movement the audience sprung to their feet and broke out into rapturous applause. The decibel levels inside the packed auditorium were ear shattering. The audience were overwhelmed by what they had just heard. Sophia stood while the audience gave her a standing ovation to a deafening soundtrack of cheers, whistles and shouts of 'bravo!!'

As usual, Sophia made a huge deal out of her curtsey, taking her time over it. She took hold of her black silk dress with her right hand while her left hand held her bow and cello upright. She slid her left foot across the stage floor, positioning it behind her right. Then she stylishly knelt and went all the way down to the floor, leaning into one knee while balancing with grace and elegance. Then, she lowered and bowed her head, holding her position for fifteen seconds before eventually standing – the audience lapped up her beautifully graceful curtsey, cheering and clapping louder and louder.

Sophia looked down into the front row at her friends and family and smiled at each of them. Then, she noticed somebody familiar out of the corner of her eye. Slightly to her left and four rows back she saw Spencer, sitting

SOPHIA

there in a halo of white Divine light. He looked at peace and was smiling at her. His mouth didn't move, but she heard his voice.

'I've got to go now, my darling. Make the most of your new life and don't spend too much time thinking about me. We shared a moment in time together, and we will again. Until then, something tells me that the void in your heart's soon going to be filled with love again. I want you to grab hold of it and embrace it. Goodbye my darling.'

Sophia looked to the front row at her parents, then back to row D, but Spencer's seat was empty – he was gone.

Epilogue

It was 10:30 p.m. at Sophia's apartment. She'd invited a few friends around to celebrate the success of the Elgar concert a week previously. It appeared that more than one person there had something to celebrate. Delphine was ecstatic, having been offered a record deal on the same label as Sophia. She and the record company had already come up with a list of classic jazz/blues songs for her to record on her debut CD.

Django was thrilled that he and Sophia were just weeks away from going into the recording studio to finally lay down the Beethoven Cello Sonatas.

'So, how long until completion on your apartment?' asked DJ.

'Well, I sold it the day after it went on the market and the solicitors have been really efficient. I expect it'll be about another four or five weeks,' said Sophia.

'What's your new place like in Cambridge?' asked Delphine.

'You wouldn't believe it. For the money I got for this place I was able to buy a four-bedroom detached house in a lovely little village just outside Cambridge. It's so peaceful and picturesque. Naturally, I'm going to invite everyone up there for a house warming.'

'Do you think you'll be happy there, away from your family I mean?' asked DJ.

'It's only sixty miles north. I drive up there quite a lot and it takes me about an hour and twenty minutes. I just feel like I need a fresh start and this will give me a chance to really concentrate on my music. I have a few friends there and my cello maker's based there, so is the man who re-hairs my bow. Besides, I just don't really like it in London anymore. Cambridge is a much smaller city. It's got everything I need and the quieter life-style will suit me better now. And the house, there's so much room in it. I've even got a dedicated music room.'

'That's great, Sophia. I'm really happy for you,' said Delphine.

By 11:30 p.m. all but Delphine and Django had left. Django got up off the sofa.

'Ok, I'm going to head off home to bed. I've got an early start,' he said.

'Thanks for coming, DJ,' said Sophia, hugging him.

'I'll see you on Tuesday at Steinway Hall – ten a.m.'

'You got it,' she said.

'Goodnight, Delphine,' he said.

'Goodnight, DJ.'

'I suppose I should make a move too. I've got to get my beauty sleep so I can look good when the photo's taken for my new CD cover,' she said, smiling.

'Oh, don't go just yet. How about a quick nightcap before you go?'

'Ok,' she said, settling herself back into the sofa. 'You

know, I'd like to say I enjoyed listening to you play at the Festival Hall last week, but "enjoyed" is just too small a word for it. I haven't been able to think of a word that can sum up your playing, Sophia. But I tell you this, your playing really moved me. I had no idea classical music could affect me so deeply. You evoked such deep emotion in me. You're my new inspiration ... Sophia Beckinsale,' she said, smiling.

'Thanks, Delphi.'

Sophia popped a CD into the CD player, turned the volume down to a neighbour friendly level and pressed play.

'Oh my God, what on earth is that?' questioned Delphine when she heard aggressive rock music coming from Sophia's hi-fi.

'Asking Alexandria' she said, handing Delphine the CD case.

'From Death To Destiny,' she said, reading the album title off the case, 'Well, it sounds ... interesting,' she said, raising a mock-eyebrow and laughing.

'Well, the tumour didn't only change my personality, it changed my taste in music too. I've been listening to a lot of rock music recently. I think the tumour allowed some of it to seep into my subconscious and now I'm left with, shall we say, a somewhat broader taste in music,' she said, smiling.

They both laughed.

If you enjoyed this novel, please be kind enough to take a moment to leave me a review on Amazon.
Thank you.

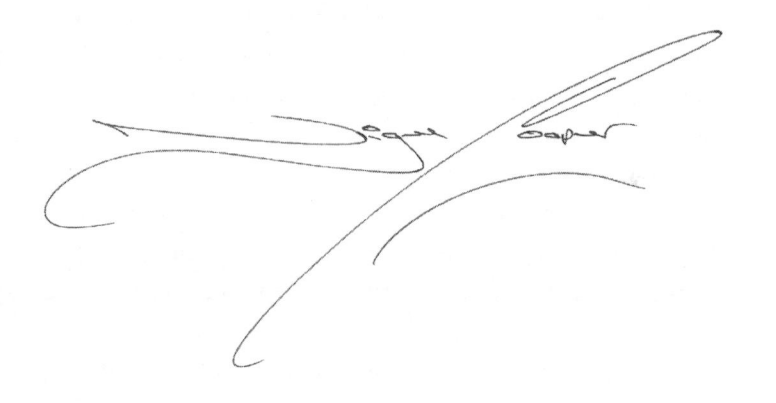

Acknowledgements

Please read this acknowledgements page after you have read the book as there are some potential plot spoilers herein.

I would like to take this opportunity to thank the many people who helped me during the research and writing stage of this novel. They kindly gave their time and expertise in helping and advising me on many subjects. Without these people, this novel would not have manifested itself in quite the same way. Their input helped make the novel come to life, made the characters more believable, and gave the story that *real* detail and *feel* that readers can relate to. It is for this reason that I would like to acknowledge all those who were kind enough to give up their time, either in person, on the phone, via email or Skype.

First I'd like to thank the photographer, Lawrence Randall, for his creative talents and imagination, and for producing such stunning imagery for the book cover. You captured the mood perfectly, giving Sophia the *look* and *mood* I wanted to portray.

I'd like to thank Lynn Mathieson for modelling for the front cover photo and bringing Sophia to life. After the photographer and I painstakingly looked through pages upon pages of models, we found you. Not only did you stand out from the rest, you were the perfect "Sophia" and were exactly how I had envisaged Sophia in my head while I wrote up the detailed synopsis, character profile and character biography for her. It's because I had such a definitive image of Sophia in my mind that it took so long to find the perfect girl amongst hundreds of other models – but it was well worth the wait.

Thanks must also go to Elvire Roux, the hair stylist and make-up artist for the day of the shoot. Thanks to you, Sophia's hair and make-up took on the desired effect required for the cover photo.

I'd like to thank Joanne Mills for lending the photographer a black dress to use on the shoot. Although he ended up using a different dress for the model on the cover photo, I'm touched by your trust. The fact that you allowed me, a total stranger, (with no ID and no security deposit) to walk out of your shop with an expensive dress was quite unexpected. People like you are unique and very rare these days and your kind act certainly helped restore my faith in the human race.

Once the photo shoot was over, the hard work didn't stop there. I'd like to thank the Creative Retoucher, Dean Feast, for his superb colour retouching work on the cover photograph. Dean, you created the perfect *look* and *feel* that I was after.

Next, I'd like to thank all the cellists who kindly gave up their time to answer my many music related questions via email, telephone, and even meeting up in coffee shops in Cambridge. I must admit this part of my research was so much fun. I thoroughly enjoyed going to see the internationally acclaimed concert cellist, Guy Johnston, performing the Shostakovich Cello Concerto with the City Of Cambridge Symphony Orchestra. I also loved seeing Katarina Majcen perform the Elgar Cello

Concerto with piano accompaniment in Cambridge. Writing this novel was just the excuse I needed to buy the complete works of Jacqueline du Pré as a CD box set - hours and hours of musical utopia to my ears. For me personally, Jacqueline du Pré is the most honest and complete musician I have ever heard; I even wrote this very sentence in the novel. The cellists who helped me get things accurate were: Katarina Majcen - concert cellist, Elizabeth Juette – lead cellist for the City of Cambridge Symphony Orchestra, Cheryl Frances-Hoad - cellist and teacher, Veronica Henderson - cellist and teacher, Kathy Whitehouse - cellist and teacher.

Next up, Cambridge-based violin and cello maker and restorer, Jonathan Woolston, who was kind enough to not only give me advice about cellos and bows and what's involved in repairing, servicing, adjustments and the like, but for also lending one of his wonderful cellos for the front cover photo. The young lady who actually owns the cello pictured on the front cover could not be there on the day of the shoot, so she sent her mother along with Jonathan to watch over the £25,000 instrument. On one or two occasions she looked a little nervous as her daughter's beloved cello sat uncomfortably close to the rough concrete steps and rocked back and forth in the model's hand in heavy wind. But, no harm came to the cello and, as you can see, the shoot was a total success. So, thank you, Jonathan, for going so far out of your way and taking the train down to London to help out - you're a real gentleman. I must also thank the excellent bow maker, Richard Wilson.

Sticking with musical people. I'd like to extend my thanks to Richard White and the staff at J.P. Guivier & Co, one of London's primary violin family dealers. They kindly gave me their time, knowledge and advice on all things cello. Also, thanks to Alan Stevenson for advising me on cello cases.

Small a part as she played, I want to thank Allyxa Ruby from AR Distribution for kindly supplying me with a cake of Andrea rosin, aiding my research still further for Sophia. Being able to see, touch, and smell (after gently rubbing a little fine grade sandpaper over the top) the rosin allowed me to write about it, however briefly, with more conviction than I would have been able to if I merely viewed a picture on the Internet. For me, it's little details like these that make the story more authentic and in turn, enjoyable for the reader. Every now and then I would pick up the rosin while I was writing this book. It proved useful for getting my creative juices flowing. I often found myself staring at the computer screen struggling to come up with a convincing line of dialogue. During these moments I took the cake of rosin, held it in my hand and rubbed my thumb across it. For those who have never held a cake of cello rosin, it is very nice to touch and it certainly helped me though some sticky moments during the writing of this book. Some people squeeze stress balls; I play with rosin.

Next I'd like to thank the many neurosurgeons who allowed me to pick their brains (yes, pun totally intended) with many questions relating to neurosurgical and neurological issues and various types of brain tumour and the effects that they can have on people. I appreciate that you are very busy people and I can't thank you enough for allowing me to pester you over the months. So, thank you to the following neurosurgeons: Mr Richard Mannion, Mr Fary Afshar, Miss Helen Fernandas, Professor Peter Richardson and Ann Mitchener.

I also want to thank Esther Linger, the ward manager at Springbank Psychiatric unit at Fulbourn Hospital, Cambridge, for giving me a tour of the secure psychiatric unit and for answering all my questions. Talking to you was not only educational, but it was also a real eye-opener. Thank you also for taking the time to read over the relevant sections of the book during the writing stage to make sure they were accurate and authentic.

Similar thanks go to Lesley Galasso, the Mental Health Act administrator for Capia Nightingale Psychiatric Hospital in London. Your help and advice proved invaluable, giving me deeper knowledge and understanding of psychiatric hospitals and the Mental Health Act. Also, thank you so much for taking the time to read the relevant sections during the writing stage for accuracy and authenticity.

Thank you also to Priscilla Masvipurwa, the hospital manager at Nouvita Community Hospital, Herts, who educated me on various psychiatric matters.

Now for the police and prison related acknowledgements. A big thanks to Mark Kelly, the CSI manager and principle SOCO at Peterborough Police HQ. Mark, I could not have written the relevant scenes with such accuracy without your in-depth knowledge. Thanks again for answering all my emails and taking the time to speak with me on the phone. Thanks to you I am further educated in police procedures, and I now know what it takes to land oneself in prison for two weeks ;)

I also want to thank Pierre Petrou, the Head of Media and Communications at Camden Police Borough Headquarters, London. Pierre, thank you for organizing my trip to Kentish Town police station. Also, thanks to Supt. Gary Buttercase for answering my many questions while I was there and for arranging a grand tour of the police station and sticking me in a cell for authenticity.

While on the theme of crime, I must thank Andy Darken, the Deputy General Secretary at the POA (Prison Officers Association). Andy, I appreciate you taking the time to explain the various prison procedures at Holloway women's prison in north London.

As we move from crime to dentistry, I'd like to thank the wonderful dentist, Georgina O'Callaghan, for filling me in (again, pun fully intended) on dental education at university. Again, this was only brief in the novel, but indispensible and without the telephone conversation with you, there would have been no mention of *phantom heads*. As an author, I find that I learn so many new things while researching a novel.

A bit about teenagers - I'd like to thank my young friend, Max Savchenko, for telling me which rock bands are hot and which are not, and for forcing me to watch music videos on YouTube for hours on end, sometimes to the dismay of the neighbours. During the novel,

Sophia found herself being strangely attracted to loud rock music. Listening to bands like Avenged Sevenfold, Asking Alexandria and AC/DC in her headphones helped drown out the memories of the horrific death of her beloved boyfriend, Spencer. I needed to know who the coolest bands were, which is where Max came in. It was because of this somewhat loud part of my novel research that Sophia ended up strutting around her living room to bands like Black Veil Brides and Heaven's Basement. Sometimes, if you want to know what's fresh and cool, you just gotta ask a teenager. Sometimes, *just* sometimes, teenagers know best. Thanks, Max.

Now for the technical acknowledgements. First I'd like to thank Ruth Ekblom for reading through the chapters as I wrote them and providing feedback and general guidance. I also owe huge thanks to Louise Wessman, Ann Ferguson, Joanne Mills and Jeremy Bonwick for all their hard work proofreading the book.

I'd like to thank my best friend and critic, Louise Wessman, for being so brutally honest with her feedback on a chapter-by-chapter basis during the writing stages of Sophia. Thanks for reeling Sophia in a little.

Last, but never the least, I'd like to thank Sylvie Bolioli and Sandrine Fresne for making sure the French parts were accurate.

About The Author

Nigel Cooper was born in England, UK. He grew up in the Lake District, but later moved down south to London.

He studied screenwriting in London, where he learned the art and craft of creative writing for film and television. In 2004 he became the founder/editor of a specialist UK-based television/broadcast production magazine. Although it was hugely successful, he sold the magazine in November 2011 to pursue a career as an author of fiction.

Nigel has had many years' experience as a writer of technical articles, tutorials, reviews, news stories and journalism, not only for his own magazine, but also for many other well known publications, magazines and newspapers.

In 2011, Nigel had an overwhelming desire to move into creative fiction writing, so he set about researching his debut novel in the dark romance vampire genre. This desire had been smouldering inside him for a few years. Having seen various classic vampire movies in the past, he decided to write a vampire story that he himself would want to read.

After extensive research and planning Nigel completed his debut novel, Email From A Vampire in May 2012.

He writes across many genres including: romance, psychological thrillers, suspense, crime & general fiction.

In his spare time Nigel enjoys playing the piano. He studied music at Trinity College Of Music, London and is an accomplished classical pianist. He enjoys photography, swimming and badminton. He also loves dogs, especially Cavalier King Charles Spaniels and small toy breeds.

Nigel lives and writes in Cambridgeshire, UK.

For more information about the author visit
www.nigelcooperauthor.co.uk

SOPHIA

GENERIC POOL PUBLISHING

ISBN 978-0-9573307-3-3